HONOR BOUND

To Cherie,
2/4/04 —
The night
I met you,
one of
the greatest
of my life.

John

Booklocker.com, Inc.
2001

HONOR BOUND

John Ratti

HONOR BOUND

One day, some of this fiction *will be fact.*

1

Sergeant Dalton Harper raised his voice, "Three of ours heading this way." He
seized a longer look with binoculars, "One has on a rancher's hat."

Captain Kasey Lawrence frowned and called her squad to attention, "We're
getting a visit from a headquarters puke who struts over spit and shine! Don't
give him a reason to linger."

The unit scrambled to appear up to regulations. Captain Lawrence never
busted them about little things, so long as the work got done. She saw it as the
only way to operate in this hoary desert near the Iraq border. They were miles
off the road running across Saudi Arabia northwest from Jordan to the Persian
Gulf southeast, a US Army chemical and biological substance detection team
working on the edge of the Empty Quarter seeking evidence of materials used
by Saddam Hussein's forces during the Gulf War.

Major Jack "Cowboy" Bowers vaulted out of a mutt followed by an attendant
combo. In rapid stride he surveyed the troops, finding something to criticize
about everyone. He ended with Kasey, her image reflecting in his mirrored
shades.

"Captain Lawrence, unbutton your coat."

Vertically embroidered along the edge of the lining, knurly stitching on top of
the finished weave, are the words - *America, One Nation, One Destiny.*

Bowers knew it. He smiled, "Your uniform is not up to code."

Kasey peered at his hat, "With due respect sir, neither is yours."

Her crew stifled smirks while Bowers failed in a search for an appropriate
retort. "You're coming with us," he finally fired off. "General Zalman wants to
see you."

She dropped command on Lieutenant Tyrone Moore and climbed into the jeep.

They moved south, toward the outpost near Badanah. The Gulf War ended
years ago, but America continued enforcing no-fly zones in north and south Iraq.
An effort mostly carried out by US personnel in Saudi Arabia, America's best
friend in the Arab Mideast. Their relationship was mature and polished in the

ways it had to be. The US provided the force to warn off outsiders with eyes on Saudi oil reserves, over one quarter of the world's total. That much both countries admitted to themselves, each other and the world. Neither dared acknowledge US presence as serving to deter internal threats to the Saudi royal family. They never went there, showing the two nations understood each other's no-fly zones.

En route, Bowers engaged in a rant disguised as small talk, criticizing in minutiae the expertise of her unit and finally degenerating into a tirade about women in the military.

"Politicians are bending over backward to curry favor with female voters and liberals. Brass is being forced to lower standards."

Kasey stared ahead, never replying, until Bowers turned to her and growled, "The fact is, you know I'm right. Don't you, captain?"

He had left himself wide open. Kasey patiently detailed, "Sir, if so, why am I, working in the field, a captain, while you, working in an office, are a major? We both graduated from West Point at the same time." She took no joy in dishing it to Bowers. Always too easy to one up him. At least he became quiet. That was satisfaction enough.

Kasey met with General Zalman soon as she arrived at the makeshift base. She noticed his white hair had grown long. Seems he's been near retirement forever. A good man but one who should have found something else to do with his life long ago, as the peccadilloes leaving his face crimson raw revealed.

"I have an order from DOD that came in on a diplomatic back channel," Zalman said when they were alone. "I am to send the highest ranking intelligence officer in the region to the Iraq border. From there Iraqi military will take you to meet an official who allegedly has information of major security interest to the region."

Kasey digested the words. Outside a window, her eye caught sight of a small plane landing and its sole occupant, a man, exit and walk toward them.

"Seems an issue for the diplomats," Kasey observed.

Zalman shrugged, "The order comes from high up on the chain. Iraq wants the meeting right away. It could be a new ploy to get sanctions lifted. DOD wants to handle this informally."

"I'm to go alone?"

"No. A comparably ranking Saudi will accompany you."

Kasey raised a brow. A very unusual pairing.

Zalman elaborated, "The matter is said to be of significant interest to them."

The pilot of the plane, Air Force Captain Nasir ibn Saud, entered the room. He ignored Kasey, quickly presented himself to the general and then went on without taking a breath, "General, it is inappropriate for a woman to attend this meeting with me. As a member of the royal family, it is unacceptable-"

Zalman, too played out for such conflict, stepped on his protest, "I will follow my orders. If you won't go, that's your choice."

Kasey moved toward Nasir and extended a hand, her first course in dealing with fixed attitudes, simply ignore them and move forward, an automatic response to diffuse negative emotions. Nasir avoided her gesture.

Zalman delivered words like a weary dirge, "Captain Saud, I won't argue etiquette with you. Saudi Arabia will have to get our briefing after the meeting."

Kasey watched an Army convoy pull up outside. Two ACAVs, a Lorry and an M113. Aged hardware, back from the Desert Storm era. Kasey walked down a hallway after being dismissed, while Nasir stayed behind threatening political repercussions. She came across Bowers loitering by the exit.

"You better watch your ass up there."

"Maybe you should come. You've been watching my ass since we entered the academy."

Kasey had a seat in a waiting vehicle. Nasir at last emerged. An angry gait launched him next to her, where he perched like a cramped animal. The caravan moved away. Zalman stared at them through a window and poured a shot of whiskey.

Kasey and Nasir didn't swap a word all the way to the border.

***

Deserts can be recent or ancient environments, as much Earth's future as past. They begin in climates where water evaporation exceeds rainfall over long periods. For a desert to evolve there must be significant open land, scant inherent vegetation and few natural bodies of water around. An atmosphere generally free of clouds is also necessary. Clouds deflect heat. High winds must predominate. Falling air warms, absorbing moisture, while rising air cools, holding less moisture, causing clouds and precipitation. Often deserts form due to continental drift and rising mountain regions. Deserts have mystery. Still unknown factors can advance their genesis. The desert in the Arabian Peninsula formed sixty-fivemillion years ago by emerging mountain range to the west. The desert in nearby North Africa is much more recent. In Egypt, the Sphinx and monuments to the pharaohs were built before the land became arid. That area became desert only a few thousand years ago, short order Earth time. Deserts are fragile and rugged. Vivid but blurred. Smooth yet craggy. Sustained and ruined. Teeming with the energy and suspense of life in a vexed setting.

***

Kasey and Nasir crossed the last guard station in Saudi Arabia before entering Iraq. A scant place watched over by two US soldiers. In the sand, borders between nations blur. Even among antagonistic states. The desert itself serves as effective sentry. Official crossing sites are rare and usually located near highways or population centers. Otherwise, border stations sit in remote territories only as far from main roads as those sneaking around dare attempt to travel. The sentries on this isolated frontier knew they were coming. They stood and watched the procession roll through. Since the Gulf War, Americans staffed these secluded margins. US soldiers are never at established border crossings. Political considerations. Citizens of Arab allies become anxious when they witness visible US military presence.

The convoy pushed north, through the time of day when motion and sun angle made the sand sparkle. Kasey looked as if she belonged here. Her pale blue eyes and milky light hair fused with the faded color values. Nasir's presence appeared distinct, even at odds, with the land of his origin. His form seemed both chiseled and uncut. Raven hair. Dark eyes. Fashioned from a clan that for eons compelled its presence on austere surroundings, defying it with their bold visage.

A waiting procession lined up like a freight train came into view on the horizon. Kasey could make out uniforms.

"Some welcoming committee - Republican Guards."

Nasir kept silent as these once warring factions came together. After a taut pause, the Iraqi in charge saluted and walked in their direction. Kasey and Nasir left their escort and converged on the officer. The man had rehearsed the few words of English he needed to know.

"Your guns, please."

Nasir wavered before handing over his revolver. Kasey remained still. Nasir glared and motioned her to comply.

"It's not part of my orders," she matter-of-factly stated.

Her reaction seemed absurd because they were facing weaponry far greater than two handguns. Kasey's refusal was a matter of principle. Iraq, a defeated enemy, never gets to impose conditions on the victor, America. Ever.

A standoff ensued. The Iraqi officer consulted with his soldiers while Nasir scowled at Kasey, "Give them your gun, I tell you!"

"You don't *tell* me to do anything!"

"I know how these people think," Nasir condescendingly said. "There will be no meeting. It will be your fault."

At the same time, the Iraqis engaged in heated debate with hostile eyes aimed at Kasey. Eventually, the Iraqi in charge signaled them to a carrier. Kasey and Nasir got into the back of a croaky Soviet transport and sat across from some Republican Guards. Kasey gawked at the interior, the rusted steel props and drooping canvas. This must be at least forty years old, she thought as the motorcade budged far inside Iraq.

Kasey absorbed every detail of the hours long ride. It concluded with the procession moving up elevated terrain. At a defended entrance carved out of stone, they advanced inside the gradient and stopped at an immense staging area. Republican Guards swarmed around, leading Kasey and Nasir on foot to a level below, passing colossal facilities constructed of marble and garnished with dense metal and down again to a darkened corridor surrounded by solid rock.

Menacing doors blocked every passageway. Kasey and Nasir followed along to a dark chamber and sat in two chairs positioned in front of a long table. Behind the table was a door. It opened and a man approached. In flat-toned English he mechanically asked for Kasey's gun. She refused. The man disappeared behind the door.

Nasir all but jumped from the chair, "This is no time to defy them!"

"It's not defiance," Kasey wished she had time to explain.

Seconds later, the man returned trailed by Republican Guards. They crammed the room, brandishing automatic weapons and chaotically forming a fast circle around Kasey and Nasir, as if to intimidate by using chaotic gestures. They set their attention on Kasey's hands. Then Saddam Hussein walked into the room.

Kasey made a quick determination. She got up, which provoked the soldiers. They tightly converged on her, guns aimed. Kasey ignored them, placed her right hand over her heart, and spoke -

"Is-saal-laam a-lay-kum." (May peace be upon you)

Saddam slightly nodded and replied without obvious demeanor.

"Wa-alaykuum is-salam." (And to you be peace)

Nasir seethed at what he viewed as an inappropriate display by Kasey. Saddam positioned himself in a chair. As Kasey sat back down, she sensed a new fury consuming Nasir as he stared at Saddam's feet.

The man who spoke deflated English stood by to interpret. Saddam declared, "I have something you need to see. It is of interest to us all."

He waved a hand and a round concrete container with a metal cover was wheeled into the room. Soldiers removed the top. Saddam pointed at it. Kasey and Nasir slowly walked over and gazed inside. Kasey masked any reaction while gently touching the pulpy mass inside and rolling the residue between her fingers. She wiped remnants on her sleeve. Nasir looked to her for an explanation, "Seems to be cellulose acetate," she said. "Used for creating plastic

JOHN RATTI

explosives. Few sources outside America have the furnace reduction technology needed to produce this quantity."

"That may no longer be true," was Nasir's obvious perspective.

The remark peeved Kasey, "We would know about it."

"Maybe now you do.

Kasey coldly stared at him, "Maybe."

Saddam's words broke their tension, "It was smuggled from Iran. Found in possession of Jordanian produce traders. They were tracked across Iraq and stopped at the border. The substance weighs 45.35 kilograms."

Saddam paused until he locked eyes with Kasey. Again, he said, "45.35 kilograms."

Nasir had another subject on his mind, "Jordan? That couldn't be the ultimate destination."

After another prompt from Saddam, a man was hauled into the chamber. Kasey and Nasir cringed at his pulpy wounds as he cowered on the floor.

Saddam didn't immediately answer Nasir's statement, "He is the only smuggler alive ... because he speaks English."

Republican Guards prodded the man with a pistol whipping. His spirit implored the outsiders, "Please ... mercy ... I have told everything. It was not for use against Iraq. We were taking it to Jordan, to a Saudi in Amman."

Nasir felt no pity for the man's obvious impending destiny, "Who was the Saudi?"

"I don't know ... a mullah there was to put us in touch." He faced Kasey, "Please, some water."

His request brought a battering. The man covered up and writhed on the floor. Kasey pushed through the soldiers, kneeled by him and addressed Saddam, "You asked us here in a presumed diplomatic setting. Witnessing violence is not a part of it. I want water for this man."

The interpreter gawked at Kasey, apprehensive of repeating such blunt words. Carefully, he translated. Saddam didn't move for a long time while Kasey wiped the man's forehead.

At last, Saddam summoned water with a hand sign. The man tried to grip the container. His finger joints were too shattered. Kasey helped him while looking

13

up at Saddam, "The credibility of your words could be better established if this man were to return with us."

Saddam wouldn't go for it, "He has no more to tell you."

Kasey pressed on, "If I could point out-"

Saddam didn't wait for translation, "He will not be leaving here."

Republican Guards forced Kasey aside and took the man. She turned away, unable to face her failure to save the man's life.

Nasir stared at Saddam, "Why are you telling us this?"

"Iraq has already fought a long war with one fundamentalist state along our border," the interpreter held up a hand to indicate Saddam hadn't finished. "Our security would be at great risk if we end up flanked by another."

Nasir resented the insinuation, "There will never be a revolution in my country."

"Consider what this could have done," was the nightmare Saddam asked Nasir to ponder.

An anxious Kasey needed to know, "What are you going to do with it?"

"I'm giving it to you. Maybe you can learn why it passed through Iraq," Saddam knew they'd find it an unexpected reply.

Kasey's struggled to contain her shock as she tried to figure Saddam's rationale. Is there another dynamic here?

It seemed less complex to Nasir. He murmured to Kasey, "Can we safely transport it?"

"In this state - yes. It is inert without a blinding agent."

Saddam briefly gazed at Kasey, "I want you to report what I've said to the president."

"I'm sure he will know," Kasey didn't want to promise anything.

"Once he knows, I will share anything else we learn. One week from today, I would like to hear the president make a public statement about desert weather. Then I will be certain he heard from you," at last Saddam revealed the outline of an agenda.

But what was it? "I'll pass that along to my superiors," Kasey remained noncommittal.

"You should know," Saddam paused, a clue he knew how to get what he wanted, "this was the third shipment smuggled through Iraq. The first two successfully made connections inside Jordan."

With that, Saddam stood and exited the room.

Kasey and Nasir burned with alarm at his parting claim but remained silent as they watched the cellulose acetate packed and loaded onto a cart. Then soldiers escorted them out. Marching through the corridor, nearby gunfire vibrated off the walls around them.

Approaching their waiting convoy, a small truck sped by carrying the inanimate flesh of the smuggler Kasey tried to save. No doubt on the way to some inglorious burial. Kasey and Nasir kept mum while returning in the company of Saddam's troops.

The US caravan waited on the spot they left them, securing the surprise freight at the rear of the procession. By the time they had moved beyond the two perimeter guards into Saudi Arabia, Nasir's seething rage finally escaped.

"Your behavior almost doomed us."

Kasey knew it was coming, "That's the main thing on your mind right now?"

Nasir wasn't listening, "Not giving up your gun ... I feared for my life ... then seeing you greet Saddam like a cherished friend–"

Kasey interrupted as Nasir began shaking his head, "I was obtaining information. I am an intelligence officer. I learn what I need to know any way I can."

He kept venting, "Americans never get it right in this part of the world."

She matched his anger word for word, "I have been in the Mideast for ten years. This is my beat. I helped defend your country when you needed us."

"Don't confuse America's self-interest with altruism."

"The same applies to Saudi Arabia."

"I have lived in America ... attended Georgetown ... spent time Benning. I know your ways."

"Your *obligation* is to know what might be happening in your country."

Kasey's language was intentional. Obligation is a word frequently used in Islam. Obligation to country is a foremost tenet. Surprisingly, her dig melted his anger. Nasir's tone became subdued, "My country is more than a religious obligation. It's my life."

The response made Kasey feel she went too far. She softened with a try at faint conciliation, "Then we are similar in one way."

Nasir kept the exchange from getting too sentimental, "Please indulge me by not announcing it."

Now they were back on ground familiar, even comfortable, in a provoking way.

"Fine!" Kasey stewed for a moment, then decided to let him have it: "Let me *announce* this to you ... The material we have has only recently been developed. The mass is small, but very dense. Probably twenty or thirty percent cellulose acetate content. C-20 or C-30 if you want to know the terminology. Mere ounces will blow the best tank to dust. Pan Am 103 was blown up over Scotland by a C-2 compound. That's least ten times less destructive than what we we're dragging now. This isn't for usual Jihad or Hezbollah activities. This is for some different purpose and we better find out what that is."

Nasir honed in on the weakness in Kasey's assessment, "That is if Saddam is telling it straight."

"Even if he isn't, the material wasn't manufactured in this part of the world. We need to find out where it came from, that's the key."

They arrived back in Badanah. Personnel surrounded the cargo while Kasey and Nasir walked away from each other to separate debriefings.

2

*A fleet of civilian cars whisked Kasey away only hours after her initial report to
Zalman.* The diplomatic security agents chaperoning her to the US Embassy in
Riyadh said little, remaining attentive to surroundings outside the tinted
windows. Foreigners are always easy to detect in Saudi Arabia, they exist so
separate from the native population that virtual cities are built exclusively for
them. Although Saudi Arabia eschews foreign cultural influences, the nation
has the largest percentage of residing non-citizens of any nation in the world.
Brimming with fossil fuel revenue (besides oil, the country holds enormous
natural gas reserves) and a small native population with a nomadic history, the
country must import workers and expertise for the enormous modernizing and
infrastructure building jobs still to be done.

Most Saudis are strict religious conservatives. Mecca, the birthplace of Islam,
is in Saudi Arabia. The nation is governed by a unique monarchy. The king
rules by consent of the governed, not by divine right. The terms of consensus
endure fixed yet arbitrary, reasoned if discrepant, enigmatic and matter-of-fact,
paradoxes that keep Saudi Arabia a stable but puzzling place, even by Mideast
standards.

Kasey arrived in Riyadh after midnight. Relatively few Americans have ever
spent time in the Saudi capitol. Even fewer American women. From what
Kasey saw, it was a modern place, yet permeated by an old ether.

The darkened embassy came into view. The Marines at the gate let them in
and Kasey got out in the heart of the compound. She had been to US embassies
before, even off-hours. This place seemed uncomfortably quiet. Approaching
the entrance to the main building, Ambassador Wilson Howe opened the door.
Curious. *Since when does an ambassador admit embassy visitors?*

17

Feeble lighting shadowed the lower level. Kasey followed Howe up to his suite where it was brighter. Ushered into a conference room, she saw Secretary of State Judith Drake sitting at the end of a long mahogany table. Kasey hid her surprise as Drake looked up from some documents inside a binder. Howe was ready to introduce them but Drake made the gesture unnecessary. She stood up and extended a hand, "Good to see you again, Captain Lawrence."

"Thank you. Good to see you again, Madame Secretary." Only now did Kasey notice someone else in the room. A man standing in a corner with his back to her, seemingly absorbed in the unremarkable wall decor. He turned around and took a seat at the table without looking at her.

Howe took a few steps in the man's direction, "Captain Lawrence, this is our new Station Chief, Alexander Walker."

Walker nodded. Kasey reflected - secretary of state, ambassador and CIA station chief. A remarkably well heeded group. Kasey dropped into a leather chair and took read of the personalities. Howe was Ivy League down to his genes. Tall, thin, and patrician. Book smart, she guessed, but life dumb. Dull gray eyes likely as neutral as his disposition. Petite Drake looked put together for a television camera. Kasey recognized her type, one who spends a career achieving all aims by roundabout and shrouded routines. This woman hardly ate breakfast without a machination. Walker projected the least artifice. No finesse or posturing evident in his bearing. She could tell he didn't care what anybody thought, which made him genuine.

Drake got down to business; "I was in Moscow when report of the encounter came. I diverted here because there are questions we need answered in order to assess the value of your information. Such as, are you sure it was Saddam you met?"

Kasey assumed it was coming, "I strongly believe so."

"He uses several look alikes," the secretary said, hunting for better information.

"He stood just under six feet tall and weighed a bit under two hundred pounds," Kasey revealed. "There was a triangular mole pattern on his right arm and a scar on the inside of his right thumb. It could have been a grazing from a bullet. It matched an injury we know he had from one assassination attempt."

Drake put her elbows on the table and a finger on her chin while Kasey capped her evaluation, "I felt fear in the people around him."

Howe smiled and nodded, "Impressive evaluation."

"I spent a lot of time in the Gulf War trying to track him down," Kasey said, more for the other two than Drake.

"This goes a way toward making him real for me," Drake said, looking around the table. Still, she had issues to talk out, "It's hard to believe he would ever reveal a hideout."

Kasey disclosed more, "We traveled four hours in a northwest direction at about fifteen miles per hour. We must have ended up in the southern corner of the Badiyat Ash-Sham. We always knew he had a lair somewhere in that area. And he knew we knew. So he wasn't revealing much."

Drake seemed to be thinking out loud, "Even so, it was risky for him."

"Maybe what he had to say was worth the risk," Kasey offered. "He has other places to hunker." She gazed around at everyone, using the opportunity brought by a long pause to make an inquiry, "Did analysis confirm the substance as cellulose acetate?"

Howe shot a look at Drake while Walker sat straight up. An unmistakable undercurrent passed through the room. Nobody said a word. The peculiar flowing electricity naturally set Kasey into a more aggressive information gathering mode. She prodded them for an answer, "I know the ratiocination takes very little time."

"Thermal neutron testing says it is cellulose acetate," Drake finally told her.

"What is it, C-20?"

"C-30," Drake's voice trailed off.

Bad news. Kasey let them know she understood the ramifications, "Likely US made."

Howe, ever the diplomat, encouraged a more indefinite view, "There are other possibilities."

Kasey regularly had problems deciding what to make of these people. But she wasn't inclined to bite her tongue, "Small chance any other country has the technology. Saddam twice mentioned the weight as 45.35 kilograms. That's

HONOR BOUND

exactly one hundred pounds. A round figure in American measurement standards."

"We noted that in your account," she told Kasey. The secretary resembled someone eager to vacillate, but at a loss how to, "You are cognizant, *that's for sure*," she finally complimented. Then Drake got up and paced, "Deception has to be considered. It might be a ploy to make it seem produced in America."

Kasey already considered that. "Saddam went lengths to show he wasn't staging an event. He made sure we saw the smuggler killed."

Drake didn't care to hear further analysis from Kasey, "Assure me you made no promise the president would acknowledge the encounter."

"Of course I didn't. It wasn't within my power to do so. But it is a condition for acquiring more information. I hope the president will know that."

"He knows. With an election coming up, he won't soil himself getting caught dealing with Saddam," the secretary grew animated when it came to political dissection. Then she fell back into her diplomatic drone, "I doubt the travel route originated in Iran. They have a more moderate government now. We've been edging toward relations with them. Saddam might be out to interfere."

Usual American policy – make Saddam the whipping boy. "Anyway, the president will be in Finland the day Saddam wants mention of desert weather. Making a reference to it there ... it's not in the cards."

Drake's clarification suggested an attempt to create a notion Kasey had insight to some inner sanctum of policy, an effort didn't fool Kasey, though she strayed from direct comment, "Madam Secretary, you once said, 'There's no place like the Mideast to learn the terms of endearment between nations.'" The words were an effort to recognize a past association, and a reminder to Drake that Kasey knew the dynamics of this part of the world.

Drake broke into a reminiscing grin, "I remember you were there when I said it. It wasn't long after my confirmation to the UN. I think you were serving on the staff at Chief of Intelligence. You gave me the first briefing from the East Asia Work Group. That's why I recommended you for the mission inside Iraq."

The revelation confused Kasey, "I heard the orders came from DOD."

"It initiated through State," the secretary quickly said after a pause. "In Algeria, the ambassador from Iraq contacted us about a meeting."

20

"And you wanted me? Teamed with a Saudi? A royal?"

"I didn't know Iraq had also contacted the Saudis. It was short notice and you were already en route to Command. Anyway, all the nations of the world have to accept me. It's time our allies accept women in any role," Drake announced with a kick in her voice.

Not having spoken in some time made Howe fidgety. It imperiled his sense of importance, "All our military here are now on alert," he interjected, aware the statement was inappropriate the moment he said it.

Walker stayed silent. Occasionally he looked away, likely digesting omens in words. His kind gives little away. Frequently viewing his head at an angle, Kasey noticed he shifted the edges of his mouth into gestures resembling snarls and grimaces. Kasey didn't want to leave without expressing real concern to the secretary, "You never mentioned any possibility the cellulose acetate could indicate something else brewing."

Drake again went ambiguous, "We're checking that out."

Kasey couldn't let it go, "It's improbable Hezbollah or Jihad would move so much explosives through one place at one time. How do the Saudis see it?"

Drake advanced the art of replying in exasperating ways, "When it comes to Saudi Arabia, it's hard to know what they really think."

Howe grabbed another chance to make an irrelevant comment, "Ever since they stonewalled us on the barracks bombing investigation-"

Drake stopped him, "Saudi Arabia is as much a family business as a country. Families are good at closing ranks. I'm not surprised they sent and officer who is family. Their military is out of the loop for the most part. The royals don't trust them."

Howe just couldn't be quiet until Drake ended the meeting, "Saddam must be lying. He's always looking for ways to stick it to us."

"He might be genuinely worried about another Islamic revolution on his doorstep and, feeling threatened, took a risk by calling the meeting," Kasey couldn't believe they weren't entertaining any such possibility.

The ambassador spit out the rehearsed view, "We don't see it happening here. As long as the oil money keeps rolling in, who wants to rock the boat?"

Kasey differed, "I'd think about that. There are a billion Muslims in the world. Saudis are among the most conservative, if not yet the most militant of the faith. This is an appropriate place for a fundamentalist revolt. Millions will soon be arriving in Mecca for the yearly pilgrimage. Something might be going on."

Drake found the view too alarmist, "The royals do a good job of maintaining the status quo. They have a pulse on things. We see no emerging challenge to them."

Kasey lobbed Drake's previous words back at her, "You said it was difficult to know what is really going on in this country."

Drake didn't address the inconsistency. She mustered Kasey out with a compliment.

Once she left, Walker finally had something to say, "Some choice you made, Madam Secretary."

* * *

Today's Mideast derives from some of the oldest civilizations on earth. For eons, the region has been exposed to external tensions and influences. Since the dawn of civilization cultures from Europe, Asia and Africa used the region as a trade route, an endless three continent exchange of humans, animals, property, ideas and beliefs fused by military subjugation and social domination. This extraordinary alchemy created the unique circumstances pervading the region today. No matter the divisions among the people now existing in the Mideast, the further back in time you go, the more shared you find their fundamental physical and social origins. Often, the deeper the people's aversions, the greater their common genesis, a peerless example of familiarity breeding contempt.

The Arabian Peninsula is suffused with the most forbidding environs in the Mideast. In the past, living there by choice attested to a fervent independence. Countless clans, tribes, ethnic groups, family dynasties and outcast cliques stayed years, decades, maybe centuries before shriveling away, choosing to move on, ending up socially devoured or shoved into exile. The peninsula's acerbic splendor includes ten thousand foot mountains on one side, the coral gardens of the Red Sea on another and the driest place on Earth in-between. It is

JOHN RATTI

the land of date palms, frankincense, wolves, jackals, baboons, kangaroo rats, honey badgers, gazelles, flamingos, storks, snakes, lizards, camels and of course, fossil fuels. Fossil fuels are vestiges from when our planet was young. Oil and natural gas are slag heaps built of ancient organic matter. Layer upon layer of stratified plant and animal life from long ago and the condensed protoplasmic energy still existing within. An example of how matter is neither created nor destroyed, only transformed. The land teemed with immense variety of life prior to becoming desert. Generations of expired organic matter entombed, layer upon layer, as uplands emerged and modified the atmosphere. The increasing heat and advancing sand formed an exceptional setting for ossifying and protecting this protozoan matter until man exploited its potential.

Saudi Arabia's foundation as a nation began around two hundred years ago. The Saud's, an extended family living on the peninsula, were converted to a rigid form of Islam by Muhammad ibn Abd al-Wahhab. Becoming a Wahhabi meant rejecting all attributed to Islam after 950 AD, regarding later additions as spurious. Islam, which literally means "submission to God" has two major branches today. The Sunni faction, about eighty-five percent of today's Muslims, approves of the historical order of Muhammad's four successors. The sect is further divided by ritual and law into four schools. The other main adherents are Shiites, making up about fifteen percent of those practicing Islam. Shiites differ from Sunnis by asserting Muhammad's true successor was his son-in-law, Ali. Wahhabis, in theory, are as puritanical as a Muslim can be, but many contemporary Saudis have eased off their ideology. Still, there are large numbers of devout Wahhabis in Saudi Arabia. Wahhabi customs resemble most Sunni practices. Shiites predominate only in Iran, although they have a substantial following in Iraq and to a lesser degree in other Mideast nations. They are often stridently anti-West and are unabashed defenders of an ends-justifies-the-means philosophy in exaltation of Islam. The Wahhabis ultimately expunged Shiites dwelling in the Arabian Peninsula.

The early twentieth century brought accelerated change to the Mideast. European colonialism and World War One played major roles in shaping today's configuration of nations. In 1902, Ibn Saud, then patriarch of the Wahhabis, set out to conquer the Arabian Peninsula. In 1923 he finished the task and declared himself king. Oil was discovered in 1936. Production began two years later. American influence in Saudi petrochemical affairs started before the resources were unearthed. Charles Crane, best known as a plumbing equipment manufacturer, made a deal with Ibn Saud in 1931 to obtain the country's mining and refining rights.

Since then, the Saudi-American relationship has been discreetly intimate. Because of Saudi resources and the Mideast situation, many treat it as America's most important foreign bond. The most visible Mideast lobby in America is Israel. They do advocating in Congress, the legislative branch of government. Saudi Arabia does theirs through the executive arm, inside the walls of the White House. Israel seeks sway in ideology. Saudi Arabia looks to affect fiscal policies, a move that proved astute for the Saudis from the beginning. In the 1950's, the US Treasury Department allowed American companies in Saudi Arabia to pay Saudi instead of US taxes. The arrangement, conferred by treaty, in effect granted Saudi Arabia financial aid without approval of Congress. That deal inaugurated an entrenched corporate association between the nations. Saudi Arabia exported oil and gas to America. In turn, they imported products and services from Ford, Westinghouse, Bechel and Chase, to identify a small number of US corporations doing business in Saudi Arabia. The US Treasury Department has an office of Saudi affairs, the only one ever in a foreign country. Saudi cash has backed American think tanks and endowed chairs at US universities. Bechel, a company with deep State Department and CIA ties, built the Trans-Arabian pipeline. US owned World Airways maintains charter contracts to fly two million Muslims to Mecca every year. Saudi banks lend to US financial institutions and control large world monetary reserves. The Saudis employ well-connected Washington lawyers, spin masters, investment consultants and public relations agencies to manage their affairs. Their representatives include former diplomats and elected officials, past generals and CIA officials, to name some.

There are deeper strata to the entangling alliance of these two entrenched political partners who act in enlightened self-interest for the regional status quo. To keep domestic peace, warn off outside invaders with eyes on Saudi oil, and contest for Persian Gulf domination (mainly against Iran), the US has nourished

Saudi Arabia's defense programs. Chiefly, the Saudi Air Force. For decades, the US has provided them with hardware such as AWAC planes, Sidewinder missiles, F-15 jet fighters and K-135 air tankers. America also prodded China to sell the Saudis thirty CSS-2s, guided rocket launchers that retain accuracy for thousands of miles. Saudis have also bought frigates and support ships from France, dozens of planes and helicopters from Great Britain, and almost two hundred anti-ship projectiles from Italy. The US kicked in again, filling a seven billion-dollar order for Tornado strike missiles. This all represents but a fraction of today's Saudi arsenal. America secretly built and maintains an intricate, ultra-modern command base in the Saudi desert. Called King Khalid Military City, it is a totally integrated air and naval facility superior to any example in America. It is complete with missile silos and buried command bunkers. One reason the Saudis selected their Air Force for foremost strategic defense is that the country has a smaller population than many Mideast rivals, leaving it at a personnel disadvantage against potential invading land forces.

There are near unfathomable political complexities to the Mideast. You would think an ally such as America in a union with an Arab state would trouble Israel. Surprisingly, some seemingly militant Arab nations have a tacit live and let live posture toward Israel. Saudi Arabia is one. Syria in ways is another. Never publicly acknowledged, these nations are comforted by stability in an antagonist. In the Mideast, the cast of characters knows well the unpredictable effect of pushing the dynamic. Even Saddam Hussein, political Dadaist that he is, knows where the lines are drawn, maybe better than anyone, seeing his uncanny ability to survive his initiated games of brinksmanship. Arab nations may condemn Israel with words and provide economic support for more benign forms of Arab nationalism, but they will not start a war. Israel, for their part, understands this and is bought off by US aid corresponding to what America does for its Arab friends.

These policies do not always proceed smoothly. In America, the relationship with Saudi Arabia has been the source of wrangling among federal agencies. The CIA routinely keeps background data on the region to itself. This creates friction with the Department of Commerce, which retaliates by not providing the CIA with export information. The CIA ends up not knowing what commodities

American firms sell to overseas nations. The CIA repays them by impounding transcripts of congressional hearings concerning foreign trade, keeping details from other agencies and the public. And the executive branch keeps intelligence gathered by the National Security Agency about the status of Mideast oil reserves away from everyone. Besides bureaucratic mistrust, other agendas blur the situation. For one, Customs gets caught in the middle trying to enforce export laws, feeling pressure from elected representatives more interested in creating business for their home districts than conducting responsible foreign policy.

Meanwhile, Saudi Arabia is encumbered with complicated internal dilemmas fossil fuel wealth does not solve. Modernizing the country, subjugating the relentless desert climate and integrating traditionalist culture while being surrounded by benefactors of radical politics is no easy matter. The royal family has had bouts with internal dissension. A member of the clan assassinated one king. Embarrassing revelations of family corruption has agitated the populace and caused some to see the monarchy rule as tentative, even suspect. There have been military coup attempts, leaving the royals uneasy and creating another reason for not keeping a large standing army. A hand picked National Guard of Beaudoin tribesmen protect the royal family and police internal matters. There is domestic religious turmoil believed instigated by Iran. Domestic tranquillity is maintained by playing to the conservative majority. The Koran is the nation's constitution. The government is quick to use capital punishment on spies, philanderers and murderers. Justice often calls for the amputation of convicted criminals' body parts. A news photograph once displayed a Saudi prince in a parking lot wielding a sword over the head of a felon. This is not enough for underground radical groups. Militants once took over the Grand Mosque in Mecca. At the time, many saw the existence of the monarchy in peril. King Khalid took swift action and had over fifty people decapitated for their role in the affair. Iranian-backed Islamic militants have assassinated Saudi diplomats in foreign countries. Saudi Arabia has countered by bankrolling friendly guerrilla armies in places like Afghanistan, defeating the forces backed by Iran. The Saudis have put aside old animosities to coordinate intelligence activities with Tunisia, Algeria and Egypt in an attempt to thwart extremists. They gave Syria two billion dollars to fund superweapon purchases, a reward for their allegiance during the Gulf War with Iraq. The influx sustained Syria's military machine for years. Completely understanding Mideast politics is easier than identifying a grain of sand in the desert. Centuries of discord, shifting alliances, religious and cultural fervor jostle with energy tender, multi-national corporations, arms dealers and countless agendas of the immeasurable individuals with ambiguous political goals. One thing you can be sure of in the Mideast - these things cover other things and there are things under the other things and all that is before you turn over the rock.

Iraq, Jordan, Kuwait, Oman, Yemen and the United Arab Emirates border Saudi Arabia on land. The Red Sea separates the peninsula's western edge from Egypt, Sudan and Ethiopia. The Persian Gulf isolates Saudi Arabia from Iran to the east. The country is grouped into four major regions. The province of Najd, in the center, is home of the ruling family. Riyadh, the nation's political and diplomatic capital, is located there. Hijaz, in the west, has the most diverse population. Mecca, Medina and the port of Jeddah are significant cities. Al Hasa is on the eastern coast. Dhahran, Dammam and the oil port of Ras Tanura are notable places. Asir is in the southwest. Comprised of towering altitudes, it receives the most rain. The oil fields exist primarily near coastal areas. The geography of Saudi Arabia also includes a massive scorched wasteland called the Empty Quarter. Bigger than Texas, it is the greatest expanse of sand in the world. Among the most desolate places on the planet, it measures in decades the duration between drops of rain.

All Saudi men are considered equal, based on their traditional self-reliant nature. Every male descendant of the nation's founder Ibn Saud carries the title of prince. When a king dies, or gives up rule, the oldest prince with the most direct male lineage to Ibn Saud takes control. In Saudi family life, the oldest male makes the decisions. Men are allowed up to four wives, but only one if additional cannot be supported. Marriage contracts prevail. Women are seeking improved social status. A while ago, a number of women drove in a convoy to Riyadh to demonstrate against prohibitions banning them from getting behind the wheel. The Matawain, the country's moral police, detained them. The king is officially prime minister and is addressed with familiarity by all citizens. He can be deposed at any time for the common good. The king appoints a Council of Ministers, yet remains final arbiter of laws. A recent development is the Consultative Council. Made up of non-royals, they advise on issues, but possess little real influence. There are no elections. Emirs are bureaucrats appointed to administer each region. Majils are daily audiences held by high officials. Everybody speaks and a consensus is reached. The country has never been invaded. The two major foreign policy objectives are to defend against hostile outside powers and to cooperate with oil producing countries. Class distinctions are never publicly exhibited. Saudis rarely socialize outside the home. Thursday and Friday are weekend days. Appointments are regularly not kept on time. Honor is everything to a Saudi. Once violated it can never be restored.

Nasir arrived in Riyadh the way Kasey did, with an escort bringing him to the Council of Ministers. He paused on the steps to look out over the city, a place in transition his entire life. Nasir liked to see what endured of old Riyadh. Signs from the days of silt paths and merchant stalls. Not that today's Riyadh appeared alien. The new city drew of on the dignity of the old. Dazzling white gypsum foundations, kinetic patterns in stained glass; the alabaster and marble patched into steel and concrete designs all inspired Nasir's faith in his country's tomorrow.

Nasir went inside to this special Majil, unusual due to the absence of managing emirs and consulting ministers. Only the family decision makers attended. Council chambers resembled a dazzling amphitheater more than a legislative chamber. Polished stone rows of cathedra aligned the room's edges facing King Khaled, who took position on his throne after leading prayers. Everyone wore traditional thobe (robe) and gutra (headdress). Perching closest to the king was his son Prince Rakan, the only one to remove his gutra when the meeting began. Nasir was on their right, among cousins and uncles and in between his brother Prince Salih and their father, Prince Sultan Abdul. King Khaled took a breath and spoke, "We will have open reflection and consensus." He turned a palm in Nasir's direction, "Prince Nasir, the Iraq matter ... How are you sure it was Saddam in your presence?"

28

Nasir advanced and faced the king, "Who else could have been so coarse, so vulgar?" He turned to the others; "He aimed his feet at me the entire time and refused to face Mecca while I was there."

Sneers filled the chamber while Khaled reflected, "In Yemen I was told Saddam vowed to never face Mecca in the presence of a Saud. To him, we betrayed Islam by letting in the Americans."

Prince Abdul cut to the core in his craggy voice, "If the explosives are real, then it probably was Saddam."

Nasir's younger brother Salih was always quick to be contentious, "America took the substance for analysis. We cannot trust them."

Rakan was openly pro-West, "That is not true. You should spend time in America. Get to know the people."

Salih did not want to hear it, "You should spend more time here and less there. Look at you ... manicured nails ... shedding your gutra so not to ruin your hairstyle, even in a sandstorm."

Nasir verbally got between them, "America should not be demonized or sanctified. They are the most important relationship our country has. It is up to us to keep it in balance."

The statement did not temper Salih, "You also have been blinded by time in America ... My brother, going on a mission with a woman."

"I objected," Nasir knew when he brother was posturing. The family gave leeway to Salih's passionate nature, but Nasir had to defend himself in front of the others, "It wasn't planned."

King Khaled had the patient nature of a good monarch as well as sense when to wield authority, "No more talk about the woman, keep it here. We had no time for other arrangements."

Salih never let issues go quietly away, "How long can we ignore the ways America influences us."

It was Abdul's turn to try and silence Salih, "Enough, son! We understand your concern."

"This from the man who resisted a Consultative Committee," Salih had no qualms about challenging even his father.

Exasperation swelled in Abdul's slow cadence, "It was used by the clerics to stir up things."

Salih was on a roll, "You have no eyes, either. The people are growing disgusted with us. When will you stop blaming the mullahs for the rot in our house?"

Rakan saw an opening, "It was the Americans who urged us to give the people more say, as you wanted. He scanned the hall, a gesture designed to inform everyone he had put his overbearing cousin in place, "Salih is bitter ... when he led the Committee it soon ended up out of control."

On the defensive, Salih took a turn addressing the group, "It was our best chance to let steam out of what is building. You are all out of touch. One day-"

The king stopped Salih with a tone that dared challenge, "Salih, end it now! Be silent or leave. We are moving far from our purpose here."

Khaled kept a furrowed brow on Salih until he sat and crossed his arms. Then the king decided it time for consensus, "Prince Nasir ibn Saud says it was Saddam. Do we agree he is correct?"

The assembly overwhelmingly concurred.

"Then what is Saddam up to? How does it affect us?"

Abdul had already given it thought; "I see no trickery on his part. It is between him and the Americans. He found explosives moving through his country and didn't want America tracing it back to Iraq."

Rakan also preferred to see little threat, "Even if headed here, the explosives were not intended for use on us. Since the barracks bombing, the Americans have separated themselves more than ever. They would be the targets. Our citizens have no worry."

Khaled had to consider every possibility, "What if Americans were not the intended targets?"

Abdul tossed a hand out toward the assembly, "What would terrorists go after here? We are well protected. Let them attack an oil pipeline or water desalination plant. Then we could then track them down and put an end to it."

A different subject was important to Nasir "Has this been talked out with the Americans?"

The king knew foreign policy better than any of them, "No. Their president has an election soon. It's difficult right now to know what they are really thinking. He would play down the threat and throw it back at our feet."

Nasir pressed on, "America knows the Hajj to Mecca is soon."

"They always are in fear of an uprising from the pilgrims," Rakan dismissed the concern with a wave.

"We oversee the pilgrims lodgings and movements from the moment they arrive," Khaled reminded. "They are under our eye. I don't worry about trouble at Mecca."

Nasir was afraid of the Majil being adjourned without considering everything. "Saddam told us previous shipments already made way to Jordan. We need to know whom the Saudi contact there is."

The king shrugged, "Do we know it is a Saudi? All we have is hearsay."

"We must take the possibility more seriously," Nasir pleaded, taken aback at what he saw as vague indifference.

"The Guard will look into it," Khaled decided. "For now, we will treat it as between Saddam and the Americans. Is there approval?"

There was near unanimous assent. Only Salih and Nasir abstained from responding.

***

The Gulf War ended in the early months of 1991 with the United States and coalition allies in Operation Desert Storm vanquishing Iraqi military forces from Kuwait. America lost 148 soldiers in combat and 145 to other causes, the lowest fatality rate of any major US conflict in over a century. US military strategists became household names and the sitting president enjoyed the highest public approval ratings ever recorded. Over 700,000 Americans served in the war, more than half positioned in the desert of northeast Saudi Arabia. The choice of location was made in deference to Saudi apprehension about foreign troops saturating their soil and alarming citizens. No matter the danger posed by Iraq, controlling Kuwait, Saudi Arabia understood the tender tango necessary in dealing with Saddam. They knew the more he stood up to America, the greater the esteem he would gain from the disenfranchised masses of the region. The Pentagon finally recognized this fact some time after the war. US Air Force strikes inside Iraq to enforce no-fly zones had failed to weaken Saddam. Congress wanted to know why. The Pentagon reluctantly admitted the more we bomb, the stronger he becomes. A logic Dr. Strangelove would appreciate and sign of the American political establishment's inability to grasp the intangibles of the Mideast. As American troops began returning home from the war, a shocking amount reported being plagued by similar puzzling maladies. Bone and connective tissue disorders, gastrointestinal problems, loss of circulation, respiratory trouble, depression, memory loss, skin rashes, chronic fatigue, insomnia, infertility and deformities in post-war conceived children were some frequently mentioned ailments.

Over time, about 80,000 Americans who served in the Persian Gulf requested special medical examinations through the Veterans Affairs Department. Due to the significant numbers, civilian leaders forced the Department of Defense to launch a study that summarily found no Americans were exposed to chemical or biological agents during the Gulf War. At the same time, many who served in the war found their health continuing to deteriorate. Former troops were wasting away from multiple sclerosis type diseases. Others became wheelchair bound with baffling conditions while more found themselves too debilitated to be productive citizens. Veterans Affairs conducted a new investigation to determine if low doses of nerve gas could be responsible for the symptoms. The Pentagon, unable to quash the new investigation, produced a past study of factory workers who were exposed in an industrial accident to low levels of the chemical nerve agent sarin. Those exposed suffered immediate muscle spasms and stomach cramps, yet suffered no discernible long-term effects. Still, VA doctors went ahead, even though their jobs were threatened for suggesting new theories into the medical mystery. The Pentagon went on the offensive by suggesting the afflictions were within the realm of psychological battlefield stress episodes recorded during other wars. Widening publicity over the matter brought involvement from other organizations. The Environmental Protection Agency declared the veterans were clearly suffering from chemical exposure symptoms. A study of 249 American Gulf War veterans published in the

JOHN RATTI

Journal of the American Medical Association concluded there were definable medical syndromes present. This led to more pressure on the Department of Defense, exacerbated by their failure to provide all the logs kept by Gen. Norman Schwarzkopf that recorded cases of possible chemical or biological agents detected by troops during the war. With political attention focusing on the Department of Defense, they finally disclosed that a new analysis of their data could "possibly" indicate there "may" have been one occurrence of chemical agent exposure to American troops. They divulged that in the closing days of the war, March 1991, US soldiers blew up a huge Iraqi ammunition depot in southern Iraq near the village of Khamisiyah. Thousands of Americans were in proximity to the blast. Some atmospheric monitoring equipment picked up "minuscule" traces of sarin or mustard gas. On the other hand, "perhaps" the monitoring results were ultimately "inconclusive" since no one was "sure" the equipment was working properly. Either way, DOD contended the amount of exposure would have been so paltry it "could not" have been any physical threat to humans. Bowing to civilian pressure, the Department of Defense at least agreed that veterans with undiagnosed ailments should be eligible for free medical treatment.

In time, the VA protested they remained hampered by DOD stonewalling. The Pentagon asserted that they did not have complete data on where particular troops were stationed and what agents they could have been subjected to. Many felt the Department of Defense had lost all credibility on the subject and its intransigence had done the veterans a disservice. The enemy was an unknown disease, not bureaucratic pretense and turf battles. Congressional and public uproar over perceived Pentagon foot dragging and their infighting with Veterans Affairs forced all future inquiries into Gulf War illness into civilian hands.

Several separate civilian panels of various experts convened to get to the bottom of the situation. The White House authorized one group, the Presidential Advisory Committee on Gulf War Veterans' Illnesses. Other groups investigating were the National Institute of Health, two advisory councils assembled by the Institute of Medicine, another sponsored by the Defense Science Board plus an unofficial one by the National Gulf War Resource Center. All harshly criticized the Pentagon. Fallout continued. Two analysts resigned

33

from the CIA claiming the agency was hiding documents suggesting thousands of American troops may have been exposed to chemical weapons during the war. The Department of Defense at last recognized that Gulf War veterans were suffering from serious health problems. The only question remaining was to define the source.

Most investigators agreed on two broad conclusions. One was that a specific disease or syndrome could not be identified and the other finding urged more research. Almost all the doctors who took part in the studies agreed that the veterans were dealing with undetermined illnesses. Many of them who went into it as skeptics admitted being swayed otherwise by the data. The investigations brought new questions. "The patterns of illness and health complaints are not consistent with just chemical agent exposure," one doctor said.

What was happening to the soldiers? Possible answers began to emerge. Researchers looking into every detail of military service in the war emphasized possible plausible "friendly" causes of the disorders. Examiners focused on a drug given to counteract potential chemical and biological agent exposure. This antidote, given as a preemptive vaccine, is called pyridostigmine bromide (PB). PB is a treatment for myasthenia gravis, a defect in the movement of nerve signals between fibers and muscles. The medication stimulates nerve signals and was believed by Pentagon doctors to be a remedy in mitigating the effects from nerve gas like sarin, which works by interrupting nerve signals. The drug had *never* been tested for such use.

At the war's onset, PB was classified by the Food and Drug Administration as an experimental medication for any use besides treating myasthenia gravis. The Pentagon managed to get the FDA to change the classification of the drug so they could meet protocol regarding use for the armed forces. Experimental drugs are banned from military use. The FDA modified the categorization of the drug, with one prerequisite, that the Department of Defense inform all taking it of its untested status as a chemical or biological weapon antitoxin. All troops in the Persian Gulf arena were compelled to take PB. In many instances, superior officers placed entire units on stand down and observed them ingesting PB to insure adherence with the directive. The Pentagon *never* told the troops of its untested status. When researchers dug deeper, they found soldiers who traced the onset of their illnesses to only hours after first taking PB. General medical literature urges caution in using the drug, even in myasthenia gravis cases. Published sources describe patterns of undesirable effects from the medication, including blockage of intestines or urinary tract, slow heartbeat, low blood pressure, nerve damage from allergic reaction, chronic fatigue, nausea, diarrhea and respiratory difficulty. These effects were noted even though relatively few people had ever taken the drug. Research centers then performed PB tests on laboratory mice. They discovered almost immediately that the animals displayed symptoms of nerve and circulatory system disorders as well as respiratory, connective tissue and fertility conditions very close to what was described by veterans. One study simulated the external conditions many experienced in the war. PB was given to mice before placing them in a setting fouled with pollution resembling the raging oil well fires that were widespread during the war. The mice's environment was then stressed to mimic the adrenaline flowing through soldiers in a combat backdrop. These factors magnified the ailments. For the mice, it was lethal.

US troops in the Gulf War may have been uninformed guinea pigs in the largest drug trial ever conducted, except no monitoring of the results was ever done by the Pentagon. They *never* established safe dosage levels or noted side effects. Simple established medical practices like basic monitoring to adjust dosage to the size of the person taking the drug never happened. A war that claimed a few hundred casualties may in reality have had almost 80,000.

Demands for answers besieged the Department of Defense. DOD was unable to supply the paperwork detailing their studies or reasoning for assuming PB effective as a chemical agent antidote. The Pentagon could not even say who approved the decision to use PB in the war. DOD had to admit they did not provide information about the experimental status of PB to the soldiers, in violation of their agreement with the FDA. Some "*accidental procrastination*" in printing the necessary information and getting it out quickly, DOD cited. Somehow, the Pentagon could brag about dropping a bomb from miles high onto a dime, yet they had not found someone capable of getting some copies made. More amusing if the results weren't likely so tragic was the incredulity

DOD expressed at public disbelief of their explanation. First, they denied a medical problem existed and refused to cooperate with those who said one did. Then they said there might have been a minor situation affecting a few. And finally they admitted likely bigger problems even as they refused to accept studies indicating they may have been responsible for it. After all this, DOD could not believe their sincerity was in question. In time, the Pentagon adopted a sheepish mea culpa that could be expressed as an "it was a war, things happen" justification while their conduct kept up a "we do not make mistakes" stance. Instead of now cooperating and trying to get to the bottom of a predicament they may have created, they said it had to be the fault of Saddam's forces. They went all out, years after the fact, trying to show that Iraq was responsible for the illnesses. DOD sent several CBW (chemical/biological warfare) detection units into northeastern Saudi Arabia, as close to the Iraqi border as they could get, to find evidence of chemical warfare by the Iraqi military in the Gulf War.

This is why Kasey, now back with her squad, was in Saudi Arabia. Moved weeks before from an intelligence monitoring position inside Kuwait to lead one of the recently created special CBW units. One reason she was chosen, besides her rank, regional proximity and assignment status, was that she was a serving officer who had not taken PB during the war. At the time, she was a lieutenant positioned in Israel, away from direct engagement, scrutinizing details such as troop activity and radar reports as well as trying to determine Saddam's movements inside Iraq.

Kasey and her company toiled under the scorching sun surrounded by two Strikers, a Bradley M2A tank, an M548 transport carrier, a sheltered Humvee and a few jeeps. A Fox reconnaissance mobile laboratory sat in the middle of their work circle. The unit probed air and soil with M-256 hand held chemistry sets, seeking answers to a bureaucratic nightmare, political morass and human tragedy. Answers Kasey, in undiscovered places, knew were not here. None of those with her served during the Gulf War, they were too young. They had little sense of futility toward their task. Kasey didn't admit any, either. She distanced herself from political issues. She had to, with the investment she made believing in great things about America. It required disconnect from other realms of thinking. It wasn't a rational choice, but an emotional one. A breach

36

no doubt jarring to witness in an intelligent person, if noticed on surface. To Kasey, they were just doing a job. She fought off any sense of functioning as governmental proxy in the cracks between integrity and deceit. She was a soldier who took an oath to protect the country. That kept it simple.

The squad took a break, slacking in the refuge of shadows cast by the Fox. Lieutenant Moore was waiting for the moment, "Captain, I've been accepted at Benning. The East Asia program. Begins in a few weeks."

Kasey gently smiled, "Taking a liking to the desert, Moore?" Looking at him, she saw a cognate spirit, "Congratulations, lieutenant."

Moore wiped his forehead, "I'm glad I had this short time to serve with you." He looked out over the horizon, "I've learned a lot about this place. The shifting allegiances and mind games. It's been interesting."

Sergeant Harper had also sopped up what he could from Kasey, "You mean, 'The enemy of my enemy is my friend' kind of thinking?"

"Right," Moore grinned and took a drink from a canteen. "It's like back in South Central."

Kasey's recent mission was on her mind, "Spend enough time here and you'll be making up sayings of your own."

Moore always wanted to hear more from her, "Such as?"

It took a moment for Kasey's words to come, "It's a kind place where your enemies will tell the truth and your friends will lie."

Harper jumped on her observation, "I get it. I always thought it was strange the Saudis would not allow the perimeter around Khobar Towers extended after the first bombing. It could have saved American lives. It always stuck in my craw."

The lookout interrupted, "Two heading for us."

Kasey had a look. Bowers' underlings. No need to call the squad to attention. Minutes later, the junior officers saluted Kasey and then dodged her gaze. They seemed uneasy when asking for a private moment with her.

One broke the news, "Captain, the general has word from home."

"Is it about my father?"

The other lieutenant nodded. Kasey dropped command on Moore and got into the jeep.

***

Kasey slung her duffel bag over a shoulder. With furlough papers in hand she walked down the corridor toward Zalman's office. The door was open. She heard Bowers inside. The general was commenting on some family photos the major was showing him: "Two girls now? Could there be a woman following in your footsteps?"

The Cowboy's voice beamed, "For the first time, I'm warming to the idea. I can't wait to see her. I'll be home in a month."

Bowers exited Zalman's office and watched Kasey approach. He looked her over, "Fix that uniform yet, captain?

His antagonism was unrelenting. "Not yet, sir," she moved by and tossed off.

The major wasn't done, "I could write you up."

Kasey had enough. She dropped her bag, turned and stared, "You won't do that. We both know why."

"Nothing ever happened."

"You were drunk," Kasey reminded him. "Lucky for you, I wasn't going to let you finish the crime."

"You're trying to rattle me with something that happened at the academy over fifteen years ago?"

Yes, Kasey was, "I wrote down everything and mailed it home. It remains unopened, postmarked the day it was sent. I record everything."

Bowers saw it as a bluff, "It's scant evidence. Any charges would ruin you, too."

"Then we'll both go down together." Kasey shifted from animosity to a neutral tone, "Stop being a bad actor about everything. I heard you in there. I'd have a hard time recommending your daughter follow in your footsteps. Would you like her to come across a man like you while serving? Think about it."

You could tell when Bowers lacked words by his dawdling jaw. He ambled away, swaggering to conceal any insult to his ego.

Kasey tapped on the open door and stepped into Zalman's office. He said nothing about the exchange he heard in the hall. Kasey put the papers on his desk. The general didn't glance at her until he signed them, "There's a transport heading out from Military City in four hours. We can get you there in time." Zalman dismissed her. Kasey saluted and walked out. It was time to go home.

3

Eastern societies tend to be high context civilizations. One needs to know boundless subtle, unpronounced indicators to negotiate effectively in everyday life. In the more recently settled West, cultural signifiers remain works-in-progress and collective experience continues under construction, often still needing obvious signs. In the East, layers upon layers must be exposed to find the seed notion behind the directives. Getting to the kernel requires comprehending reasons behind reasons.

To understand Saudi Arabia, it is essential to grasp complexities behind the idea of "separateness" within their world, a practice clearly established in their relationship with foreigners. It may appear culturally judgmental of them to virtually cordon off non-natives, but the bolder the discrimination is, the easier to understand the intent. Yet the nuances to how it exists in Saudi life takes much study to comprehend. "Status quo" is the underpinning behind Saudi "separateness" and it further exists there within a dichotomy. Saudis outwardly revel in shared cultural life. A citizen never publicly flaunts class or status. A billionaire Saudi prays next to another in rags and waits his turn for service at a local shop. Cite tenets of Islam, or studied social policy meant to keep things as they are, or the long tradition of individual autonomy among the people as motives for this conduct and you begin to see the intents and designs existing behind high context culture.

Separateness is practiced in unshared aspects of Saudi life. The extended royal family numbers about six thousand. They live on the outskirts of Riyadh, old home of the Sauds. Beaudoins of the National Guard patrol the gated communities and never socially mix with the royals. A loyal Beaudoin can provide security for a prince over decades without an invitation into his home.

No offense intended and none taken. A mere invitation violates the social codes of both. Ironically, the separateness of the royal family in the name of status quo has brought change inside their sanctum. Extreme wealth and absolute privacy have given free reign to rampant excess. Tales of wild parties, drugs and group sex have reached the public, leading the royal family to hire a staff of public relations experts to advise them how to act regal.

Elsewhere, the moneyed business class resides in separate areas near port cities such as Dammam and Dhahran. The merchant class separates itself near the large market areas. Clerics and religious conservatives separate close to the sacred places of Medina and Mecca. And the Beaudoins separate into the remote places. Synonyms for the word separateness are detachment, isolation, division, split and disunity. All describe factors stirring behind life in Saudi Arabia.

***

It was a Thursday, the preferred day for Saudis to engage in their favorite recreational activity, getting together with extended family. About forty people circulated inside Nasir's home, a place modest by royal standards. Sixteen wide rooms supported by broad adamantine polished granite columns, decked in glazed hand-painted tile floors under gold dust lacquered argil stucco ceilings and finished with silk drapes, custom upholstery, antique auction house furniture and effects compiled by personal shoppers from around the world. Mercedes SUVs and BMW sedans lined the quarter mile cul-de-sac outside. A fifteen feet high rock wall bordered by manicured thicket of rosebush, lilac, briar and oak vine bordered the estate. Nasir's three cars and truck sat parked near the guest house courtyard near where his camels often strayed.

Inside, males and females gathered in separate areas. Nasir's wife Waddhi provided dates, yogurt and figs for the women as young girls played by their feet. The women, in abaaya (black cloak) and kohl (veil) peeled off bits of concealment to decorate themselves in favorite jewelry and fix dark eye shadow of henna on each other. Beneath wraps and shawls, the wife of a Saudi royal

HONOR BOUND

could easily be adorned in enough set gems and precious metals as to make a
simple millionaire into a pauper.

In another roor.:, the men sat on the floor in a broad loop eating lamb, rice and
vegetables. Nasir watched his seven-year-old son Ibrahim struggle to keep up
with other boys running in and out of the house. A year ago, the boy developed
what appeared to be a cyst on his foot. After surgical removal, doctors
discovered it to be ossified ligament, a condition no Saudi surgeon had seen.
Since the procedure, more bursa has formed in Ibrahim's leg. Imaging showed
likely additional tissue solidification. Pressure from the growth twisted the boy's
foot inward, causing him to limp. Saudi doctors remain baffled. Another
operation would danger the entire leg.

Salih spied concern on Nasir's face. He moved next to his brother and held his
hand. Nasir pressed it hard, "The doctor returns from America today. He will
be coming over."

"The boy has been through too much."

Nasir frowned, "What kind of life will he have if I do nothing?"

"You have done enough. Surgery hasn't helped." Salih slid an arm around
Nasir, "Leave it up to Allah."

"Yet Allah provides doctors," Nasir immediately regretted his snappish tone.
He turned away and met the gaze of his son. Both smiled.

Nasir looked at his brother, ready to apologize. Salih gestured at their father
Abdul dozing in a corner, "Look at him. He liquors up before coming here. Our
family has strayed far from its world. You in your way, he in his."

Salih's tone of sincere disappointment saddened Nasir, "We are the House of
Saud. Our family is good from the inside out."

They retreated into inner worlds. Salih then looked so deep into Nasir's eyes
he saw his own reflection, "I am giving everything to the clerics."

This information would have been a shock if they didn't possess unclouded
insight into each other. "Think before you do," Nasir warned. "You will lose
command over the Guard. It is all you have left."

"Let it happen. One day, it will be the family who loses what it has left."

They retreated again, Nasir wishing for Salih to reconsider and Salih longing
for Nasir to yield to faith.

42

Nasir heard a vehicle approaching up the shale driveway. He walked to the door and greeted the doctor with a sweeping embrace. Isolating themselves, the doctor informed Nasir, "For two weeks I consulted eight doctors in three cities before I found one familiar with Ibrahim's condition."

Parental optimism burst forth, "Then we will immediately go to him." Nasir was certain that if a doctor somewhere knew anything about his son's condition, then something could be done.

The doctor winced, "It was the operation which made things worse for Ibrahim. The shock of surgery accelerated the localized petrifaction of tissue into bone. I'm sorry."

Nasir heard the words, but they didn't settle in. The doctor knew the only one way to get it into his consciousness. First, the whole detestable truth, "If we try surgery to remove the new growth, it might stimulate more ossification." Next, give something positive to hold on to, "The transformation of tissue to bone going on now should end soon. If we leave it alone until he's fully grown, then it can be removed with little chance of again starting the process. Ibrahim could end up with nerve damage that therapy can compensate for, or it could be so bad as he'll lose his lower leg. There's nothing we can do right now. He must endure the condition."

Both were quiet. Nasir finally understood. The part of him wanting to fight on forever went limp with a deep exhale.

Nobody had anything to say to Nasir until long after the doctor left. There was no need, the look on his face answered all their curiosity.

Nasir called his son. Holding a hand on the boy's shoulder, they moved to another room to be alone. Waddhi, out of sight when Nasir spoke with the doctor, already put a pot of coffee there. Saudi women have ways of knowing their families that husbands accept, if not understand. Ibrahim and Nasir sat across from each other on a rug. The son poured coffee into a small cup and handed it to his father. Nasir finished it and tried to clear his throat, "Ibrahim, no more doctors or trips to the hospital. They cannot help until you are older. Soon, we will take you to a special school, a place you will live, where they help boys with problems."

43

Nasir acted true to the Saudi way. Ibrahim was now anointed as different, another form of separate in their world, this time serving as a defense mechanism to hide shame.

Ibrahim stared at his father. It was the distance in his timbre that made the boy's heart cringe. Ibrahim swallowed hard. Father and son knelt and prayed.

***

After the military plane landed in America, Kasey caught a ride to a commercial airport for one more flight, finally ending up on a bus for the last leg of the trip. Little more twenty-four hours after leaving Saudi Arabia, she was let off about a mile from home. Indeterminate connections gave scant opportunity to arrange a ride. That's what she was prepared to tell her father. She preferred not to talk to him until she was back. They had gone at it more than once lately over her furloughs. Ted didn't want her taking too much time off. His view was that frequent personal time might interfere with her career. It could lead to loss of a favored assignment or slow a promotion. Anyway, showing up home without notice was her preferred way of coming back. Even when time back home was cheerful. Kasey wasn't fooling herself though. Even without notifying him, somehow her father knew she was on her way.

Kasey noticed her heart swelling as she walked alongside the dark road. Vivid emotions seemed to come less frequently as she aged. But not the ones for her father. She wasn't sure why she had come to limit herself this way. Was there less new in life to encounter and coax out feelings? Had her cerebral nature rooted neurons and dendrites so deep unfettered sentiment became buried? She withdrew from confronting the divide between heart and mind. Kasey never learned how to confess, let alone reconcile this part of her existence. Who knew where it would lead? Best to experience only safe emotions, ones for people and things from way back. Her abiding passion was for country. An inanimate ideal. Easier to place attachment on things insentient. Better than confronting intense genuine stirrings. Her experience showed there was no fulfillment there.

Kasey slowed for a chance to deeply inhale scent of the ocean, so distinct after time in the desert. The hard, nippy late winter air and frozen mud under foot completed the sensations of being in a crisp new surrounding. Kasey turned onto a gracious, wandering lane of modest homes fringed by soft woodlands. The path led into a village out of time, dimly lit by electrified gas lamps. The neighborhood was part of a town bisecting a shallow salt river, emptying into the sea not far away. Kasey passed a modest cemetery on a hill with a flawless, gleaming Civil War monument poised in front of the street below.

Already, there was something different about this trip home. Unfamiliar impressions filtered in, as though this place so well known had new things to reveal. She absorbed everything, aware for the first time that one day, this place would be here, but she would not. Maybe she would be on to another world, maybe not. The more the thought stayed, the more she sensed the unseen all around. Kasey felt the underground verdure waiting for spring and grub larvae clinging to tree branches eager to hatch in the first warm sun. She envisioned people she long knew inside their homes, almost knowing what they were doing at the moment. She stepped onto a small curved path lining the quiet cove. Some homes had candles burning in the windows, confirmation they knew she was coming home. At the end of the path was a three hundred years old foot bridge that spanned the river a few feet above the water, connecting to a street on the other side of the cove. She walked into the yard next to the bridge. An American flag flew on a pole in front of the house. On the porch, a red cooler sat next to the door. Kasey opened it, picked up the foil wrapped plate and went inside. She dropped her duffel bag, put the china on the kitchen table and stepped into the living room. Her father sat alone in silence on a recliner. Ted slowly got up with tears in his eyes when he saw her. They embraced, both squeezing so fiercely they near crushed the other. While holding on, Kasey's gaze moved around the room, a virtual library of American history books and a near shrine to her military career.

Kasey held her father until he pulled away, "You shouldn't be here. I'm all right."

"No you're not. You didn't even have your dinner."

"I'm not hungry right now."

No matter what they talked about, behind it was a whirling riptide neither wanted to face.

"You need to eat. There's meatloaf here. I'll heat it."

Ted followed Kasey into the kitchen and watched her turn on the microwave, "Rick's wife must have left it."

Kasey expected him to say more about Rick. And he did, "Did you hear Rick won a national award for newspaper reporting?"

"You told me in letters. Twice."

"I think he had you called home."

She was sure of it, "Well, everyone seems to know I was coming. I saw candles in the windows."

Ted smiled, "I made sure they knew."

Kasey got some things from the refrigerator and took the food out of the oven, "Where's Gary?"

"He has his wanderings. In his way your brother is like you."

She wasn't happy with the comparison, "Is he taking good care of the business?"

"He does the best he can. It hasn't been easy on him."

It wasn't a father's apology, but Kasey saw it that way. She set the table and gestured for him to sit. Walking to the chair, he pulled open her coat and beamed when he saw the stitching – *America, One Nation, One Destiny.* Ted tapped her on the cheek.

Kasey poured him a glass of milk, settled across the table and took a good look at him. Ted wasn't yet sixty. Barely gray around the temples. Maybe a bit thinner than last time she was home. *How can this be happening to him?*

One of them had to brave the undertow. She knew he never would. So, she had to, "How are the treatments going?"

Ted began eating, letting the question dangle. *Suddenly he's hungry?* Her father savored another bite, the silence packed with roaring emotion. Then he dropped his fork, "They make me feel lousy and I'm tired of feeling lousy. And don't you give me hell about what the doctors say."

She was ready to give him hell but Ted gave a signal she well understood. It was a command to desist. Kasey surrendered, but stared until it made him uncomfortable. Ted decided to inform her, "Nothing's going to help ... It's spread to my liver."

Kasey was crushed, frozen until adrenaline propelled her up from the table. She turned away, standing over the kitchen sink and looking out the window, bursting apart imagining what her father was going through. The things he'd never talk about.

Kasey faced him. Ted resumed supper, "Guess I was hungrier than I thought."

"Why didn't you notify me about this?"

"I would have ... eventually."

"How long have you known?"

"A week or so."

"Then how-"

Ted cut her off in his no compromise voice, "We won't be talking any more about it."

Kasey stood with arms folded until Ted finished eating. She seized his plate and turned on water in the sink. Layers of craving and fury occupied the cloistered depths inside each of them. Kasey's anger ebbed by the time she put everything away.

"Come on," Ted headed for the living room, "I want to hear what has been going on with you." There was so much Kasey wanted to express and little she needed to say. But it was a time to show respect for her father by doing what he wanted. Kasey sat on the edge of the couch, "Dad, I've taken five seconds of my mile even though it's over a hundred degrees where I run. The guys in my unit call me the Roadrunner. You know how he was always dashing through the desert ... "

Kasey talked on deep into the night. Her father pushed back his recliner and grinned as she detailed unit command assignments, hardware, weaponry, politics, gossip, even rations. Ted loved hearing everything, thrilled his daughter was part of military life. Kasey didn't recall most of what she said. She only remembered the desperate passions and aching sorrow that stirred when she looked his eyes.

Ted eventually had a hard time keeping his eyes open. Kasey helped him from the chair and they joined arms walking upstairs to the bedrooms. Before splitting up, they hugged. Kasey kissed his neck before he pulled away. Ted always was first to pull away.

Kasey watched him walk down the hall, "Dad, want to go fishing tomorrow?" Ted turned and broke into a soft smile, "Sure, let's do that." He closed his bedroom door. Kasey went back downstairs for her duffel bag, then up into to her room.

She turned on a light. The room remained nearly as it did when she went off to West Point eighteen years ago. The only change to the precise order was the uneven stack of diaries scattered in one corner. She dropped the bag on the floor and took out a journal. Then she sat at her desk and started to write.

An hour later, she took a pair of scissors and a roll of tape from a drawer, went to her bag and pulled out a shirt wrapped in plastic. The one she wore when she met Saddam. Kasey spread it on the bed and carefully nipped off the sleeve she wiped cellulose acetate on. Back at her desk, she taped the cloth inside her diary and continued writing.

Much later, Kasey stopped. A need to pause, not in search of words, but to head off a battle with things she kept in a willfully unaware place. Her unmet self. She closed the journal and had a look at a framed photograph on the desk. Taken on her high school prom night, Kasey stood beaming next to a young man. She searched the image, wanting to know if she was the same person now as then. A long yawn broke her focus. She got up and pushed her duffel bag under the bed, kneeling to move aside the old .22 sitting there, the gun her father taught her to shoot when she was a teenager. Then she went to bed.

Kasey went out running shortly after dawn, her breath floating and dissipating in front of her face in the chilly morning. Even at the early hour, she came across many she knew. Buzz paused in his truck to give quick regards on the way to a day of lobstering. Third generation in the business, Kasey went all the way through public school with him. Barber Sal stopped his car and got out. He was on the way to his shop, open at 6am six days a week for over forty years. He stood there, without words, arms open. Donna, another school chum, gave a honk on her commute to work.

Kasey chose a route passing her father's business. Ahead, she could see the sign, *Lawrence Garden Supply*, above the store. It emerged between bare trees up on the edge of a hill. At the bottom of the hill was *Uncle Moe's*, a breakfast and lunch place. Uncle Moe was behind the grill and Jack the letter carrier sat at the counter reading a newspaper when Kasey jogged by and waved. They were outside in seconds.

Uncle Moe shouted, "Not even stopping in to say hi, are ya?"

Kasey pivoted and came back, "Sure I was. But first I wanted to have a-"

Uncle Moe put a bear hug on Kasey before she finished. One so tight, she couldn't speak even if she needed to. "I'm glad you're home," he finally let her go. "Come in for breakfast."

"Not this morning, Uncle Moe. I'm going fishing with my father," Kasey loved Uncle Moe, but not his food.

"It's good to see you back," Did Jack sound openly relieved Kasey was home? Her father never came to the door for his mail anymore and hadn't been at his store in a while.

Jack's tone left Kasey with an uneasy feeling everybody knew more than she did about what was going on with her family. It made her eager to get up that hill and have a look at the store.

"We'll talk later," she promised, hoping they didn't sense her anxiety.

They nodded and Kasey raced toward the store. Uncle Moe raised an eyebrow and Jack gently shook his head as they watched her.

She reached the parking area, her stride furiously pounding the asphalt after noticing the delivery truck had a flat tire and crumpled rear bumper. The shrub rows and plant stalls, by now usually ready for spring planting items, sat empty. In disgust she set hands on hips and marched to a window outside the store. She noted near empty shelves inside. Kasey uttered, "Bastard," turned around and dashed away.

Uncle Moe and Jack pretended not to be watching when she ran by.

Kasey noticed Gary still wasn't home as she raced into the empty driveway. She barged through the front door and stopped in the kitchen for a drink of water, slamming the glass down once it was empty. Then she heard a car pull up. Trying hard to stay composed, Kasey stared at the screen door as it slowly creaked open. Gary ambled in holding a can of beer, his eyes cherry veined from a night of carousing. He grinned at Kasey and saluted, "Good morning, sir. I mean big sister Army captain."

"Where have you been?"

Gary finished his beer, "Unlike you, I am always around."

"You're supposed to be caring for dad."

"I am."

Kasey lost it, "The hell you are!" She got into his face, "Thank god the neighbors are leaving him meals. I just went by the store. What have you been doing? The place looks like crap."

"I'm doing all I can," Gary tuned her out.

"He raised us by building up that business."

Gary spun toward the door, "It's been nice seeing you. I'll come back when you are gone."

Kasey stepped in front of him. Gary pushed her away. She cuffed him with a right. Gary slapped at her. They wrestled each other, ending up on the living room floor after knocking over lamps and a table. Gary banged his head hard on a cabinet and Kasey backed off. Both stood and eyed the other for a long time.

Gary erupted in a tirade, "Who are you to say anything about what goes on here! You're never around. I wish you'd stay away forever! Even when you're gone it's, 'Kasey has done so well, we all love her,' that's all I ever hear! It's always Kasey, Kasey, and Kasey! Hasn't she overcome so much? She's the debating champ. Tops in the state in cross country. Number one at school. Then off to West Point. Then all over the world. I'm sick of hearing it! You don't see dad every day like I do. Look at this room! It's Kasey's temple. Do you see anything about my life here?"

For the first time, Gary forced her to see his perspective. Kasey didn't know what to say. Gary sat on the sofa feeling the bump on his head. She studied his face. His always neatly trimmed beard was bristly and uneven. She looked down and noticed his stomach now pitching over his belt. Kasey went to the refrigerator for some ice, rolled it up inside a towel and returned to the living room, "Let me look at that bump on your head. Then you can get some sleep."

Kasey leaned over him and gently pressed the ice on Gary's bruise. Both knew how to vent anger. Neither was sure how to declare affection. They both looked up at the same time and glimpsed their father standing on the stairs glaring at them. The anguish in his face bridged an emotional common ground between Kasey and Gary. Both froze in shame.

That afternoon, Kasey and her father were fishing off the bridge next to their house. They sat with feet dangling over the ebbing river that was shimmering beneath the sun. Kasey pulled in her line.

"I thought I had something."

Ted laughed, "Have we ever caught anything?"

"Yes ... once ... remember? I was five. It was the fourth of July. Not long after you started taking care of us. Later, we all went to the parade. I can still see you in uniform."

"You remember that?" The day held a different significance to Ted.

Kasey often thought about that time, "Sure, I do. I know it was hard for you to leave the Army after going all the way through ROTC."

He was surprised how well she knew his life, "That was the last day I ever wore my uniform." Ted left it at that, not wanting to dwell on his past. His children's future was on his mind. "Gary, he has this idea in his head that your mother left us because of your problems, that it was too hard for her to care for you both while I was away." Ted knew his time was short. He needed his son and daughter to understand each other. "I tried to explain the late 60's to him. Your mother and I got married too young. She decided life with a career military man wasn't for her. She had things to learn about herself. She just lost us on the way."

She knew her father was too good a man to speak unkindly about his ex-wife.

"I don't want to talk about her," Kasey's voice trailed off and she looked away. There was a lull. Ted listened to a distant songbird. Spring was nearing. He wondered if he would see it.

Kasey had something to reveal; "Dad, I'm leaving the Army."

Ted covered up the injury he felt, "Kasey, don't do it for me."

"I should be here with the two of you."

"Don't make a decision you may come to regret."

"No regrets. It's time for me to be here. We'll straighten out the business and spend time together. I have been gone too long."

Her father wanted to be blunt about his future, but held back, "In my heart, you never left. The proudest moment in my life was when you decided to serve the country."

"Now it's time for family," Kasey said it quickly to hold off stirring emotions.

Ted put a hand on Kasey's leg, "Let's go up to the cemetery."

They left the fishing gear behind and walked toward the hill. Halfway up, Ted experienced shortness of breath. That's what he told Kasey. It was really a sharp pain in his side that almost knocked him over. Kasey put an arm around him, "Let's go home."

"We're making it up this hill," he said, more commanding his body than dictating to Kasey.

No enclosure surrounded this burial ground. It was too much a part of the community to be separated from it, a fact obvious from its meticulous appearance. They gradually made it to the back row. The first headstone, carved from a white tablet, was a memorial for a soldier entombed on a battlefield. Kasey saluted. Then they bowed heads in silence.

Pvt. Casey Lawrence
Union Army, Antietam
1862

A moment later they moved to the next marker, another memorial for a family member who never returned from war. Kasey saluted and they both bowed their heads.

Sgt. Casey Lawrence III
United States Army
Perished From Wounds of War
In Ypres, France
April 1918

Another stone, this one of polished granite, commemorated one more family member interred elsewhere. They enacted the same simple ritual before his memorial.

Sgt. Gary Lawrence
US Army
Gave His Life
Shores of Anzio, Italy
1944

The last epitaph in the row was above the only entombed soldier.

Lieutenant Casey Lawrence IV
US Army
Died in the Battle of Pusan, Korea
1951

During their silence, Kasey focused on the words etched on the bottom, an admonition that appeared at the end of each memorial.

A Sudden Death, A Striking Call
A Warning Voice That Speaks To All
To All Who Wear The Uniform
Be Prepared To Die
America, One Nation, One Destiny

Kasey looked out the corner of an eye at the empty spaces in the row. Thoughts she didn't want to consider forced her to turn away. The cemetery had the best open view of the entire town. Kasey's gaze followed the river's aim to the sea. Neighborhoods clustered along the shore. Downtown was the ocean harbor. She could see the streets extended like spokes on a wheel away from the waterfront. Dusk cast a golden tint on the scene, resembling a sepia photograph taken long ago. They were impressions that nurtured Kasey, made her draw

HONOR BOUND

dazzling breaths. Her heart expanded as she took in the panorama of her home,
a special place in an extraordinary land.
Ted stood behind her and sensed feelings he shared, "You're the first Lawrence
to make captain."
Kasey had made peace with her dreams, "Fulfills our family's tradition. Each
generation rising higher in rank than the last."
Ted knew when that was not enough, "You wanted to make general."
"I want something else now."
"For the moment you do," Ted tried to point her toward the future.
"I belong here," Kasey simplified her priorities.
"No you don't," Ted found a way to be direct about the matter without bringing
up what he was going through. "When you graduated from West Point, I saw
the destiny our family sacrificed lives for come to pass. The promise of
opportunity America meant to all of them was alive in you. Another Lawrence
was serving - a woman. Now you've gone on to a higher rank than anyone in
our family ever has. We're military people. You'd never be happy in civilian
life. But you'll love being a general. Stay in the Army. I want you to. It's
where you belong."
"I have made up my mind. That's it."
"Do it for me. Stay in the Army," there was a desperation in Ted's plea that
Kasey wouldn't hear.
Kasey waved a hand in a command to desist gesture she inherited from her
father. Ted said nothing more. They linked arms and walked home.
Inside, they found Gary sober and rested. He stood over the oven stirring a
sauce. Ted went upstairs. Kasey lingered in the kitchen, "Something smells
good in here."
"I made dinner," Gary knowingly smiled as he rummaged through the
refrigerator, "in case you didn't catch anything."
Kasey couldn't keep a spoon out of the sauce, so Gary finally tried to seize it,
"Can't you wait a few minutes?"
She pulled it away. Gary tried to reach over her for it. Their proximity ignited
a kinetic reaction. They stared at each other and embraced. Kasey held him
tight. She wasn't going to let go until she was sure she wouldn't cry.

54

The television was on in the living room. It snared Kasey's attention over Gary's shoulder when a news reporter stood in front of some important looking building and began, "*The president was in Helsinki, Finland today, his last stop before returning home from a whirlwind European* swing. *This is expected to be his last overseas trip before gearing up for a bruising* re-election *campaign, one not made easier by figures out today. Inflation and unemployment numbers are up for the sixth straight month, a major factor being rising oil prices, highest since the early 1970's when inflation is factored into the equation. Diplomacy to get OPEC nations to increase production and lower wholesale crude prices has so far failed.* Add American troop casualties from the peace keeping commitment in Indonesia and ongoing investigation of campaign finance irregularities during his lastt campaign, and you have approval ratings for this president at a new low. Yet he did find time for some levity today ... "

The screen flashed to an image of the president earlier in the day making a statement for reporters outside as snow swirled around him, "*This is my sixth country in four days. I was ready for this. My bags were packed for anything, even desert weather.*"

Kasey stared at the president's face, her mind racing into overdrive. *He said it? The president wants to hear more from Saddam? Why he must believe that ...* Gary brought her focus back to the here and now, "Kasey, let me go now. I need to boil the water."

She released him, wondering how long she had been holding on. Gary put a bowl on the counter, "Want to start making the salad?"

Rinsing and cutting vegetables were good things for her to do right now. She needed time to think.

Late that night, Kasey stopped writing in her journal and went for a walk outside, stopping on the bridge next to the house. She leaned with her elbows on the railing and gazed at the moon's reflection illuminating the river, her ears open to the ripple of water against the pilings. In time, she heard footsteps on the planks. Kasey casually glanced sideways and saw Rick emerge, her feigned detachment betrayed by the sparkle in her eyes.

Rick stood a few feet away and looked out over the river. "I thought you'd come by and see us," he eventually said.

"Only got back yesterday." Kasey regretted seeming cold. She gave Rick a lean smile, "You just found me first."

He faced her, "I always know where to find you in the dark hours. How are you, Kasey?"

"I am ... enduring. How are you? And Denise?"

"We're both well. She wants you to come over for dinner."

Kasey ended the small talk, "You're the one who had me called home."

"Ted would never have told you."

He was right. Kasey took a long pause before saying more, "I am coming home for good."

"Talk it over with your father?"

Kasey moved the discussion elsewhere, "Congratulations on the award."

"The governor was going to go down sooner or later. I was only doing a public service. How could anybody have ever voted for the guy?"

"Is life different for you now?" Kasey didn't mean it to sound sarcastic, yet it did.

"No. It's an overblown award. Who cares?"

She wanted to make up for the tone of her last comment, "He was in office since we were in high school. You mu st have really taken on his machine."

"He got careless, that's all. Anyway, nobody reads newspapers anymore."

Kasey smirked, "Even in success, cynicism remains."

"Leave it to you to notice."

These two always found a way to rush up to the barbed wire fence that emotionally separated them. Kasey had too much respect for Rick not to retreat, "I shouldn't criticize. It has served you well."

"I'm glad you're still the same," Rick sounded nostalgic. "I'm always afraid I won't recognize you when you come home."

Kasey was surprised, "Why wouldn't I be the same?"

Rick wondered why he said what he did. Kasey scrutinized him while he thought it over.

Rick didn't seem as muscular as he once did, but there was scant indication his body had begun yielding to time. His hair had its same light color and appealing texture it did in the prom picture sitting on Kasey's desk. Rick's words sounded like an attempt to clarify things for himself as much as Kasey, "I admire the life choices you've made." He stopped and searched for each phrase before speaking, "You have the courage to believe the best about our country ... I wish I was that brave ... I guess if I knew that somehow your years in the Army made you as mistrustful of the powers that be as I am, it would confirm my way of seeing the world."

Kasey broke his reflective tone with a teasing smile, "Wouldn't you like that?"

"No," Rick remained solemn. "There are demons there."

"I have bad places inside, too."

Kasey had never said such a thing to anyone. She didn't know why she said it now. Rick knew it and was curious what was behind the candor, "Where are they?"

"Poor word choice on my part," Kasey backed off.

"Try again," Rick chased.

"You're relentless," Kasey half joked. "It's comforting to know you haven't changed."

"Forgive me for wanting to see at last what lurks behind that reserve of yours."

So different in every way, these two cared so *deeply,* so *strongly,* about each other, it hurt. *Who* they were required a distance from each other. That's what they had in common today, the similar wound that never went away. Neither could stand to focus on it. Rick extracted something sweet from the bitter realization, "Standing here makes me think of the summer after we graduated from high school. Remember the love letters we wrote every day and left under the bridge? What a pair we were. You - on your way to West Point. Me - a rebel without a cause pushing every button I could."

"I always think of those days when I'm out here," Kasey wouldn't mention all the other times she thought of them.

"That's why I never come here," Rick gently laughed, "even though I live two streets away."

There was quiet. A particular thing about Rick and Kasey was how occupied the silences were between them, better defined as an intense hush those witnessing it easily perceived as a surging current.

"I'm leaving the *Tribune*. Starting work at the *Examiner* next week," Rick so far only told Denise.

"So life is changing for you."

"Still a journalist. Only with a bigger newspaper."

Kasey's tried not to sound worried, "Are you moving?"

"It'll be only an hour drive." Rick understood what was behind the question - was he was leaving?

"The *Examiner* asked me to join their *In Depth* team. It's a chance to do bigger investigative pieces. They have great resources. And four Pulitzers."

Kasey felt genuine delight, "Fantastic! With you, they'll soon have five."

Rick swore he could feel her heart racing, "Thanks. I'm searching for my first story now. Any suggestions?"

She deflected the question, "You'd know what makes a good story better than I do."

These two knew when it best to take leave of each other. Rick gave Kasey a long look, "I told Denise I'd be back in a few minutes. Please come by. If there's anything I can do for you or your father, let me know."

"Thanks. You'll see me soon. Send my best to Denise."

Fog rolled in from the sea while Kasey watched Rick begin to dissolve. Something forced her to shout his name. When he turned around, words burst out of Kasey like an uncontrolled reflex, "If you want to look into a something, check out the production of plastic explosives. Cellulose acetate. American chemical companies manufacture most of the world's supply. You might want to research the distribution process. Where it ends up, how it gets there."

He was intrigued, alerted by the way Kasey hurried to unburden herself, "Think there's something there? We'll talk later." Then Rick vanished into the mist.

Kasey remained motionless. What was this she emptied herself of? She pushed away confusion and had a last look over the river. It was hardly visible now. Wintry drizzle dabbed her face. She put her hands in pockets and headed home.

On the way back, the faint gleam of a light on in her bedroom grabbed her attention. Walking into the yard, she saw her father in the window. He smiled down at her and gave a hint of a wave.

In the living room, Kasey was taking off her coat when a sound she absolutely identified thundered down the stairs. Kasey dashed up the steps as Gary hurried from his bedroom.

Both sprinted into Kasey's room.

Their father had shot himself with Kasey's .22.

Gary ran to the phone. Kasey cradled her father's head and prayed.

***

The final vibrant trace of ancient Riyadh is the Old Marketplace. The growing city was configured around this bundle of canopied emporiums and penned stalls. Goats and chickens roamed the sawdust floors. Aromas of grilled lamb and saffron shared the air with a snarl of voices bartering payment for goods and wares. Supermarkets and malls abound in Saudi Arabia, but the Old Marketplace was a tradition they anchored to as a way to deflect the jolt of finding themselves in an affluent, swiftly modernizing society. It represents a collective memory of their self-reliant character. It also provides a backdrop to sustain the perception of equality among men. Disappearing free space in the flourishing city forces a mile walk to the bazaar from the parking lot, yet even the king continues to shop there.

Nasir brought his favorite camel to the Old Marketplace. Another reason the parking area sits far from the market is most Saudi men insist on taking their camels when they shop. They haul them along in the back of pick-up trucks or in attached trailers, requiring ample land for parking. Keeping camels is one more way Saudis recall their nomadic history and independent nature. A Beaudoin would drape all his family's possessions on the animal's back and move to the next oasis. In modern Riyadh, seeing a man walking on the side of the boulevard loosely holding his camel's harness as vehicle traffic hums along indicates he's on the way to the Old Marketplace.

HONOR BOUND

Entering the market, Nasir and his camel moved in step with the crowd drifting through the center, a spontaneously formed browsing aisle. Nasir glanced left and right at the first merchant stalls, which sold bulk household commodities such as rice, coffee, flour and sugar. Snaking down alleys behind these shops were butchers, produce sellers and chefs roasting vegetable kebobs. The price of everything was negotiated, another familiar and comfortable Saudi tradition. It took Nasir only a few seconds to agree on terms for two forty kilogram bags of rice, which were tied together and suspended over the camel's back. He then went back and forth with a coffee trader, finally allowing the man's preferred price after being offered a new brewing pot with the bulging canvas sack filled with beans. Farther ahead, rug and textile salesmen perched in booths surrounded by tall spindles of woven fabric while the side paths were packed with cubicles selling appliances and electronics. Nasir pinned his sight on a trundled Persian broadloom patterned with octagonal geometric designs. It featured graduated degrees of monochromatic red, a tint he favored. Nasir cued by a nod and the dealer spread it open on the floor. Nasir crouched and stroked the material with his fingers, closing his eyes to use a tactile sense to judge quality. Then he brought the carpet close to his face, analyzing filament count and braid quality. The shopkeeper handed him a magnifying glass, assured of his merchandise. Nasir and the businessman stood over the rug and haggled. The salesman lowered his price once, even though Nasir raised his offer three times. Nasir realized he had given too much away when he first spotted the carpet. The shopkeeper maybe observant of a gesture that was a fraction too brisk or a drool in his eyes he didn't hide well enough when he noticed the rug. Nasir fingered his worry beads and increased his offer one more time. The salesman refused to move off his price. Nasir stared at his camel as if seeking telepathic advice. He looked at the carpet, shook his head, frowned and walked away. The shopkeeper rolled up the rug. Nasir looked over his shoulder. The man was sitting on a stool. Nasir kept on, gazing back one more time. The merchant met Nasir's eyes, slightly bowed his head and looked away. The camel stopped in its tracks. Nasir sauntered back and the retailer tossed the rug on the camel. Nasir paid the man and finally both smiled. The more agony in the bargaining, the greater the sense of accomplishment for each. The camel bent its head toward Nasir's face. He rubbed its ears and spoke in a dear tone, "That's right ... you knew we were going to get it now ... didn't you?" Nasir paraded with a boastful swagger as he jostled toward the far bounds of the market. His pace enlivened the camel, doubtless expectant of favors waiting at the end of the trip. The last quarter Nasir set foot into was the Brilliant Emporium. From its ragged stalls was sold as much precious rock and metal as any one place on earth. Saudis are per capita the greatest consumers of rare stones anywhere. Energy wealth has empowered their voracious appetite for gems of such high quality that the rest of the world makes due with their seconds. Nasir, like any moneyed Saudi shopping at the Old Marketplace, regularly stops by the Brilliant Emporium.

When Nasir approached, a guard yanked open the towering silk curtain barricade dividing the Brilliant Emporium from the rest of the Old Marketplace. The moment dealers noticed Nasir, they hurried to complete deals with buyers or abandoned browsers to rush to the edge of their cubicles. It rapidly became an assertive cacophony crying out, "Ibn Saud! ... ibn Saud! ... " while open palms filled with sapphires, rubies and emeralds beckoned him. Nasir glanced at one merchant displaying inventory of long, thick gold chain hanging over his fingers, "Ibn Saud ... 999 absolute, many times sandblasted, 14 grams weight by centimeter ... "

Nasir moved along as the man continued his pitch, "Would you like to see platinum? If you buy gems I can set them in PT 950, forged in Argentina ... "

Nasir kept walking. He usually knew what he was shopping for when he came here, but today he wanted to be lured to a gift he would buy for Waddhi.

A shop owner Nasir didn't know dumped a pouch of diamonds on a tray and aimed it as he passed. He stopped and fondled the stones. The proprietor was fast to claim, "You see ibn Saud, internally flawless. From Rwanda. The mines there are again open." Nasir wasn't impressed with the assertion. No rocks from Rwanda had been genuinely flawless since domestic problems there. He pulled out his loupe, put it to his eye and held up the biggest diamond. Nasir rotated the stone and counted under his breath. His suspicion was correct. "This pebble is notably spread. Indeed, it's not an F1."

HONOR BOUND

Nasir left the diamond on the table and went his way. The shopkeeper kept up his annoying jabber, "Ibn Saud, not that one! Come back, have a look at this ..." Maybe the man did have quality stones. But buying jewels was serious business. Easy for even an experienced shopper to pay too much for too little. A consumer who bought as much as he did required some faith in the dealer. Sellers need choose carefully what they say at first meeting. Nasir committed the man's face to memory. He had no chance of ever making him a steady customer.

The bedlam of noise leveled toward Nasir compelled him to focus visually. For a royal, visits to the Brilliant Emporium often ended up a tumultuous promenade. Nasir shut out the din and cast his view on the precious wares exhibited before him. Nothing delighted his fancy until he was by the exit. Roosting on stacked vegetable crates, he spied old Hassad, better known as Black Patch, slowly rotating a noble sized diamond between his fingers. Nasir hadn't seen him lately and noticed his booth was gone. He thought Hassad must have retired. Black Patch had been a diamond broker for over half a century. A renowned talent with the knife, he created remarkable quality diamonds with his unrivaled faceting skills. He was so emphatically fixated on his microscopic craftsmanship that he covered over his favored eye to protect it from overuse, injury and the elements. Hence the name many knew him by.

Nasir stopped in front of him. The ringing blare ceased to reach his ears when he gaped at the diamond. He could see the exquisite geometrically spaced angles glisten at exact intervals as it turned in Hassad's hand. No lens was necessary to know it was the work of a master. This diamond wasn't *spread*, it was a genuine *cut*. Hassad grinned, "A princely piece, no doubt ibn Saud?"

"Too well off to toil, Hassad?" Nasir flashed a wide smile, "We miss your work."

Black Patch stood up on creaky knees. When they embraced, Hassad slid the diamond into Nasir's hand. Nasir supported Hassad when he eased back onto the makeshift bench.

"I have the spirit, but my bones are weak," Hassad lamented. "So I come a day here and there, looking for a rich man like you."

Nasir settled his monocle on the radiant bit, more to regard the handicraft than analyze distinction. He savored the classic magnificent alignment of all 58 keen serrations. Low-grade diamonds are bluntly scrapped and unevenly arranged, classified as spread. With compromised proportions stones end up weighing more, so one pays a higher figure for a lesser diamond.

"Planing to leave all the profit from this to your children, Hassad?"

"Wouldn't be much at the price you'd pay, Nasir."

These two knew how to splendidly bargain.

"Hassad, how many riyals you want? I can't spend much today."

"Then you cannot afford even the shavings."

They danced around like this for half an hour. A rich man many times over going at it with a simpler man of means trying to assess the value of a rock. Hassad at last declared opening terms.

Another half hour of wrangling went on until Black Patch removed bands of metal from a pocket, potential settings for the stone and a sure sign a deal was near. Nasir desired a braided gold and platinum mount. Hassad began labor before the worth of the diamond was agreed upon. He pulled out jeweler's habiliments tacked inside his thobe, removed his eye shield and began fashioning the ring. Black Patch used no table, only his hands and lap. He knew Waddhi's size from memory.

"So Hassad, I will pay your last figure if you set it with trillium edges." Nasir understood it would never happen.

"I might as well give it away." Hassad's knuckles cracked when his pawl twisted the metals into one band, "Twenty percent more for the trimming, Nasir."

"Five. You're already making me a vagrant."

"Five? To edge a four-carat asscher cut? I should have stayed home today and not put myself through this."

"I'll give you ten percent if you stop complaining, Hassad."

Hassad opened his hand and Nasir dropped the diamond in it.

"Fifteen, ibn Saud. Only because of past business."

"Eleven, so you can tell your wife you took me."

Black Patch held the ring between his knees and placed the stone in the readied aperture,

"Thirteen. An old man needs money for medicine."

Nasir paused for effect, "Twelve, since you made me feel sorry for you."

"Twelve and one half, and only if your family doesn't come looking for the same deal." Hassad completed his work with a pry bar and crush press. He posed the ring inside a silver box and passed it to Nasir.

This had been a good day for Nasir, "I'll give you a check." He felt satisfied, almost beaming, over the result of negotiations.

Together, they left the Old Marketplace. Black Patch hobbled away to meet his driver and Nasir took his camel to the grooming pen where it was given a soaking. Then it was massaged and brushed while fed bananas, melon and sweet ice as Nasir lounged at a cafe, drinking coffee.

He observed a mullah holding court nearby. A few men sat on the ground listening to him recite the Koran. In the market aisle, a father instructed his son in the basics of commerce. Next to him in the cafe, an elderly man swallowed cup after cup of coffee he poured from a steaming kettle as he stared off into space. Then Nasir's eyes widened in surprise. He spotted Salih walk by carrying a briefcase, his lean frame locked in a tight stride. He came within feet of Nasir, yet didn't even notice him. Nasir watched Salih stop in front of the cleric, kneel and open the briefcase. Passers by circled, blocking Nasir's view.

Nasir walked over and witnessed Salih piling up gold bars on the ground before the cleric. In shock, his voice strained even in the hushed tone he used to call, "Salih ... Salih ... "

Salih smiled when he looked up. Nasir made a hand signal and Salih followed Nasir down an alley to an isolated area behind merchant booths.

"What are you doing, Salih! Everybody was watching. Soon, all will know."

"I am fulfilling my obligation to charity."

Nasir had never seen Salih so at ease. "Doing it this way will stir things up," Nasir couldn't believe he had to inform him of this.

"For doing what Islam preaches?"

Something more coalesced in Nasir's mind, "I went to the bank today. They had little cash on hand. If you are going to drain the bank, give us notice."

"I haven't been to the bank," Salih informed, "I took it all from my safe."
Nasir frowned, "Then why so little money on hand?"
Salih hesitated, "Ask the family." He believed Nasir still could finally grasp what he always chose to ignore.
Nasir was thinking, but Salih couldn't tell about what. Behind them, two men ducked into the other end of the alley, their conversation just loud enough to be overheard.
"The school is closing," one said in a low voice. "I'm losing my job."
The other was more nonchalant, "I'm not surprised. Most chemical engineering students study in America now."
"All the oil here and not one school for petroleum engineering?"
"So what are you going to do?"
The man grew manic, "They said go home to Jordan. I have been here twenty years. I don't want to leave. Something is going on."
The other was worried for his friend, "You are thinking crazy!"
"Am I? Listen, my apartment is near the port in Ras Tanura. For months now, few tankers there leave. Before, always busy!"
"You are not always watching."
"I know when they are empty, they sit."
"How do you know if they are empty?"
"They sit deep down in the water when full. The ones sitting there are window dressing. There is more, I-"
The agitated man was about to continue when Salih yanked his pistol from under his robe and ran after them. Nasir hustled behind. The rumbling footsteps startled the men. They darted out of the alley in opposite directions.
Salih took aim at the closest man weaving in and out of the crowd and shot him in the back. The man fell face down and was motionless when Nasir stooped beside him. Throngs of shoppers shrieked and jumped away as Salih gave chase to the other, but the commotion allowed the man to become lost in the market maze.
Salih returned and stood over the dead man. Nasir was confused and angry, "Salih, what have you done?"

"Some things are too dangerous to speak of," Salih crouched next to Nasir. "Even quietly," he softly added.

"It was the other man spreading rumor," Nasir launched a wail that shook his viscera, "This is the wrong man! You killed the wrong man!"

***

Kasey wore full dress uniform on the day of her father's burial. Mourners grouped in her living room before a banded trip to the funeral home. Kasey rummaged through a closet in her father's bedroom until she found a picture of him and her brother taken long ago. She brought it downstairs and arranged it on the mantel, pushing aside memorabilia devoted to her achievements. She stood aside and looked at the image with regret. It should have been done long ago.

Rick gently shared abiding disbelief with acquaintances while Denise sat alone. She was a stranger here until she married Rick. Her shyness had more to do her natural reserve than lack of personal history with those around her. Uncle Moe enlivened some with amusing tales about Kasey's father. There was no gloom in his corner of the room, only bursts of robust laughter.

Donna put an arm around Kasey, "I admired your father. He gave up so much for his family. I always thought about brownies when I saw him, how he always baked them for us when we had a sleep over."

Gary was in his bedroom hopelessly trying to compose himself. He listened to another car pull up. There were too many people around. He needed time for private grief. That is, until he heard a voice outside, one he missed for ages but never forgot. He looked out the window to be sure her head right. It was no mistake. His mother was back. He charged downstairs past everybody in the living room and dashed into the yard. His mother barely set eyes on him when he bounded into her arms. His tears of sorrow shifted to ones of longing and elation.

"I'm glad I could make it here in time," Cutty at last said after pulling from Gary's grip. "Let me look at you, my darling, wonderful, cherished son."

66

Cutty had gotten rounder since Gary last remembered her, though her appearance left no doubt she had preserved her usual style.

Gary again squeezed her. This time Cutty needed to hang on to her broad hat. She then introduced him to her traveling companion Alice, who followed along as mother and son walked inside the house holding hands.

One of Uncle Moe's stories had Kasey smiling for the first time since the tragedy. Then Cutty walked in. A nasty surprise for Kasey. Cutty grinned and Kasey sneered when they caught sight of each other. They stared at each other as Cutty approached and those near Kasey drifted away.

Cutty stood in front of Kasey hoping for physical contact. It wasn't going to happen. Kasey fought to harness her anger, "Who invited you?"

Cutty clasped her lavishly decorated fingers in front of her face, "No matter the words, it's a happy melody to hear my daughter speak." Kasey relived the distance she always felt from her mother, even before she left them. She could never tell if Cutty was being caustic or just had difficulty sounding sincere. Cutty gestured to those nearby, "My, how far she has come. Just look at her."

Should I curtsy and pirouette? Kasey shuddered at bad memories, "How did you find out?"

"Gary didn't tell you he called me?"

Kasey shot daggers at Gary who was advancing with his new friend Alice. Cutty took her companion's hand, "Kasey, this is my lover Alice. Alice, my daughter Kasey."

Alice's condolences went off awkwardly because of Kasey's burning stare at her mother. Gary wisely moved Alice away.

"I wish you had stayed away." Kasey doggedly established there would be no gushy eunion between them, "We've seen you one in twenty-five years. I don't even know you."

Cutty accepted her daughter's view, "I haven't traveled three thousand miles to get into this with you." However, she rejected what she saw as an attempt to heap shame, "As you see, there were factors you probably didn't know about that kept your father and I from being together."

"You left when he needed you. You wanted to put me in a home."

Kasey never came to terms with that. Cutty long ago did, "I was wrong and I am sorry. We saw eleven doctors by the time you were five. They said the birth defect you had would never be overcome. When a child is born with no passageway between their nose and throat, they are usually destined to never speak. You could hardly breathe on your own."

"They were wrong," Kasey declared in vindication. "You just didn't want to deal with it."

For Cutty, it wasn't as black and white as Kasey so passionately believed, "It's all we had to go by at the time. I wanted you to be in an immersed environment so you could learn how to deal with being mute."

"A year after you left, I was talking. Thank god he didn't lower expectations for my life." Kasey's voice grew louder, "He raised them!" She knew this face to face had to end.

"He was an extraordinary man because of his obsession. That's why I am here. For *him*, not you." Cutty had a lump in her throat, "I know you don't like me. This probably means nothing to you, but I am proud of you."

"You're right," Kasey said walking away, "it means nothing to me."

Cutty watched her for a moment. Kasey's words hurt more than she thought possible. Her resentment spewed out, "We are a lot more alike than you would ever believe."

"I don't see how that could be true," Kasey fired over her shoulder.

"No? You left him, too." Cutty immediately wished she hadn't said it. She was glad Kasey didn't look back.

Kasey led the gathering outside. They traveled in a motorcade to the funeral home and joined others waiting for the casket to be loaded into the hearse for the trip to the church.

There were so many intense, clashing emotions for Kasey to struggle with she hardly remembered the service in the church. Her adrenaline never stopped pumping in response to danger. The peril was vulnerability, an encumbrance she fended off to keep things covered in her psyche, the undiscovered self, too consuming to encounter.

She followed the casket outside, trailing the stream of flowers. Before the door of the hearse closed, the funeral director looked at Kasey and pointed behind her. Kasey turned and saw two Army officers, a major and lieutenant, get out of a car parked close by.

The procession waited while Kasey walked over to them. After an introductory salute and expression of sorrow over the interruption the major informed her, "Captain Lawrence, effective this moment your leave is terminated. You must come with us, *now*. I'm sorry."

For the first time in her military career, she considered disobeying an order, "Let me bury him ... I need one hour."

The major's voice cracked, "You must leave now. I'm sorry."

"Captain, we only have time to go home and get your gear," the lieutenant couldn't look her in the eye.

Kasey took a deep breath and stared at the hearse. The driver stood waiting for a signal. This was as far as her goodbye would go. She scrutinized the faces and felt the ache in the air. It seemed forever before Kasey motioned for the hearse to leave, using the same hint of a wave Kasey's father gave her the last time she saw him alive. The vehicles moved away. Kasey departed in the opposite direction.

4

For years, three American presidents considered Saddam Hussein an ally. Their administrations provided financial aid, weapons and materials for producing chemical agents of war. The US State Department furnished cover for unsavory conduct by his regime, cloaking it with media spin heralding his role in "balancing" the region. Checking press reports in the US media from the pre-Gulf War era, Saddam is regularly depicted as a firm ruler from a long standing political party who revived Iraq through modernization and ended Soviet influence in his country. He was saluted for opening Iraq to corporations from the West, improving infrastructure, bettering literacy and access to health care and creating more opportunity for women than was found in most Arab countries. This portrayal of Saddam changed literally overnight on August 2, 1990, when his military forces invaded Kuwait. Forthwith, he became known as the "Butcher of Baghdad." President Bush's State Department initiated a press campaign to direct the perception of Saddam to that of a brutal dictator. The mainstream American media went for it hook, line and sinker. Suddenly, Saddam Hussein was a man who committed wholesale massacre of political opposition, put down ethnic minorities with use of biological weapons and built an enormous military machine designed to conquer the Mideast. The US was gearing up for war, and Iraq needed to be demonized if the American people were to support it. Early command of public consciousness was achieved by painting any public utterance of doubt about the government's position as unpatriotic. Americans had to "support the troops". After the war, some truth about US government media deceit emerged.

One case in point was a widely reported alleged Iraqi atrocity. Supposedly, in Kuwaiti hospitals infants were removed from incubators by Saddam's occupying forces. Accounts went so far as to say the infants were tossed out windows. The source of the story was a Kuwaiti woman testifying before Congress who claimed to have witnessed the event. She then went on American television networks and recounted the story many times. After the war, it was discovered she wasn't even in Kuwait when Iraq invaded. She was in fact a member of the Kuwaiti royal family who fled before Iraq invaded and was residing in New York at the time of the occupation. A public relations firm hired by the Kuwaiti royal family in exile concocted the tale for US public consumption to boost support for American military intervention.

To grasp the relationship between America and Saddam Hussein, start at the 1979 takeover of the American Embassy in Iran by Islamic activists loyal to religious leader Ayatollah Ruhollah Khomeini. Before Khomeini's return from exile, the United States had a decades long cozy alliance with the family dynasty that ruled Iran. After World War Two there was intense competition between America and the Soviet Union to gain influence in the Mideast. Shah of Iran Rezi Pahlavi was one of America's best friends in the region. He brought Western style social liberalization and economic change to the country, but political opposition was not tolerated. In the late 1970's, conservative Muslims began openly protesting the Western influences personified by the Shah. The Shah's violent crack down eroded his domestic support. Martial law was declared. Oil workers then went on strike. Other industries followed. A military government was appointed to deal with the crisis. Riots ensued. Most public trust in the shah evaporated. His health deteriorating, he fled Iran in January 1979, leaving the country in the hands of an appointed civilian government. Khomeini, in France, named a provisional government in exile to prepare for his return. Clashes between Khomeini's supporters and government troops led to the rout of Iran's elite Imperial Guard and the fall of the civilian government.

Khomeini chartered an Islamic constitution that fixed ultimate civil authority in a Faghi, the Ayatollah Khomeini. The modern world had its first doctrinal Islamic state. However, the transition did not proceed smoothly. Battles between clerical forces and secular intellectuals combined with regional ethnic revolts left the new on shaky ground. To increase public support and consolidate power, Iranian militants seized the US Embassy in Tehran on November 4, 1979, taking 62 US hostages. For America, it became a degrading quagmire that went on for almost fifteen months and included an aborted military rescue attempt.

The humiliation was ultimately alleviated through a superpower's preferred rejoinder -payback by proxy.

Iran and Iraq had for years been involved in a minor dispute over a small part of the Shatt al-Arab waterway that divided the two nations. A barren, uninhabited bit of land called Karg Island sits in the middle of the channel. Title to the ground was a subject of bickering between the countries. The island's worth was entirely symbolic. Control of the terrain epitomized authority over the straits, an emotional source of pride and indication of regional superiority to each nation. The United States saw ascendancy of an Islamic regime in Iran as threatening to provoke revolution in the region. America viewed Saddam, with domestic opposition under control and in an enduring squabble with Iran, as likely surrogate to keep Iran in check. Saddam, for his part, saw Iran as preoccupied with internal strife and the hostage crisis. Opportunity was ripe for him to take Karg Island.

Beginning with the hostage crisis, American military aid to Iraq skyrocketed. Less than a year after Iranian seizure of the US Embassy, the conflict between Iraq and Iran erupted in open warfare. Iraq made a move to capture the island, bombing Iranian ports and even Tehran airport in an attempt to cripple their military. Iraqi troops went so far as to invade Iranian coastal cities. Iran, brimming with nationalistic pride and energized by their revolution, eagerly went to war with old adversary Iraq and repressor of clergy Saddam. Saddam did America's bidding and did it well. The Iraq-Iran War lasted eight years, with casualties numbering millions. Devastation wise, it surpassed any conflict since World War Two. A reason the embassy crisis was eventually resolved was Iran became preoccupied by their war with Iraq. Over three million young Iranian men were killed. Many were responsible for Khomeini's rise and were the brain trust who engineered the embassy takeover. Which is why at the dawn of a new century Iran is demographically a very young and predominantly female country.

The war served US purposes by eliminating the most militant champions of Islamic revolution, slowing down its export to neighboring countries. The war ended after Iran retook Karg Island only to have thousands of troops occupying it gassed by the Iraqi Air Force. Over ten thousand died. Both countries ended up shattered and exhausted, finally signing a treaty to share the waterway. It was, in effect, a victory for Iraq. Iran went into the war with over three times the population, greater industrial capacity, more oil wealth and a better equipped military.

A noteworthy incident occurred about halfway through the war. Senior US officials secretly visited Iran and traded vital spare parts needed to supply the Iranian war machine. It was done and in exchange for Iranian help in obtaining release of US civilian hostages being held by terrorists in Lebanon. Iranian weapons were primarily American made and obtained during the shah's regime. Iran needed replacement parts to continue the war. Only America could provide them. One by one, American hostages were released, and each time new inventory made its way to Iran. The US ended up equipping both sides, an Alice in Wonderland logic that illustrates the entangling alliances, enlightened self-interests and superpower foreign policy that predominates in the Mideast.

Kasey knew of all this and more about her country and its involvement in Mideast affairs. Nonetheless, denial produces a curious material in the psyche. There is sorcery in play ruling the disconnect between truth and delusion. A conjurer-self lurking with a wand over a hat, taking stage in our core until its magic is lost. Whenever that is.

That charmer remained alive inside Kasey as she again sat in an Army convoy moving toward southern Iraq. Nasir was next to her. Fellowship remained non-existent between them. Kasey felt a need for some sincere contact, if only to favor effectiveness of the mission.

"Captain Saud, I know you're upset about being teamed with me-"

Nasir interrupted, "Iraq said they would meet only with the two of us. Since they may have information vital to my country's security, that's how we will do it."

For Kasey, the response was as close to a truce as she could expect. She unbuttoned her coat to gain relief from the heat. Nasir caught an angled peek at the words inside the lining – *America, One Nation, One Destiny.* Then he looked directly at it, "That can't be official."

"I wear it to respect my family's military tradition," Kasey was happy to inform him. "These were the words inside the lining of President Lincoln's coat when he was killed. The first member of my family who came to America died in the Civil War."

Nasir quietly thought about it. Kasey sensed he was impressed and believed she knew why, "My family has served in five wars. Lost members in four of them. Surprised to find that military history in the family of a woman soldier?"

Nasir torqued his head away. He wouldn't admit she had read his mind.

The caravan went by the final outpost inside Saudi Arabia they passed earlier. The same two US Army servicemen were on duty. This time, one coupled his gaze with Kasey's and saluted. She noted him by returning the gesture. They moved toward the horizon where they could make out the awaiting Iraqis. The first thing that happened when they joined up was a replay of what went on previously. The same Republican Guard leader asked Kasey and Nasir to forfeit their weapons. Kasey again declined. Nasir wiggled his feet as he deliberated. He reached for his gun, stopped, folded his arms and nodded in refusal. Again, the Iraqis huddled and again they finally relented. Kasey and Nasir climbed into the Iraqi convoy and were whisked away, this time traveling in a different direction. Kasey, in surveillance mode, perceived an altered dynamism radiating from Nasir.

Maybe now they could connect. Kasey's attempt relied on something they shared, "You mentioned attending Georgetown. I went there in a special curriculum for Mideast studies."

"My uncle endowed the chair," it was the first time Nasir spoke to her minus an attitude.

Kasey had to take advantage of it, "When you were at Benning, did you study the effects of extended foreign service?"

"It emotionally disconnects personnel. Even more so when heightened cultural differences are involved," Nasir summarized what was committed to memory.

"I wrote that section of the manual." She guessed he was impressed when he looked away.

He was. Also confounded at finding his life so in circuit with the existence of this woman. He didn't openly admit it to himself, yet it was near enough to the surface for him to keep quiet so additional discoveries wouldn't befuddle him.

Two hours later the motorcade took a road bisecting abandoned oil fields, heading for the empty buildings that made up the refinery complex. They were being watched as they moved along. Unseen around them spread along the route were scores of women who wore military fatigues with green scarves tied around their heads. Closing in on the main complex, Iraqi troop presence grew intense.

Nasir leaned toward Kasey and murmured, "This region once pumped a half million gallons a day. Now, no activity at all?"

"They remain under sanction. If it can't be sold, why should they pump it?" Kasey had it all calculated. Or thought she did.

"This refinery produces oil for internal consumption. It is always operating. They want us to notice this, that's why we're here," this time Nasir had the shrewd analysis.

The convoy stopped near the main building. Kasey and Nasir left their transport. Following escort, both witnessed the gallows set up in front as they neared. A dead man swayed suspended from a noose. Kasey flinched at the bulging eyes and distended neck of the corpse. Her overall impression was Nasir's insight was correct. The display was theater. Passing by, Nasir noticed cleric's robes. He squinted and had a close look. He faced Kasey as they entered the building, "That was Ahmed Saghi. A mullah who fled Saudi Arabia years ago. He was preaching revolt."

Inside, Republican Guards were everywhere. Kasey and Nasir were led to a windowless room and seated at a table in front of a door opposite them. As before, the man who spoke rehearsed English came through the door and asked for their weapons. Both refused and he went back through the door. Then what seemed to be an endless flow of soldiers marched in and surrounded the room, aiming rifles at Kasey and Nasir. There was no surprise this time when Saddam walked in with the same interpreter. He sat at the other end of the table, near the door. There were no formalities this time, creating a vague sense of immediacy. Saddam's pronouncements sieved through quicker than before, "I know what I tell you goes to the right place. That's why you are back." Saddam addressed Nasir directly, something he didn't do previously, "Ibn Saud, take notice as you entered?"

"Did I see Saghi? Yes. He was wanted in Saudi Arabia." Nasir pursued the dialogue to gain answers, "If you protected him, why kill him?"

The question seemed puzzling to Saddam, like the Saudi in front of him should know better. "We weren't shielding him. After our meeting, I sent agents posing as the smugglers into Jordan. They were led to Saghi. We were able to get information about where the explosives were going," Saddam explained. He then dropped a bullet on the table and pushed it toward them. Nasir picked it up. Kasey leaned over and examined indentations in the lead.

Nasir peered at Saddam, "The imprints on it? Do you know what they are?"

"Teeth marks," Saddam answered. "Saghi gave my spies the bullet and told them to wait in a cafe. The man taking possession of the explosives was to declare himself by matching the marks on the bullet with his bite. He never showed. Must have been tipped off. So we took Saghi and brought him here for interrogation."

"Did Saghi confess who the contact was?" Finding out instantly consumed Nasir.

"Saghi said his work was done. He begged for death." Saddam paused, "He told us it is now inevitable."

The way Saddam said it worried Nasir, "What is inevitable?"

"Revolution," Saddam suspended his remarks until they absorbed the news. "The long planned uprising in Saudi Arabia. To install a Faghi and form a state ruled by the clerics. It is due to happen soon. During the pilgrim's visit to Mecca."

The information was not startling to Kasey. She had expressed the possibility to Drake. For Nasir, considering it would pierce his armor of denial. Like Kasey, Nasir had unmet places inside that he avoided. His mind raced in every direction but the true one. *Is this a fabrication of Saddam's? Did Saghi lie? Is it all a diversion of some kind? Why are the oil fields abandoned?* Nasir sought to hold on to any explanation except the idea of deep dissent brewing at home. Saddam went on, "If revolution happens, it will not benefit any of us. A new fundamentalist state would surely inspire more revolution in the region."

The remark roused Nasir's defenses. He became dubious, "You should have turned Saghi over to us. How do we know he told you this?"

"My concern is the security of Iraq," Saddam comprehended what boiled inside Nasir. "We needed to know who was smuggling the explosives through our country. The only reason it was done is to disguise the real source. From Iran to Jordan through Iraq? No need to do that. We are being set up to appear involved. That is why I tell you all this. I do not know who is behind it. I want the president to know we are not a party to the events underway."

It made sense to Kasey. But this was the Mideast, where the train of logic can enter a tunnel and never exit. "I will pass along what you say," was again as much as Kasey could promise. She thought it was a good time to make a request; "Can we take this bullet?"

Saddam assented by thrusting his palms forward, "I want to know what America learns. The *other matter* facing us will wait."

The remark baffled Kasey and Nasir. They looked at each other. When they did, Saddam got up and left the room. No chance to press for more. Kasey put the bullet in her coat pocket.

They left the building and got into the waiting transport. As they began the trip back, several of the uniformed women who watched their arrival were now concealed only yards away.

There was plenty Kasey and Nasir needed to discuss. They didn't wait until they were away from Iraqi escort.

"I suspected this was happening," Kasey wanted Nasir to acknowledgment she was correct.

Nasir was still wary, "We will check it out."

"Better move fast. Thousands of Americans are in Saudi Arabia. As soon as our embassy hears from me, they will warn them."

"Word would get out everywhere. A panic makes things worse," Nasir wanted it kept under wraps for now.

"If something like this goes down, you can bet Americans will be targets," worry was starting to eat at Kasey.

"We don't know if Saddam is telling the truth," Nasir remained guarded.

Their contrasting allegiances were exposed. Kasey understood it was a grim idea for Nasir to ponder, "Still, better safe than sorry. We can't afford to assume he's lying."

"Our view is that Saddam is playing games with America. Probably trying to get sanctions lifted," Nasir said, as if saying and believing it could force it to be true. "There has never been the disgrace of rebellion in my home. Saudi Arabia is the jewel of Arabia. Never tarnished."

"Don't be blinded, it won't help your country." Kasey plainly saw the process underway in Nasir's psyche. He turned away. Kasey already determined this was his way of reacting to what he didn't care to hear. She let go pursuing their testy exchange. They were now on the road dividing the oil fields. Kasey surveyed the area. Disturbing speculation trespassed on her observational quiet. Kasey wondered if Nasir was similarly contemplating, "Saddam asked if you took notice. Maybe he was referring to more than the body of Saghi. You mentioned the oil fields being empty. Saddam referred to the other matter facing-"

Before Kasey finished, an abrupt barrage of artillery fire erupted at the refinery complex behind them. Then rapid, extended salvos from automatic weapons rang out. Kasey and Nasir quickly looked behind them and saw Republican Guards frantically flowing into the building where Kasey and Nasir had just left. A battle was underway. Some of Saddam's troops appeared engaged in open revolt. A part of the convoy peeled away and hurried back. The three remaining vehicles rushed Kasey and Nasir away from the conflict. In no time, a wailing cacophony told of a furious struggle underway. Tanks rolled into the refinery from encircling territory accompanied by armed soldiers on foot and in trucks.

All Kasey and Nasir could distinguish about them was the green scarves worn on top of their uniforms. The battalion dashed toward the fray. Nasir spoke rapid fire Arabic to their driver, a frenzied plea to move faster. He was desperate to reach safe haven, based on innate understanding of the many things that could quickly befall a Saudi royal and American military officer astray in Iraqi wasteland.

At a secluded hillside encampment off road ahead of them, the leader of a gang of armed civilian men watched the unfolding events through binoculars. The man riotously motioned while reporting the episode. He jumped up and down when he saw artillery shells begin to rain down around Kasey and Nasir's convoy. The band readied weapons and vaulted into their trucks.

Kasey and Nasir ducked when they heard the roar of a screaming missile. The projectile obliterated one of the escort vehicles. Moving at top speed, a mortar fusillade burst in torrents around them. A direct hit sent another chaperoning transport into flames. Only their carrier now survived. The terrified driver zigzagged along to escape aim. Kasey kept peering behind. As long as no one was following, they had a chance. When Kasey twisted forward, she detected trucks ahead on the road moving toward them. The trucks veered off to each side as they neared. Closing in, passengers in the trucks leaned out and shot at them with rifles. Kasey and Nasir were under siege from all directions. They drew their pistols. Before they could return fire, a bomb exploded only yards away, overturning their carrier.

The driver was crushed beneath the wreckage. Nasir was thrown some distance away. Kasey crawled fom her seat with gun in hand. The mob swarmed Nasir as he came to. Other men searched around the debris of the transport for Kasey. She surprised one man from behind and demanded he drop his gun. He gave in. Kasey ordered his hands up and walked behind him, revealing herself to the others. They had guns pointed at Nasir. A standoff was underway. She commanded them away from Nasir. They countered with a demand she drop her gun. It went on for seconds but seemed an eternity. The head of the gang did the math. No way she could take them all out before they would get her. He bent over, cocked his gun's trigger and held it to Nasir's head. "He will die right now," he barked and grinned at the same time.

Nasir's eyes pleaded with Kasey. What she was expected to do violated everything she had learned. Never give up your gun, it is sole leverage in a stalemate. She pressed her pistol into her hostage's back. He twitched. She had to keep from looking at Nasir, couldn't stand to witness his expression. She stared into all of the others and shouted, "We are on a diplomatic mission. We are not part of any military action." As she spoke, she was sizing them up. They spoke English. *Definitely not soldiers.* Maybe not Iraqi. Some looked alike. *A family militia? How do we escape this situation?*

The leader signaled his bunch aside. He was about to blow Nasir's brains out. Kasey gaped at his nervous finger. Nasir's face begged her. These were not circumstances where a man would ever be held accountable for murder. Not in this place and not with hostilities raging down the road.

Kasey dropped her gun.

Men flocked around her as others lifted Nasir to his feet. Their hands were tied, and then they were blindfolded and shoved into a truck. As the rabble dashed them away, they whooped and hollered like ebullient game hunters who had bagged big prey. The gang shot off the road in a northerly direction, away from the Saudi Arabian border and away from the refinery behind them that was now in flames.

5

The kidnappers sped through the desert until evening. Kasey depended on whatever leaked through to her ears for information. She sensed they were criminal thugs, which was worse than them being political operatives, who at least usually had a formal agenda. It may end up being harder to gain release from this bunch. Who knows what terms will satisfy them? She came to label the voices of those in the truck. Raza was the one who threatened to kill Nasir. He seemed to be the decision maker. Abbas was his right hand, relaying orders to the following vehicles. Raza's brother, younger she believed, always spoke loudly and moved nervously. He was the one who tied Kasey, staring with a lecherous grin as he secured the rope as tight as he could. She calculated they had moved south, due to the way the vehicles were facing when they shot off. She used the angle of the sun reaching her skin to corroborate her reckoning. Kasey still had the bullet, having foresight to hide the evidence after dropping her gun and before being taken away. She aimed to preserve it at all costs. The characteristics in the soft lead being the only evidence who may be behind what could be underway in Saudi Arabia. With thousands of Americans potentially at risk, she would do everything possible to extricate from this situation. She could tell it was now night. Lack of sun, drop in temperature and passage of time made that clear. She had quickly alerted her under employed senses to compensate for her situation. Her unending hunt for details explicit in her nature and honed through her training was going to be her best passage out of these straits.

Nasir also applied his ears to gathering what he could. The captor's speech was faint due to the blindfold covering his ears and the grumble of the old truck

HONOR BOUND

engine. They spoke concocted Arabic and primitive English, as if to disguise their identity. Nasir knew neither was their native tongue. The man called Hani once let his guard down and slipped into Persian. He stopped after what must have been a silent warning from the others. So, maybe they were Iranian? Then again, Nasir's abiding suspicion was they were Iraqi and he was a victim of Saddam's intrigue. Like Kasey, he identified the two called Raza and Abbas. They hadn't stopped to pray, so they were not devout Muslims. Nasir, even in his situation, made sure he carried out his daily prayer requirements. His big worry was they would discover he was a Saudi prince. There was no lack of enemies for the Saudi royal family, even in the Arab Mideast. Anyone from hoodlums wanting to make a name to factions in surrounding countries vying for regional influence to Muslim fundamentalists angered by what they saw as Saudi wealth so extreme it violated Islamic tenets of social justice. That's just to name a few.

The pack finally paused at the bottom of a sandstone crest. Some made camp while the rest marched Kasey and Nasir up a path and to a cave at the top. A few took up lookout positions outside as Kasey and Nasir were led into the winding cavern. The gang knew every nook and fissure in the desert wild.

Kasey and Nasir were spilt up. Raza, Hani and a few more shoved Kasey to the ground at the end of one fork in the grotto. Raza ripped her blinders away. Kasey adopted an aggressive stance. She demanded they identify themselves and recited international law compelling them to notify the US government of her captivity. She warned them any charges must at once be described. It was a prisoner of war strategy, as her military standing decreed.

Raza chuckled. His clique was amused. Hani dropped a new outfit at her feet. He grabbed a long knife from his boot, cut her ligature and tore her uniform off. Kasey kept quiet as the men flocked closer, watching Hani let his hand linger near her groin as he yanked up a pant leg of her new clothes. His elbows pressed her breasts while pulling the jersey over her head. He forced Kasey on her stomach and held a foot on her back while she was again restrained, this time with sharp wire. The numbness in her hands and feet began almost at once. Hani rolled Kasey over and skimmed the back of his hand against her cheek. With his other hand, he put his knife to her face, resting it on her jaw. He

82

leisurely ran the blade it down her neck, just deep enough to leave a long scratch.

Hani knotted the blindfold around her face and whispered in her ear, "I can do anything I want to you. Remember that." Then he dragged her to an old fire pit and kicked her in. They all stood over and watched Kasey for a while before leaving. She was cold. Her discomfort was magnified by attention her constraints forced upon every ache. She was so dehydrated she couldn't swallow. More than anything else, she needed to relieve herself. She had no choice but to soil her flesh and try to writhe away from the ground it seeped into.

Nasir was squat against the wall in a different recess of the cave. When Raza and his toadies entered, Abbas had stripped Nasir of his uniform and draped him in new clothes. Nasir addressed Raza, "I do not know who you represent. Our countries ordered us to a meeting Iraq. They will know we are missing-"

Raza booted Nasir over before he could finish. He tried to continue as they bound him. Abbas snatched up handfuls of dirt sprinkled with rodent droppings and shoved it inside Nasir's mouth with it until it bulged. Then they gagged him. Raza picked up Nasir's uniform and closely examined it. He looked down at Nasir, "We are holy fighters. I call to Allah for Jihad against all enemies of Islam!"

Abbas smirked, "You, ibn Saud, have much to answer for."

Nasir's heart sank. They knew who he was.

Then Abbas spit in Nasir's face, "Look now at the House of Saud!"

They pushed Nasir on his stomach and rolled boulders on his back to secure his position. He couldn't move. Nasir felt the weight compress his organs on top of each other, an agony that allowed no rest.

***

When General Zalman marched into the US Embassy in Riyadh early the next morning, there was no hint of anything but business as usual among the downstairs staff, a group regularly made up of out of the loop personnel engaged in mundane duties. The general's arrival was relayed upstairs. An aide came down and accompanied Zalman in the elevator. As soon as the general stepped out, he instantly perceived a different charge in the atmosphere. Senior managing and policy assistants rushed around with precise resolve and the dizzying whir of faxes, phones and computers made it clear something serious was going on.

Ambassador Howe knew Zalman was coming. He dreaded meetings with the military. Especially one on ones. Howe was comfortable only with career diplomatic or bureaucratic types like himself. People who used circuitous phraseology and weighty pauses to subdue torturous encounters. The military breed had no curtsy to their style. That made Howe nervous. He didn't know how to tamp down their impetuosity. When Zalman entered, the ambassador turned away for a moment to brace himself while his deputies left office.

Howe faced the general, leaned over the desk to shake his hand and signaled Zalman to a seat. Howe seized the initiative in an attempt to soothe the general's anticipated bluntness. A charted strategy to usurp a belligerent inquiry and show solidarity in dealing with the problem facing them.

"We are trying to contact the Iraqi government through the Algerian back channel," Howe disclosed. "No reply yet."

Zalman unerringly presumed Howe's tactics. He didn't wait for the ambassador to continue. The general dropped a series of satellite photographs on the ambassador's desk. Howe gazed at the spread, resting a finger on his chin to seem in reflection even though he had no idea how to interpret what he was seeing.

The general figured this from Howe's eye movements, "We pulled these off the southern no-fly reconnaissance bird. It looks like combat broke out between segments of Saddam's troops when Captain Lawrence was there. Might have been a coup attempt. It happened after their meeting. She was stopped by a small group coming from the other direction."

Howe nodded. He had even more data about the event from other sources but did not intend to inform Zalman. Howe waited to see what else the general knew.

Zalman revealed no more, "What do you hear from up the chain?"

"The secretary of state has been notified," Howe began to dole out what he was allowed to, eased that Zalman had nothing else to confront him with. "She was about to see the president when she was notified. I'm sure he's aware of the situation."

"I expect all their focus to be on the safe return of Captain Lawrence," Zalman stared at the ambassador after the demand.

The remark was too much of a browbeating for Howe, "You take orders, not give them."

Zalman got out of the chair, "Not from you."

The ambassador took a deep breath. He resented his superiors who expected him to stonewall the general. "I'm sorry. I know you are concerned about one of your own being missing," Howe's background steered him to a conciliatory remark.

The general took it as a patronizing remark, "She isn't one of my own. She is our own."

"Of course she is," poise in this situation required validating Zalman's ire. "General, I'm afraid too much of what I say seems inappropriate to you. Since yesterday, all I have been doing is dealing with this problem."

The stance only paid off because it made Zalman accept that Howe was only a point man, "Ambassador, I just want her back."

"We all do," Howe felt the waves of tension subsiding. "The nature of her mission requires stealth until learn more. We are working on every front to make that happen. The secretary is anxious to know what happened during the meeting. If nothing else, that alone will keep full attention on the case."

The ambassador felt he did a good job finally quashing the general's antagonism. Zalman gathered the photos into his briefcase. There was a prolonged lag by the door before they joined eyes, Zalman's reflecting vague contempt and Howe's shielding suspicion.

"I'll stay in contact. Every few hours," Zalman informed. It had the sound of another command, but Howe let it go.

As the meeting at the US Embassy was underway, an emergency Majil was going on across town at the Saudi Council of Ministers. Again, the provincial emirs were absent. This was strictly family business.

Salih was speaking and most of the clan had given up disguising their fatigue as his harangue was winding down, " ... He should have never been on the mission with a woman. I saw it as no good from the start. After he returned the first time, I knew he was forever blind to what he needed to see. Until then, there was hope."

King Khaled was growing impatient of Salih's claims to moral virtue, "You agreed the Americans needed to cover themselves."

"With my brother's blood?"

Prince Rakan smiled. He had his chance to detail the clear irony in his cousin's argument, "You all but disowned him for being like them. Now you complain as though he was ripped from your arms."

The king searched for common ground, "Maybe it is good Nasir is not here. Who would want to see his face when he discovered the truth?"

"If only my father had not extracted a promise to keep Nasir out of it. It has turned out to be his downfall," Salih ruined the king's attempt at conciliation by fixing blame.

But Rakan came to his uncle's defense by returning criticism, "You Salih, are pushing too hard and too fast. Kneeling and giving gold in public to those who are against us. Killing a man at the market and claiming idle talk a security threat. You are eager to nourish your ambition."

Heartache was ripping Prince Abdul apart, "Enough! I have one son missing and another against the family. I want both back."

"We will get Nasir back," Khaled tried to calm the passion ready to melt the chamber. "The Americans will see to it because they will do everything to find their soldier. Let them handle it." The king was also offering a sense of distance to comfort them all should the worse happen.

Salih wasn't good at knowing when enough was enough, "I killed the man at the market to protect all of you. If people heard his words, they would be at these doors now-"

Khaled pointed a finger to silence his nephew, "Beware. I think you crave too much, Salih. You must hold off until our business is done. No more talk about the woman. Keep it here."
Salih brought his strident tone down a notch, "How long will that work? Nasir asked why the bank had no money. Others will soon find out. Things could get out of control fast."
"Everything must occur smoothly and according to the plan. We guaranteed it. Pray for the return of Nasir. Let us expect Saddam will not be a problem. We cannot let the Americans become nervous. Who knows how their president will act with an election near?

While the Majil of the Saudi royal family was happening in Riyadh, a bus full of American engineers and oil refinery employees arrived in the port city of Ras Tanura, site of a major US operated crude processing and cargo loading complex. It was a trip made every work day from the separated virtual city a few miles away. A routine undertaken with escort by a hired detachment of the Saudi National Guard. Since the Khobar Towers barracks bombing and the terrorist attack not long before directed against US military personnel, greater safety precautions were deemed necessary. Until then, workers made their way back and forth unaccompanied. The Guard now saw them to the entrance of the complex and came back at the end of the day to guide their return.
Arriving inside the facility, the crew was told the pipeline was down and they were being sent home. Not an unusual event, thousands of miles of oil and gas transit ducts crisscrossed Saudi Arabia and interruptions in the flow were frequent. Breakdowns in conduits, areas discovered to need immediate maintenance and suspicious activity detected along the route were a few reasons behind the shutdowns. The workers knew this and never asked for or were given more information. Even if the no work days had numbered many lately, it was paid time off. Which was why the American oil company employed the Guard escort only to the facility, then scheduled them later in the day for the return trip. Not hiring a full time detail was a way to save some money. This led to a security flaw. When the Americans left early, it was without Guard protection.

HONOR BOUND

The employees filed back onto the bus and the vehicle made its way past the refinery gate and into boulevard traffic leading to the highway. As the bus moved along, the passengers heard faint chants in Arabic emanating from somewhere nearby. The noise grew louder and one American pointed out the window at a number of men emerging from a side street next to a mosque. The crowd was walking behind a mullah, the one Salih kneeled at the feet of and placed gold bars. The mob turned and headed toward the bus, swarming the avenue and forcing cars aside.

A rider looked at a colleague who knew Arabic well, "Do you know what they are saying?"

The man tilted his head and carefully listened, "They are saying ... Behind every fortune is a crime."

The mass behind the cleric swelled. Men seemed to appear out of nowhere to join the spontaneous demonstration. Reaching the bus, the mob jammed the route and flanked the vehicle, forcing the Saudi driver to stop after an attempt to maneuver around them. The mullah was raised up on the shoulders of the horde directly in front of the vehicle.

The swarm started banging on the sides of the bus. The Americans on board, nervously observing until now, pleaded with the driver to move ahead. He shrugged and threw up his arms. Suddenly, a rock crashed through a window and the Americans ducked under the seats. The voices outside took on a furious disposition, obvious even without knowing the language. The emboldened crowd started hurling bottles, rocks and whatever they could get their hands on in a barrage that sent a blizzard of glass flying around inside the bus. Fragments lacerated one American's face and another howled when shreds of glass were launched into his eyes. Someone bent over to shield him and desperate passengers finally rushed the driver, screaming for him to get them out of there. Some outside climbed onto the roof of the bus and whacked away at the metal with bats.

The terrified Saudi driver opened the door and vanished into the crowd, leaving an opening for the multitude to stream inside. The bus passengers made their stand at the doorway, kicking and pushing the intruders back.

One American jumped behind the wheel of the bus and pounded the gas, daring the mob in a test of survival. The crowd leaped aside, parting the way so the bus could speed off, tossing those clinging to the roof onto the ground. The throng chased the bus as it veered down the boulevard, crashing into parked cars.

***

The kidnappers spent most of the day curving east through Iraq. They dodged the inhabited regions along the southern rim, the fertile land permeated by overflow from the Tigris and Euphrates Rivers. Raza kept the caravan within the orbit of scorched sand, the path of their frequent wanderings. Most thoroughfares in Iraq were tiered in a North/South alignment, a substructure dating back to ancient Mesopotamia. The times they needed to crosscut a major access road, they did it at lonesome cusps where only the dubious rambled. By sunset, they had crossed into Iran and arrived at a forsaken settlement near the brink of the two countries. A place north of the Persian Gulf war zone between the two nations, yet situated critically enough to have more than once been site of planned attacks, entrenched resistance and hit and run guerrilla forays during the conflict. The hamlet was once a modestly vital, self-sufficient place. Now it was a ruined habitat of emotionally devastated and resentful extended families who never recovered from the war.

The entire citizenry rushed to the edge of the village when they spied the gang speeding their way on the horizon. It was native home to the band and everyone there were kinfolk supported by their criminal enterprises. The community had a survival interest in the spoils brought by the group. Parents, aunts, uncles, cousins and children of the roamers queued along the road as they went by and then followed along to the vacant plaza where a market once thrived. When the convoy stopped, the residents surrounded the trucks and embraced the pack as they got out.

Kasey and Nasir were positioned in the back of an open pick-up and paraded in a circle for everyone to see. Raza stood between them broadcasting the account of their capture. A severe tirade meant to rivet attention on himself that ended up motivating the citizenry to pelt Kasey and Nasir with rocks and garbage, forcing Raza to jump off the truck. The sermon vividly attributed blame for all the town's problems on the two. So much so that the people riddled the truck with a furious onslaught, focusing years of simmering rage that had no outlet on them and leaving Raza delighted by his oratorical genius.

Kasey was taken to a crinkled tin shack Raza's family called home, while Nasir was brought to a shattered barn, ripped with bullet holes and split beams from plundered lumber.

Inside Raza's shanty, Kasey was tied to a chair. Hani removed her blindfold and stood by as Raza lectured her with a pointed finger in front of his approving family and friends. It took time for Kasey's eyes to recover clear vision. She felt less hampered now that she had reacquired another sense and immediately went to work devouring every impression she could. Raza called America, "A shrine to Satan" and threatened Kasey with a trial that could result in a death sentence. Raza didn't know it, but he was giving much about himself away. He gave Kasey information that he was likely Iranian, and from the amount time that went by until they arrived at this place plus the resemblance of the people cramming the room, she calculated they were at his native home in Iran. Bolstering her conclusion was his word for word rhetoric used years ago by Iranian militants, old notions exposing his current social unawareness. He began an overwrought interrogation, theatrically revealing his knowledge of her meeting with Saddam. Kasey knew he would ask what the encounter was about. How she answered would be important. She would never reveal the truth to them, but needed an answer that would match Nasir's, who was bound to be asked the same question. When Raza demanded to know why they were seeing Saddam, she explained they were there to negotiate with him about the conditions tied to US support for lifting sanctions against Iraqi oil exports. She fabricated details. The rendezvous was done in secret due to current US policy of no diplomatic contact between the countries. A Saudi was included because they were America's ally in the region and would need to sign off on any policy change. Kasey knew Raza liked her answers. He faked doubt and made a show of menacing her for more, yet she could tell he was pleased. Raza's witnesses were dazzled by his ability to reap intelligence the country would surely reward them for.

The grilling was, in fact, Kasey's exploration of Raza's character. He undoubtedly was the theorist of the gang, which wasn't saying much, yet it made him the most stable and likely to be swayed by reason. The others never questioned him, meaning they ceded decision-making. The assessment gave Kasey a bit of comfort, more as something to anchor hope for a way out to than anything else. His conduct reflected a man seeking admiration. He already had showed himself useful to Kasey by keeping his younger brother Hani in line. Hani stayed next to Kasey during the questioning. She could tell when he was looking down at her because his breathing turned into a heavy pant. She was aware from the first moment he saw her what was on his mind.

Hani put Kasey's blindfold back on. Again, he took his knife and scraped the blade across her cheek, moving the edge up near her eye and stopping it on her forehead. The impression Kasey got was that Hani was branding her as his through visible imprint, the way an animal leaves a marking like scent or urine. Raza finally barked for him to back away. He eventually obeyed, but only gradually, after sliding the tip of the scalpel down the other side of her face. He complied so leisurely Kasey wondered for how long Raza could control him.

Inside the barn, Nasir's limbs were knotted to corral posts. Villagers drifted in to watch Abbas put on a performance. He began by thrashing Nasir with a strap. Then he went into a long rant about crimes committed against Islam by the Saudi royal family. Nasir was also threatened with a tribunal that could lead to a death sentence. Occasionally a member of the gang would pull Nasir's head back by the hair and another would jab at him. Abbas' interrogation wasn't about procuring homage. It was about trying out means of torture and enjoying the fulfillment it brought. Especially satisfying when it was leveled at one who by accident of ancestry had so much more than he did. Abbas had the anger in him to kill Nasir. It was a fury combined of indignation over inequity and whims of fate joined with pompous egotism. Nasir had innate radar for people such as Abbas. Most born into wealth and advantage comparable to Nasir's soon mastered such ability. It was a survival mechanism rooted in apprehension of the payoff someone like Abbas could deliver in the right circumstances. Nasir was living those circumstances now. He refused to grovel. It would be dishonor and only likely to further ignite Abbas' obsession. It was better to suffer. Even if such poise only inspired more agony. They could kill him, but they would never crush him. Not men like Abbas, who had no respect for anything or sincere faith to live by. Nasir deduced what Kasey had, that eventually they would want to know why they were meeting Saddam. When Abbas finally insisted on the facts, Nasir slowly responded it was to bargain conditions necessary for Saddam to fulfill in order for sanctions to be removed. Logically, that answer that made most sense. Like Kasey, Nasir invented particulars about how Saddam wanted a direct contact with the significant players in the region unfiltered through the UN, and hoped if he made some concessions privately things could move faster, allowing Iraq to sell more oil. Nasir hoped the comprehensive remarks would seem credible. He couldn't tell if they were seen that way. Abbas' lash of the strap had the same vigor it did before the explanation. This time Abbas invited the gang, even the villagers to join in. It became a communal frenzy. Fists pummeled Nasir, knocking his head around and thumping so hard on his chest and back he could feel his organs quiver. Blood ran from his nose into his mouth, caking like a paste when it evaporated. He was relieved when they became tired or bored and put the blindfold back on, leaving him alone to deflect his searing anguish with prayer. Foremost, he implored Allah that the answers he gave matched Kasey's.

Late that night, the community built in bonfire in the square. Kasey and Nasir were marched through the village by the gang and down to the plaza where men surrounded the blaze with an air of expectation. By the light of the fire, Hani ripped Kasey's clothes off while Abbas did the same to Nasir.

They stood naked. The guns trained on them cast broad shadows, stirring the horror Kasey and Nasir felt, that this was to become their funeral pyre. These two, so different in many ways, again made the same decision. They would never go out this way. They would resist, not to escape, but to make them execute them another way, with guns, knifes, clubs or even bare hands. Kasey and Nasir swapped a look, a penetrating current transmitting their shared thinking. Nasir refused to move his eyes downward. He wouldn't disgrace modesty with an extensive look at her uncovered body. Kasey defiantly scowled at the men who were now crowding closer. Both were ready to die. They were propelled next to each other. Nasir swallowed hard and got ready to run. He preferred being shot in the back so he wouldn't be looking into their faces as he perished. He quickly gazed at Kasey. She gave him a slight nod. Nasir bent his legs the moment Raza emerged from the dark holding a camera.

"You two will make love now," he grinned.

The order was so bizarre, created so deep a chasm from their expectation, that Kasey and Nasir froze, unable to absorb the words. When it finally kicked in to Nasir, that some kind of blackmail was the intent and he was no doubt the victim, he was furious. The prospect of the shame to his family, country and faith was equal to being tossed into the fire, "I will do no such thing!"

Raza pushed him into Kasey, "You will! Right now!"

Nasir growlded, "This is extortion. It will not happen!"

Abbas jammed his pistol against Kasey's head, "Then you both will die. She will be first."

Kasey took the initiative. She pressed against Nasir and slid her arms around his head. He tried to pull away, but Kasey held firm. She began to kiss him, beginning on his cheeks. She could taste the dried blood on his face. It left a metallic tinge on her tongue. Kasey's mouth lingered on his cuts, her belief being the saliva she left behind might help mend his lacerations. Eventually she positioned her lips on Nasir's locked mouth.

The noise of the camera's shutter clicking away between the crackling flames made Nasir wince. The spectators gaped while Raza framed Kasey and Nasir in the viewfinder. To the lens they appeared alone, the inferno pitching volumes of light and presenting a dramatic image of glowing sensuality.

Nasir's conditioning kept demanding he yank himself away. Kasey moved her lips to his ears and whispered, "Don't resist. Do what they want. It might keep us alive."

Nasir bowed his head and angrily muttered, "Such pictures would be a scandal in my country. Adultery means a death sentence. I would rather be murdered right here."

The throng was barely far enough away and just enough enthralled for Kasey and Nasir to cloak their conversation with the sound of the crackling fire.

"We have vital information. We need to return with it," Kasey couldn't believe she had to reason with him in this situation. "Your family will understand."

Hani was crouching with wide eyes and open mouth. He edged closer to Kasey. Raza gave a brusque wave and Abbas hauled him out of the frame. Abbas then bumped Kasey onto the ground and the rest of the gang threw Nasir on top of her. Kasey held him near, "Can't you see? They don't plan to kill us. What good will extortion be if you don't return alive?"

Nasir softened his attitude. He pecked at Kasey's lips, animating Raza who gyrated above them with the camera.

Kasey and Nasir needed to use this encounter for as much knowledge exchange as they could. Nasir nibbled at Kasey's ear, "Did they ask about meeting Saddam?"

"I said it was about lifting sanctions."

"Good. We are reasoning alike."

They faked more foreplay to keep Raza from closing in. Kasey wanted a deduction validated, "Do you know where we are?"

"Iran. What about the bullet? Lost?"

"I still have it. Don't ask where."

Nasir slightly nodded his head before Raza swooped in with the camera.

Then he was done.

Hani jumped in and pulled Nasir off Kasey. Both were tugged to their feet and covered up. Their hands were again bound and they were hustled along back to separate confinement. The villagers dispersed, an excited hubbub energized their walk home. A few followed along behind Kasey and Nasir, squeezing every memorable moment out of the event. Raza reminded Abbas, "Say nothing about the pictures when we meet with the Foreign Ministry."

***

Rick took Kasey's suggestion and ran with it. During all her time in the Army Kasey never brought up any subject he might pursue for a story. And until their encounter on the bridge, he had never asked. He knew her job involved covert matters obligating her to uphold silence regarding things he could only guess. Kasey's intense patriotism alone was reason enough for him to realize she would never be the source for a snooping reporter's account that might shame her country. But something in their lives that always diverged had converged that night on the bridge. Kasey's brief statement about plastic explosives shocked Rick in a quiet way. He knew she wasn't going to say more. It was up to him to take it from there. He also had a sense there must be something serious, or disturbing, maybe even personal, for Kasey to have mentioned it. Particulars in Kasey's life somehow intersected with Rick's that evening. He was a journalist on the way up and on a hot streak. The *Examiner* was many times the size of the *Tribune*. The kind of paper that won Pulitzers, instead of regional awards. Not that Rick would ever admit he thought about such things. He innately hid denial by blending cynicism with propriety. He would only admit being motivated by professionalism. Never ego, or desire to impress a new employer. A US Army intelligence officer urged him to look at the production and distribution process of cellulose acetate. Any good reporter would do what he did, which was immediately go to work researching the subject. Rick learned that American chemical companies did, as Kasey said, manufacture most of the cellulose acetate produced in the world. Most of it was done at the Wall Chemical Company located in New Jersey.

Denise accompanied Rick on the trip to the airport. He had an appointment later in the day at Wall with their public information office. On the road before dawn, neither said much until the coffee they stopped for got them going. They were married for two years. Rick was four years older than her. Denise was an archivist at a museum library. The executor of its donated collection and expert in acquiring missing gaps in its documents. Denise had a highly refined, almost uncanny ability to notice the fissures and lags in things she focused on.

Rick first saw her while researching a story at the library. She grabbed his eye while going about her business. Something about her gave him the impression she cultivated her workplace persona. The way someone in a distinctive setting gives off a sure, if difficult to describe bearing uncharacteristic to a specific environment. Denise had a sweeping mane she tamed with breezy twists and piles that looked different every day. She wore glasses with antique frames and had a radiant style that blended old things and new ways into something cleverly neither dated nor trendy. In the library, she moved more softly than others. Rick had to find pretense to keep twisting around so he could see if she was near. Rick made unnecessary trips to the library hoping for cause to have an extended conversation and if the vibe was right maybe ask her out for coffee. It never happened. Finally, he was too busy, too adult and the library was too far out of the way for such adolescent behavior to continue. Besides, he wasn't even aware what her relationship situation was except that she didn't wear a wedding ring. A grumpy smile and shrug in his step described his bearing as he paced to his car.

While driving out of the parking garage, his attention was distracted by something that fell onto the floor of the car. He reached to pick it up the as a motorcycle turned the corner in front of the garage. Rick looked up barely in time to swerve away as the operator of the bike spun out trying to avoid a collision. The motorcycle was moving slowly enough to keep the driver from a sprawling fall. Rick got out of his car and approached, already apologizing before he had a good look at the woman with wild hair in a leather jacket who was driving - Denise. She was inspecting her bike and ready to berate the dimwit driving the car. Disdain and sorrow went into arrest, then flowed into a surprise, confused silence when they stood face to face. Denise had watched Rick in the library and once caught him looking her over. Her notion of him was similar to his impression of her. Denise thought he seemed somehow out of element in an indescribable way while inside the library. She was curious enough about him to observe his activity when she was nearby and pay attention to the research material he poured over. It took seconds that felt an eternity for a new dynamic to sift out of the hush. When it formed, it happened without conscious effort.

"You're going to have to convince me you didn't plan this," were the words that raced from Denise's mouth.

If only Rick were so clever.

He laughed.

So did she.

A year later they were married.

Denise moved into the house Rick inherited from his parents. It was the place where he grew up but moved from after college when he was previously wedded for a brief time. His parents died years ago, but Rick stayed in the house from time to time. For some reason, he couldn't sell the place. Something tied him to the spot. Denise wanted them to live there. It wasn't that far a commute and the lot had enough land for her to indulge in a passion for gardening she hadn't explored for a long time.

Those in town who knew Rick saw how good she was for him. The house never looked better. Rick made improvements and Denise filled the inside with plants and the yard with wildflowers. Rick's friends liked Denise's quick smile that fronted an amiable nature. Neighbors grinned seeing him riding on the back of her motorcycle along the shore roads on summer days.

Nearing the airport, Denise was pondering the exuberance she witnessed in Rick as he attacked the subject of plastic explosives after meeting with Kasey. She had met Kasey only on a few occasions. Once before they were married, then at their wedding and a few times since during Kasey's visits home. Rick told her Kasey was a childhood friend and high school sweetheart. A nonchalant, simple description Denise never viewed as suspect. She never felt threatened by their past. She was more curious about Rick's earlier marriage he explained as breaking up due to each being "much too young." It wasn't the only thing about Rick's young adult life yet to be clarified. Denise tried to believe some matters are revealed only when the time is right. The view was at odds with her intellect that sought to connect gaps in things. Maybe it was simply her nature to exist within the dichotomy. Perhaps it was a murky area in her psyche where qualities such as defense and denial entomb. She looked at Rick, who was behind the wheel. The moment nudged her to a place she hadn't gone to before.

"Were you and Kasey always so different?"

Her inquiry wasn't met with a pause. It was a deliberation.

"How do you mean?"

Rick searched for what was behind the question, also buying time to structure a reply.

"She seems so ... " Denise stopped, needing to label it for him as well as herself, "flag-waving, apple pie American."

Both grinned at the cliched profile. Denise proceeded, "You're such an anti-establishment rabble rouser. Were you both that way when you were younger?"

"Pretty much."

"Did you think you'd always be together?"

"I guess there was a time we did," Rick tried to sound loose and easy. "We almost went to the same college, until she was accepted at West Point."

The answer was more revealing than Rick probably wished. It filled an information breach for Denise. There were emotions he couldn't conceal behind the way he tossed off the words. She was learning things about Rick. Disappointments. Vulnerabilities. She pictured a young man experiencing feelings of losing someone to a way of life he didn't share. Denise wasn't sure why the empathy stirred up some sadness about their marriage. Maybe it opened a new abyss to be bridged. Now new facts were at some point going to be necessary and she wasn't sure why her intuition was wary. A vague and unsettling something brewed on the horizon menacing their relationship. It was a preposterous sensation, she knew, and staggeringly opposite of what she was feeling only moments ago.

The sun was rising as the airport came into view. They had been silent for a while. Denise saw it as a good time to bring up what they hadn't discussed lately. Good because of the little time it remaining to get into a fidgety subject.

"Are you planning to see a doctor about that soon?"

Before her question, Rick was mulling over a similar puzzling conclusion of a troubling dynamic in the air. But his more complex system of negation kept it at a better distance.

"Soon, yeah," Rick's voice fell like a boulder hurled from a cliff. He turned away, removed from the unmet old demons. "I don't know if it's going to be possible to do anything about it. It's been so long."

This was a different opinion. Denise never heard him so sullen. It hurt. When he proposed, he was buoyant about their future. Now, as they arrived at the terminal, she wanted to probe.

It was too late. Rick opened the door. Denise slid over to the driver's side. Rick stepped out, leaned in and gave her a kiss. Denise watched him head inside. A craving moved her to call his name. He quit walking and curved her way. She got out of the car. They walked to each other and fell into a prolonged and rooted embrace, at last parting without a word.

George Campbell, the executive supervising public information at Wall, gave Rick a tour of the vast facility. Rick knew he would be spending time hearing the company line before he'd have a chance for an interview. He told Campbell he was researching a story about modern chemical production and changing environmental standards. A subject agreeable enough for Wall to permit an audience. Campbell's ramble around the premises lasted four hours. None of it supplying any details Rick was after. He didn't expect it to. Neither did he expect the tour to go on so long. Rick spent most of this time thinking about Denise, still hoping to make the last flight back so he could be home that night. He feigned interest in Campbell's presentation by occasionally asking enthralled questions and scribbling notes.

By late afternoon, they finally sat down in Campbell's office. Rick glanced at the memorabilia in the room. It told Rick that George was a company lifer. He informed Rick he started at Wall as an engineer. Campbell's stomach swelled over his waist as if an unmetabolized tire lodged there. Rick presumed it was an effect from being behind a desk for a long time.

Rick started asking about the evolution of recent chemical manufacturing techniques, progressing to a query about challenges Wall faced with as environmental law developed. Campbell's words took a long time to come out. He seemed to breathe only through his nose, often pausing to inhale. It slowed his answers and filled the silence with strikingly obnoxious sounds of respiration.

Rick perked up when Campbell revealed Wall received waivers to exceed legal standards when providing military contracts. This was the opening he needed to shift his probing.

"So Wall manufactures chemical materials for the private and government sector? What's the balance in ratio?"

"Almost twenty percent of our contracts are from the government."

"Military?"

"Mostly."

"For weapons?"

Rick tapped his foot waiting for Campbell to store up enough oxygen to answer. "Yes. Wall innovated the newest generation molding polymers used for incendiary components."

"That meaning what in lay terms?" Rick asked quickly, hoping George might respond before needing another breath.

"We provide pliant synthetics - plastics, for combustible casting. I can't say much more about it."

Rick was where he wanted to be and got there without Campbell suspecting a different agenda. "How long has Wall been doing that? What controls are on the production process? I've heard small amounts can be very destructive."

The questions were asked in sequence to give Campbell time to catch air. Campbell immediately replied, "Years ago Congress shut down a number of military bases, some that were manufacturing the materials. Federal law mandated all but research be outsourced. At the same time, it put detailed new restrictions on substances used in the process. Everything is micro managed."

That was as long as Campbell could talk. Rick had figured the rhythm. It was his turn to speak. "Can security ever be that good? This is a huge place. Only a tiny bit sneaks out or someone in the chain does creative paper shuffling and what happens? Multiply it all by the other chemical companies with similar contracts ... " Rick laterally pitched his arms.

Campbell was ready, "The control link being what it is, a vast number of people would have to be involved. From CEO to plant workers, security, government auditors and our suppliers. All of them would be risking prison time. Even minor honest mistakes can result in fines and loss of careers."

Rick waited. He knew there would be more. Campbell was such a company man, he was glad to narrate what he saw as achievements. His smile was one a person with obscure expertise shines when finding another curious about their specialty. "Wall today is the only *legal producer* of pliant synthetics with incendiary potential in America. The contract was awarded to one company so security and technology access could be monitored and managed. It really is near impossible for any funny business to go on."

Campbell was silent, not from oxygen need lack but because he said all he could about the subject. Rick's journalistic instincts told him there was a trace of something useful here, yet whatever story there was to unearth in Kasey's words was not going to be found at this place.

***

Raza and Abbas waited in a Teheran cafe. A friend of a friend had put them in contact with the Foreign Ministry and after outlining details of the situation, they were given a name, place and time for rendezvous. The contact was already hours late. Raza and Abbas lingered all morning, musing over expected glory and frowning about changes they noticed in the city. More women were in public jobs than since before the revolution, and many were lax in traditional dress. Abbas was taken aback to have a hostess welcome them and more confounded when she looked him straight in the eye. He was ready to question the waiter about this, but had to withhold complaint when a boy came to take their order.

Raza kept checking the clock. He was fretting over leaving Kasey and Nasir in the charge of Hani and the others. They stayed a while longer until Raza decided there must be some mix-up. He decided they should go to the nearby home of Raza's distant cousin until they could find out what was happening.

Stepping away from the table, a man seated close by leaned over and pushed Raza down into the chair. Raza glared and pushed the man's hand off him while Abbas geared up to pounce. Another man slithered into a space at their table and announced, "I am Hashemi Rajavi. Where are the two?"

This was the name they were waiting to hear, but Raza and Abbas shot each other a look that said they didn't know what to make of the greeting. Rajavi spoke in a seething pitch through clenched teeth and his hulking silent associate added a threatening, browbeating air with his unblinking stare.

Raza and Abbas noticed them earlier come in separately and be seated at tables beside them. Rajavi spent the time seemingly reading a newspaper and drinking juice while his associate had companions with him who now were nowhere to be seen.

Rajavi impatiently tapped his fingers. Raza was at first insulted, then chose to see it as a misunderstanding, "We have something valuable for you. A treasure for the cause. Already, we have gotten important information."

"I asked you, where are the two?"

Abbas discharged his indignation, "We risked our lives to-"

Rajavi cut him off. He knew the kind of people they were and how to deal with them, "Answer my question, where are your hostages?"

Suddenly, Raza wasn't sure he wanted them to know.

Then Abbas blurted out, "They're back home."

Rajavi and his associate communicated through eye contact. Raza watched and decided he didn't trust them.

Which made it a bad time for Abbas to become talkative, "We saw Saddam arrive at a refinery that is now deserted. Then Republican Guards brought the American and Saudi-"

Rajavi again wouldn't let him finish, "What were you doing in Iraq?"

Why was Rajavi more interested in their activity than the spoils they had? Raza hoped Abbas would shut up.

"We saw some of Saddam's troops move from our border," Abbas was becoming a windbag. "Last time that happened they tried to destroy him. We trailed way behind to see."

"A lie," Rajavi knew. He spent all morning listening to them

"You were slinking around, robbers in the wasteland."

Abbas wanted to deflect the truth, "We are telling what we saw, you need to know we-"

"Following them so far into southern Iraq? It could have been the end of you or started the war all over again."

Raza's ire erupted, "This is how you react to our bravery? We have an American officer and Saudi prince for our country."

Rajavi ignored the protest, "Do the hostages know where they are?"

"No," Raza spit out, "we tried to find out why they were seeing Saddam. Each said it was about removing sanctions."

The associate snickered. Rajavi shook his head, "Fools. Of course they know where they are."

"We blindfolded them right away," Abbas disagreed. "Green Scarves were around, so we got out of there fast. They were going to Saddam's aid."

"Green Scarves?" Rajavi raised a brow. "You were fortunate. If they weren't busy they would have cut you to pieces."

"We are not stupid," Raza claimed.

Rajavi wasn't sure about that. He was finished with them, "Return home and stay with the two. Do not leave there. You will hear from us."

The silent associate got up, kicked his chair aside and followed Rajavi. Raza and Abbas were left pouting, slouching and enfeebled.

Raza roused himself by shaking a fist, "If they won't give us due, there are others who be happy to take them off our hands."

The villagers slit the throats of some goats and drained their blood, usual Muslim practice before eating meat. When Raza and Abbas returned, a victory feast roasted in the plaza. A celebration based on the promise of reward Hani filled local hearts with while they were gone. An expectation Raza and Abbas raised further when they arrived waving hands over their heads. The community flocking around boosted their injured egos. Both were certain they deserved such exalt. No matter what their government decided to do, they had pictures that were going to make them rich.

People crowded deep in a circle and Raza regaled them with details of the visit to the Foreign Ministry. How their presence in the corridors of power was treated like a pageant with ayatollahs, leaders of the assembly, even the president rushing to greet them and shower them with praise. Abbas supplied details about the paved roads and health clinic the country planned to provide for the village. They even pledged to fix everybody's house! Abbas paused after announcing each particular, soaking in every cheer and wringing every second from the wide eyed adoration directed his way. No one seemed to grasp these were the exact promises made to them by Teheran after the war ruined their lives. Promises made repeatedly and never met. All chose to bask in the expectation as if they were hearing it for the first time. Their existence was so decrepit inwardly and outwardly that a moment of old, bogus hope was better than unremitting misery, no matter the future disappointment.

It grew late, but only the least forlorn had left. The rest huddled closer by the fire in the victory ring. Raza and Abbas intended to go on so long as one person listened. Their dignity, like the town's, needed every crumb it could be fed.

Abbas was the first to tilt his head toward the faint vibration. Raza stopped talking when it became an approaching echo. Hani scrambled to the top of a ledge and looked off into the darkness while the sound expanded into a girdling clamor. He spotted a line of headlights piercing the night. They were moving fast. By the time Hani rushed to the square, the ground was shaking. A row of Iranian Army troop carriers emerged, barreling around him and coming to a jarring halt. Soldiers began leaping out.

Rajavi's silent associate led them. He was no longer silent, or a civilian. He was leading the stream of troops. He pointed out Raza and Abbas. A band of soldiers rushed them. The gang went for their guns, which served to identify them as the agitators. They were quickly dissuaded from confrontation by shots fired overhead and the enveloping show of force. Troops confined the pack in a corner of the square while more soldiers fanned out and into homes and buildings, pushing aside shrieking women and children. The army probed every inch of the community and forced all the men down to the plaza. One soldier inside Raza's house came across rolls of undeveloped film. It became part of a number of things collected by the regiment. A squad discovered Kasey and Nasır secured and blindfolded in their separate prisons. They sent word to the commander.

The commander paced in front of the gang, who glared at him and whispered to each other. Once the square was full of the village males, a mission secured signal made way to the commander. The gathered men had no anger. They were used to being routed or herded by some force or another. And they didn't think the gang had lied. They saw it as another deception by a greater force. Something ordinary in their world.

But Hani couldn't take it anymore. For him, they lied to his brother, causing his entire family to lose face. He jumped at the commander who in an instant flung Hani to the ground, put a boot on his neck and shoved pistol in his mouth.

The commander looked at Raza, "Get the hostages. Bring them over here. Have your men get your vehicles ready."

The gang brought trucks to the square. Raza went one way and Abbas another, each taking a few men to fetch Kasey and Nasir. Soldiers followed along as Kasey and Nasir were hustled to the plaza. Their ears were sensitive to a ruckus they couldn't identify, and their shattered nerves absorbed new insult when they were hurled into the waiting caravan. Raza and Abbas got into the front rig. The commander at last removed his boot from Hani's throat. Hani dashed into the nearest truck. The commander walked over to Raza, "They were never here. Do not come back with them. If you do, it'll be the end of you all."

With that, the commander flung his thumb ahead and the train slowly moved away, flanked by troops who escorted them to the edge of the village. Raza leaned out a window and howled at the commander, "It's fine for us! Just fine for us!"

The commander and squad leader watched the lights disappear as the gang headed back into their desert haunts. The commander shook his head, "Scum. They could have ruined everything."

***

Julius Cunningham and Clayton Amfrick perched in their usual positions across the president's desk in the Oval Office. It was only 7:30 in the morning and the president already looked tired. Not overworked exhausted, more worn from the tonnage of his soul's unease. Cunningham and Amfrick prepared for this. Since the president began having trouble sleeping, they were in the habit of inquiring mornings with Secret Service agents stationed at the White House about his night activity. The agents could tell he was up and around during the night by the creaking floor boards upstairs as he wandered the living quarters. It was worse with no guest was over to occupy his growing anxiety. Doubly worse when, as now, his wife was away. At least she kept him in bed, increasing odds he might eventually nod off. Americans were somewhat accustomed to seeing their president with dusky circles under his eyes. The worry for Cunningham and Amfrick was his energy level for the upcoming convention and his autumn re-election campaign.

They gave each other a look when the president yawned for the third time in five minutes. Cunningham and Amfrick were his senior political aides. They controlled access and set his daily schedule. The time when genuine policy advisors and those involved in the business of the country had the sincere attention of the president was long gone in America, especially during first terms. The political people would immediately burrow in, citing another election four years down the line, and encase the president's perceptions to an extent they had mastery over his sentience.

Cunningham leaned over the desk and began summarizing the report he put in front of the president, "Wholesale crude prices went up eight percent yesterday. That makes twenty percent in two weeks. The Press Office has been instructed to blame commodity market speculation."

They could tell the president wasn't reading the pages. He turned them over too quickly. Amfrick condensed its proposition, "Psychologically, people won't be paying attention until winter. But market watchers are all over it. We'll stick to the story that OPEC has cut back production to raise price and, unusual for them, all member nations are sticking to it. There is going to be another spike in inflation because of the increases."

The president was good at discerning the simple things that affected his popularity, "What number will it rise to?"

"For the year, it's over twelve percent."

"What's it doing to unemployment numbers?"

"It'll probably send it up to nine," Cunningham softly told the president.

The president's eyes lit up, "Gasoline will be expensive for people's summer vacations.

Should I open the tap on the Strategic Petroleum Reserve?"

Amfrick always loathed the president's ideas. That supply was to be kept under wraps until the election campaign was in full swing. The president asked the same question yesterday. Amfrick answered it again, "Let's take the hit now, while we can still blame others and save the reserve for when the cold weather starts. It's the best option."

"Can I see the schedule for the Lincoln Bedroom?"

Cunningham and Amfrick were relieved he got off the subject. Better he worried about guests to help relieve insomnia than be reminded why he couldn't act on an issue.

"We'll get that for you, sir," Amfrick smiled.

The president pushed the report aside, "Oil ... oil ... oil. I'm tired of thinking about it."

Cunningham replaced the report with a copy of a speech, "You should look this over. It's the speech for tonight's fund raiser." He stood next to the president and pointed out underlined sections. The president moved his lips while reading.

The president's secretary entered, whispered in Amfrick's ear and left the room. Amfrick signaled Cunningham and the two excused themselves.

Outside the office, Amfrick told Cunningham, "Drake's in the building. They lopped off her entourage. She's heading this way."

The peculiar looking duo marched down the hall. Cunningham was unusually tall and abnormally thin. Amfrick was round and walked with his feet pointing outward. He had a fashion sense talked about behind his back. His glasses had colossal hooplike frames and he finished his appearance with trademark brightly colored bow ties.

They almost bumped into Drake when she came around the corner. Cunningham and Amfrick adroitly obstructed her way. "I spoke with the president last night," the secretary explained. "He's expecting me."

The president hadn't mentioned it to them. More upsetting, she seemed to have a way to reach him they didn't know about.

Cunningham leaned toward Drake. He had to lurch over to talk to just about everyone. Whether the gesture contributed to or only emphasized his condescending nature was something one could only theorize. "He's in an important meeting at the moment," Cunningham kept Drake cornered. "He said to talk with us." Amfrick pointed to his office and they all stepped inside.

"The Iraq ambassador at the UN has notified me that Saddam remains in control," Drake quietly said.

Amfrick wasn't convinced, "Then let us see him in public."

"He said we will," the secretary already had stipulated the condition. A career diplomat knows exactly the roles Cunningham and Amfrick serve. She didn't like them and they knew how she felt, mainly because they felt likewise about her. The mutual antipathy was plainly understood to be underlying their encounters. What the secretary misread was the importance of the hostage matter to them. She wanted them aware she carefully assessed the situation and wasn't to be played for a fool, "Somebody must demand the CIA come clean about activities inside Iraq. Where they behind the coup attempt against Saddam? We must get Captain Lawrence back. The Army isn't happy."

"Neither is the president," Amfrick knew how to handle Drake. "It's all he talks about. He's in an intelligence meeting about the situation now."

"I want to go to Saudi Arabia and manage the situation until they are returned."

"The president suggested that," Cunningham jumped in. It was a good idea. Get her out of Washington, away from friends in the press, foreign contacts, bureaucratic leaks and the president. Easier to keep her out of the loop there. "Clear your schedule and go as soon as you can."

"Say little to the CIA when you're there," Amfrick added. He and Cunningham were always on the same page. "Keep them out of it. We don't need any internal bloodshed with the president free falling in the polls. We are all going to have to dance around this or else there will be a messy debris field."

Cunningham almost waved his finger at her but stopped and held it on front of his face, "Remember, the correct line *is* and *always* will be that their meeting never happened." He could tell by Drake's expression he was too close to lecturing. He toned it down, "It is, after all, why the meeting was done unofficially, to maximize deniability. For all of us." A gentle hint of her inclusion in the grid of culpability. Or was it a warning?

Drake noted, "If we had officially met with Saddam, as I suggested, this would have never happened." Underlying thrust of her comment - I was right and you were wrong.

Amfrick put spin out so relentlessly he had no bearing to tell him when it was wasted on one who knew better , "You know we can never deal with Saddam publicly after the number we've done on him for years. He should have been finished off long ago when we had our chance."

There was only so much even a diplomat could take of these two before bursting into undisguised contempt. That moment had yet to arrive for Drake, but for the first time she thought it one day could.

"We'll omit your schedule to the Press Office. If anyone asks, word will be you have no current itinerary and are out of Washington," Cunningham's words signaled end of their business.

Drake usually exploded when they tried to hijack control of her agenda. But the Lawrence matter was too important. She pivoted and quickly got away from them.

***

Borders are ephemeral assumptions in the Mideast. No doubt surprising to many from the West, who lack insight arising from extended history in a location and are besieged by reports of endless strife in that part of the world. In the Mideast, nation perimeters have been established and severed countless times. The people there have ancient blood and cultural bonds that innately transcend fleeting lines drawn in the dirt.

If the written word represents the beginning of human history, then the first chapter would start in Mesopotamia, now Iraq, some six thousand years ago. Sumerians, the world's initial authors, lived in the Fertile Crescent spawned by the Tigris and Euphrates Rivers. Over subsequent millenniums usurping cultures surged out and shaped the entire Mideast. Some of the arising civilizations became the Amorite, Akkadian, Hammurabi, Assyrian and Babylonian societies. These groups gradually spread into what is Iran and were assimilated by people of Indo-Euro ethnicity infused with Aryans from India. This combination became the Parthian and Sassanian cultures and later were absorbed by the Turks, who were related to the Mongols. Then Greece, in the era of Alexander the Great, left another civilization's imprint on the area. This synthesis created Persian society. During this time, other tribes and races left marks elsewhere the Mideast. Syria was dominated by Hittite, Phyrgian and Byzantine cultures. The territory that became Israel was ruled by Seljuks, Mamluks and then Hebrews.

Meanwhile, in the watered highlands of Yemen on the southern end of the Arabian Peninsula, a land and sea trade in frankincense and myrrh linked Minean, Himyarite and Sabean influences, connecting Far East communities to the Mideast. Even the Roman Empire dug in for a time in its last days. This is but a short account of the astonishing invasions of humanity that have washed over the area. After the Roman Empire, Islam burst onto the scene and while the rest of the world was in the Dark Ages, a golden era of Muslim culture lasted for centuries. The Crusades marked the beginning of the end of that epoch, which led to the expanding Ottoman Empire gaining control for centuries.

The configuration of today's Mideast was formed by circumstances that almost two centuries ago. The British, French and Russians moved in as Ottoman Empire control declined. These new powers in the region formed alliances with friendly native sovereigns and started sculpting borders in ways beneficial to their imperialist hegemony. Britain carved Afghanistan out of Iran in 1857 and favored modest family dynasties that grew into Kuwait and Quatar.

In the Twentieth Century, accelerated modification came to Mideast borders. Internal opposition to the czar caused Russia to withdraw from the region by the time of the Bolshevik Revolution. World War One found the disintegrating Ottoman Empire allied with Germany and Austria on the losing side of the war, allowing the British and French victors to apportion boundaries virtually to their will. At the Paris Peace Conference in 1919, the Treaty of Versailles sanctioned a new map of the Mideast. British, French and Arab dynastic manoeuvering created the monarchies of Iraq and Transjordan under British rule. The remaining Ottoman Empire in Turkey was shredded into what became Syria and Lebanon and placed under French mandate in the 1920 Treaty of Sevres. In 1917, Britain became the first to call for a Jewish national homeland with the Balfour Declaration, leading them to gain edict over the land that became Israel. The one condition was recognition for a Palestinian state to be created somewhere in proximity, a condition taking nearly another century to complete. The World War Two Jewish holocaust in Germany spurred immigration to Israel, a compelling situation speeding creation of the Jewish state. Perceived international favoritism toward the creation of Israel ahead of a Palestinian state produced riots between Jewish settlers and Arabs who had been established in the area for centuries. Until that time, the two groups lived in tolerance of each other. After the riots, land was divided into Jewish and Arab sections. In 1948, Israel became a nation and since has engaged in four wars with Arab neighbors.

After World War Two, victorious allies the United States and Soviet Union became involved in a Cold War over contrasting ideologies. British and French control over the Mideast was replaced by the rivalry of the modern superpowers against a backdrop of increasing Arab nationalism. Growing political parties and new monarchs supported by America and the Soviet Union overthrew former governments or forced them to rush into superpowers' arms to retain power. Kings and sultans were deposed and replaced with modern family dynasties. Secular republics and authoritative regimes came into existence. In the first decades of the Cold War, the majority of Mideast Arab nations aligned themselves with the Soviets. But after Soviet military equipment and advisors came up on the short end in four wars against US backed Israel, Arab Mideast nations began tilting toward the West.

A major event in the Arab Mideast's lean toward the West was the fallout from the 1973 Arab-Israeli War. At the time, OPEC was led by Saudi King Faisal, an Arab hard liner. He fashioned the policy of cutting crude oil production and raising prices to punish the West for supporting Israel.

This was reason for the long remembered gasoline shortages in North America and Europe. Even though Arabs lost the 1973 war, tensions remained higher than ever in the region. Embargoes urged by King Faisal occurred regularly to 1975. During that summer, Faisal was assassinated by his nephew Abdel Aziz at the Royal Palace in Riyadh. The new Saudi monarch refused to support the embargo, in effect opening the spigot. Saudi Arabia, as world's largest oil producer can, on its own, cut the world price of crude by increasing production and flooding the market. Even today, Saudi Arabia regulates the price of world crude by endorsing or refusing to be a part of the OPEC fixed price.

Since the assassination of Faisal, the Saudi monarchy has been close allies of the United States. Some wonder about what really was going on behind the scenes with the two countries during that time. It wouldn't have been the first time America pulled the strings on Mideast events. A known example happened in Iran. In 1951, Iranian leader Mossadegh nationalized the country's British owned oil industry. The CIA admitted orchestrating Mossadegh's assassination, overthrowing the government and installing a US friendly monarch of dubious sovereign claim. Shah Pahlavi ruled Iran until his death when his son, Shah Reza Pahlavi took over, eventually being toppled by the Ayatollah Khomeini. A history seldom cited that brings perspective to the 1979 US hostage crisis with Iran.

The dissolution of the Soviet Union and decisive American victory in the 1991 war with Iraq has solidified US influence in the region. Persistent Arab nationalism and religious fervor are today's threats to US interests. Traditional Arab disunity impedes the danger to major energy resources. There have been several failed attempts at fusing the region into a United Arab Republic. Arab nations are often on opposite sides in one conflict, then on the same side in another. Kuwait supported Iraq in the Iran-Iraq War and ended up being invaded by Iraq not long after it ended. Syria financially supported Iraq against Iran but became an enemy after the Kuwait invasion. An opposition so impassioned that Syria began talking with bitter foe Israel and sending infantry units to fight with the US coalition in the war. At the same time, Syria remained on a US State Department list of nations said to engage in state sponsored terrorism. Saudi Arabia went from friend of Iraq to friend of Iran after the Kuwait invasion. After supporting Egypt in more than one war with Israel, Saudi Arabia and Egypt found themselves backing opposite factions in a civil war in Yemen.

These are but a few instances of how politics is practiced in the Mideast. New coalitions and adversaries can pattern in an instant. Mideast borders today remain unstable. Palestinians now have their homeland. Israel may one day return land on the West Bank and in the Golan Heights taken in previous wars, making new borders into old ones until who knows what factors change the dynamic. Viewing the entire Mideast as one entity may be more useful than seeing it as many shifting ones, in order to avoid bewilderment at finding the captors of Kasey and Nasir back in Iraq, slithering carefully northwest in the desert. The sand and wind served as their compass. So long as the horizon kept its shriveled tan cast and the breeze out of the south had a fruitful scent from the sodden basins, they knew they were on course. It took only a day for the gang to reach the craggy slab plateaus slightly east of the Tigris River marking three borders - Iraq, Turkey and Syria.

The caravan slowed descended the heights, twisting one way and another between boulders and cavities on the tight path shaped by sporadic previous vehicles. They located the road of gravel binder leading to an isolated border crossing into Syria.

In the crisp night, they came to stop at the station. Raza got out of the lead truck and had a talk with the sentries. Soon, he returned to the convoy and they were waved through. They moved up the slope of the mountain range dividing the wasteland of northeast Syria from temperate climate and population centers of the south and west. Creeping by the side of the crest, the truck tires pitched rocks off the ledge to the valley below. Fajid Mohammad, sometime farmer, full time outlaw, one time Hezbollah warrior and lifetime leader of an extended family militia that commanded the desert wild of Syria waited with his clique, ears tuned to the announcing convoy.

Fajid was expecting them. When the procession pulled in, Raza and Abbas jumped out and embraced Fajid while their entourages converged.

Fajid squeezed Raza's hand, "Cousin, how is the family?"

"Even more prosperous than we asked Allah," Raza fibbed.

Abbas clasped Fajid's shoulders, "My fellow soldier, I miss our days in Bekka."

Fajid broke away when his eyes came upon Hani, "No more a boy, now a man." Fajid embraced him, "Hani, so much like your brother."

Raza was too keyed up to wait any longer. He motioned to Hani, who led a few away to drag Kasey and Nasir out for presentation.

Fajid squinted and his garrison crowded in when Kasey and Nasir were dumped on the ground in front of them. Kasey and Nasir, quickly practiced at heeding their unconstrained senses, could tell they were in a new place. ~~Fajid fingered Kasey's hair.~~

Fajid leaned over and fingered Kasey's hair, "An American?"

"A soldier ... an officer," Raza's voice strutted.

Fajid pulled off Nasir's blindfold and near drooled after scrutinizing Nasir's features.

"He is ... a Saud?"

Raza grinned and nodded. The gesture sent Fajid's heart racing. It was like discovering a gold mine. Fajid looked at his men. They were already grinning. Fajid acted like someone who had found a wallet with a lot money inside. He peeked around to see if anybody might be coming for it. Raza and Abbas were thrilled at impressing Fajid. Hani was watching Fajid's band, wondering if they were going to be after Kasey.

"Lock them in the bin," Fajid called out. He beckoned his visitors, "Come into the house. We have business."

Hani supervised the arrangement of Kasey and Nasir inside the nearby grain hut. Piles of harvest were shoveled aside, creating space on opposite sides to secure Kasey and Nasir. Hani insisted on being the one to bind Kasey. Stronger rope and rigid blindfolds replaced worn out restraints. Both were gagged with rags and buried waist high in milled wheat before being left alone with guards outside.

Neither Kasey nor Nasir knew they were in the same place together for the first time since being kidnapped. Nasir prayed. He was overcome by an image of his wife and son. His heart ached recalling the last emotions he witnessed in them - anguish over his will to close off the boy from the world. His torment was the way he ignored his son, never asking his feelings or even explaining the decision he made. Nasir still wasn't questioning his actions. But he was stirred by the vision, praying intensely to shield the perforation in his conditioning from reaching the more intimate realm of denial. He begged Allah to save his family and country, imploring so fervently he perspired and wilted into senselessness.

Kasey's body had time in the quiet to finally scream for rest. She couldn't give in because there was disorder in her mind. She had lost track of time. How many days in captivity now? Yes, it was night, but which one? Third of fourth? She had to figure it out. The passing time increased risk to those in Saudi Arabia unaware of the possible impending uprising. Even worse for her, the doubt in a mind that absorbed and chronicled everything was intolerable. The disarray opened her psyche. Things from who knows where gushed up. A picture of her father developed in her mind's eye. He was back home, in their house, shaking a fist at her. She strangled a moan, sure he was damning her for

114

wanting to leave the Army. He killed himself over it and it was all her fault. She apologized and pleaded for forgiveness. He waved off her appeal. He didn't want an apology. Again, he shook a fist. He looked young, powerful, and right into her soul. He was urging, no demanding, her to prevail. It was a signal, a forceful transfer of mettle. Her mind started questioning the picture, her reasoning asserting control. Of course it wasn't really him. It was a hallucination. A survival trick. The picture faded, slowly lingering until a soft caress brushed across her face. The sensation was followed by movement of airy feet along her torso. She was being tickled by a rat's tail. Kasey became stationary. Before long she felt motion all around her. Then the noise began. Gnawing sounds, at first like a hum, then buzzing and vibrating. Rats were swarming, crawling over her body and burrowing into the grain pile. There must have been hundreds coming to feast.* They coated her. Kasey tried to shake them off, but her constricted defenses were no threat for a feeding frenzy. Her gestures were a mere irritation the rats reacted to by nipping at her flesh. It was a collective enthusiasm that could devour her. The only way to survive it was to remain inert and hope the dawn was not far away. Kasey could feel the grain pile diminishing as the rats gorged themselves, biting at her skin trying to get at the granules and leaving excrement in her hair and on her face. Even breathing too deeply was met with stings from needle-sharp teeth. Kasey endured, not until daylight, but until stress and exhaustion drained her waking consciousness.

***

At the Saudi National Reserve Bank in Riyadh, accountants poured over the daily opening invoice of capital assets. The treasury director frowned when his aide entered his office and placed the figures on his desk. It didn't take long for the director to frown, "Shut the door."

In seclusion, the director wanted confirmation, "Are you *absolutely certain* these rollover numbers are correct?"

His aide was waiting to finally hear the question, "Third time in a month. Last night it was seven hundred million that moved out overnight."

"What are the royals up to?" The director pondered, "Once, maybe even twice, but three times?"

"My source in Zurich tells me they are grabbing it there as soon as it hits their accounts," the aide already was on top of the situation.

They're moving it again? Usually they inform us when they do this," the director was baffled. He groaned, "Some banks will need to shut down today. The royals can do what they want to do, but if this continues, whispering will begin. They must know this. Change the access code so only the two of us can see the morning numbers until I find a way to bring this up with the royals."

***

"*We sense that we are being watched.*"

Marine Corps Lt. Gen. Anthony Zinni
US Persian Gulf Commander

In November 1995, the bombing of a US-run military training complex in Riyadh killed five American servicemen. In June 1996, a huge truck bomb parked outside Khobar Towers, an apartment complex housing US military personnel in Dammam, blew the face off the building and killed nineteen Americans.

Subsequent investigations by the FBI, US military and Saudi government ended up being excellent models of ass-covering politics.

The Saudis learned soon after the Khobar bombing that five of their citizens, believed to have been trained and possibly financed by Iranians, fled to Teheran after the bombing. The FBI gathered information linking them to Hezbollah, or Party of God, a terrorist group with strong ties to Iran. When other suspects were arrested in Saudi Arabia, the FBI traveled to Riyadh to become part of the search for truth. Upon arriving, they were denied access to the investigation by Saudi law enforcement. Diplomacy failed to resolve the impasse. The FBI found it so disturbing they publicly complained, causing the Saudis to relent, but only to a degree. They allowed the FBI to observe, not participate, in *some* interrogations of the suspects.

The FBI, unhappy with the conditions and what they came to see as a half-hearted Saudi inquiry, proceeded on their own track. Their investigation pointed to involvement of Iranian government officials in the attacks. When the FBI was ready to announce their report, somebody tipped off the Iranian government. They became so alarmed they placed their military on high alert, expecting US retaliatory attacks. The final FBI report never became public. On behalf of Saudi Arabia, the US State Department successfully lobbied to have it suppressed. They cited Saudi concerns about Muslim pilgrimages to Mecca and Medina that yearly includes 70,000 Iranians. Effects from outright condemnation and military retaliation by a Saudi ally could lead to internal public safety threats. The Saudis urged the US to wait for the result into their inquiry into the bombings. Their eventual account blamed a few Saudi dissidents, not Iran. Behind the scenes, the Saudi and American governments sought to reconcile their summaries. The result was politics intervened with reality and it was the truth that was compromised. The outcome of both investigations concluded the bombings were done by Saudi renegades, with help from Iranians, but *not* the Iranian government. Saudi Arabia has since markedly improved their relationship with Iran.

That's how things are in the Mideast.

The Saudi government has always been skittish about domestic perception of their ties to America. Many of their citizens share the anti-Western views common in outwardly militant Mideast nations. Osama bin Laden, under indictment in America for attacks at US embassies in Kenya and Tanzania that killed 224 people, is a native born Saudi. US intelligence later discovered evidence that a number of Saudi Arabia's top businessmen had transferred personal funds of several millions of dollars to out of country bank accounts controlled by bin Laden. Bin Laden, whose family owns the largest construction firm in Saudi Arabia, has made public statements calling for overthrow of the Saudi government, as if his outcry might deflect suspicion of Saudi establishment involvement in his activities. The Saudi government, when faced with the US evidence, claimed it was protection money that was being paid by Saudi executives to stave off terrorist attacks and interference with commerce.

The deeper you go, the more peculiar it becomes. Equally as curious was the US military investigation into the Khobar bombing. At first, a task force led by an Army four-star general issued an account criticizing the Air Force general in charge of base security when the nineteen airmen died. The report noted intelligence warnings the apartment complex was a likely terrorist target were ignored. The Air Force general was also held liable for failing to make base security a higher priority. But an in-house Air Force version of the incident was much more forgiving of their general. They maintained that unlike Army officers, Air Force commanders are responsible for security up to the perimeter of their base, but *not* beyond. For the Air Force, this was the key issue, since the bomb was parked on the street outside the apartment building, technically distant of base perimeter. Frustration over bureaucratic hair-splitting and inter-agency finger pointing led one Senator to declare, "The Department of Defense has become an excuse factory." The remark came at a hearing where the Air Force general in charge of security at Khobar was about to be *awarded his second star.*

Twenty-four Americans dead.

To date, no one held accountable.

The only result of the military investigation was a quietly issued internal directive making all commanders responsible for base *and* perimeter security. Commanders established invisible boundaries to be defended. Which was likely why the four men sitting in a car on the outskirts of Damman, site of the Khobar bombing and still a major virtual city housing US military and civilian oil workers, weren't aware they were being watched.

They spent almost an hour staring through binoculars at the layout and jotting notes on a pad. They drove around the periphery taking photographs, unaware of the Air Force police sneaking up on them in a jeep.

At a vulnerable moment, the Americans made a charge toward them. The spies noticed barely in time to race away, heading off road down an embankment. The Americans got up their rear, when one man leaned out the window and fired a quick volley from an AK-47 at them. The soldiers reacted with a barrage, notching the car's frame with lead. Another burst from the spies ended up wounding an American in the shoulder. The soldier pushed for them to continue pursuit, but military policy forced a decision to call off the chase and bring the wounded guard to the hospital. The Americans kept staring back at the operatives, who stopped to watch the retreat, a gesture of casual unconcern and taunting bravado.

***

In a scant Saudi town on the edge of the desert, a man walked up to the entrance of the National Commercial Bank as an employee inside finished locking the doors. The customer tapped on the glass when he couldn't get in. "We are closed," the employee raised his voice to be heard through the glass.
"Closed? Again? So early?"
"We are out of cash."
"You are the only bank for kilometers. I need to buy provisions," the customer was more frustrated than angry.
The employee shrugged and withdrew into a back office.
A pair of passing men observed the exchange. "The same thing happened two days ago in Nafi," one said.
The three grumbled about the inconvenience. More men converged on the scene. Further expressions of dissatisfaction were voiced.
"I'll bet they don't lock the bank on the king," one remarked and the rest agreed. The spot in front of the bank became a focus area for the complaints of an increasing crowd. As their numbers increased, so did their scowls and jeers. A man kicked at and rattled the bank's doors. Others pounded on the window and shook their fists. A bank employee inside peeked at them from the lobby and then disappeared.

HONOR BOUND

There was a lot of throaty mumbling. Then silence. They had gone as far as they could with verbal griping. They milled around in front of the bank, sulking and peering inside. Someone took a bottle from a garbage can and threw it at the window. The sound of breaking glass propelled the episode from oral protest to riot. Collective fury was unleashed. Almost simultaneously, the horde started flinging rocks, bottles and whatever they could grab near the bank's facade. Two seized a litter barrel and used it as a battering ram on the door. Seemingly out of nowhere, more appeared to join the swarm, their shouts becoming a tumultuous clamor.

Inside the bank, nervous employees watched the bank manager scream into a phone, "Where is the Guard? We need the Guard!" Fear made him drop the phone and herd employees into the walk-in safe and lock themselves inside. A moment later the mob broke through the door and stampeded in, turning over desks, rifling cash drawers and wrecking the place.

After demolishing the bank, the upheaval spilled back out into the street. Uncontested by law enforcement, the crowd tore down the avenue sending store owners fleeing, and leaving a wake of looted and demolished emporiums. Cars were overturned and a blaze was kindled at the end of the block. It was an event never experienced in the town, such civic turmoil. More threateningly, it was a belligerent airing of resentment over social conditions, striking to the merchants for the utter absence of establishment force to challenge the situation.

⁜ ⁜ ⁜

In the morning, Kasey was removed from the grain shack and brought to a barn on the other side of Fajid's homestead. Hani was up early preparing her new prison. Iron shackles were secured to corral planks above a pile of straw. During the night, Raza, Hani and Fajid made plans that would take them and most of the gang away for the day. Hani stayed behind, in charge of the hostages and a few of Fajid's men left behind.

Kasey was rigged into the stockade. Hani was consumed with orchestrating the arrangement as if particularizing his vision of a fantasy. After fixing things

120

to his satisfaction, he went outside to complete a task Raza wanted done, fueling the trucks left behind.

Fajid's gang stayed in the barn guarding Kasey. At first, they were dispersed around the periphery, lurking by the door and in the shadowy corners. All eyes were on Kasey, who sporadically tried to shift into a less agonizing position. She gasped when her muscles reflexively contorted and groaned when the deadening numbness in her limbs became unbearable.

The pack gradually enveloped around Kasey. They talked to each other, blanketing the air with blunt sexual remarks. Slowly, a dynamic was fusing, at last activated by one thug who crept next to Kasey and started stroking her hair. Another advanced and thrust his arm down her jersey, fondling her breasts and squeezing her nipples. Kasey's heart surged, assuming the nightmare in the back of her mind since being captured was about to begin. Not recognizing the voices denied her indication of the personalities she was dealing with, but Kasey detected the gyrating dynamism of group arousal. The rest closed in. Kasey could smell them. Someone pulled her pants down to the irons and started rubbing her groin. Their ravished, moist tongues communicated impending debasement. Kasey heard a belt untie and felt ramming pressure. Whoever was mashing her flapped his arms holding off others wanting at her. Kasey clamped her mouth when her legs were held apart. The man pinning her readied to slide inside Kasey when a gunshot rang out by the barn door.

It was Hani, furious at what they were doing to the one he coveted. He dropped the empty gas can he was holding and aimed his pistol at them, "Step away! She is not your prisoner."

The men sheepishly but leisurely slinked away with expressions like children caught with their hands in the cookie jar. Their voided sexual ferment was slow to abate. A shaky current continued flowing as Hani rushed to have a look at Kasey.

"Angry Hani? You must want her all for yourself," one said with a bitter smirk.

"You violated Hezbollah principles," Hani bared his teeth. "We arrested her and we decided her fate!"

121

The band retreated into a broad circle around Hani and Kasey. Hani wanted to diminish the tension by getting them out of the barn. "I cannot locate any petrol," he told them.

"Lately, it has been hard to find," someone shrugged.

"Go and find fuel for us," Hani barked.

For a while, they stood around. Hani kept his gun ready until one of them rambled toward the gas can. He grabbed it, glared at Hani and swaggered away. Eventually, the others followed.

Hani watched from the door until they disappeared. Then he kneeled next to Kasey. "I should have never left you alone with them," he said, taking off her blindfold.

It took Kasey a long time to regain sight. Even the dull sunlight filtering into the barn hurt her eyes. Hani yanked her pants up and fixed her shirt. "They are animals," he said almost apologetically.

Kasey knew they were alone. "Please, I need water," she pleaded.

Hani nodded and left the barn. Kasey could hear him pumping from a well outside. She took a good look around and listened.

He came back with a canteen and set it to her lips. Kasey drank it dry.

"Thank you. I'm so glad you came. I was afraid."

Hani nodded with a twinge of guilt.

"Please, more water. And some food," Kasey whispered.

Hani settled the pistol inside his waistband and left her alone.

Kasey used the time to think and focus her senses. She paid attention to the quiet, tilting her head to detect sound.

He returned with a bowl of figs and more water. Kasey motioned for the water. Hani gave her a long drink.

"I wanted to bring some sooner, but my brother said no," Hani explained.

Kasey slowly pulled her lips from the canteen, "I knew you weren't like them."

Hani sat on the ground and fed her. Kasey stared into his eyes. He tried to give her another drink. Kasey turned away, "Please, I can't do it this way."

Hani got up and took a key from his pocket. He unshackled one arm then left the bowl and canteen within her reach before putting the keys back in his pocket. Then he went to shut the barn door.

When his back was turned, Kasey probed the range of motion her free arm allowed. After, she tossed the canteen just out of her grasp. When Hani came back, Kasey was crouched at an angle over the food. She was, in fact, *coiled*. Hani picked up the canteen and leaned over toward her. Kasey selected the perfect moment to whip around with all the force she could muster and strike Hani in the throat with her elbow. The blow propelled Hani backward onto his behind. He stared at her. There was a stunned pause, then distress contorted his face. Hani placed hands on his throat and hopelessly tried to inhale, gasping for air that wouldn't come up his windpipe. His esophagus was crushed. He labored to get up, but never made it to his feet. His eyes bulged and face turned ash pale while he flailed arms and furiously attempted to gulp oxygen. Rapidly, Hani was suffocating and he knew it. His face grotesquely distorted before he descended into dry convulsions.

Kasey calmly waited for him to die. She felt nothing for his plight. Her mind was busy plotting and her ears were pinned toward what she couldn't see. It was unwavering focus on getting out of the situation and finding a way to return with the crucial information she had. Nothing else mattered. The desolate expression of betrayal on Hani's stirred no compassion. He fell over on his side facing her, unblinking. The void soon took his eyes. Kasey waited for his body to be still and concentrated on the next obstacle.

Hani's corpse appeared to be slightly out of her reach. Kasey extended her free arm and verified the assumption. She needed the key to her shackles that sat in his pocket. She wrenched forward and stretched her hand to no avail. He was an inch too far away. She tugged on her chains, frenetically jerking ahead striving to clutch Hani's foot and pull him close to her. He remained barely out of reach. Again she tried, shrieking in pain when feeling her bones crackle against the restraints. Once more she elongated, this time with such strength the planks fastened to the shackles began to waver and finally buckle, just enough for Kasey to grab his foot with the tips of two fingers. Kasey held on, even through the agony piercing her wrists and ankles, raw from chafing. She yanked at his foot until angling his body close enough for her to seize the key from his pocket. She freed herself. Time was precious, but her body insisted on a moment to savor liberation.

Now she had to find Nasir. She already figured a likely place to locate him might be near where she was previously was held, a place where grain is stored. She took Hani's gun and checked the chamber. It was one bullet shy of fully loaded. She ran to the door and peeked outside. The barn sat in a lot among a curving tangle of buildings centered by Fajid's home. She picked out the lean hovel that looked to be not much more than a bin and fled toward it, holding the gun in one hand and hoping Nasir could be freed with Hani's key. She stopped at the door and listened. There was no noise. She carefully tried the door. It was unlocked. Kasey softly opened it, aiming the gun, alert to what she might encounter. She stepped in and quickly looked around. In a grain mound against a wall she spied Nasir, buried neck deep in the pile. He was blindfolded and inert. She dashed over and started digging him out, ecstatic to discover he was only bound with rope and wire. Removing his blindfold seemed to stir his consciousness.

"Nasir ... Nasir come to," Kasey said, trying to shake him out of his stupor.

He couldn't open his eyes, so encrusted were they with residuum. Kasey wiped his face to get a good look at him. His skin was withered from dehydration. Nasir pried apart his eyelids barely a fraction. "Nasir, we must get out of here," Kasey was determined to get moving. "I need you ready to go. Now!"

Nasir understood. He whispered, "Water."

Kasey finished extricating him, grabbed a pail and dashed to the well while holding the pistol.

When she came back, Nasir was sitting up rubbing his face. She began giving him little sips of water and splashing drops on his face. "Nobody's around," Kasey explained. "I killed the one guarding me. We need to get out of here before they come back."

Like Kasey, Nasir's body needed to adjust to the freedom. Kasey knew he was gaining strength when he snatched the pail and downed all the water. His vision remained blurry when he stood up. But he was sharp and ready, "Let's go."

He tottered with lurching limbs as he followed Kasey to the shed door. They stepped outside and Kasey gave an exacting look every which way on the horizon.

The sunlight burned Nasir's eyes when he tried to do the same thing, "Where are we? Which direction do we go?"

Kasey saw sloping pastures and mountains off to the north, past a range of what looked to be uncultivated pistachio fields. The land was level in every other direction. Probably desert, she calculated. Their survival depended on making the right choice.

"I think I see fields of wild pistachios. We could be in Syria. That would mean Turkey must be beyond the mountains," Kasey reasoned. "The hills will provide cover," Nasir added. "That's where we need to go." Without any more talk, they advanced toward the distant high country, moving in silhouette amid the thicket with increasing vigor inspired by the prospect of rescue.

6

Rick barely made the late flight back after his visit to Wall Chemical. It was after midnight when the plane landed. He didn't call Denise for a ride, preferring she not head to the airport alone at such a late hour. That was a considerate explanation. The more honest one had to do with what stayed with him from their ride earlier in the day. He didn't want a reminder of what seemed to be ruffling between them, even though he wasn't sure what it was. He believed they could get back on good footing if he simply saw her when he got back. So, he took a long cab ride home.

Denise was awake in bed when Rick came in. She listened to him come upstairs and shuffle around in the bathroom before quietly sitting on the edge of their bed. She turned over and found him looking at her. The moonlight through the window cast a soft glow on their faces.

"I wish you had called. I wanted to pick you up."

Rick caressed her face, "I had to rush to catch the plane."

"You have your phone."

"I didn't want to make you stay up so late."

"I stayed awake anyway."

Rick slid under the covers and put his arms round her. Denise wanted to apologize for sounding testy when she meant to seem caring. He kissed her before she could say anything, keeping his lips against hers, his tongue slow waltzing inside her. He eventually pulled away to say, "I love you."

He said it so gracefully, so deliciously, the emotion behind the words permeated the air, rising to the ceiling and floating Denise along. Her heart quivered and head reeled, as if looking down from a rising hot air balloon.

126

They made love for a long time. Yearning love, raw with silent feelings they kept to themselves. Matching sentiments, experienced alone, leaving a melancholy undertow to their union at the same time spilling into a fervent passion, both puzzling and inspiring. Only later, as they held onto each other, did each reflect on what it both protected and predicted. They were aware of a growing distance and were so engrossed by it they couldn't see they were in the same inner place.

Not long after they fell asleep the alarm told them it was time to get up. Neither said much getting ready to go to work. Afterglow, persistent contemplation and knowing it was going to be an ass-dragging day from lack of sleep left them quiet during a quick breakfast. They left the house together and went separate ways after an embrace in the driveway.

Rick went to a meeting with Carl Patina, his editor at the *Examiner*. They analyzed Rick's visit to Wall Chemical.

"You got a lot of corporate line," was Carl's opinion.

Rick agreed, "I knew that's what I was going to get when he drove me around in a golf cart for half the day."

Carl tapped a pen on his desk as he looked over Rick's notes from the Campbell interview, "But it does seem as though there are thorough checks in place to keep any of this material leaking from their end."

"I checked out his account of the laws and supervising controls," Rick assured. "He is right."

Carl looked away. Rick still found him hard to figure. They hadn't known each other very long and Carl seemed to keep a lot to himself. Only now did Rick figure them as about the same age. Rick glanced at award after award framed around the office. He envied Carl's career, and felt excited about working with him.

Carl knew how he would proceed as reporter on this kind of story. He wanted to gauge how Rick would do it. Tough to know, even with the reputation Rick came with, how methods at a more modest newspaper stacked up against the major leagues. Carl leaned toward Rick, "What's next? What direction do you want to go?"

•

"Wall only represents the commercial segment of the field," Rick began to sum up his approach. "Now I want to scrutinize the science. Learn about what all this stuff is. Get the facts from academia, where there's no corporate spin."

Carl was smiling inside. It was the choice he would have made, "Do it. Let's see what you come up with."

It was a good story meeting, Rick thought on his way home. Always tough for a new employee to negotiate his way. Rick felt pumped about his career move. Every time he was at the *Examiner,* there were more reporters and editors to meet. They had so many, and they all had big reputations. He idly dreamed that someday he'd be the one a new reporter would be awe struck to meet.

Rick arrived home before Denise. Before going to his office upstairs, he sat in the living room and thumbed through a phone book until finding the section heading: Physicians-Specialists. He paused after he began to set the open book on a lamp table. Instead, Rick placed the book on the coffee table in front of the sofa and headed upstairs to search for an appropriate member of the chemical engineering intelligentsia to ply for information.

Rick got off the phone and came downstairs when he heard Denise come in. She had planting bulbs in her arms, "I stopped at Kasey's father's place. It's time to start thinking about the garden. Gary has painted the store inside and out. It looks good."

"Let's have him over for dinner soon," Rick took the rosebush and lilacs and took them to the cellar. "I thought you'd be too tired to do anything but come right home," he called up to her.

"There was too much feel of spring in the air. We haven't talked about your trip. How'd it go?"

"I'm not sure," Rick trudged up the stairs and started brewing a pot of coffee. "I doubt there's a story at Wall."

In an irrational way, Denise was happy, "So, is that it?"

"Not yet. I'm pursuing another avenue, talking to a college professor."

Denise wanted it to lead nowhere. She wanted Rick's career at the *Examiner* to start with a bang. But the story he was working on made her think of Kasey, and since their trip to the airport, she hadn't wanted to.

128

Rick sat in the kitchen drinking coffee. He watched Denise notice the open phone book and linger over the page. He turned away before she looked at him. He expected her to be smiling when she came into the kitchen. She wasn't. It was hard for him to define her expression. A deliberate non-expression, maybe? Rick was stumped.

Denise wanted to smile, but intuition forbid the response. Something about the image of the phone book on the table and Rick's lack of mention about it. There was a gap there, between the picture and lack of words. Some kind of vague, yet important space.

She shook it off. Maybe she was more tired than she realized, "I don't think either of us wants to cook. Why don't we call out for something tonight?"

Rick nodded, "It's all right with me."

***

"Modern chemical engineering began in 1839 when Goodyear accidentally spilled sulfur on raw latex rubber on a stove. The fusion created a stable elastic-like substance. Their molecules linked in a spider's web design," Professor Anton Lem told Rick. "That was the first industrial polymer, combinations of matter's building blocks united into more or less complicated chains."

Rick stopped scribbling notes. He could tell details were going to be lost on him if he didn't exactly record the professor's terminology. He pulled a sound recorder from his coat pocket, "Mind if I use this?"

It must have been a rhetorical question to the professor because he kept talking, "You may be surprised to learn that incendiary plastics date from not long after that time."

Rick was pleased to find the expert he needed only a few hours drive from home at Bennett University, a technical college in the western part of the state. He was a bit nervous about the interview and labored hard to absorb the concepts tossed off by the professor. Rick didn't have a technical mind and was afraid of becoming lost in the subject matter. It was mildly surprising to discover the ambiance in this scholarly chemical engineering setting. When

HONOR BOUND

Professor Lem led him through the laboratory to his office, Rick sensed intense energy from an international array of students. There was runaway ebullience in room. Excited dialogue about theory and rapt attention on experimentation charged the setting. And Professor Lem was younger than Rick pictured him being.

Rick asked for clarifications as he needed them, "Can you elaborate on your description of polymers?"

Lem seemed to never tire of answering questions he'd been asked many times in different ways, "Since the era of the cave man, humans have used naturally occurring biochemical building blocks like amino acids and sugars, making useful things from hair, skin and fur. Frame that analogy in your mind. It's creating new substances from appropriated sections of others."

"Tell me more about the early history of ignitable plastics."

"After inventing modern rubber processing, inventors began mixing binding substances glues, resins, shellacs with substances like paper and linen." The professor twirled his fingers like he was stirring something in a bowl, "Someone eventually mixed an adhesive derived from a by-product of cotton called colloidon with nitric acid. It dried into a thin, clear film that was unstable and highly flammable. It was aptly called guncotton. After adding sodium chloride, inventors learned it had a bizarre propensity to capture a photographic image. Photography and later motion pictures were born from this first commercial plastic, called celluloid. Early film stocks were highly ignitable. They actually exploded if users weren't careful."

"I seem to remember hearing that," Rick felt Lem could deliver a semester's lecture if the information flow wasn't directed. "So, today's plastic explosives are not much different from what was created back then?"

Lem paused, "Yes and no. There are very new pliable synthetics with nightmarish destructive capabilities."

Rick was still trying to find the meaning behind Kasey's urging. The dread raised by the professor's last remark led Rick to ask, "Could terrorists manufacture them?"

"It would be seriously difficult."

"What does it take to construct them?"

130

"Heavy chemical engineering and production ability. A developed nation's industry," was the professor's view. "But it's every government's fear because losing account of small amounts could lead to it being used against them as much as an enemy. There's good evidence those who blew up Pan Am 103 years ago probably did it with plastic compounds originating in the West."

"I never knew that," Rick said, shocked and excited. Reporter's instinct finally kicked in on this story.

"It's well known to the chemical engineering community. Some in law enforcement believe terrorists may have scoped out Materials Research Society conventions in America. Chemical engineering professionals from industry, governments and schools meet every year at an exhibition. It attracts sales representatives, venture capitalists and other interested parties who check out things like mass spectrometers, nanoscopic ceramic powders, biomemetic materials, whatever is new in the field."

"Isn't it mind boggling to think terrorists might attend something so public?

"I know the government didn't think so," Lem plainly stated. "A few years ago they started a National Defense Preparedness Association to impose security classifications on these meetings."

Intriguing, Rick thought. "If a terrorist saw something they wanted at this convention, how would they get hold of it?"

"There's a black market in export controlled technology. The convention was one place those up to no good could meet. Buyers hooked up with sellers who would set up dummy important-export companies in foreign countries to ship it. Then the company would disappear. It was a shell game, not so easy to do today. Supple conductive materials manufacturers need deep political connections to get a production license. Controls inventory every gram, so there's little chance of seepage, if you know what I mean."

Rick got the hint. Plastic explosives ending up in terrorist hands likely came from politically connected legal manufacturers. He'd have to check out the politics behind it. His line of line inquiry began to flow naturally, "Is there any way to trace production?"

"Indeed. Technology today can read the molecular tag in any batch processed. Every lot is unique, with unalterable microscopic variations in its bonding pattern."

Rick now doubled back to what they touched on earlier, "Can you explain why it is so difficult to manufacture?"

Professor Lem squinted, leaned over the desk and picked a piece of lint off Rick's shirt, "Would you believe this piece of cotton fiber has something to do with it?" he smiled. "Tiny particles of honeycombed cotton separated from the plant by linters, machines that do the processing, play the biggest role. Huge amounts of these spongy filaments are heated by miniature blast furnaces, then treated with chemical solvents, forming it into a mushy pulp called cellulose acetate. Blend in a ratio of your powdered combustible of choice, compress the atoms until they fuse together, and you're on the way to having a wonderfully pernicious creation."

"Cellulose acetate," the words now had a fully sinister connotation to Rick. "That's all there is to it?"

"One more process," the professor held up a finger. "Take a colossal amount of cellulose acetate, treat it with formaldehyde and phenol, pressurize and heat it again and you end up with a bendable plastic that has no resistance to conductivity. Then it can be formed into anything made from plastic. The proportion and class of explosives in the micro architecture decides what spark is needed to make it ignite. On Pan Am 103, the likely plastic explosives probably cast as a tape player only needed the low level battery voltage from it being turned on to create an explosion big enough to blow a hole in a jumbo jet," Lem stopped, as if in remembrance of those lost.

Rick absorbed it, but knew he had work to do to really understand all the abstraction.

The professor added, "Today, you can add a high degree of more concentrated ignitables. And today's pliable synthetics are 'smart' meaning they can adapt, making themselves close to undetectable."

An unsettling thought. But Rick wanted to know, "If it begins with processing cotton, couldn't any mill produce it?"

"Not so easy," Lem explained. "Sale or export of miniature blast furnaces and amalgamating atom smashers are only by government license. It's high tech, very expensive machinery. Also, an enormous amount of cellulose is needed. It takes tons of linted cotton to make an ounce of plastic explosives." Rick shut off the recorder. He had what he needed to know.

***

Raza, Abbas and Fajid led their seedy entourage south down the Qunaytra Motorway into Damascus. They passed the ancient Roman cobblestone walls outlining the oldest continually inhabited city in the world and pushed through traffic by the covered souks (markets). Modern Damascus unfolded ahead after they turned into Umayyades Square. They pointed and laughed at the American flag when they moved by the United States Embassy and impatiently leaned on the horn after becoming snared in more traffic on busy Youssef al-Ameh Boulevard, the heart of Syria's political and business activity.

It may have seemed brazen for them to pull over directly in front of the Foreign Intelligence Bureau. Yet it was less bold than the Bureau scheduling their appointment at agency headquarters. Not surprising from a nation with a reputation for conducting political affairs without nuance. As if obstinate audacity was all that was left to substitute for pride after decades of bad policy decisions. From cozying up to the Soviet Union in the Cold War to the humiliating forfeiture of land to Israel after losing one of several wars against the Jewish state.

The gang hit the sidewalk, jostling among the throng of students, government workers, businessmen and tourists (some of them American, courted by the Syrian Tourism Bureau, even though the US State Department lists Syria as government sponsoring terrorism). Raza, Abbas and Fajid paraded into the Foreign Intelligence Bureau while the rest of their pack visited Hamam al-Novry, the public baths.

Fajid related the story they wanted known to Director of Foreign Intelligence Hassan al-Sayah. The director sat at one end of a long conference room, surrounded *or* propped up by aides. It was hard for Raza and Abbas to tell which. Al-Sayah seemed to lean on the associates that hemmed him. He was already seated when they entered, probably to disguise some sort of wobbling debility. A depiction of inadequacy potentially lethal to entrenched power. Al-Sayah spent a long time whispering to aides after hearing the particulars. Raza and Abbas were nervously recalling their previous meeting with government officials. They watched the Director's face closely from the moment they set foot into the room and hunkered beside Fajid. It was hard to interpret al-Sayah's mood. All he did was frown. Abbas was becoming worried.

He tilted toward Fajid, "You said they would be pleased."

"Quiet," Fajid didn't want them to act grouchy or be heard at the other end of the room.

Fajid held a hand near Abbas' ear, "He always looks troubled. I know - I told you he is my mother's second cousin."

The Director's head drifted in their direction. An aide asked, "How come you did not take them to your home in Iran? Why bring them to Syria?"

Raza stood and cleared his throat, "Syria is a reliable Hezbollah ally." He was indulging their national egoism. "Iran does business with America behind everyone's back. It would not surprise me if they collaborated on the attempt to kill Saddam."

They needed the lie to seem plausible. The three labored to stay calm, but the effort was making them perspire. The wait for a reaction after another round of murmuring between al-Sayah and his inner circle felt endless.

"Intriguing story," another associate told them. "We have seen indications of unusual events underway in both Iraq and Saudi Arabia."

Fajid jumped in, using the tone of a salesman trying to close a deal, "Having a stake in our hostages allow you to bargain for information."

The Director consulted his aides. Finally, he spoke, "They cannot stay in Syria. If our hands are discovered on them, we will face rage. We will give you passage to Lebanon. You will take them to the Bekka. Jihad crusaders there will hide you."

A sponsor, guardian and vested interest had joined them. It was a relief. Raza, Abbas and Fajid were ushered out smiling.

Hassan addressed his clique, "It could help us. If we "rescue" their officer, the cost to America will be leaning on Israel to return the Golan. And the Saud's will repay us with a bankroll for new weapons."

***

Kasey and Nasir scaled the stone face of the mountain ahead, supposing the woods and shrubs on the crest provided a measure of protection from discovery. There were footpaths through wilderness on the summit. For them, it marked routes to avoid. They pushed forward on the lateral rim facing away from Fajid's place, scrambling around boulders and ducking under flogging branches. Their footgear was taken away when they were stripped of their uniforms, so it didn't take long for their feet to get gnarled and bloody. At least their hardened soles toughened up fast. Adrenaline and survival instinct obliterated any pain. They moved faster when the night came. The shroud of darkness inspired them to move bravely in a direction set to the North star. It was well after midnight when they lulled between marble chunks on the edge of a dribbling stream, drinking water and eating fistfuls of grass. They knew they had a long way to go. Some time was necessary to end the panting and gather energy. Both felt a moment of serenity under the dazzling night sky. They slipped into private worlds. Eventually, they linked eyes. Kasey smiled and asked him, "What were you thinking about?"

"My son," Nasir bowed his head. "I never told him I love him."

His answer revealed that like her, he spent the moments in personal reflection. "You'll have your chance," she told him.

Nasir stared into the trickling brook. He wanted to know, "What were you thinking about?"

"My father," Kasey wasn't sure she could say more that would make sense. She paused. Nasir waited for her to go on. So she did, "When I was young, on Sunday mornings he would fry an egg and put it on top of a jelly doughnut for me."

After observing the culinary revulsion on Nasir's face, she probably should have held back the detail. Maybe elaborating would clue him to the logic, "I wish it was one of those Sunday mornings now."

Nasir's grimace dissolved into a soft, kindly cast. He understood.

They probably should have been moving on, or talking about how to get back with the information they had, or what to do with the bullet Kasey had tucked away in a body cavity. Instead, they plunged deep into their inner realms and in time dozed off.

An unfamiliar odor agitated Nasir enough to force open his eyes. He was wondering how long he had been out when he caught sight of a huge dog sitting attentively in front of Kasey. It began to growl. A feral canine, Nasir knew from the look and sound of the animal. A creature with no inbred fear of humans. Before Nasir could warn Kasey, the dog spread its jaws, ready to snap at Kasey's face. Nasir threw an arm in front of the dog. It's teeth cut into and held Nasir's arm as tight as a vise. Kasey woke up to Nasir's scream, which also incited other hounds nearby to begin yapping. Quickly, a pack of them raced down the side of the ridge at them. Kasey jerked out the gun and shot the dog holding onto Nasir. It released him, running in circles and squealing a death wail. Kasey and Nasir jumped on the rocks as the dogs surrounded, barking in delirium. They started leaping, snapping and climbing in attack. It was a brutish onslaught staved off only when Kasey started shooting them. She killed one, then another and another, agonizing at every bullet she was losing. She killed two more, thinning the pack enough for them to change dashing away. Nasir headed off first, trying to race toward the basin below. Kasey held the hound's focus until Nasir disappeared. Then she raced in his path with the dogs on her trail. One hurdled onto her back, knocking her to the ground. Before the rest could swarm, she shot it with the last bullet, got up and ran until reaching the end of the tilting underbrush. She came to a dead stop when she saw the steep vertical drop of rock leading down. There was no sight of Nasir in the darkness, and no place left to run. She tried to hold off the dogs by tossing rocks. It didn't work. They circled her, nipping at her legs.

Nasir was just below the ledge, intently positioning his feet. Kasey again looked toward bottom. She didn't like her chances, until one dog burrowed its fangs into her thigh. She screamed.

Nasir yelled up to her, "Kasey, come on!"

"I can't climb down. My ankles have swelled up."

"Put your feet on my shoulders. I'll do the work."

She leaned over, fending off the pack and searching for Nasir's shoulder with her foot. Timidly, she placed one, then the other on him and crouched, bracing her hands against the granite. The dogs took turns trying to slide over the ridge in pursuit, but couldn't overcome the instinct it was too steep.

Nasir sustained Kasey's weight and delicately sought cracks to set his feet. Covered with seeping wounds, they gradually made way below until Nasir lost balance trying to find footing. His equilibrium collapsed, sending them toppling down and reaching for each other until impacting with jutting slabs under them while being pelted with a boulder avalanche dislodged by the energy of their fall. They gained velocity hurling down until crashing into a mud stream at the base of the mountain. They were unconscious for a time. Kasey was first to awaken. Groggy, she spied Nasir face down in the mud. Quickly forcing off her fog, she crawled to him, calling, then shouting his name, her dread intensifying at his inert torpor. She turned him over. He wasn't breathing. The dogs above made frenzied attempts at making their way down to them, snarling and barely stopping short on the ledge. Kasey hoped they hadn't been oblivious for long. She shook him and got no response. Wasting no more time, she gave him mouth-to-mouth resuscitation, stopping to message his chest and asking, begging, demanding him to breathe. She heard a noise from inside him. A gurgle? Convulsion? Or moan? Let it be anything but a death rattle, she begged. She filled his mouth with air, pulled her lips away and watched his chest rise slightly on its own. She was ready to do it again when he hacked and took a real breath, opening his eyes with a vacant stare. Kasey shook him again, needing to see some consciousness registering. She shouted into his ear, "Nasir, do you hear me?" His face remained blank. Kasey was afraid a lack of oxygen may have caused brain damage. She sat him up, "Nasir, can you hear me? Speak to me!"

Nasir help up a hand, indicating he wanted her to cease. Opening his mouth stimulated an involuntary gagging reflex. A rumble erupted from his viscera, then a flow of mud ejected out, surging down his chin like larva from a volcano.

It poured onto the ground, the flood interfering with Nasir's breathing and making him gasp. The spew in time became diluted with saliva, resembling a nectar by the time it emptied. He fell over on his side in relief.

Kasey continued unsure of his faculties. She grabbed his lapels and again yelled, "Nasir, can you hear me?"

He pushed her hands away and finally spoke, "Yes ... Yes ... Yes! I hear you. Will you be quiet!"

She backed off. Nasir got on his feet. Both of them were coated with muck. Nasir looked at Kasey and shook his head in disbelief, "You're relentless, do you know that?"

She turned her back to him, folded her arms and scanned the environs while Nasir composed himself.

***

As the gang made its way back in the dead of night, Fajid wrangled with the unease he felt at the sight on the horizon. Things looked too dark ahead on his homestead. Shouldn't his men be visibly on guard with the lights on? He gave in to the sensation, kicking at the gas pedal and shooting a worried look at Raza and Abbas.

They raced into the compound and jumped out of the trucks. Raza's pulse throbbed when he spotted the open door of the barn flapping in the breeze. Someone handed him a flashlight and he ran toward the barn, followed by Fajid and Abbas. Those armed went in first. One man shouted and waved to them. Raza clamped his fists when he saw the body on the ground. Kneeling down, somebody held up a light, revealing Hani's corpse. There was silence but for the rattling empty shackles Fajid held up. Tears poured from Raza's face. He wiped swarming insects of the body and cradled his brother.

Outside, someone checking the grain shed began wailing, "He's gone! He's gone!"

Speeding into the barn, the man stopped in his tracks.

Raza was sobbing, "My brother ... they have killed my brother ... "

Abbas and a few others charged outside when they felt the ground shake from the tremor of nearing vehicles. The fuel gofers were finally returning from a long search for gasoline.

Abbas screamed, "Where were you?"

"Hani sent us to find petrol," he was told as they started to unload the cans.

"You left him alone?"

"He demanded it."

Abbas kicked over a container and marched back into the barn. The crew looked puzzled and trekked behind.

Raza hissed through his rigid jaw, "They will pay! I want the criminals' blood!"

Rabid fury electrified the pack. Fajid went for shovels so they could bury Hani before sun up. When he returned, Raza was thrashing the one who left Hani alone. He threw a shovel at the man, who was nursing a black eye, "You who left him will bury him."

The remaining gasoline couriers warily grabbed the scoops and moved away from Raza. There was no time for Raza to punish the others. He stormed away with the gang, leading the way to the trucks. The caravan thundered away, fanning out to scour every inch of land in pursuit of Kasey and Nasir.

***

Drake called an immediate meeting with Ambassador Howe and General Zalman once she arrived back at the embassy in Riyadh. The three of them convened in Howe's office. It was Drake's order that no one else be present. Narrowing the information loop would help root her control of the situation. Power in diplomacy and politics is based largely on adept maneuvering of data flow. Isolating, dividing, hoarding and sharing data soon becomes basic nature. And Drake was at it right away.

Howe told her, "We pulled video from international satellite news. Saddam was walking around Baghdad. Someone with him was holding today's newspaper, so we know it is a current photo op."

139

The secretary checked it off in her mind, "That issue is settled. We *know* he remains in control." She faced Zalman, "General, I know your assignment here is winding down. Can I ask you to postpone retirement until the Lawrence matter has ended?"

He knew he was being asked only to keep a new officer from becoming involved, "I wouldn't think of leaving until she's back."

"I will be staying in Riyadh," Drake announced. "Cooperation between agencies will be done through me, so one hand will know what the other is doing. The best hope for getting Captain Lawrence back and avoiding a foreign policy disaster for the president is that we all be on the same page. I want to talk to you both about what the CIA has been up to-"

There was a knock on the door. Howe opened it. A courier put a sealed pouch in his hand and walked away. Howe looked at it, "It's for you. From the Algerians. Might be a message from Saddam."

He handed it to her. Drake went to a corner of the room, broke the seal and turned her back when she looked at the note that said:

Re: Your question - Where are the two?

Reply: Only you can answer.

She remained facing away as she walked to the document shredder. Diplomatic strength - it pulverized the letter into dust.

When she looked at Howe and Zalman, she was shocked to find Station Chief Walker standing by the door. She bit her tongue in anger at his audacity. There was much she wanted to say, but she only placed a hand on her hip. Always best to be mindful around the station chief. They have allies and agendas that are hard to figure.

Drake chose to sound detached rather than act surprised, "We didn't ask for you." He stepped forward with a bone-locked stride, his coat draped over his shoulders like a cape. Even more disturbing was the interval he took before words. He absorbed the entire space before speaking, as if phantasms only he could see shared the room.

Howe stared at him, but Zalman refused to give him attention.

"I will not stand for another government department humiliating the agency," Walker coldly established. "We will not be your fall guys."

The secretary was not going to tolerate being lectured, "I have no idea what you're talking about."

Walker reeled around and exited.

What maddened Drake was knowing how his visit had the effect he no doubt wanted. She asked herself, does he know what I know? More? Less? Was he being tipped off from inside the White House? Or was he the one informing them? Much more raced through her mind. She thought all he wanted was to snare her in a net of insecurity and indecision, bogging her down in corridors of dead ends and mirrors. That was his skill, wasn't it?

Drake knew Howe and Zalman sensed her resentment. Suddenly, she wasn't sure she should go on with what she had started to say about the CIA. Would it get back to Walker? If not from someone present, then by Walker having a way to hear what goes on in Howe's office. After all, Walker was based in the embassy and certainly had motive and opportunity to know what was happening anywhere on premises. She was frustrated that Walker had unnerved her. She couldn't get the image out of her head of Walker cracking a smile after leaving the room, laughing inside at her. An odd picture because she never saw Walker smile.

Drake chose to scrap the rest of the meeting.

***

The Saud's held their next meeting inside the Royal Palace. Family only, outside members of the Council of Ministers were told official Majils were postponed due to intelligence citing a terrorist threat. It was a decision the king made to merge Guard units defending the palace and Council of Ministers into a single corps to tighten the ring of security around the family.

The director of the National Reserve stood in the antechamber cautiously wording his concern about the nation's economy, "I kept banks in the cities open and closed some in the rough country," he explained. "In some villages, citizens became wild. Think what would happen in Riyadh. I can plan if you give us notice before large withdrawals."

King Khaled saw how the director couldn't take eyes off the throne. Even in muted light, the jewels embedded in the pure gold glistened. "It was an oversight on our part," Khaled smiled. "We are creating new portfolios to invest in robust Western securities. The entire country will benefit. There will be more shifting of capital for the next two weeks. Plan accordingly. I praise your decision to restrict who sees the count. It will stifle rumors."

The director felt relieved. He made his point and was treated with courtesy. The king dismissed him with a genial hug.

"See what happens in the hurry," Abdul spoke up after the director was gone. "We are risking chaos."

Khaled agreed, "We will transfer property in arranged order. If there is another riot, people will make a run on banks.

It was an easy decision for the king, but one that made the others nervous. Rakan expressed what they were thinking, "How shall we do it? Time is growing short."

The king probed faces then issued his decree, "Transfer will be done in progression by standing. Mine first, then Abdul's and-"

His ruling was swallowed up by an uproar. It was a paroxysm of self-interest, the tumult of an imminent family brawl.

Rakan was the one the king heard over the bedlam, "Why not allow all of us to move portions at the same time?"

The king raised his voice, "I have made my decision!"

Salih challenged him, "Your decision is not for the good of us all. It favors only you. Your judgment carries no weight."

Khaled's authority was rapidly disappearing. He stood and paced toward Salih, "I will show you my prominence! Salih, you are dismissed as Director of the Guard."

It was the bluster of a monarch witnessing respect slipping away, something Khaled never experienced in his reign. He bared his contempt for Salih, "Where was the Guard when the bank was looted? Where were they when the Americans were attacked? This is not the transition agreed to. If you were doing your job, it would be happening evenly, and we all would still be here when your brother is found."

Salih sneered, "As if you care about Nasir! You haven't brought up his name for two days. Wait for him? To me, he was lost long ago. America is the doom of all of you."

The king shouted in Salih's face, "They're the ones who made the deal you wanted! You don't want their military involved. If things spiral out of control, they will step in to protect their own. Rakan will now lead the Guard!"

"Rakan? They won't listen to a dandy," Salih laughed. "The Mecca pilgrims arrive in two weeks. That's all the time you have."

Salih thundered out of the chamber. The king demanded order, but the scene had long degenerated into finger pointing, name calling and venting of simmering feuds. Khaled was forced to elbow through his carping kin, fretting over propriety likely forever lost. He mounted his throne and sat silently with tears in his eyes. He was begged to change his decision. When he refused, the family put aside strife to unite in disregard of his edict. The king finally flinched in panic. He threw his hands over his head and snapped his fingers, a sign to the Guard commander incredulously observing the shocking events. Soldiers rushed in, but were reluctant to use riot control until the king ordered a show of force. The regiment launched into the warring royals, knocking them aside with rifle butts and pushing them out of the palace hall, all the while in wide-eyed in disbelief at what was unfolding.

* * *

The runway at the private airport in Damman belonging to the USA Oil Company was crowded with corporate jets. One was boarding passengers, largely wives and children of executives stationed in Saudi Arabia. Inside a hangar, the maintenance supervisor called another plane in for a check. Two American mechanics took a break while waiting. One seemed puzzled, "I've never seen so many planes here at one time, all flying out. Do they know something we don't?"

The other brushed off suspicion, "You are too paranoid."

"But the other day the soldier was shot and-"

His friend cut him off and spoke quietly, "Isolated things like will happen in this part of the world. You'll know once you've been here long enough. The company is sending the families on a vacation. They rent a resort every few months as a reward for them putting up with the foreign duty."

"I was told that in Saudi Arabia wives need permission from husbands to leave the country, even for foreigners. An Air Force policeman told me no one has gone to the embassy in a week."

"The company probably took care of the paperwork. If something was going on, the government would have us all out of here."

***

The Republic of Turkey is the naked paradox of the Mideast. A country of dazzling bewilderment arising from remarkably glaring incongruities. Straddling the continents of Europe and the Mideast, the republic was formed in 1923, a remnant of the Ottoman Empire. After being on the losing side in World War One and surrendering massive territory, the sultanate was overthrown and a civil government established. It is a nation where the population is more than 99% Sunni Muslim, and recently *led by a woman*. A North Atlantic Treaty Organization member that has been at war with *another* NATO nation, Greece, while both were included in the treaty. Turkey is an almost exclusive trading partner with the West, yet with strong foreign policy ties to Iran and Iraq. An allegiance that springs from a major oil pipeline inside Turkey that transports *both* Iranian and Iraqi crude. Moreover, the three nations' have an interest in repressing nationalistic impulses of the Kurds, who inhabit each country in substantial numbers. The Kurds are a two thousand years old ethnic population today numbering twenty million who, despite international promises, have never had a sovereign state in an area they have lived in for ages. After World War One, the British in Iraq drove them into Turkey. Turkey pushed them into Iran. Iran forced them back into Iraq. Kurds are transients in a region where they pre-date the current populace.

Today, the Kurds primarily exist in a remote triangular area among the three countries, causing strife in them all. Turkey has also been plagued by other erupting streams of ethnic and religious tension. Even through the republic long ago officially renounced the Caliphate, spiritual leader of Islam, religious fundamentalism has challenged ruling authority. The civilian government is watched over by the military. In the 1960's and 80's Turkish armed forces stepped in to quell domestic unrest. In the mid 1990's, the first pro-Islamic fundamentalist government was elected, causing nervous tremors in the US State Department over another Islamic state in the region. It resulted in the European Union rebuffing Turkey's membership bid and America withholding monetary aide. The US went so far as to threaten military intervention to protect the oil pipeline. *The pipeline that transports Iranian and Iraqi oil.* Again, the Turkish military, closely aligned with America, stepped in and thwarted formation of an Islamic state overwhelmingly voted in by the Turkish people.

Currently, the situation is at an uneasy standstill. The military has quietly backed creation of a moderate civilian coalition. The West for now has stifled a new Islamic state. But what will be the eventual result?

Kasey and Nasir desperately hoped they were now in Turkey. It took the better part of two days to cross the mountain range that must have extended well over fifty miles. Welts covered their heels, slowing progress. They knew they were heading in the right direction. From their elevation, they twice spotted foot caravans below, armed men with backpacks, obviously carrying processed heroin from Turkey into Syria. Heroin traffic radiated from Turkey like spokes from a wheel, branching into the Mideast and Europe.

The highlands gradually leveled into a vast basin. Exhaustion and physical adversity had taken its toll. Kasey and Nasir remained silent for hours, too weary to expend energy in conversation. They winced with each hobbling step until Kasey became aware of the pasture they trudged through, "Poppies," she said with feeble delight. "Wild poppies, Nasir."

Nasir ran his hands over the plants, "We must be in Turkey. In Syria, the Bluecoats eradicate them."

The insight put energy in their step. Miles later, the meadow configured into cultivated fields. Kasey and Nasir moved discreetly. Trespassing through a poppy crop was potentially as deadly as being captured by a Jihad band. Ahead, there was a pond between a grove. They stumbled toward it, collapsing in the water, drinking and drenching themselves. Nasir finished first. He sat on the ground, shielded by the trees.

Looking around, he saw a young girl peeking at him through the trees. He stared hard to be certain it was no mirage. She smiled at him. Nasir called to Kasey and pointed to the girl at the same time voices were heard close by. Kasey and Nasir jumped out of sight lines and observed a woman guiding a group of young children emerge from a path. After watching long enough to believe they might find help, Kasey and Nasir revealed themselves.

The woman was startled. She huddled the children behind her. Kasey and Nasir approached, but stopped far enough away to let it be known they were no threat.

Kasey anxiously asked, "Do you speak English?"

The woman took a long look at them. Kasey tried again, "We mean you no harm. Can you speak English?"

The woman decided to answer, "Yes, some ... I am a teacher."

"Are we in Turkiyie?" Nasir advanced toward her.

The teacher's gestures made the children a bit wary, but they gawked curiously. "Yes," she said.

Her answer produced overflowing emotional relief from Kasey and Nasir. They rushed to her.

"Please help us," Kasey begged. "I am an American. He is a Saudi. We were kidnapped and escaped in Syria. We need to reach our embassy. Can you take us to government authorities?"

The teacher needed time to absorb the meaning of the words. The children started to play hide and seek with Kasey and Nasir. They ducked between the teacher, hid behind the trees and covered their faces grinning when Kasey and Nasir looked a them. Gradually, they moved closer to the strangers.

"Come with us to the school," the woman finally said. She turned began walking down the path. Kasey and Nasir followed, hiking with the children who

146

started falling behind their teacher, surrounding Kasey and Nasir, giggling, reaching for their hands and grabbing at their legs. The teacher said something, leading the children to begin offering their snacks of nuts and raisins. A famished Kasey and Nasir nibbled from the small open palms.

Ahead, a schoolhouse emerged, sitting at the base of a knoll in front of a valley. Once inside, Kasey and Nasir plunked into undersized chairs. The teacher sent the children out to do chores.

"The farm below has a radio. Only I should go. I will call the gendarmes."

Nasir looked at Kasey, both reflecting on the plan.

"Please, don't let-" Kasey paused.

The woman was already nodding, "I will not tell others you are here."

Kasey nodded back and the teacher left them.

They watched through a window as she walked away. She flung her arms forward to push the children along ahead of her.

Nasir wanted his worry eased, "Can we trust her?"

"Turkey is an ally to both our countries. Unrest is mostly in Kurdish areas and large cities."

"There are poppy farmers around here," was Nasir's real concern.

"I know," Kasey didn't like considering that wild card. But she already figured it in her calculations. "They are controlled by the military. And America manages the military. Farmers would turn us over to soldiers."

Nasir didn't reply. He didn't like how sure she was. They fell silent. Nasir recited prayers in his heart. Kasey kept her eyes peeled out the window and took brief, labored breaths.

Both were so drained, they lost consciousness for a time. Kasey knew it happened, but the span felt like it was only the blink of an eye. She looked over at Nasir. He was upright in the chair with his eyes shut. She focused her gaze through the window. Everything was quiet. Too quiet, something intuitive told her. She got out of the chair, walked to the door and looked outside. Nobody was around. She jumped when she felt warm air on her neck. It was Nasir, looking over her shoulder.

"I don't like this," she told him.

Nasir was thinking the same thing, "Let's get out of here."

147

When they stepped outside, Raza, Abbas and their pack swarmed from around corners, down the roof and out of the woods. Nasir was bashed to the ground and pushed ahead on all fours. Kasey was kicked onto her back and towed by her locks. Other accomplices rushing headlong screaming abuse.

Raza leaned over them and shouted, "Butchers! Assassins! You will stand trial for your crimes!"

Behind a hill, Fajid and his men waited in the trucks. The children and their teacher stood in a row as Kasey and Nasir were dragged by. The children threw rocks while the teacher scowled.

Abbas bellowed, "Praise Allah! Praise Hezbollah!"

The invocation brought all to their knees. Abbas led a liturgy, falling forward with arms outstretched.

Kasey and Nasir found themselves again tied and blindfolded by the time prayers were done. Abbas jumped behind the wheel of a truck and the caravan dashed away, spurting through lowlands beneath the high country. At the Syrian border, they joined up with the waiting Syrian Army unit ready to escort them. They were on the way to Lebanon, the Bekka Valley, and headquarters of Hezbollah and Jihad. The most hostile place in the world for a heathen American soldier and Arab royal perceived to be an Islamic heretic.

7

The old man who dozed every afternoon under the sun on a stone bench in the plaza of the kidnappers' native village was the first to sense distant rumbling. The rattle in his brittle bones awakened him. He tilted an ear toward the groaning rumble. The noise had a fortitude that disturbed him. He tottered to his feet and leaned on his cane, attentive to the organ-like dirge as he ambled to the outskirts of the hamlet. He said nothing to those he passed. They were acting as if they heard nothing. It wouldn't be the first time his ears had played tricks on him.

He gazed into the desert horizon, fastening his eyes in the direction of the echo. He tuned his sight to penetrate the vista that quivered from rising heat.

The old man realized the roar was not from any returning family caravan or tormenting government officials. What at last emerged on the horizon churned his fear. It appeared instantly and in colossal totality, a looming dynamism and distending panoramic spectacle, an immense human force storming his way. A crackling, thundering clamor started vibrating his torso. The man searched for details about the figures covered with dust kicked up by tanks, artillery and troop transports. He finally identified the soldiers by the green scarves they all had tied around their heads.

He turned toward the village and lurched toward the square in a panic, crying out, "Green Scarves! Men be warned ... the Green Scarves are coming!"

Nearby men who heard his gasping warning dropped what they were doing and ran shouting, "The Green Scarves are coming! ... Green Scarves are near!"

Men hustled out of buildings, pushing aside their children to flee in an every male for himself fury. A number of them crammed into the only working truck and tried to drive away. The suspension quivered and gave way. The lilting truck tipped over as men jumped off. They tried to catch up on foot to those spurting ahead while women directed girls into shelters and tried to hide remaining boys. Some women and girls defied the desperation by lingering in public. They had an idea what was about to happen.

An artillery barrage preceded the Green Scarves arrival. Some too late for the exodus had to hunt for hiding places. One forced a woman with her son from a hole next to a building foundation and crawled inside. The old man ceased being messenger and nestled in his secret space, careful to remain unnoticed by other men seeking cover.

After the artillery barrage, tanks rolled into the village, strangling the perimeter. Infantry followed. The lead squad fired bullets randomly into buildings, a terror tactic to discourage any struggle. The Green Scarves performed textbook Western military strategy combined with established Mideast tactics of acting erratically to inspire panic. The place was theirs the moment they set foot into the village.

Infantry units scoured dwellings for men. Another unit plundered supplies of food, fuel, weapons - anything potentially useful to them.

A teenaged girl grew awed and inspired by the women strutting toward the square flanking the prowling tanks as gunfire seemed to bounce from every direction. She cast off her chador, left it on the ground and ran to the soldiers, pointing to the hole next to the building foundation.

The first tank stopped. Out of the driver's hatch burst Maryam Moghavi, honcho of this army that displayed no rank or insignia. She scrambled down the turret and jumped onto the ground. A long sword dangled inside a sheath tied to her waist. It dragged along the ground when she marched her five-foot tall frame over to the hole and watched a lithe soldier disappear inside and haul out the terrified man by his collar. He was thrown on his back.

Moghavi stood over him with a boot on his chest, "When did Raza and his scum leave?"

"I don't know when he was last here," the man lied, hoping he might be saved by denying any connection to Raza. "They stay in the desert."

The man tried to sit up and beg. Moghavi kicked him down into the dirt and

Pressed a boot on his chest, "If you tell me where he is now, you won't have to die *slowly.*"

"Mercy ... please," his eyes grew teary at Moghavi's proposition. "They left two days ago. The Guard kicked them out. They went back into the Iraq desert."

"Thank you," Moghavi smiled. She pulled out her polished, needle-sharp sword, "I do keep my word."

The man shivered. Soldiers held his head firm on the ground. He let out a scream when Moghavi kneeled on his chest. Quickly, with surgical precision, she slit the man's throat.

It was all over for him in seconds.

Moghavi stood up and thrust out a hand. A soldier placed a handmade bouquet of black silk roses in Moghavi's palm. She dropped them on the corpse.

Female villagers crowded in awe around Moghavi. They followed her to a well and watched her wash her sword. The girl who shed her chador approached Moghavi, folding her hands and pleading to join them. When Moghavi embraced her, other girls threw off their veils and raced to Moghavi.

She welcomed them all into her army. The girls blended with the soldiers as Moghavi climbed back into her tank. She led them away, blasting apart what remained intact in front of her. The Green Scarves sauntered off, leaving the looted village a smoldering ruin.

***

At a concealed intelligence post burrowed into a craggy plateau in northern Israel, two Mossad analysts reflected on fresh data designated for review. In silence, they inspected minute-by-minute satellite photographs, searching for critical details under a magnifying glass.

One was talking out a fluid interpretation, "Seems as though ... earlier today ... a Syrian division moved into the Bekka, then immediately left the way they came."

The other formed a similar conclusion, "Berets ... dropping something off?"

He was intrigued by a dynamic he saw evolving, "Several divisions sitting inside Iraq made a raid into Iran."

"Green Scarves, no doubt," his associate decided. "Now they're moving on a collision course with the Syrians."

Both grinned.

Their supervisor came into the room with latest intelligence, "Some very unusual things are going on." He set new photos and acoustic graphs from listening stations on the table. "Headquarters brought it up with the Americans. Their State Department claims none of it seems curious."

The three frowned. The supervisor went on, "Events could spin our way or get too hot to ignore." He sighed, "It's much harder to find out what we need since the Pollard case. No access to ECHELON, or the Seven Dwarves. Mossad is prepared to spend hard capital sending America a message. They'll be persuaded to open up again when they see we know they're lying."

"What's the deal?"

"We are going to mobilize our deep cover in the Bekka."

The look the two agents gave each other said something unusual had to be underway.

Their supervisor decided to insert himself into the affair, "If the diplomats try to freeze us out, we'll deal with it Mossad to CIA. Neither of us can trust security to the smoothies."

***

Call Lebanon the storm drain of the Mideast. Almost every banished, tormented, persecuted or miscreant roving mass with a political agenda ends up scoured out and rinsed into this perpetually shattered country. The blame starts with Lebanon's official birth after World War One. Formed of five former Ottoman Empire districts and administered under French mandate, the first foible sealing its fate was the apportioning of all government positions among religious communities. This National Covenant afforded most status and rank to the minority Christians, even though the population was overwhelmingly

Muslim. That antagonism of the majority is root cause of all the misery that has followed.

US Marines intervened in 1958 during a Syrian backed Muslim uprising, further suppressing the majority and provoking anti-American sentiment in the Arab Mideast. Muslims fought back with guerrilla attacks against America's regional ally, Israel. Israel artillery pounded the Arab opposition and Palestinian camps inside Lebanon, becoming an occupying force in the south, which led to a skittish Syria invading and holding the North. This cycle of raids, counterattacks, bombardments and occupations has gone on for decades. The chaos was an invitation for any area expatriate multitude to settle in, intensifying the ruin of Lebanon by using it as base for their agendas, leading to more insurgencies, offensives and bombings between ever widening factions.

These incessant, feverish conflicts finally plunged the country into a civil war that erupted in 1975, leading to the deaths of over 60,000. Palestinian exiles and leftist Muslims fought against the Maronite militia and Phalange Christians. Village garrisons, mercenaries, criminal bands and family defenders, many of which flip-flopped loyalties by the day, or even hour, joined the main warring parties.

Terrorism became a way of life. Fifty Americans were killed at one US Embassy bombing. In another, 241 Marines. Kidnappings of foreigners became common. US, British, French and Soviet citizens were the primary victims. Some were released, some never returned. Today, Lebanon is recognized as a legitimate state. Yet it remains a siphon, draining the wringing perspiration of the region into its cedar basins, lush plains and cosmopolitan Beirut. A place where no one publicly speaks of yesterday, not from superstitious dread of repeating it, but because the trials of the past have always been its tomorrow.

The Syrian outfit, two hundred strong, left the kidnappers on the outskirts of Baalbek, the heart of Hezbollah dominated territory in Lebanon. The unit had orders to exit the area quickly. Syrian regulars, called *Helmets,* defended Northern Lebanon. The battalion escorting Raza and Abbas was one of the Syrian elite, dubbed *Berets.* Berets were ordinarily exclusive protectors of high government officials. The sight of them pushing by threw open every grunt supervised checkpoint so fast the caravan never had to brake. The Berets began their trip back when the kidnappers disappeared from sight. It wasn't a good idea for them be to away from Damascus for long. Political leaders were concerned that decreasing their protection for long might encourage something. In the Mideast, one never knows where enemies lurk. Besides, the presence of Berets in Lebanon would fast be noted by Israel, a tip off something extraordinary was happening.

The kidnappers were on the way to Yanta, a Hezbollah training center sealed deep in the valley. Along the way, they passed dazzling Roman ruins, lush vineyards and wild cherry orchards before bouncing down dusty roads staffed every few kilometers by Hezbollah fighters. The guards also operated remote controlled roadside bombs, usually disguised as simulated rocks made from plastic. This explained the overturned personnel carriers occasionally blocking the road. Usually wreckage of South Lebanese Army vehicles destroyed during hit and run raids against Hezbollah. The South Lebanese Army is a mercenary force hired by Israel to bolster their control of south Lebanon. The SLA and Israel rule southern Lebanon from headquarters at a crusader-era fortress known as Beaufort Castle, while Hezbollah and Syria command the north. Erected next to some of the upended wreckage were sculptures made of stones and rocket fragments, with the gear of dead soldiers impaled on poles as both warning and victory symbols. Behind a hill that obstructed the village was a small airfield, its cobblestone runway overgrown with weeds. Long dormant, the strip was built for crop dusters back when the canyon was center of wine country. Emerging around the hill was a bundle of tents used to house Shiite Muslim warriors during military exercises. A giant billboard stood in the middle of the camp, portraying an Israeli soldier with wolf-like features ripping to pieces Jerusalem's Dome of the Rock mosque. Beneath the image, writing in Farsi and Arabic propagandized: *Israel Must Be Destroyed.*

Mottled clay dwellings and creaky plywood shacks emanated in awry patterns from the only thoroughfare. The remaining municipal infrastructure was a stucco building, the jail. Wilting posters of Ayatollah Ruhollah Khomeini drooped off its wall. The tolerable habitats were for Hezbollah leaders, who changed whereabouts frequently and without warning. They are never safe from

Israel's reach, even in the Bekka. A conspicuous Soviet provided, Cold War era artillery network looked down from the surrounding highlands. A long ago gift to protect Imad Mugniyeh, founder of Hezbollah, who was from Yanta.

The Bekka Valley training center has also served, at one time or another, as meeting ground for many belligerent pariahs, or freedom fighters, such as the Turkish Kurdistan Workers Party, Abu Nidal's Palestinian Terror Squad, Osama bin Laden's Holy Fighters, Afghanistan's Taliban, the Irish Republican Army and the Japanese Red Army Faction, to name some. They find their way to the Bekka from Arab contacts in London, New York, Toronto, Bonn and Singapore, then are led to Hezbollah emissaries in Teheran, Damascus, Beirut and Tripoli. The Bekka Valley was where Western hostages were held in the 1980's. Citizens of Yanta grow up with inveterate hatred of America and Israel. Their heroes are the martyrs trained in the Bekka who perish in truck bombings and commit civilian massacres. People who are rewarded for sacrificing their flesh with sainthood and a cash payoff to relatives left behind. Hezbollah maintains their Bekka stronghold by harsh persuasion of the illiterate population, teaching them to blame the West and Israel for their poverty, lack of education, repression of Islam and world social injustice.

Raza led the caravan into the village square. Everyone seemed to know they were coming. Men lined the route and followed behind. Others dragged a pair of wire cages, used for previous hostages, to the end of the road. As the crowd peculiarly managed to at the same time chuckle and sneer, Kasey and Nasir were tossed onto the back of a rusting flatbed and towed around.

Men and boys glared with flaring nostrils, shouted and pitched rocks, stabbed at them with spikes and sticks, even hurled an animal carcass at them. In Yanta, a strict Muslim fundamentalist place, women were seldom seen in public. They peered from doorways and windows. Raza drove the truck around in circles, honking the horn, until he got dizzy. Then Abbas got behind the wheel.

For Kasey and Nasir, it was another round of sensory deprived torture. They were barely conscious when they were caged. Nasir prayed and Kasey again focused on a strategy of escape until the abuse began. It was part defense mechanism and part relentless patriotism that sent one into faith and the other into self-reliance. They had a complementary sense of belief and conviction, secular and religious, which merged in the certitude that their nations were doing everything possible to get them back.

The truck stopped. Raza jumped on the back and quieted the chanting throng. "Send word all through the valley," he bellowed, a shriek stained with grief from losing a brother. "A trial will take place. The charge is murder. Every man shall be a juror."

The excitement incited by his announcement made Raza forget his sorrow. Esteem provided by the limelight took priority over his pain. He wasn't very sure where he was going with this. The Syrians told him to wait in the valley with the hostages. He never told their escort commander what happened to his brother. Where would a trial lead? If Kasey and Nasir were put to death, there would be no material gain, only revenge. What was more important? And what would the Syrians do? His advertisement of an impending trial might lead to things getting out of his control. None of it worried him now. Not while he was center of attention.

Boys ran away on foot to spread the word nearby while Fajid and his band to kicked up dust speeding off to notify far regions of the valley.

The howling mob circled Kasey and Nasir. They both guessed they were in Lebanon. Kasey by depth of the hostility she felt directed at them. It was so much greater and more sincere than the other places they had found themselves in. She clung to the fact that Western hostages had in the past been released from the Bekka and ignored the truth that they were just as often killed. Nasir's conclusion about locale was based on how the crowd blended Farsi and Arabic. He wondered if Kasey knew what Raza said about putting them on trial. No Saudi royal had ever been brought to the Bekka. His fear was that Hezbollah would make an example of him, venting their frustration at Saudi royal family wealth and their perceived indifference toward Arab nationalism.

One man joined the rabble, straggling along the rear, chanting and pumping his fists, yet scrutinizing with detached, keen eyes.

Stockades were constructed in the plaza. Kasey and Nasir were locked in and the clothes on their backs ripped off, exposing their skin to the scorching sun.

Raza pounded a whip handle into his palm, "They escaped once," he told the inspired crowd. "Under Hezbollah law, we can do anything to deter another attempt."

He walked behind Kasey and Nasir. At least being blindfolded held off sight of the looming horror. Raza began with Nasir. The first lash was a surprise. Nasir's body convulsed, then buckled. Raza lashed him again. The delay between the crack and the whack felt endless. Then he whipped Kasey. She tried so hard to scream she near swallowed her gag. Raza alternated strokes until their bodies almost as red as the sun above. Rising welts bubbled up, cooking in the heat.

Raza offered the strap to the mob. Fathers helped sons onto the truck and showed them how to grip the handle, then helpfully stood by and beamed when the boys got off a good stroke. The flogging continued through the afternoon heat. Fortunately, Kasey and Nasir passed out early on.

The man with the keen eyes took a turn with the whip and lashed them as hard as he could. Then Raza called off the thrashing. Unconscious, Kasey and Nasir were carried on top of the throng's shoulders and secured in different cells at the jail. Guards were stationed inside and out while the rest of the community was absorbed in prayer. Awakening in the night, Kasey and Nasir hurt so bad they dared not move a muscle or breathe too hard. The short time they spent aware was consumed with praying and plotting. They had little inkling about the futility of their inner defiance. Along with those protecting their prison, every resident of Yanta was a sentry. As were all in the surrounding villages. Not to mention the constant Hezbollah checkpoints, patrolling Syrian troops and assorted militias that attended the valley. For Kasey and Nasir, this was a place of no escape.

***

Prince Rakan led a procession of Guard vehicles onto a runway at the airport in Jiddah. An armored car stopped next to a private jet. Soldiers formed a defensive ring around it as a team began loading trunks and vaults into the jet's open cargo hold.

157

Not far away, early arriving Mecca pilgrims were disembarking a chartered plane. Inside the lone terminal, they were greeted by waiting friends and family. A pair of soldiers lost grip of a trunk on the loading ramp. Gold bars, jewels, artifacts and other valuables spilled out.

In the terminal, a pilgrim's eye was captured by the gold twinkling in the sun. He pointed it out to the others. One squinted at a profile he recognized, "That's Prince Rakan." The comment raised eyebrows. "Since when does a Saud use a public airport?" somebody asked. They watched the armored car unload so much property it backed up the chain of laborers and ended up stacked on the pavement. There was a buzz among the crowd, an undertone of astonishment that took shape when two men walked out of the terminal and headed for Rakan. A few others followed, then many more.

On the airstrip, some were still collecting the strewn treasure. Rakan noticed the pack heading his way. Members of the Guard intercepted them. Rakan glanced warily on the animated discussion going on between the Guard and the curious throng.

The crowd finally sidestepped the outnumbered Guard who merely stood by after a feeble attempt to stop them. Rakan saw them coming. He ordered the workers to hurry while the horde started circling.

A man folded his arms and questioned Rakan, "Why are you rushing to put your valuables on a plane?"

"It's none of your business," Rakan said as he motioned the Guard to stand by him. He was annoyed at their presumption. "They are my possessions, I'll do what I like."

A group splintered off and took a good look at what was going into the hold, "Some of this belongs to the Saudi people, not the royal family."

One was bold enough to try to open a trunk. Rakan fast grew jittery. He was violating the king's decree by moving his wealth out prior to authorization and now was being challenged by a multitude, most not even Saudis, and the Guard was oddly indifferent.

Rakan was relieved when a loyal Guardsman fired a gun into the air to force the crowd back, but the act only fired up anger and suspicion.

"You're robbing the country in front everybody," was the remark that provoked greater audacity. People took position in front of the ramp, blocking the Guard. They kicked at a strongbox until its cover loosened.

"Look at this," the man who kneeled and tore off the cover said, waving people over. The trunk was full of Muslim artifacts dating back to the Middle Ages. Some of it borrowed from elsewhere, most of it acquired on the black market.

"These cannot belong to you," one of the bunch fumed as hands grabbed at the items.

Some of the Guard hesitated. Rakan saw the outrage in their eyes. A few tried pushing people back. It was a deflated effort.

Rakan dashed into the plane, finding the pilot in the cockpit, "Get ready to take off with what's already on board!"

"We can't," the pilot threw up his arms. "We are waiting on a fuel delivery."

Rakan rolled his eyes and looked outside through a window. The situation was getting out of control. His property was being looted. He was growing poorer by the minute, cringing at the sight of a pair making off with a safe while the Guard watched.

"Where did they all come from? I was told there were no flights scheduled to land for hours."

"They didn't arrive commercial," the pilot had to tell him. "It was a contract flight. It doesn't appear on the schedule."

Rakan couldn't endure his disbelief. He ran back out onto the runway and collared the nearest soldier.

"Fire on them!"

The soldier turned his head away.

The prince grabbed the soldier's rifle and aimed it at the crowd, "Thieves! Drop everything or I'll shoot!"

The crowd ignored him. Rakan was furious. He set the gun sight on a man trotting by with gold bars in his arms. He stopped a few feet from Rakan and boldly stared. The attention of the Guard was on Rakan.

Rakan wanted to put a bullet in him, he really did. His finger wobbled on the trigger. He couldn't pull it.

His inaction drew quiet scorn from the Guard and only encouraged the plundering.

The troops decided to retreat. They headed for their vehicles.

Rakan was taunted by the mob:

"This is what you deserve for stealing from the country!"

"The Saud's are not worthy to lead!"

"Your relatives are cowards!"

These were the insults hurled at Rakan. People gradually began to envelop Rakan and demanded answers. The Guard started driving away. No chance they would intercede to stop those they were coming to share sentiment with.

A man stuck a finger in his Rakan's face, "Our time is coming."

Alone, and sensing threat of violence in the air, Rakan feared it the gathering might decide their time was now.

Rakan flagged down a Guard jeep racing by. It passed him, but then stopped. Rakan hustled over and jumped in, the crowd giving chase. An out of breath Rakan pleaded, "Hurry! Get me out of here now!"

The people emptied the cargo hold, ransacked baggage and seized Rakan's vaults. The pilot inside the plane watched the unruffled crowd walk away admiring their spoils. Some dragged off suitcases weighed down with gold. Others stuffed pockets with diamonds and rubies while a few struggled to haul away furniture and artwork.

***

General Zalman deposited the latest series of reconnaissance images on a desk at the US Embassy. Secretary Drake peered over her glasses at Ambassador Howe, "Do you need to see these?"

Howe reacted with an ambiguous gesture. Drake pushed the data back at Zalman, "Give us a summary."

Zalman paused to frame the presentation of facts. The delay made Drake notice how tired she felt. Fatigued at this situation and all the others she had to deal with in these unusual times. The weariness punctured her guard by way of vulnerable introspection. Such contemplation was usually held in check by all the activity around her. Meetings like these, with no aides, media, envoys or public event to occupy her left nothing to hinder restlessness. How would history view her term as secretary of state? She wondered. Especially with what was underway in the world now. Drake spent most of her life in academia, a professor of foreign affairs and diplomacy. At Georgetown and Tufts, she taught many who worked at State over the past two decades. Several years ago, she was named interim American ambassador to the UN, replacing an ill predecessor. She ended up on the job for three years during the last president's administration, impressing world diplomats and the newly elected president enough to be offered the job of secretary of state. It was an exhilarating experience for a short time, but if she knew then what she does now, she would have gone back to academia. She longed for that road not taken, the time she could have spent with her grandchildren and husband. Patriotism was why she stayed on, a sense that right now it was her job to do the best she could to help America during events those who knew better never admitted was coming. She was too astute to believe history would view her role in this unfolding episode that way.

Zalman began interpreting, "A new Syrian division moved in and out of the Bekka Valley. Some forces inside Iraq made a quick raid into Iran. Likely Moghavi. Now they're heading west. Right now, they're on a collision course with the returning Syrians."

"Moghavi acting up ... that's all we need," Drake sighed. "Is there new information about their size?"

"It's a tough call for me," Zalman hedged, seeing an opening for a grievance. "Department of Defense is only providing the exact recon I ask for. I think they're unhappy about lack of information from you. They feel left in the dark and might be more forthcoming if-"

Drake stopped him, "It's out of their realm."

"Maybe they feel some accountability for what happened to Captain Lawrence?"

"They're not involved."

"When I gave Captain Lawrence her orders to go to Iraq, I was told they came from a DOD back channel."

"That must have been a communication muddle. I originated the order but they had to be transferred from a civilian to a military command."

Zalman wasn't buying it. He had been lied to and then he lied to the soldier under his authority. And now that soldier was missing. The general was seething and Drake knew it.

Howe perceived the tension in the sudden silence. If it went on for long, something was going to give. He remained curious about Drake's last question, "General, give me a ballpark figure on Moghavi's strength based on what's in front of you."

Finally, a good move on Howe's part.

"Look as though they are more than twenty thousand strong," Zalman said after glancing at the pictures.

Drake was shocked, "They are growing, fast. At this rate, they will be a big problem to Iran. And maybe to others. They're known to affiliate with anyone who'll help their cause. They've bailed out Saddam more than once."

"Maybe they were around when Captain Lawrence was lost," Howe speculated. "Maybe they are some piece of the puzzle now?"

"Doubt it," the dismissal showed how little Drake knew about them. One thing she did know, "Their beef is with Iran."

Zalman's concern about his soldier was eating at him more than ever. Things were murkier now than when the meeting started. He was still puzzled by the station chief's antagonism last time he was at the embassy, "What about Walker? Have you made a truce with him? He has to know something."

Drake was being squeezed, "He knows nothing that will help."

Nobody knows anything except for the three of them in the room? It was either another lie, or maybe it was the secretary who knew nothing. Zalman was becoming disgusted, "Spinning wheels ... that's what's going on here. Do either of you have any idea where Captain Lawrence is?"

"The president is ready to move a division to the Iraq border. He's deeply concerned about Captain Lawrence and thinks the action will pressure Saddam," Drake announced, without answering the question.

Howe impassively swiveled his chair in Zalman's direction.

To the general, it was a bombshell, "That's risky. The whole region will see it. It's like setting a fuse. And what reason will Defense be given for the order if they're in the dark?"

"I didn't ask for your assessment," the secretary coldly said. She paused to let air out of her words, realizing tension would only increase as this went along unless she clarified something. "I'm sorry to be brusque. General, let me tell you something about America's foreign policy - ascendancy of Islamic states in the Mideast is an absolute inevitability. What started in Iran has spread to Afghanistan, Libya and Sudan. It is underway in Egypt, Tunisia, Morocco, Syria, Jordan, Algeria and Iraq. Soon it will happen here in Saudi Arabia, even in Turkey, a NATO ally. The plan is to quietly accommodate this certainty and inhibit hostility toward America in an important part of the world. The American people have not had this explained to them yet. We haven't found a way to present the concept. They are not ready to hear it."

Zalman found the information curious and astonishing. Curious because it seemed to have little relation to what they were discussing, as though something was festering in the secretary that she had to get out by giving utterance to, and astonishing for its repellent hoax that was official policy. His disdain was clear, "Moving troops is a cover for *somebody* to say they did all they could to get Captain Lawrence back. That's the only purpose it serves. It will do nothing to bring her home."

Who was that somebody? The general wouldn't outright condemn his superior. It was as far as he would go with candor.

* * *

Rick needed to find a wonk, someone with a passionate knowledge about a topic. Usually a person buried in the bowls of an organization who has accumulated measureless, never used data. The wonk has a fetish he will gladly share, for few ever seek his expertise. For Rick, finding the right wonk was key to vivifying his raw data and coaxing it into a story.

Finding the needed wonk is a challenge. It takes penetrating a bureaucracy. Sometimes bureaucrats provide good information. Find enough in an agency who do and you have a collective wonk. Often bureaucracies are staffed with people who have no clue or don't care. Usually appointees of some sort, who don't need to know anything because they are protected by some higher-up know nothing. Or else they are the well intentioned who have simply risen to the level of their incompetence, faking it in a position well beyond the grasp of their qualifications. It's also important to understand that the aim of every bureaucracy, above all else, is to perpetuate itself. Never seem a threat to the bureaucrat. Tread lightly, be polite and most of all kiss-up. If you can manage to do that, you may find your way to the wonk, the investigative reporter's Holy Grail.

Rick wanted to know how many export licenses were granted over the past few years to US companies allowing them to sell reduction furnaces and amalgamated atom smashers. Rick gathered a list of corporate contributors to the major political parties. His goal was to find names on both lists and trace the exports from there.

He contacted the Office of the US Trade Representative, an executive branch agency in the federal government. They weren't repositories of the export data. No surprise. Rick knew it was seldom that a fishing expedition hooked something at first cast. They suggested the Commerce Department. Commerce said to try the Export Administration. They couldn't help but pointed him to the Export Enforcement Department. Somebody there was vaguely familiar with the subject, enough so to urge Rick try the Office of Export Technology. They faxed him a briefing paper noting prohibited exports. No reduction furnaces or amalgamated atom smashers were sold to outside countries over the past eight years. Rick decided to go deeper into the past. The Bureau of Economic Statistics, Export Branch, couldn't help. They said maybe the National Archives and Records Administration could. That agency urged him to contact the Bureau of Economic Analysis, who in turn speculated the Federal Trade Commission might have the data. FTC passed him to the Trade and Development Agency. Rick was worn out by the time they advised him the Customs Service might have the data. Their Press Office and Statistics Bureau blew him off. On a lark, Rick tried the Enforcement Division. They had the facts and emailed them to him. Rick learned that only Canada and Great

Britain had ever been allowed to import reduction furnaces and amalgamated atom smashers. Besides that, Customs, of all agencies, also sent along a federal talking points directive on plastic explosives. Obviously from their Press Office, somehow a heedless or iconoclastic bureaucrat messaged it to Rick. The regulation advised media inquiries about the subject be met with a narration of how, years ago, Czechoslovakia's first post-Communist president, Vaclav Havel, revealed that his country's former regime had sold Libya one thousand tons of Semtex, a then state-of-the-art plastic explosive. That one sale was enough to support terrorist activity for a century. To date, these explosives have turned up in North Korea, Afghanistan, Iran, Lebanon, and the Far East and are believed by the US Government to be the source of all plastic explosives used in world terrorist activity today.

Rick checked out the presented facts. True, the president of Czechoslovakia did make such an announcement. But it was the US Government maintaining that *all* plastic explosives used by terrorists today comes from Czechoslovakia. It was contrary to what those outside government told him. He was lost and disappointed. No such exports for eight year, which ruled out all the new "smart" explosives. Only Great Britain and Canada receiving the machinery, a smaller list than Rick expected. It defeated the idea of indexing a large group of political contributors with export licenses. Professor Lem, who sent the search in this direction, just didn't have the correct information. Rick didn't fault him for that. It took him three days of phone calls, faxes and e-mails to ooze through the bureaucracy. Of course, the export information he learned didn't account for all the past illegal dummy company set-ups. That wasn't something you'd get from a government agency.

Again, his story stalled. If only he could find a wonk who could break the logjam, if there was one to be broken.

Looking for different sources for information about plastic explosives, he tried the American Institute of Chemical Engineers, the Chemical Manufacturers Association and the American Chemical Society. All to avail. The National Cotton Council of America was a long shot that didn't pan out. The Association of Energy Engineers recommended trying the American Society for Industrial Security. They were of no help. The Society of Plastic Engineers never got back to him. The Society of the American Plastics Industry had no expert on the matter. The American Textile Manufacturers Institute had no idea why he would call them about plastic explosives. However, they casually suggested contacting a labor union called the Leather Goods, Plastics and Novelty Workers' International. Rick hung up the phone with a mean laugh. He sat at the desk in his home office, surrounded by reference works, magazine articles, newsletters, directories and a pile of faxes on the floor.

He sat quietly for a long time before picking up the phone again. This was it. Last try. He found the number for the union and dialed, expecting little.

Rick almost hung up when the elderly woman with the tiny voice picked up the phone at Leather Goods, Plastics and Novelty Workers' International, "LGPNWI, this is Molly Allard. Can I help you?"

He went ahead with the sure to be useless question, "Is anyone there a good source for information on materials manufactured from plastics?"

"I can help you."

"I'm sorry, ma'am, I doubt you can," Rick didn't want to broach a subject like explosives with ˜omeone who sounded like she could be his grandmother. "I am a reporter looking for information about plastic explosives. I'm sorry to have bothered you."

"You're not bothering me. I might be able to help you."

"I really don't think so."

"My family organized unions in plastic manufactories for almost one hundred years. Today, only one plant, Wall, in New Jersey, can legally produce the substances. Over two hundred jobs in this industry niche has disappeared."

Maybe she did know something.

Molly turned out to be the guru of all things plastic.

They talked for over an hour. Molly knew all Rick did about the subject and more, filling in details about the history of plastic explosives manufacturing. At the end of their conversation, she did what a wonk does. She told him something he didn't know that he didn't know.

" ... Skilled workers in ignitable plastics are near gone. Besides Wall, the only place providing training is in the military."

"They're not in plastic explosives manufacturing anymore," Rick informed her.

"Yes-it's all been farmed out to Wall. Except what they make at the Army Materials Research and Development centers."

"They're manufacturing plastic explosives?"

"Some. To develop them."

"Where?"

"I'm not up on the locations of Army Materials Research and Development bases."

When Rick got off the phone, he quickly became one.

Online, he culled a list of the installations. Further research revealed the ones closed in recent years. He opened a map of the country and outlined locations of the bases still in operation. He took some time to think. If such a facility was producing plastic explosives in greater than research quantities, how could they get the restricted raw materials without it being noted? The only answer was obtaining it from cotton processing.

Where would it come from?

He put his finger on the map at one location in North Carolina. The only Army R&D base in cotton country. He found a more detailed map and discovered major textile manufacturers and cotton processors surrounded the facility. More inquiry about the base described it as a *former* R&D facility that was transformed into a training ground to avoid closing. A telling fact was that the facility changed over occurred when plastic explosives production was given over to the private sector.

Was there something going on there?

Maybe he should see for himself. Was it worth a trip? He called Carl at the *Examiner* and gave him specifics. What did he think? Could there be something there?

Carl's intuition said yes.

Rick said he'd leave for North Carolina tomorrow.

Denise was in the kitchen making dinner. She knew all about Rick's story problems. She hoped more than ever he would be forced to drop the subject. He had been holed up in his office for days, engrossed, slightly irritable and saying little before sinking into bed after midnight. They hadn't made love once

167

this week, nor had they talked about him seeing a doctor. She never mentioned the open phone book she saw days ago sitting on the table. She wanted to, but made a decision not to nag. She was encouraged to believe it must be on his mind if he was looking up doctors.

What was grating on her was Rick's determination to find a story in Kasey's words. Denise was concerned by the energy he put into the search. She felt Rick was trying to prove something. Prove something to Kasey? She felt guilty about the emotion. It was bizarre and had to come from a peculiar place. It was bewildering, this unexpressed obsessive pondering. Did Kasey know Rick would be acting as he has? Did she hope for it? What exactly was this thing between them? Maybe she was only searching for an illusory issue to keep away a potential real rift in their marriage. Dammit! She had enough. She heard Rick coming downstairs. It was time to bring up the doctor again.

Rick was smiling. He gave her a kiss and began setting the table. Denise was about to ask if he had made an appointment, but Rick spoke first, "I may have a story. I'm going to North Carolina."

Denise disguised her plunging heart, "Have you found out something?"

"Maybe ... maybe not. Carl wants me to go and check it out."

Both were quiet. Denise hesitated. What she intended to do a minute ago now didn't seem a good idea. But why? Why not just bring the subject up again and see what he says? They were going to have to deal with it eventually.

Denise opened her mouth, then stopped. She was seized by a thought. Maybe she didn't want to know the reply he would give right now. She lingered over the oven, thinking.

There were footsteps on the porch. Gary walked in. They had invited him for dinner.

Rick hugged him, then stood a few feet away, "You're looking great!"

Denise and gave him a kiss. Gary appeared more together than she had ever seen him. He deserved a compliment, "Everybody's talking about how the store is shaping up."

Rick and Gary helped Denise get dinner on the table. As they all sat down, Rick asked, "Have you heard from Kasey?"

"Not since they Army whisked her away before the funeral," Gary shrugged. "Old Uncle Sam must be keeping her busy."

***

"Thanks for the nights we can't remember."

A Sign Inside Tabasco Charlie's
Manama, Bahrain

Bahrain is the anything goes, free trade zone and liberty port of the Mideast. Call it Bangkok on the Persian Gulf, right down to the Malaysian barmaids serving beer and whiskey in dimly lit pubs where the music is so loud it permeates the rooms for rent by the hour upstairs. A place where racketeers and outlaws openly do business on the boardwalk with financiers and diplomats, surrounded by revelry and garish neon. It's only place in the region to really party. And party they do, from soldier to sheik.

Bahrain is a small island nation a few miles off the eastern Saudi Arabian coast. Ruled by an emir and with negligible oil resources, Bahrain has transformed its former pearl and fish economy by building refineries for Saudi crude, attracting international shipping to its no duty ports, enacting liberal banking laws and most of all by being a tourist haven. It is also home port for the US Navy Fifth Fleet of 19 vessels. For the 12,000 sailors, being stationed in the vice capital of the Mideast is as good as it gets if you must be in the region. In Bahrain, you can pretty much hook up with anything, or anybody. Americans, British, French, Russian and Germans in the Mideast for whatever reason often escape to Bahrain and end up bumping elbows with Saudis, Kuwaitis, Iraqis, Iranians, Syrian and Lebanese letting off steam from the rigid lifestyles back home. You might say the place is something of a no judgment zone, citizens from antagonistic nations put conflicts aside and let their hair down. Barrooms and dance clubs are packed with military uniforms, white robes, black chadors, mini-skirts and halter-tops. Civilians and US soldiers based all over the Mideast will charter planes and arrive one after another to carouse for as little as a day. Americans will get off flights and walk past arms dealers moving cargo containers filled with implements of war headed for likely intended use against them.

Deals for portable grenade launchers and Chinese rockets are made in dark alleys next to American soldiers buying Lebanese hashish. Bahrain is where the native Hezbollah faction, after beginning an arson and bombing campaign to ruin tourism, had all support withdrawn by its sponsors. It was just too unfair. The Mideast needed a place for everyone to get away from all that.

Major Bowers walked into a Manama dive called The Seeking Spirit. He had some liberty due him, even though he was soon heading back to the US for extended time off to see his new daughter. He had half planned to go to the virtual city in Dammam and hang out with Air Force buddies until he ran into a pilot who was ferrying a Black Hawk helicopter to an aircraft carrier in Bahrain. Bowers made a spot decision to hitch a ride. He knew he'd find Army friends in Manama he cold tag along with back to Saudi Arabia.

When he walked into the bar, he immediately spotted Lieutenant Moore, Sergeant Harper and a few others from Kasey's outfit. They had pushed some tables together in a corner by the jukebox. Moore waved him over and bought him a drink. Bowers could see the crew already had few.

"Didn't think I'd see this place for a while," Moore said, like he found the environment soothing. "First they told me I'd be commanding Captain Lawrence's squad indefinitely, then they pulled us out and gave us time off."

"Something's going on," Harper was certain. "We saw an infantry company and battery corps moving toward the border."

Moore was hoping the major could shed light on an issue he was wrestling with, "I'm due to be transferred to Benning, but I'm getting worried they'll make me put it off. Have any idea when Captain Lawrence will be back?"

Harper interjected, "I have a funny feeling she's involved in whatever is going on around the southern no-fly." The soldiers moaned. Evidently Harper had been railing about it.

There was pause before Bowers said, "She is."

The blaring music and jumble of voices faded into the background for the squad.

Bowers took off his rancher's hat and ran a finger along the brim. The men leaned in, waiting for him to decide what he wanted to say.

"She's gone missing. She was inside Iraq on an assignment and now we have no idea where she is. Zalman isn't happy with how DOD, State, or the embassy are handling it."

"Can't depend on them," Moore shook his head at the unsettling news. He finished his drink, "We need to take care of our own."

Everyone thought so. Bowers bought the next round, filling them in on some details. An American sitting at the bar overheard bits of their conversation. He walked over, needing to know if he heard right, "You say Captain Lawrence is missing? She caught a ride home on my transport a few weeks ago. She was going to see her father."

"They hauled her back for a mission inside Iraq and she hasn't been heard from," a somber private told him.

"Something is up," the pilot had a seat and added what he knew. "After going state side, I brought a fighter to Germany. When I got there, they took me out of uniform and on a privately chartered L-32. It's basically a Lear jet with extended capacity. I flew the secretary of state to Dhahran. She must have been heading for Riyadh. I think she's still here, but I can't say for sure. It's all on the hush."

"She's still there. General Zalman has been meeting with her every day," Bowers clued him.

Scattered pieces of a puzzle. There was fact to what Harper was ridiculed for saying. The soldiers remembered particulars of recent assignments, incidents that seemed trivial at the time but now had significance. They were getting angry at the emerging picture.

While waiting for more beer, a man nobody previously noticed appeared in their midst. "Excuse me," he spoke English with a slight accent, "I know you are American servicemen. Do you have an officer missing?"

Moore examined him, "Who are you?"

He was the supervisor of the mountain intelligence post in Israel. The man responded with a gesture that was a request to join them. Nobody refused, so he pulled up a chair.

His manner made it seem he was about to try and sell them something, "I'm with Mossad," were his unexpected words. "We have confirmed intelligence that a female Army officer of yours is a hostage in Lebanon with a Saudi. We brought it to your State Department and they *denied it*."

There was appalled silence. Carefully, they looked him over.

The Israeli let it sink in with them. Mossad knows if you want to get information from American troops in the Mideast, head to Bahrain." He admitted, "I was sent here to find out the truth."

Bowers had him come over to his end of the table.

Mossad Man's timing and presentation were superb. The soldiers listened to the Israeli share what he wanted them to know. It was a sublime performance, the way he dispensed facts that entirely corresponded with what they knew. He did it with terms that bolstered their prevailing attitudes and provoked rising emotion.

Harper was furious, "Why the hell aren't they doing anything!"

"We wanted to offer support," Mossad Man whispered. "We can get her out with some help. We activated our deep cover close by them. I don't know why your government is acting this way.

I guess smoothies are the same all over. That's why I'm here. Thought you might know something. Soldiers care about their kind."

As a corporal erupted into an alcohol inspired rant, Moore and Harper glanced at each other and Bowers stared at them. It was the beginning of collective deliberation.

The Israeli knew that was going on, "There's a small airstrip near where she is held. The place has no anti-aircraft defenses and only aging artillery. A small plane could fly under Syrian radar and pick her up. Five minutes on the ground. That's it. We can take care of her guards."

Mossad Man searched their eyes, stroking his beard to fill the pause, waiting for his delicate urging to guide their passions.

Selection D3 played on the jukebox, a song about crying a mountain of tears. Moore expressed what they all were thinking, "I have half a mind to put together a squad and go get her."

"Why don't we?" Harper said, not casually, but with resolve.

There was more silence. The soldiers were dealing with wavering emotions. The pilot finally stabilized his, "You know we could." Everybody turned to him. "I'm taking the L-32 back to Germany soon. It would only take a minor detour and the plane is small enough to fly under radar. I could take a dozen men."

One private was afraid and intrigued, "The logistics, how would we coordinate? How do we know you're really Mossad?"

"Come back to my hotel and I'll prove it," the Israeli wasn't upset at the challenge. "I'm not here to urge you to do anything. I only want you to know we can't understand why your country is denying what we know. In Israel, we go to the ends of the earth to save our own."

Again, he was focusing on their loyalty and concern, this time adding a gentle affront at their nation's commitment.

Bowers must have been seriously considering a rescue, "We don't have weapons, radios, or any other mission supplies with us."

No problem, according to Moore, "I know a guy down the street who can get us all anything we need."

"I have a credit line at a bank here," Mossad Man added.

Harper mused with a smile "Imagine getting off a plane in Germany with Captain Lawrence in tow?"

They were excited. And drunk. It must have been the alcohol arousing this crazy inkling of a scheme. They ordered more drinks and everybody huddled closer.

"It's a very dangerous thing to try," Bowers reminded them. "Let's think this out."

"I spent over ten years in the military," the Israeli prodded. "I know what how you feel about one of your own."

The soldiers probed each other. How they would approach such a mission, what situations they saw arising and possible circumstances they didn't. Mostly, they were checking out each other's mettle. A real plot was shaping up, spreading over their dissection of each other.

"Israel would have south Lebanon infantry on alert ready to dash in if there was aproblem," the Israeli fed them what they needed to form a strategy. "Mossad can direct the whole thing with the intelligence we have. Of course, I'm crazy for even offering. I know it can never happen."

Mossad Man was throwing down the gauntlet. It was dare from Israel, the country that tackles any obstacle, takes any risk, to protect its citizens.

The Americans either had to show their patriotism, or realize they had a few too many.

"I'm in," Bowers pledged. "What the hell, if we don't take care of our own nobody else will."

All the Americans declared themselves ready. Harper ordered another round as soon as their drinks arrived. Bowers and the Israeli began sketching out diagrams on cocktail napkins.

Of course, by morning, or whenever the Americans would wake up, wherever that would be, they were sure to comprehend the witless idiocy of the night before. If they remembered anything at all.

***

It didn't take Rick long to arrange a meeting with Fort Sellers Public Information Officer Lieutenant Andrew Ward. He hopped a plane to Raleigh, rented a car and went to the base in western North Carolina that skirted forest rising into the Appalachian hills.

"I'm working on a story about military base closings," Rick told the lieutenant when he saw him. Ward insisted on meeting Rick at the entry gate. "I want to feature Fort Sellers as an example of a facility that transformed itself to stay in operation."

Ward took Rick around, explaining what was happening with the recruits that he saw going through practice drills. "Luckily for us, it was an easy transition," Ward volunteered. "Mainly due to our location. Besides training enlistees, our grounds are used to launch survival exercises and combat maneuvers in the mountains."

Rick feigned interest by writing down quotations, a practiced cover for his exploring eyes. He immediately grew curious about a chain of brick buildings isolated in a divided corner of the base. There was a staffed gate in front, but no activity. Instructors kept trainees clear of the area.

"What modifications were done to convert the base?"

"Few, which was our key advantage." The lieutenant pointed to a long field strewn with crumpled metal debris, "That artillery range was mothballed after World War Two. What was there to do?"

"So, what else goes on here?" Rick was slowly rambling toward his real topic of inquiry.

"Those buildings behind the other gate, what are they used for? Classrooms?"

"No," Ward aimed his hand in the opposite direction. "That goes on over there in the quad complex behind the barracks."

The lieutenant began to move to another subject. Rick wanted an answer, some official reply, "Then what goes on behind that gate?"

"Right now, nothing," was the response. Rick sensed the dismissive wave he received meant that was going to be the end of it. But then Ward added, "In the past, that was the war materials R&D zone."

Ward should have stopped before elaborating. It heated Rick's interest.

After the tour, Rick got into his car parked in the visitor's lot just inside the main gate. While he waited for the guard to let him out, he peered into the rear view mirror and saw sentries motion a small truck out of the former R&D area. It stopped in the exit line behind him. Rick angled his mirror until he saw the words on its side - *Coleman's Commercial Laundry.*

Rick left the base and turned onto an artery. The truck followed. Rick slowed and it passed in another lane. He got behind it and trailed it onto the highway. There was a pair of windows above the walk-in back door. He grabbed binoculars from his briefcase and was able to get a partial look inside. He could see racks of clothes - lab coats and protective outfits. What did it mean? Maybe nothing. It was a commercial laundry truck. Possibly making several stops many different places. It was intriguing enough for Rick to take his camera, zoom in and shoot some partially obstructed pictures. He stayed with the truck until it drove into its scrub plant behind in an industrial area behind a strip mall. A sign above the entrance facing the road had advertised HELP WANTED to passers-by.

He drove back to the Fort Sellers area and found a motel less than two miles away with a view into parts of the base. He fell asleep in a chair for a while after settling in. It was dark when he woke. He went to the window and applied the night vision feature on his binoculars. Checking the map he made in the margins of his notes, he searched the grounds until he could make out a light on inside the guard station in front of the former R&D zone.

Raising the sights, he identified the buildings behind the gate. It was near midnight and the covered windows in this supposedly inactive sector were illuminated.

Rick watched for hours, spinning in his head all it might mean. Maybe there was maintenance underway? Perhaps it was in use for a one-time event? Who knows, could be a guard was too lazy to turn off the lights? Then again, he was kept away from the place while he was there. He was told the section was dormant. He observed a commercial laundry truck leaving. The truck had apparel inside from an industrial manufacturing environment.

Only when Rick finally went to bed did he remember he told Denise he would call. Too late now, he thought. He spent the remainder of the night dozing off for periods, waking up to scribble down notes, and forming questions in his mind. By dawn, he had set down all he wanted to know. It was how he would find out that became the labor at hand.

***

A Beret nervously pulled binoculars away from his face. The commander didn't like the expression he saw on the soldier. He grabbed the lens and locked on to the moving speck ahead on the horizon.

The commander swallowed hard at what he saw.

He immediately stopped the division in its tracks. "It's the Green Scarves," the commander broadcast after clearing the lump in his throat.

The Syrians were traveling through a ravine between pebbly hills. Already out of Lebanon, they were expecting to be back at their post in Damascus by the next day.

The commander took another look toward the skyline. By the time he focused, the image ahead expanded from a row of tanks to trailing personnel carriers, jeeps and trucks that were kicking up dust towing artillery.

The commander probed the landscape for a long time. His troops watched an anguished look spread over his grimace. There was a decision to make. Unfolding ahead was a force that was vastly bigger, making it futile to dig in and take them on. Retreat? Where to? They were in a tough position, hampered by the narrow gorge that already forced them to file in a tight line.

"I don't know what they're doing in Syria," he said, almost to himself. He ordered the division, "Stay calm and they won't engage us. Their war is with Iran."

The Berets continued moving ahead.

Green Scarves on foot began appearing on the enclosing crests and pushing down into the canyon. They swarmed alongside the Berets, slowing so their impending armor could catch up. The women hiked by the Syrians, who couldn't help gawking. Everybody knew about the Green Scarves, but few ever encountered them. Few men, that is, who lived to talk about it. The women glared back at the Berets, in scorn of their fascination. Moghavi led the armor column by, inspecting the scene from the open hatch of her tank. The Green Scarves and Berets moved parallel in opposite directions.

There was a taut hush in the air. The Berets grew apprehensive. Moghavi and the Syrian commander eyeballed each other when they passed. He knew who she was and knew enough not to let his visual curiosity linger. He looked away. So far, so good, he thought. Just a short distance to go.

A woman holding a machine gun raised an arm to wipe sweat from her brow. One jittery Beret misjudged the gesture and went for his gun.

Big mistake.

Before he got a shot off, an energetic massacre was underway. The Green Scarves, acting as a collective entity, started with a thunderous barrage of automatic weapon fire that echoed throughout the canyon. They seemed to

177

possess aggregate telepathy, the way they knew who would mow down which soldiers. They were lithe and quick compared to the Berets. They were a hungrier army. And more joyous. Some near somersaulted on top of the Syrian troop carriers and pitched grenades inside as others scaled tanks and dropped pipe bombs down the hole, vaulting off before the shielding rocked. Wounded Berets were finished off when they were found. This meticulous army took no prisoners. One woman's job was to fire bullets into every motionless adversary to be certain none were playing dead. They grabbed the commander early on and kept him corralled. He fell to his knees in prayer with tears streaming down his cheeks at the sight of men he led into this situation being turned to tomorrow's dust.

Some Green Scarves got busy confiscating the Syrian's weapons and armor. Others picked through the dead men's pockets while a few held the commander on the ground as Moghavi charged from her tank.

She placed a foot on his chest, "If you don't want to die *slowly*, tell me where your company was returning from."

"Bekka," the commander's heart raced. He couldn't avoid looking at the dead around him. "We were in Lebanon. I'll help you, I'll do any-"

"What were you doing there?"

"Supplying Hezbollah," his tone begged.

"Did you *supply them* with two people?"

"An American woman and Saudi prince."

Moghavi's hand grabbed onto her knife. She gradually slithered it from its casing. Pulling it out too fast dulled the blade.

It was agony, that slow sound. The commander didn't wait to see the sword, "Please ... mercy ... don't kill me ... "

Moghavi moved faster when she heard him beg. She was no admirer of weakness in people who in other circumstances flaunted aggression. It was appalling hypocrisy.

She kneeled beside the commander, quickly yanked his head back and slit his throat. A perfect straight line. She got up and wiped her blade on the clothes of a dead Beret while she waited for the commander to stop writhing. It didn't take long, which was good because these women had places to go and things to do.

Once the commander expired, Moghavi cast out her arm and a woman placed another bouquet of silk black roses in her hand. She leaned over and fixed them to the corpse.

The Green Scarves moved on. Now in greater formation, each a human neutron Bombs doing all she could to annihilate men in combat while preserving the arms and supplies belonging to their foes. They came out of the skirmish only destroying three Syrian tanks and two personnel carriers. They rapaciously went for the remaining. In this part of the world, a scavenger army can do more than get by, it can thrive.

***

Friday afternoons are the quietest work times in the West Wing. Employees thin out for early weekends and those who stay behind loaf by the water cooler reluctant to get busy on anything new - that's a Monday task. Usually the only item on the president's schedule is recording his weekly radio address to the nation that is broadcast the next day. Only the White House press corps remains on alert. Whenever possible, recent administrations have taken to announcing unfavorable news just before 5:00pm on Friday, calculating that most Americans won't get word of it. Friday newscasts are the least watched and Saturday newspapers are the most sparsely read. Senior press corps usually let the second stringers linger in wait for these bad news briefings.

Clayton Amfrick's Friday afternoon routine was to call in the lunch take-out order for the press room then join them for repartee with pizza or Chinese. Although they were stand-in reporters, one day some would end up featured players. It was a good way for Amfrick to make friendly contacts, even if he tended to bore this mostly younger set with his passions for opera and classical music. Common topics of conversation among this set were extreme sports, tech stocks and most of all gossip. Amfrick would feign inattention while listening to every word. Pressroom gossip was a way to take the real pulse of Washington, based on what they were talking about and what they weren't.

Amfrick began his political career as a caterer on the Washington party circuit almost three decades ago. He witnessed political and business lobbying organizations spend fortunes on the most awkward, boorish galas that yielded limited influence for the buck. Not only that, but most professional party planners were awful at figuring the details of how to connect one clique to another during these affairs. They used blunt, pedestrian methods practiced for so long nobody knew how ineffective they were. Amfrick knew he could do better. He registered as a lobbyist, for him really meaning a hosting specialist and event organizer. He created extensive files on everybody in the Washington social scene and developed a legendary skill at knowing who needed to have an audience with whom while providing as charming a social environment as possible for it to all happen. He got considerable notice working for clients with uphill agendas and fame from the success they achieved with his help. He socialized his way up the power ladder, adding corporate and organizational titles to his vast list of influential friends. In time, he became seen as an inveterate Washington power broker. Nobody remembered how he got his start, or they didn't care.

Amfrick was the image-maker. His duties were to make the president seem warm and fuzzy, to glisten and glow.

Julius Cunningham was in the Oval Office working with the president on the phrasing of his radio address. Cunningham highlighted in neon marker words the president would emphasize and where he would pause. Cunningham had a Ph.D. in linguistics. Perfect for a presidential advisor. His sense of word structure, inflection and its cognitive perception made everyone he ever worked for sound immeasurably more profound than they were.

Cunningham got into politics only a decade ago. He was working at a commercial think tank studying the variables of subjective perception for advertisers. He helped a friend running for local office and it was onward and upward from there. In time, he consulted with nineteen candidates on state and national levels. All won election, creating a mythical aura around his skills. The current president never publicly uttered a word that didn't first pass through Cunningham.

Cunningham was the substance. His tasks were the essence and themes that made the president appear human, caring and wise.

Technicians were testing the microphone on the president's desk when Amfrick made his way up from the pressroom. He conferred with Cunningham in the vestibule outside the Oval Office. The president remained in view through the open door.

"Everything remains under control," Amfrick passed along. "The timing remains true."

"What's happening with the Lawrence matter?"

"We took a scattered division and moved it to the Iraq border. They were so spread out it'll be hard for anyone to notice the shift. They'll only stay long enough to cover us."

Cunningham nodded. "Is the press sniffing around?"

"Not a bit."

These two had a routine of reminding the other of how situations are expected to play out.

"The president must look as though he did everything he could to get her home," Amfrick underscored for them both. He was slightly anxious about one thing: "The longer she is gone, the bigger the problem her return will be. She might come back knowing too much."

"What if," Cunningham paused and almost cringed at what was on his mind, "we find out she's going to come back?"

"Not a problem," Amfrick was confident. "We know where she is. Israel told us. So long as we have track of her, we can do something about it."

Cunningham absorbed the reply. He was a bit puzzled. Amfrick didn't want to say more, so he compromised by talking without revealing, "Don't ask anything. Plausible deniability is the operative term. You can't testify about what you don't know."

"I hear you."

"The real events aren't even underway yet."

"All I'm going to worry about is how to make the president rise in the polls and win another term," Cunningham asserted like a mantra. "I've broken it down into a simple hypothesis. Turn culpability into victimization."

"That's good." Amfrick smiled. "Something the electorate can identify with."

The technicians were ready. Cunningham stepped inside the Oval Office to watch the first of many takes that will necessary before the president suitably performs the brief address.

***

Nights in the Bekka are seldom quiet. Barking dogs, munching locusts, wandering gunfire, explosions of indeterminable origin, shouts, ghostly screams, marching feet and rumblingvehicles pierce the darkness, blending with and reverberating through the syrupy haze that sits over the valley. Kasey and Nasir were shackled, blindfolded and behind bars in the Yanta jail. Five men guarded them inside and five more sat around the outside perimeter. It was late when the man with the keen eyes pulled up in a truck and got out with a steaming cauldron, bread and some bowls.

The men converged on him, grabbing at the bread. Keen Eyes put the pot on the ground.

"We've had no food all day," an angry guard complained as Keen Eyes ladled soup into a crock.

"The village is filled with visitors here for the trial," Keen Eyes said, handing him the bowl. "They had to be served."

The guards tore at the bread waiting for the stew to cool. Keen Eyes took the pot inside the jail and spooned the cauldron dry for the guards. As they drained their bowls, Keen Eyes walked over to the cells and studied Kasey and Nasir. It was impossible to know if they were conscious.

A guard grinned, "Nothing left for them?"

Keen Eyes walked by him on the way out, "They'll be dead before they starve."

They all had a good laugh. Keen Eyes left the jail and went by those outside without saying a word. He got into the truck and drove away. When he was out of their view, he pulled off the road, parked in a concealed spot and turned off the engine.

Shortly after their meal, the guards outside became drowsy. It wasn't an abrupt sensation, more like a burden to be on their feet. It led to them seeking ease, attributed to the late hour and full stomach. They gradually spread out, sitting on the ground against the jail and finding makeshift repose on crates and cinder blocks. They were quiet and breathing in slow motion when they lost consciousness.

Minutes later, a similar event took place inside the jailhouse. A guard leaned back in a chair, put his feet up on a desk and passed out, falling over onto the floor. Another guard laughed as he strolled over to him. He keeled over halfway across the room. The remaining three knew something was amiss. One tried to hurry over to his fallen cohorts and felt his numb legs wobble. Light-headed, he slumped against a wall, closed his eyes and slid to the floor. Two were left. One turned to the other and found him comatose. The last guard ran outside. At the door, he dropped and stopped breathing.

Keen Eyes looked at his watch, started the engine and calmly headed back toward the jail. Kasey was lodged in an abyss. The torture, sensory deprivation and hallucinatory imagery inside her head left her in a freakish realm, no longer able to determine reality from phantasm. She never moved after being unshackled, never opened her eyes when the blindfold was removed. She merely curled up.

Keen Eyes looked down at her. In one hand he had the cell keys he fished out of a dead guard's pocket. In another, he held a finger on the trigger of a gun. He filled a cup with water and tossed it on Kasey's face. She twitched and began a struggle for consciousness while Keen Eyes opened Nasir's cell and went to work freeing him.

Nasir took less time to come around. Maybe it was the fierce concentration on prayer he maintained throughout the ordeal, a repetition that empowered his bearing. Almost immediately, he investigated the range of motion in his deadened limbs. He opened his eyes, things had no definition, but he heard only one person in the jail.

Keen Eyes grabbed Nasir by the hand, "Muster your strength and come with me." Adrenaline shot through Nasir's nervous system. He tried to stand too fast and collapsed. Rising to his knees, he could make out vague forms of inert bodies. Keen Eyes pulled him up, kept a hand around his wrist and led him to Kasey.

•

HONOR BOUND

Kasey was battling to open her eyes. Keen Eyes yanked her to her feet, "Come with me, now!"

Nasir held Kasey's hand and the three of them, clasped together in a chain, stepped outside. Kasey staggered half blind and Nasir shivered. It seemed very cold to him, an impression that faded when his feet struck a dead guard. Looking down, he saw more corpses.

Keen Eyes helped them into the idling truck, then he jumped in and drove away.

Nasir looked back at the receding village. He spun around to Keen Eyes, "Who are you?"

"I'm with Mossad. We'll talk later."

His answer inspired Kasey to shake off her stupor. Her voice rasped, "Israel is getting us out of here?"

"With help. You'll soon see."

Keen Eyes stopped near the old airstrip, "Stay in the truck." He got out and went to work marking the outline of the runway with flares. Then he fired one into the sky.

Bowers, Harper, Moore and another six from Kasey's squad were approaching from above in the L-32. They finished locking and loading their hair trigger automatics, rickety Czech 10-3's, circa 1960's, with loose pieces rattling around inside. Two Pakistani rocket launchers sat in front of them. Everyone in the plane had two South African made grenades on him. Bowers walked into the cockpit, "How are we doing?"

The flare was twinkling ahead. The pilot looked down and spotted the landing strip,

"They're there. We're going down."

"Two minutes is all we need," Bowers said, holding up fingers.

The pilot angled below. The soldiers crouched by the exit.

Keen Eyes stood beside the runway. Kasey and Nasir heard the plane and looked up. Kasey squeezed Nasir's hand in relief.

The plane touched down and rolled toward them. Keen Eyes excitedly motioned Kasey and Nasir out of the truck. Before reaching full stop, the jet's door opened and troops jumped onto the ground, weapons ready. Two fitted the grenade launchers and waited while the rest spread around the runway.

Kasey and Nasir dashed ahead of Keen Eyes. Nearing the jet, Kasey almost froze in astonishment when she saw the soldier in the rancher's hat ready to boost them on board.

It had to be Bowers.

That goddamn leering chauvinist, ball-busting, bullet-headed, incessantly obnoxious nemesis.

It was a moment when judgment of another is turned upside down in an instant, swinging around all the way in an opposite direction, upsetting the earth and stars, taking breath away in elation at the infinite wonder of human character.

Bowers!

Kasey let Nasir get inside first. Then she came face to face with the Cowboy. He was leaning over waiting to give her a boost. She couldn't take her eyes off him. He smiled at her. She smiled back.

"I never thought I'd be happy to see your face."

Bowers briefly smiled, then waved her on, "Come on, get in!"

Keen Eyes was last, then the soldiers began climbing back in, lifting those behind them. Moore and Harper hugged Kasey.

Nasir noticed Keen Eyes slip into a corner. As the troops started to close the door, Nasir was shocked to witness Keen Eyes pull a grenade from a pocket, activate it and drop it on the ground. Disbelief temporarily paralyzed Nasir, as though he couldn't persuade his mind to accept what his eyes were seeing.

The door was closing. Keen Eyes raced by them and jumped out the same second Nasir began screaming, "Live grenade! Live grenade on board! Everybody out! Now!" Nasir flung himself out the door, pulling Kasey with him. Keen Eyes was already speeding off in his truck.

Kasey looked up at the plane. Bowers was set to leap out when the implosion began. A chain reaction ensued. The grenade exploded above the fuel tank, igniting it and exploding the weapons on board. Almost instantly, the jet became a flaming metal shell. Nobody else made it out. Bowers by the doorway was the last picture burned into Kasey's head before a huge blast threw her and Nasir into the air and rendered them unconscious. Everybody in the plane was incinerated. The village immediately came alive. A blowing fury charged their way like a tornado. The entire valley seemed to be dashing to the airfield, the towering bonfire serving as a beacon.

On top of a distant hill, Keen Eyes photographed the wreckage, zooming in on particular details of the plane.

He drove off before the enraged horde descended on Kasey and Nasir. When report of what happened at the jail reached the crowd, they were kicked and stomped. Some fell on the ground, crying in anguish and rocking in grief over lost loved ones. Raza buried his head in his arms. There was no way he would procure gain from his hostages. They did nothing but bring death and distress. And now they were going to be killed. For justice, revenge and to purge everybody's suffering.

8

Kasey and Nasir awoke to find themselves on top the shoulders of the raging mob carrying them back to the Yanta jail. New arrivals from around the valley chanted slogans and took turns whacking at them with clubs. Kasey still felt heat from the burning debris and could smell her singed hair and puss blistered face. She saw the dead guards lying in the back of a truck following men walking with shovels.

It was time to stiffen defenses. Fajid left to direct a group hurrying to staff the hillside artillery batteries as Kasey and Nasir were flung into a single cell. Abbas goaded emotions to more fervent levels, cursing so vehemently the roaring throng shook the walls of the building.

Raza nudged Abbas aside. *He* was a directly aggrieved one, having lost a brother. If he gained nothing else from the hostages, he would at least have attention of the crowd. "The felons sent by America could not save them," he bellowed, shaking a fist. "There is no escape."

Abbas stepped in front of Raza and addressed the glares, "Their trial begins at sunrise. Eleven charges of murder." He pivoted toward Kasey and Nasir and spit at them, "Prepare your defense!"

Friends and family of the dead filed away to mourn at the burial. The rest looped around outside the jailhouse, keeping a riotous vigil.

Both knew any trial was only vacuous spectacle. The rabble wanted theater, some drama to mollify their burdensome loathing.

"They disgrace Islam," Nasir ranted as he paced. "They are demons! This is a circus!"

187

Kasey was quiet, unable to shake the image of Bowers in the jet and the anguish at what happened to those who came to save them.

The two of them were so devoured by inner passions they shut out the suffering endured on the way back to the jail. It became easier to bear the torture with each new round, the inverse of what is expected. Perpetual pain dispossessed the shock of it.

Nasir kicked the wall and kept circling.

"The men who came to rescue us were my friends," Kasey said, trying to understand what happened. "Why them? If they knew we were here, then my our governments must know, too."

Kasey sat on the floor against the wall, wanting, eagerly needing Nasir to say something to keep her logic from arriving at a place she didn't want to go. Nasir continued moving back and forth. Kasey studied him, hoping to fend off her relentless analysis. Was his hair turning white over these past days? His face was ashy and a bizarre shade of blue. Scabs and cuts ravaged his face. He probably wasn't aware his arms swung at grotesque angles and that he was walking with a broken gait. She had to turn away when she wondered how she must appear to him.

"It was a set up," Nasir said. "To take us all out."

It was explanation Kasey didn't want to hear, one she still chose not to consider. Nasir briefly stopped and added, "There was no Saudi involvement."

Nasir's inner process mimicked Kasey's. There were chains of reasoning he wouldn't, or couldn't consider.

Kasey clenched her teeth, irritated by Nasir's perceived insult. Did he mean it was an American set up? Or was it possible her friends found out where they were and undertook the mission alone? Why would they do that instead of informing superiors or civilian officials who could threaten massive force or carry out a larger rescue operation? Were they aware of the information she was frantic to bring back? She felt some relief picturing the US government evacuating Americans and warning the Saudis just in time to stop revolt and bloodshed. Kasey kept asking herself questions in quick succession to keep from having to answer them.

Kasey tried to find a way out of an inescapable conclusion, "Who was the man who brought us to the plane?"

Nasir was agitated by her unending inquiry "He was an accomplice.

His answer led her to another question, "Then why-"

Nasir firmly motioned her to stop. His eyes were wide, his upset off the raging scale, "I *shall not* grovel! I *will not* dishonor my country or family. There will be no defense! Let Allah judge me."

Kasey knew what he meant. It no longer was about survival, but honor. All strategy and interpretation vanished in face of his courage to embrace that reality. All agony faded when she liberated herself by agreeing with him. Maybe it was the ultimate defense mechanism, meeting with death by execution rather than possibly living to discover a truth neither could face.

They looked at each other. The rhythmic hum of the hissing chorus outside was jarring their viscera. Kasey decided it was time for it all to end.

Kasey got up, "Then we shall present no defense."

She held out a tight fist. Nasir pounded it with a closed hand.

***

Frequently, Israel and the United Stated are agnostic allies. There has never been a more picayunish, emotional or dramatic political tie for America than its relationship with Israel. Moments of exultation ultimately are tempered by aggravation and sometimes sorrow. Call it a tempestuous romance.

The sizable Jewish population in America, along with Mideast energy resources and the region's history of attracting competition between world powers has made Israel an important bond for America. For Israel, a young, tiny nation trying to survive in a bad neighborhood, the gist of its relationship with America can be stated simply as: America has many allies in the world - Israel has one.

Yet there are problems. Power blocs within both countries are often at odds, a telling illustration of the axiom that no nation has "friends," only mutual enlightened self-interests.

To cite one example, use an event that occurred in the 1967 Six Days War between Israel and its Arab neighbors. Before it began, Israeli intelligence discovered Syrian, Egyptian and Jordanian armies amassing near its border. Expecting an imminent invasion, Israel decided to strike first, but US President Johnson, claiming surprise at the situation, urged restraint so America could attempt diplomatic intervention. Israel refused and went ahead with a pre-emptive attack that virtually ended the war in its first day by obliterating Egypt's Air Force. During the conflict, Israel bombed and torpedoed the US Navy spy vessel *Liberty* stationed off the coast of Egypt. Thirty-four Americans were killed. Israel asserted it was a mistake and paid reparations. Many American military officials said it was no accident. They believed that Israel concluded Johnson's alleged surprise at the Arab build-up had to be a lie since there was a US Navy surveillance vessel in the region. Even today, some in the military suspect Israel was delivering a message by the attack - "friends" better deal from a straight deck when Israel is at risk was the statement.

On the Israeli side, there has always been measured distrust of the US State Department. A faction Israel calls "Arabists" is seen as an enemy camp. They are the employees and diplomats who have had posts in Arab capitals, speak the language and hold the "British flaw" of romanticizing the Arab world. The mistrust is so great that any US State Department employee or diplomat who has been posted in an Arab country is "officially" unwelcome in Israel.

For decades, Israel won the public relations war for the hearts and minds of American citizens. That changed forever when America formed a determined bond with Saudi Arabia beginning in the mid 1970's. The US government was architect of a plan, enacted by a massive influx of Saudi fossil fuel currency, to change American opinion of Saudi Arabia, and by extension the entire Arab world. Many millions were spent courting the media, employing elite Washington lobbyists and Madison Avenue marketing geniuses, funding university academic programs in Arab studies and contributing to munificent charities. The Saudis shrewdly remained in the background while their proponents went to work. It was a masterful campaign that culminated with the US Congress, despite intense Israeli objections and counter lobbying, voting in 1981 to sell Saudi Arabia F-15 fighter planes, tanks and several Airborne

Warning and Control Systems (AWACS) aircraft. It was the first time the US government provided arms to an Arab nation. Saudi Arabia, like most Arab nations at the time, was technically in a state of war against Israel. The sale was an unsettling event for the Israel and from that day onward the United States has engaged in a more "balanced" foreign policy between Israel and Arab nations. The "balance" might be defined as whatever material aid the US provides to any Arab nation is offset by a corresponding extension of benefits to Israel.

Another dividing influence between Israel and America was the 1981 Israeli invasion and occupation of Lebanon. Called Operation Peace for Galilee, it was a military operation to flush Palestinian terrorists, or freedom fighters, from encampments in south Lebanon.

Assuring America the operation would last only a few days, the Israeli military was (as usual) so effective that in short order they found themselves approaching Beirut, far north of their original mission. As Syria mobilized a massive response ready to contest the offensive, America pleaded with Israel not to for the first time conquer the capital of an Arab country. Israel refused and pounded Beirut day after day with bombs and artillery. With all hell threatening to break loose once Syria became involved, the US government assisted the American media, pointing them, even transporting them to the scenes of civilian casualties caused by the Israeli attacks. For the first time, the American public was seeing images of Israeli aggression. The disturbing imagery played out across the world. Israel stopped their assault, but took three years to retreat.

The US sent peacekeeping Marines to Beirut and 241 of them ended up killed by a terrorist attack. The US military was again angry at Israel, blaming them for the American involvement that led to the casualties.

Then there was the Jonathan Pollard matter. Pollard was a US born Navy civilian intelligence analyst who used high security clearance to obtain information from restricted archives. Over the course of two years, he passed along highly classified intelligence to Israel from Pentagon databases. Eventually he was caught spying and was tried and convicted of espionage, the first time an American was sent to jail for spying for an ally. The situation further damaged American-Israeli relations.

Not to say Israel hasn't had cause to be angry with American policy. The US furiously twisted Israel's arm to keep them out of the Gulf War after Iraq began firing Scud missiles on Israel. It was the first time Israel didn't respond to an outside attack. America felt Israeli military action would shatter the anti-Saddam coalition the US created with other Arab nations. Many in Israel hold a grudge against America for the threats made by high US officials, coercing the Israeli government to forgo a military policy seen vital to its existence. These are reasons why Keen Eyes felt no remorse and never for a second meditated upon the result of his actions. There was no need to justify anything. National preservation is a tough business, many times more so in the Mideast. The operation went perfectly, right down to his escape. He knew every crevice of the Bekka, how to avoid the Hezbollah and Syrian Army checkpoints and how to elude all the roving militias. He smoothly negotiated the way since most men were in Yanta for the trial. Shortly after dawn, he arrived at the boundary of South Lebanese Army territory. It was classic Mideast irony, America's ally Israel having a proxy force so close to Kasey and Nasir. A waiting unit rushed him to the Israel border. A few hours later, he was in Tel Aviv, leaning over a darkroom tub and waiting for the photos to develop.

Keen Eyes lifted the first one from the bath and clamped it to a hanging line. Mossad Man stood behind him, inspecting the picture in dim light until he was satisfied with its detail, "Good job," he patted Keen Eyes on the back.

"See the jet's markings," Keen Eyes pointed at a maturing photo.

"Let's show him," Mossad Man smiled and opened the door.

Alexander Walker slinked in and squinted at the pictures.

"Nobody survived," Keen Eyes told him.

"They'll know whose plane it was," Mossad Man said, using a that-will-teach-them tone.

Walker collected photos into a satchel as they developed. "My, what a tragedy," he frowned. "I feel for their families."

"We could have saved them from the bastards who killed them," Mossad Man was getting their story straight. "If only the diplomats had been honest with us."

Walker nodded in a corroborating gesture of unity as he walked out the door.

***

Alexander Walker was a shadow man born and bred. Son of a CIA man who was the son of an Office of Strategic Services (OSS) operative killed in World War Two. OSS was precursor to the CIA and Alexander's grandfather was a friend of OSS founding director "Wild Bill" Donovan during the unbridled glory days of American intelligence, when the fate of the nation hung in the balance and nobody questioned the methods of espionage. Walker's father was recruited for the nascent CIA in the 1950's after graduating from college. He served as station chief in four countries before finishing agency service as an adjunct to the Pentagon. Young Alexander spent his childhood in Costa Rica, Argentina, South Korea and Egypt. He attended American operated schools with the children of embassy employees. Alexander's father took the Washington assignment after his son completed high school. Alexander then attended the University of Virginia, majoring in psychology. After graduation, he was recruited into the CIA. Recruiting within families provided the agency with prospective employees who knew what to expect from the career and who came with an essentially inbred security clearance. Alexander obtained a Master's Degree in International Studies before taking a post in data research and analysis in Germany. Then it was on to Cypress where he trained in methods of information assemblage. After four years away, he returned to America to attend his mother's funeral. He was disturbed to find a deteriorating public perception of the agency. It was the mid 1970's and Americans were hearing testimony before Congress about CIA transgressions such as gathering information on American citizens and plots to assassinate foreign leaders. Combined with the concluding Vietnam fiasco and ongoing fallout from the Watergate scandal, the American public was becoming disbelieving and angry at its government institutions.

Alexander's father believed the Church Committee hearings were an attempt to divert attention from the foibles of other government branches onto the CIA. At the time, the agency was inexpert at public relations and easy whipping boy for its reluctance to defend itself and risk exposing covert activities vital for American defense. Not long after Alexander returned to Cypress, his father suddenly died. Maybe he gave up on life after his wife's death. Maybe it was simply his time. But Alexander blamed it on the heartache he witnessed tearing his father apart. His father was never the same after the organization he revered lost prestige.

After that, Alexander vowed he'd never tolerate vilification of the CIA from the public, media, or any government representative. After a term of service in Cypress, he was awarded his first station chief position, in Portugal. He made his reputation within the agency once he was promoted to the Philippines. There he was part of the embassy team that persuaded Ferdinand Marcos and his crumbling regime to peacefully relinquish power, leading to an orderly transfer of government, protecting American interests and maintaining stability in the region. Then it was on to Greece, an advantageous station chief position for gaining Mideast contacts. A European country in proximity to the Mideast is fertile ground for establishing Arab and Israeli connections. A station chief in such circumstances could gain trust and curry favor with many Mideast nations by not being directly associated with a term of service in an unfriendly country.

US diplomats considered Walker unrefined and contentious, which made CIA superiors hold him in high regard. He protected agency domain and could be an utter pain to bureaucrats. Walker, like most within the agency, believed that politicians and the media misled the American people about the CIA. Americans just didn't understand what was necessary behind the world stage to protect the nation's security. Elected officials and the press were quick to let the public know about agency fiascoes, well aware the agency couldn't defend itself. They all knew that if the CIA could reveal all it did to safeguard America, there would be many stories of bravery, sacrifice and lives saved that would more than offset the mistakes. Intelligence life is often one of thankless perdition, pitiless and uncompromising, with peculiar logic and rules. Walker new this even better than most inside the agency, with the loss of life and emotional ruin two generations of his family endured.

In Greece, Walker ran afoul with the US ambassador, a close friend of the at the time president. The State Department insisted on a new station chief, and in a rare case of State winning a standoff with the CIA, succeeded in having Walker recalled to Washington.

A rankled Walker simmered in hostility for three years while assigned to agency headquarters in Virginia. The only way to be a real player and rise in the ranks inside the agency was through the Foreign Service. Walker felt his career was derailed. He stayed on only because he knew the political variables that cut him down could some day change.

And one day they did. Without notice, the director of the agency escorted Walker to Camp David to meet presidential advisors Amfrick and Cunningham. They told him a new station chief was immediately needed in Saudi Arabia, one who "takes no prisoners" and could "master the reactive mode in rootlessly progressing eventualities." Walker took the assignment and after a week's briefing arrived in Saudi Arabia when Drake did, the day they met with Captain Lawrence at the embassy in Riyadh.

Drake's State Department "microgroove" gave her the scuttlebutt on Walker. They reported he harbored a bitter, almost paranoid grudge toward those who represented institutions he perceived as having a vendetta against the CIA. Drake never knew this until they met for the first time, minutes before the Lawrence meeting. Replacing a station chief without notice was not unprecedented. CIA, even to State, provides information only on a need-to-know basis. That's why State keeps up an active internal pipeline tracking civilian intelligence personnel. CIA and State may work out of the same embassies, but each group stakes out their territory and is wary of the other based on a history of often conflicting agendas. Buried details of the suspicions and rivalries, sometimes going back decades, usually play out way above the heads of ambassadors, who more than likely today are appointed to their posts due to individual relationships and political fund raising abilities. Frequently they have no diplomatic or foreign service experience and are in the dark about complexities of the countries they serve in. Ambassadors don't make policy, they are merely window dressing led by competing agencies and business influences established long before they arrived and that will continue long after they are gone.

Ambassador Wilson Howe was a former college roommate of the president. A blue blood with a law degree who never practiced judicature. He never had any real job at all. He spent his adult life directing his family's philanthropies, using

195

his connections to raise large sums for the president's election campaign. His reward was the Saudi Arabian ambassadorship.

Shortly before Walker returned from Tel Aviv, Ambassador Howe received an order to send most of the embassy's three hundred plus employees on leave until further notice. Non-essential personnel such as clerks, researchers, secretaries as well as liaisons for commercial affairs and science were sent to their homes in the virtual city. Howe was told it was an attempt to prevent leaks about the Lawrence matter as events moved into a sensitive stage.

To Drake and Walker, it meant something else. The embassy was closing ranks, leaving the two of them naked of the mass of employees who provided inside scoops on each other through the embassy network of loyal tattlers. Most of them were now gone.

Ambassador Howe was out for lunch when he got a call to return right away to the embassy. When the Marines let him on the grounds, he was shaken by the bustle he saw underway once he was within the enclosure.

Quickly moving inside the center of operations, he was almost knocked over by the deluge of activity. The remaining staff was scurrying around with binders and portfolios crammed with reports and communications, while others huddled over computers, stood over humming faxes and dashed to answer ringing phones. Anarchy reigned, as staff bumped into each other, distracted with tasks at hand.

Things were quiet when Howe left only an hour ago after the daily conference with Drake and General Zalman over the Lawrence matter. In fact, Howe remembered thinking the place seemed peaceful, with no new news on the Lawrence front and so fewer employees to smother the premises.

He still hadn't adjusted to the scene when he hurried into his office. He shut the door, silencing the racket outside. Walking to his desk, he detected Walker sitting alone at the long table in the suite's appointment chamber. Marching in, Howe saw Drake in a corner whispering on a phone. Walker's satchel sat open on the counter with a series of photographs scattered around.

Howe approached Walker, "What's going on?"

Walker only stared at the table.

Howe picked up the photos. He paused, trying to act as though he understood what he was looking at. A burning plane. What did it mean? Something important, evidently, because everybody was frantic.

Drake finished her call, sat down, and rubbed her forehead.

"So, what's happening?"

"What's happening, you ask?" The secretary fumed, "What's happening is that my plane is down. What remains of it is sitting on the ground in Lebanon and we have soldiers missing. Soldiers from Captain Lawrence's unit. They were probably on board."

Howe plopped down into a chair, "What were they doing there?

"Probably trying to save Captain Lawrence, who I find out now Israel said was being held there," Drake was petulant. "We're hearing they are all dead. How they knew she was there, I don't know."

That's what was tormenting Drake. How did they know? She looked at Walker. How able a phantom he was, so quiet and inert, as though he wasn't even there.

Howe became fidgety. The swirling agitation was spreading to him, "What happens now?"

Drake jumped up, circling and sighing, "I just got off the phone with the president. Moving troops to the Iraq border hasn't intimidated Saddam. He remains out of sight. Reports show the action has boomeranged on us. Iran is moving units toward Iraq. Syria is sending troops to bolster their presence in Lebanon. Israel is doing fly-overs above Syria, Jordan has closed its border with Lebanon and Kurdish refugees are trying to get into Turkey. The whole region is a tinderbox waiting for a match."

Howe stood, amped up with arms akimbo, "What is the president going to do?"

Drake hated dealing with crisis mode when she was away from home. Ambassadors were always in the way because they needed everything explained, "He's pulling the troops back," she calmed him. "Now we need to come up with damage control and something to tell the soldier's families."

The answer was so simple Walker decided to materialize for a moment, "They were on the way to Germany to train troops scheduled for duty here. They grabbed a ride on your plane and it was accidentally shot down. We use that story all the time."

"It doesn't factor in settlement of the Lawrence matter," Drake had to have all the answers.

"Don't say anything about her right now, just sit on it," Walker was becoming, for him, long-winded. "She was an officer on a mission. Say nothing to the military and don't address rumors. Later, say she was lost and call her a hero."

Walker, Howe and Drake looked at each other, asking themselves the same questions - *What do they know that I don't? Do they know what's really happening?*

The secretary again took a seat. She tilted her head and pointed her eyes toward the ceiling, contemplating.

"Sad to say," Walker went on, "but having her out of the picture solves more problems than it creates."

Drake snapped her gaze on Walker, "Depends on what's going on with the Saud's."

***

King Khaled kept his hand on Prince Abdul's shoulder for a long time. The tears persisted, so the king crouched in front of Abdul and wiped them.

Abdul turned away in embarrassment. So did everybody else at the family meeting in the Royal Palace. Abdul seemed to at once age after he heard the news. Could be they were all looking old lately.

"It was Allah's will," Abdul near mumbled in a cracked voice. "Better Nasir be dead than see what he cherished torn apart."

The king searched for something to say, but finally settled on the truth, "Who could have explained to him our disgrace?"

Salih ruined the grieving, "As Nasir's death was Allah's wish, so is a new Arabia."

Khaled pivoted toward Salih perched across the hall, training a finger and bellowing, "You will speak only when I say!"

198

His words echoed. The palace was quieter than it ever had been. Servants and most of the staff were no longer there. Even the Guard was kept out of the building. It was an attempt to hinder talk about what might be overheard or witnessed, a decision made after the squabble that broke out last time they all met.

Salih paused, then mouthed off again, "Khaled, will you stand on ceremony even as you linger at the door?"

The king ignored him. He had business with Rakan, "Your first action as head of the Guard was to move your own wealth? You disobeyed my decree. I cold have you executed."

Rakan stood up, unstrung but grinning, "I was only checking on the allegiance of the Guard. I couldn't allow you to risk your wealth on such a test, so I sacrificed some of mine." Nobody believed him. Rakan refused to acknowledge the rolling eyes as he continued, "I am happy to report the Guard remains loyal. I stopped them from firing on the thugs. We were swarmed, so I let them take my things rather than have bloodshed."

It was silent until somebody coughed.

The king approached Rakan, "I should build you a monument."

Salih snickered, "I told you, they won't obey Rakan. You must hurry getting affairs in order. Squeezing out every riyal will be the death of you. Mecca pilgrims are due, their passions ready to be inflamed by word of the birth of Allah's Arabia."

"Not another word, Salih," the king said, using a steely pitch.

Salih began to say something. Khaled marched over to him while pulling a gun from under his robe. He pointed the pistol at Salih's face, "Not one word."

Some recoiled. Others covered their faces or looked away, but most watched. Khaled kept hard aim directly between Salih's eyes.

They stared at each other for a long time.

Salih gave a feeble bow. Then he smiled.

***

HONOR BOUND

"I love you," were the first words Denise said to Rick when at last he called. After passing out before dawn, Rick woke up too late to reach her until she returned home from work.

Of course she was bothered he didn't call the night before. She decided not to stay up waiting to hear from him, but that's not how it worked out. She couldn't sleep soundly, tossing and turning in speculation at what was going on between them. This invisible space cleaving away at them was eating at her. She suspected Rick's failure to call was a sign he was consumed by the story, which for Denise was coming to be synonymous with Kasey. Was she ever going to find out if this was based in fact? Or was it a substitution for other relationship issues? As much as she dreaded what she might learn if Rick found a story, part of her felt it might be worse if he didn't come up with one and her curious examination of his bond with Kasey was left hanging.

She found a way to put off thoughts about it while at work the next day. For Denise, anger manifested as the less obtrusive emotion of disappointment. The quiet places and spaces in her essential nature impeded the torrid connections necessary for furious sentiments. A manner that set the emotional tone in their marriage. Rick never saw her angry, chalking it up to an affable disposition that attracted him to her. Yet nobody is unconditionally good-natured. Her calm and her parted regions were shock cushions for white- hot passions that settled in her tingling plexus.

On the way home, Denise banished introspection about Kasey. She concentrated attention on the question she needed Rick to get answered. Was he putting it off? Before this story he was working on he said it was time for them to know. Is the story an excuse to delay? Then she would back off, questioning whether she was obsessing on the subject. Then the topic would again intrude with her saying to herself that he intended to get the answer soon. Didn't she see a sign he was searching for a doctor?

There was no waiting message from Rick when she got home. She sat at the kitchen table, longing to hear from him. Fact was, she didn't care, not about his seeing a doctor, the story, Kasey, any of it. She only wanted to hear his voice and dream of looking at him and feeling his arms squeezing her.

That's when the phone rang. She knew it was him. She didn't even say hello, just hit him with the three words.

"I love you, too," Rick couldn't wait to say. "Sorry, I didn't call. I was busy until late, then I fell asleep. I miss you."

When Rick woke up, he headed for Paragon Fabrics, the closest cotton mill to Fort Sellers, about forty miles away. Rick orbited the plant a few times, getting an idea of the layout and searching for the means of egress. He expected it to be larger than the four or so blocks it took up. The facility was located near the edge of approaching suburban sprawl. It looked as though much of it was built before the area was settled, judging conditions of the factory, although there seemed to be some recent expansion. Anyone could drive onto the property, park in the fenced in lot and gain admittance to the grounds. Not a characteristic of a place where tight-lipped events were happening. Rick lingered in a coffee shop across from the main entrance, listening and watching for a lead. Denise kept grabbing at his thoughts. He knew she wouldn't be angry, but this wasn't the time in their relationship for him to be screwing up.

It was warmer here than back home, causing him to imagine Denise spring planting in thegarden. The fragrances of blossoms and sun baked soil made Rick recall the times they made love after she worked in the yard and how he once tasted earth under her nails when he put his tongue on her fingers.

Even now, he pushed away asking why he misled her by leaving the open phone book on the table. The act didn't come from a mindful place. He didn't know why he was stalling. He couldn't picture life without Denise. He had to have her in his life. In some way, he knew that eventually the cost to keep her would be giving up a demon.

Rick left the coffee shop and found a low-profile place to park not far from the rear of the mill. He had a good view of the service access. Back doors are where you find out what you need to know, even when you don't know what you need to know.

When sitting there waiting, it was time to call Denise.

"I can't stop thinking about you," Denise had to let him know.

"So, how's it going?"

"I took a tour of the Army base."

"Find out anything intriguing?"

"Can't say. I'm checking something out."

"What?" Denise hated needing to know.

"Might mean nothing, only something a little unusual," Rick didn't want to say more about it, telling himself wireless phone calls could be monitored. The truth was he could tell Denise was threatened by the story. "It's killing me not to be with you."

She was sure he meant it, "When will you be back?"

Rick's eye captured a ten- wheel truck with trailer departing the access road. It quickly increased speed as it turned onto the artery and rumbled by him. What interested Rick was the canvas covering its ample load and the vehicle's identification - *Olson Waste Disposal.*

It had to be the mill's waste. Instinct told him to chase the truck. He didn't realize his long delay with Denise on the line.

"Rick? Are you there?"

"I need to catch up to a truck. I'll call you later," he didn't wait for Denise to say goodbye.

The tone of the dead connection tore a new quiet between her thoughts, eventually prompting what she was struggling to let go of, the worry about his lust for this story.

Rick didn't remember if Denise said goodbye. He was consumed with getting close enough to follow the truck. He managed to find it taking a ramp onto the highway. He jumped a light and cut off traffic, keeping it in sight until he could get near.

He merged into the lane not far behind the truck, clutching his camera and keeping one hand on the wheel. Rick maneuvered to a suitable angle of view and took a few pictures. That done, he trailed the truck in a northwest direction for almost an hour, ending up in back country at the Appalachian foothills. The truck exited the highway and made its way through the main streets of increasingly scrawnier towns. Rick saw a vast, enclosed and stationed landfill ahead. He knew that's where it was going.

Rick continued straight ahead as the truck turned inside. Driving by, he pivoted his head for a glimpse. He had to continue on almost a mile before finding a street parallel to the landfill. He pulled over. Woods surrounded the area. He jumped out of the car with his camera and binoculars and ran toward the landfill. It was twilight, but he could make out the truck crawling along a dirt road and disappearing behind an expanding mound. Crouching, he hustled to keep it in view. The truck stopped behind the mound. Rick had to creep to the edge of the woods to put binoculars on it. He watched the driver get out of the cab, climb into the back and begin rolling off the canvas while Rick tried to interpret the scene. Other trucks inside the landfill took their loads on the widening trajectory leading to the top of the mound, obviously the authorized dump spot. What was the driver doing and why was he doing it there?

It took the driver a long time to peel back the cover. When he finished, he went back into the cab and started the hydraulic booster until the trailer was slightly raised. Then he got back out, climbed again into the back, freed the tail hitch and began pushing fifty-gallon drums out onto the ground.

Why was he leaving it there? The barrels seemed to easily rotate off. The contents couldn't be too solid. An impression confirmed when the driver jumped onto the ground and started aligning the drums in a row.

Eventually the truck left, but Rick didn't. He kept peering at the metal drums sitting there. In the dark, Rick moved close enough to zoom in with the low-light lens and flash for a series of photos.

What was in those barrels? Why were they left there? Rick reloaded his camera and waited.

* * *

Islam was revealed to Muhammad about AD 622 in Mecca. It is a monotheistic faith asserting God is omnipotent, impartial and forgiving. Muslims see humanity as God's supreme creation, but man is irresolute, narcissistic, neglectful of life's purpose and continually entranced by Satan. God revealed the Koran to Muhammad to steer man toward truth and justice. Those who repent and sincerely submit to God attain salvation and enter the Paradise, while the wicked burn in hell.

Since Muhammad was both prophet and political leader, Muslim leadership is frequently linked to both civic and religious functions of society. Predominantly Muslim countries are held together by common religious law, enforced in matters of morality only. In social arrangements, there is leeway for the individual and cultural histories of particular nations to distinctly shape civil life. Islam is inherently democratic, distrustful of totalitarianism and cultural lfe tends to be dominated by the religious establishment.

Besides the everyday moral guidance, there are "Five Pillars of Islam": affirmation of faith (oneness of God and the prophet Muhammad); prayer five times a day; social charity and devotion to nation; dawn-to-dusk fasting in the month of Ramadan; and if possible, a once in a lifetime pilgrimage to Mecca.

The two major sects of Islam, the Sunni and Shiite, differ philosophically chiefly in one regard: Sunni's believe in pre-determination while Shiite's embrace the idea of free will. Sufism, the mystical frontier of Islam, includes both groups and emphasizes a personal relationship with God. Islam is the fastest growing religion in the world, gaining a million new adherents every month. It has much in common with Judaism and Christianity. The story of Moses appears verbatim in the Koran. Islam's building blocks of faith are similar in substance to the Ten Commandments. Islam mirrors Judaism in maintaining that God does not take corporeal form, a difference from Christianity the two religions share. For them, Jesus is not the literal Son of God, but an inspired human prophet and divine messenger.

The similarities beg the obvious conclusion:

Religious canon does not turn people against each other.

Political doctrine does.

For centuries, the Ottoman Empire was as close as the Muslim world came to having social and spiritual unity. Since the end of the Ottoman era in the early Twentieth Century, the precepts of Islamic civic and social existence have been subject to fractured wanderings, sometimes by sincere believers and sometimes by political opportunists. The loss of Islam's cultural hub, the two World Wars, discovery of oil in the Mideast, superpower expansionism and Western media ignorance have played major roles, as has Islamic tradition of promoting social justice, in how non-Muslims see Islam.

Viewing Arab Muslims as terrorists is akin to judging Christians as murderers because a handful of anti-abortion activists have murdered doctors. As much as Arab nations, particularly Saudi Arabia, have done to present a more balanced picture of the Arab world to the West, the few incidents of terrorism in the name of Islam is played up by Western media and ignorant foreign government officials to give an impression that Arab Muslims are major sources of international strife.

Many Arab Muslims today are well aware who among them exploits Islam for political purposes. Those who do so incite a unique rage in traditional Muslims, like the violent disgust Nasir was now experiencing. He defiantly glared at the screaming mob as he stood next to Kasey on back of a platform truck in the Yanta plaza. Guards toting AK-47's pushed the surging crowd back, until they were again provoked by the rhetoric from Raza, Abbas and Fajid, circling Kasey and Nasir on the platform, acting as accusers in this bogus trial.

The anger boiling in Nasir equaled the fury of the horde. As much as he hated their stupidity and gullibility, he despised even more the masterminds who used them as pawns, duping these fools into notions of victimization and loathing. Nasir was prepared for it to all be over, ready to kneel before Allah and let him judge the truth. He ached at Kasey's plight, suffering over what was going to happen to her in the name of Islam. Her terms of service predicated no sentimentality over whatever fate duty brought. He knew that's how she would see it. But now, set loose of status, conditioning and future, he recognized his awe at her. She wasn't a friend, or a woman, or an American, she was a *soldier* he was proud to have known, a soldier her country would be diminished by losing. He couldn't dwell on the emotion, the agony knowing that she was going to be murdered was too much to bear.

. " ... They were alone with my brother," Raza was going on, his voice quivering. "When we returned, he was dead!"

Abbas put a comforting hand on Raza's shoulder and took over as prosecutor, "They killed him! It could only have been them."

Raza covered his face to hide tears. Abbas embraced him and Fijid took over, shouting, "You are all witnesses to the slaughter brought on by the American plot! This harlot and her adulterous infidel planned the deaths of our people!"

After hearing the charges for hours, the noise from the crowd was expanding to a teeming crescendo. Fajid stopped before exhausting the mob's fury, spinning toward the accused, "American and Saud, your defense!"

The gathering jammed forwards, rocking the truck and near crushing the guards until they gave up pushing them away. Keeping them off the platform was the best they could do.

Kasey retained an unbroken serenity. Some of it was due to acceptance of fate, yet some of it was based on a churning hope that now, more than ever, there could be a chance they would be rescued. She never stopped reasoning. If her cohorts undertook the mission on their own, their absence would have to be noticed. They must have told *somebody*. There were thousands outside at this public event. They came from all over the valley. There had to be ground intelligence or sky views picking up what was going on.

The only power Kasey now had was forcing the rabble to expend its energy. She kept quiet until they menacingly swarmed, as if sensing her attempt at one upsmanship. Kasey walked to the edge of the platform and roared, "I do not recognize these proceedings as actions of a legitimate state!"

Nasir was right behind her, "We will not reply!"

Security shoved Kasey and Nasir away so a composed Raza could take the center stage, "So be it. I ask the jury for a verdict ... "

"Guilty," the mob shrieked when Raza held out his arms. Their prolonged howl of "Guilty! ... Guilty!" ... became a savage mantra that bulged with wild frenzy.

Raza growled, "The penalty?"

The throng clamored ... "Death! ... Death! ... Death!" The demand continued while celebratory gunshots were fired into the air and fists waved in rhythm.

A scowling Abbas screeched over the chaos, "American filth and criminal Arabian, you both will be hanged at sunrise!"

206

His declaration propelled the mass to an orgasm of festive fury. Kasey approached Raza. The guards on the platform surrounded her, pointing their weapons. She looked Raza in the eyes and said, "We want our uniforms."
Raza was taken aback. Her earnest tone almost made him see her as human. He stuttered until noticing Abbas and Fajid looking at him. Then he grinned, "You shall have them. We want you to die in costume. It will make a good picture for your country and familyto see."
Then he laughed and did a spontaneous dance to the beat of the chants, happy hands whirling above his head. The gesture drove the multitude to a level of ecstatic derangement.
Men jumped onto the platform, grabbing at Kasey and Nasir until the guards gave up trying to hold them back. Kasey and Nasir were heaved on top of the drove while calls for their demise rumbled through the canyon.
Abbas drove the truck away so construction of the gallows could begin in the square. Raza led a pack searching for lumber, their exuberance so great they tore apart the nearest building for its planks.
Kasey and Nasir were hauled to the dump at the end of the village and flung to the ground. Fajid brought shovels and ordered them to dig their own tombs. They refused until being stomped and whacked into surrender. The crowd clapped, prodding them whenever they delayed. Gradually, groups split off to prepare for the carousing that would go on until late into the night.

***

What the CIA is to human information gathering, the National Security Agency (NSA) is to electronic intelligence. Yes, the CIA does amasses electronic data and the NSA does collect information through human contacts, but each agency has a specialty, acquired mainly from the time and circumstances of inception than due to design or charter. The organizations are cousins at war, sparring jealously for influence with and the assets of their doting uncle. Each agency uses their strengths to protect their jurisdiction and takes every opportunity to exploit the other's weaknesses. The CIA, in existence longer, has a labyrinth history of affiliations within the government and excels at analysis of data.

Their shortcomings include the baggage they bring from failures and embarrassing episodes. The NSA, formed later, used CIA mistakes to its advantage in crafting an agency even more secretive than its kin. Its strength is its ability to grab hold of virtually any electronic or person-to-person communication going on anywhere in the world it focuses attention on. One weakness is its upstart status compared to the CIA. It may not carry the CIA's baggage, but it lacks the CIA's inter-government connections. Another deficiency is its flimsy capability to analyze what it collects. They continually lobby for a greater mission in intelligence explication, but the CIA successfully pressures otherwise.

Randall Gross was the National Security Advisor designated as the NSA's advocate inside the executive branch. Over the past few days, his calls for a White House meeting became filled with more urgent verbs and excited adjectives until Cunningham and Amfrick finally scheduled an appointment for the middle of one afternoon, when the president was under wraps, napping upstairs after lunch. They knew what Gross wanted to talk about and were experts at feigning absorbed interest. They stared unblinkingly at Gross, eyes peeled on his every gesture as he summarized his report inside Amfrick's West Wing office. They gave him half an hour. Neither had to look at a clock to know his time was almost up.

" ... What we've accumulated is irrefutable. An insurrection is at hand inside Saudi Arabia. We strongly urge evacuation of all American civilian personnel and a chance to discuss this with the president and Joint Chiefs. Decisions must be made about our military there. You know they will be immediate targets. A soldier there was shot the other day after encountering suspicious activity. It may seem to be an isolated incident but-"

"Other intelligence we have says it is," Amfrick interrupted. He was somber and muted, "It's the Mideast. There will always be these things going on. We've told our troops and American companies to be on the alert."

Gross knew this and more, "I know executives sent their families home. But the workers haven't been told. Saudi media is censored. If we don't tell them, they'll never know. A delay is courting disaster. I expected to see the president about this. He needs to know how dire the situation is."

"He's busy," Cunningham stood and looked out a window. "He wanted us to handle the briefing. Anyway, he already knows everything you've said." Cunningham walked to the door and opened it for Gross, "Keep us informed."

Gross knew they were blowing him off. He was more upset that the CIA obviously had won their ear than what ignoring his information might mean. He crowded papers into a briefcase and left without looking at either of them.

Cunningham closed the door and drifted around the office while Amfrick sat at his desk with hands folded. Cunningham took a seat, "He won't stay in the dark forever."

Amfrick nodded. Then he raised a finger, "But we don't need forever. It's time I did a little sightseeing."

***

It ended up being another no-work day for American employees in the Saudi port city of Az Zahran. Empty tankers floated high in the water by the docks, an indicator to the arriving end line crew that no crude was making way to port. After one more morning of make- work labor the foreman sent everybody home, citing corporate word that a leak up the flow area still needed repair. Three days straight with no crude heading out was beginning to make the personnel grouchy. There simply wasn't enough to occupy their free time back in the virtual city. That's why a few lingered behind at a restaurant catering to Americans outside the entrance to the cargo gate. They knew about the attack on Americans at the Ras Tanura refinery. Security concerns were addressed by alternating transportation routes and hiring Saudi Guard full time during work hours. That way, there would be escort available whenever the workers went home and a constant enforcement presence visible around facilities where foreigners worked. A Saudi Guard platoon lingered outside near the one bus left behind to shuttle the Americans when they decided to head home. Inside, a dozen men were eating pizza and watching basketball on satellite television.

In another part of the city, Saudis driving into a petrol station found it wasn't open. They headed for the other fuel depot in town and joined a queue of vehicles extending into the street until the proprietor announced there was no more gasoline.

Angry motorists complained to the attendants, who could only shrug their shoulders andsay come back later. A man in the back of the line yelled that he drove kilometers from home where all the petrol stations were closed. Drivers listened to his protest until one pointed at the tankers in the port, "None for us, all for the Americans."

That visual image became a focus as the motorists collected into a pack, their griping dilating into bolder expression of discontent as they glanced around to find no Saudi Guard to constrain them. No petrol. Banks closed. What was next? They stared at the shipping facility, still half expecting the law to disperse them.

Somebody finally slammed his car door and began marching toward the port. Most of the others joined him. As they progressed, Saudi men along the street overheard the snarling and united with the bunch. Motorists passing by pulled over to find out what was going on and left their vehicles in the road to become part of the march. Visiting Mecca pilgrims garbed in white linen swelled the gathering further. Voices grew louder as they turned onto the avenue leading to the docks. They broke into a trot, the mix of spontaneous protest and mob psychology ignited as the men began hunting for solids to use venting the energy. They quickly rummaged through trash barrels and bent over to pick up rocks without lagging the collective gait. The electricity spiking the air was as untamed as a bolt of lightning. When the Guard stationed outside the restaurant saw them approaching, there was no showdown. The Guard abruptly and silently disappeared.

The Americans inside didn't have time to notice the Guard's absence before a rock crashed through the window. There was a pause, not a stunned one, more bewilderment at something out of the blue. One American sitting at a table stood up to wipe off shards of glass when another rock bounced off his head. Everybody hit the ground. A man whose face was bloodied by shattering glass braved the shouts of fury outside and rushed to the door. Before he opened it, the mob rushed in and started beating whomever they could lay hands on and trashing the place. A few Americans escaped in the chaos, seeking refuge in the port facility, which was closing its gates. The Saudi restaurant workers fled into the street, screaming for the Guard. The Americans trapped inside the restaurant hopelessly tried to defend themselves. One fell unconscious. Like an injured animal downed by a wolf pack, he was descended upon, kicked and punched until the mob had rendered whatever level of mutilation and destruction the aggregate perceptual mind deemed sufficient. Then they emptied back into the street, stopping traffic, searching for Americans and crashing the barriers of the port.

* * *

Rick spent the night lurking on the edge of the woods. The temperature dropped to near freezing after midnight. At one point it rained, or he thought it did. It really was a rolling mist sweeping down from the hills leaving a moist sheen on the budding foliage when the moon peeked through the clouds. Rick paced back and forth, occasionally sitting on the ground and leaning against a tree. It wasn't the cold, or fear of nodding off that made him get up after a few minutes. It was noise in the woods. Unidentifiable sounds of nocturnal things, sometimes mingling with a gently rustling underbrush. He kept attention on the landfill, fixing the night scope on the occasional truck clamoring up that expanding mound. It became silent in the wee morning. It was close to dawn when he saw the next rig rolling in. Watching it motor away after dropping its load, he saw three trucks parked in a semi-circle by the metal drums. He never heard them arrive. When and how did they get there? Struggling for a good view, Rick saw that they were delivery trucks with walk-in back doors, like the Coleman's Commercial Laundry vehicles. Even with technology's help, it was too dark and he was too far away to see any denoting name on them.

  Rick detected three men rotating the containers to the trucks and hoisting them inside. He had a good look at the man who seemed to be directing the action. Late middle aged with white hair, rather tall, standing ramrod straight with an athletic build. Rick did get a few pictures, but he needed to hurry. They were working fast and he wanted to catch them as they left. He dashed through the woods back to his car and raced to the entrance of the landfill only moments before the trucks drove away. Just what he surmised - it was Coleman's Laundry. The streets were quiet, so Rick stayed a distance away to keep a low-profile. He followed them onto the highway moving in the direction of Fort Sellers. But they got off the highway before reaching the exit. The sun was rising and there was more activity on the streets, so Rick closed in and took more pictures. Winding through suburbia, the area seemed familiar. Then ahead he noticed the strip mall in front of Coleman's Commercial Laundry. That's where they went? Intriguing. The trucks turned into the lot in front of the long building. Rick drove by and made a U-turn, stopping in a donut shop parking area across the artery. He could see the back of the scrub plant.

He watched the trucks park next to each other in a far corner and the three drivers exit and head for the building.

There is no way to describe the powerful excitement Rick felt snapping more photos, this time zooming in on the men. A story was breaking open due to all his effort. He couldn't say where it was leading, but he now knew for sure it was real and it could be big. It was a fulfillment at unearthing the proverbial needle in a haystack. He had taken Kasey's few, vague words and made something from it. Now he had to turn it into something he could prove. To his editor, the world and Kasey!

He sat in his car for a long time looking at the above sign facing the street inside the Coleman's lot. The HELP WANTED notice was still planted on the bottom. Rick intended to get inside the place and find out what was going on.

***

Outside the Yanta jail, scores of men spent the night yelping like dogs. It was a dirge of death. The howling incantations were slurs directed at Kasey and Nasir mixed with jubilation at their imminent execution.

Raza walked into the lockup with their uniforms. The accompanying crowd wedged between a ring of guards, watching Raza drop the clothes on the floor and step on them. They cheered when he used a hard heel to whisk the ground and then kicked the sullied uniforms through the cell bars. Then Raza was

212

followed back outside where he was subject to attention from many more than the numbers who could be crammed into the jail.

There was no humiliation remaining for Kasey and Nasir to experience. What did it matter in these last moments? They did their best to stroke clean their uniforms, then stripped and dressed in front of the guards.

Outside, under exiting moonlight, a train of robed and veiled women appeared out of the dark haze walking toward the jail. Some veered off into the hills toward the men stationing the artillery batteries. The women carried wash clothes and water pitchers to scrub the men's hands and feet before their morning prayers.

Inside their cell, Nasir was facing Mecca and praying. He knew it was his final petition. He begged Allah to watch over his family, preserve his nation, and render Kasey glorious afterlife. Sitting on the floor, Kasey listened to Nasir and felt the burning emotion in his cadence. She realized it was his final plea to God. It was time to release the clinging hope she had, that there was a way out for them. She then said a brief prayer in her head, asking safety for the Americans she wouldn't get to warn. Then she apologized for her role in her father's death and for selfish insensitivity toward her brother. When Gary came to mind, the lump that formed in her throat made her stop. She was never again going to see the person in this world she was closest to, the first time she confessed to herself such an emotion for Gary. Kasey searched for a different focus. Fingering her coat, she looked at the words stitched inside – *America, One Nation, One Destiny.*

Somebody opened the jailhouse door and told the guards the women had arrived. They stepped outside, leaving Kasey and Nasir alone.

Nasir finished praying. There was a drawn-out silence before they looked at each other.

Kasey speculated what was on his mind, "Thinking about your son?"

He stood up and said nothing.

Kasey walked over and gripped his shoulders, "Nasir, you did say you loved him. You told me."

He grabbed her hand. Then they embraced, ready to die.

HONOR BOUND

The men sat in front of the jail while the women sponged their feet. A slight woman with smiling eyes glanced up at the artillery batteries, where the same action was underway. For the first time that night it was quiet outside. A deep hush permeated the ether, as if suspending breath and motion of every living thing in a static foreboding.

In unison, the women rapidly pulled out knives from under their robes and began stabbing the men, aiming for hearts and throats. Brisk, efficient thrusts that gave no time to reach for a gun or even scream as the valley's dynamism returned with the hell that broke loose when the massacre commenced. The men unlucky enough not to die quickly had their moans swiftly stifled by a hand over the mouth and steel in the gut. The woman with the smiling eyes made way along a row of stretched out men, drilling their flesh with her dagger for good measure.

Witnessing the Green Scarves in action, it's unfathomable how they function. They behave with a supernatural coherence, like the entirety had a collective psyche.

The women up at the artillery batteries finished off the men in no time. After a lanky woman climbed down a ledge to finish off the one escaping man, the women turned the artillery on the Hezbollah training camp and barracks where men who chose to get sleep before the execution were resting. They waited for a signal from the women outside the jail who were searching clothing looking for keys to the jail cell. They came up empty.

Green Scarves in uniform appeared on peaks surrounding the valley and streamed into Yanta and its environs, strangling egress. Then they dashed into homes and started massacring every man they found.

Detecting the roaring armored column thundering into Yanta from the north road, the artillery battery waited no longer to begin shelling the men's quarters. The first direct hit ignited propane stored in a kitchen area, bursting the entire camp into a swelling inferno that broadcast for miles what was underway.

The tanks, troop transports and gun carriers surged into town confident the advance company did their job. They had already cleared the route for the armor, leaving a chain of corpses at Hezbollah and militia checkpoints. The first tanks ringed the jailhouse while big guns were set up on open land with a clear shot at near reaches of the valley. The units started battering the surrounding settlements as dazed and wounded men staggered out of the barracks only to meet waiting Green Scarves. The women cut down those aflame or badly injured before finishing off the lesser mangled. For Green Scarves, compassion extended no further than mercy killing.

The delirium of slaughter seemed to have no culminating point, as if sight of blood only pitched the frenzy to greater gluttony. Sometimes the Green Scarves stormed a home, other times they kicked open a door and fired away or tossed a grenade inside. Then they would wait for unfortunates to run or crawl outside. Once the bloodbath was announced, some men barricaded themselves inside buildings. Their protection was shattered to bits by the muzzle-loaders on the ground or in the hills. Surviving men trying to hide or flee were chased down, sometimes with bullets and other times by a pack who drove them down and slit their jugulars.

Inside the jail, Kasey and Nasir listened, at the beginning curious, then astonished. It was a cacophony of gunshots near and far, shouting, hurrying feet, screaming, rumbling tanks and blaring howitzers, barking dogs, bursting grenades, sobbing women and sickening moans.

They had no idea what was happening. It was too confusing for any sharp ear. Whatever was going on was monstrous, but neither dared jinx with words the hope of rescue that electrified their psyches.

They felt vibrating earth and ricocheting bullets among stomach-churning shrieks and cries until it all became a roaring stream of boundless, unintelligible noise.

Kasey and Nasir stared at the door and prayed.

Outside, the artillery in the hills pointed at further regions of the valley, pummeling home a message to anyone considering a challenge. The Green Scarves started scouring every inch of land for hiding men, sidestepping women mourning the dead but heeding other women who hurried to them, eager to show where the men were. As the sun came up, the occasional stray gunfire indicated it was strictly a mop up operation.

Thousands of dead men littered the canyon. Green Scarves controlled every inch of territory. They were above, below, inside, outside, everywhere. The

HONOR BOUND

smoke cleared and the morning haze burned off as a fresh breeze blew in the valley. A new force ruled undisputed in the Bekka.

The Green Scarves!

In front of the jail, one tank turned, faced the door and accelerated. The entire wall came crashing down with a mighty clamor.

Kasey and Nasir had no time to react to the commotion. A speeding tank was heading for them. They jumped into a corner and covered their asses as it crushed the bars of the cell and came to stop inches away. Kasey and Nasir looked up. The above hatch flew open and Maryam Moghavi climbed out on top of the debris.

"Hope I didn't scare you," there was never irony in her voice. "We couldn't find the guy with the keys," there was no accent to her English. "Then we had work to do."

Kasey and Nasir were flabbergasted beyond reaction. They slowly pried hands from heads and straightened up.

Should they be ecstatic? Relieved? Afraid?

Moghavi stood over them and smiled. Then she walked away, treading over the rubble. She tossed an arm over the back of her head and waved, "Come on out."

Kasey and Nasir probed each other's eyes for an explanation neither had. Gradually, they drifted toward the open air. As they dodged wreckage, the valley unveiled, bringing jaw- dropping stupefaction. Yanta was a ruin. Bodies were everywhere. Far ahead, men were still being hunted down and killed in plain view. It was barbarity beyond anything the two of them could ever imagine. Only the bracing sense of liberation staved off the scent of putrefaction settling into the lowlands.

Moghavi was leaning against a pile of crushed metal, holding one hand on her hip as she scanned the vista. Kasey and Nasir approached as curious Green Scarves edged over. Kasey and Nasir didn't know what to say. What words were in order? Thank you?

Moghavi took a deep breath, "This is our first big road trip." She turned and grinned at Kasey and Nasir, "Awesome. I've been wanting to test our muscle."

The images, Moghavi's words, it was far beyond weird. It was too hallucinatory to assimilate. Kasey wasn't responsible for what came out of her mouth, "Is this a dream?"

"No," Moghavi aimed a finger at the ground, "*this* is Lebanon." The she stretched an arm toward the valley floor, "*That* was Hezbollah." She hit her chest with a thumb, "*We* are the *National Liberation Army of Iran.*"

Just as Kasey suspected. Maryam Moghavi. She knew who she was. Every player in the Mideast did, even if few ever encountered her and lived. Kasey was astonished by the size of the Green Scarves. She nodded at Moghavi, "Commander."

"Don't call me that," Moghavi fired back. "We have no rank. That's the second rule. The first is to believe we will free Iran from the clerics or die trying."

Kasey absorbed Moghavi's presence, surprised she was so small, a stature emphasized by the long sword hanging from her belt with its tip scraping the ground. This was the woman so feared? Kasey scrutinized Moghavi's face, noting her thick, unbroken brow. She looked away when Moghavi sensed her nosy eyes.

Nasir also knew who Moghavi was. That's why he was quiet. Tense and more than a little apprehensive, he was driven to say *something*, if only to calm himself, "The mullahs in Iran fear you, they stay out of the south." He knew when he said it was an irrelevant comment.

"Don't try to flatter me," Moghavi growled. "I tell you right now ibn Saud, your country needs to change. I promised we would tolerate you. Just don't think you know everything. Because if I was a Saudi woman ... " she never finished. She didn't need to.

"I will be no trouble," he affirmed, looking at all the dead men. "I promise."

Kasey noted how Moghavi addressed Nasir, "You know who we are?"

Moghavi laughed, clipped but loose, "Everybody knows who you are and where you are. Why do you think we are here?"

Kasey wasn't sure what Moghavi meant, "It looks like you came to take out Hezbollah."

Moghavi grinned, "Puts a smile on your face, doesn't it?"

217

Far from it Kasey thought. Yes, she saved them from execution. Yet what she saw of this revolutionary army out to overthrow their native government for right or wrong political reasons made her cringe. As much as Kasey had reason to hate these men who tortured her, there was something unbelievably disturbing about her rescuers. Their action in the Bekka was close to being a hate crime against a gender. An international hate crime, since they crossed borders. An international hate crime of genocidal proportions based on the annihilation in front of her.

Kasey watched Moghavi sit on a pile of debris, then stiffen her back like a cobra rising to strike. It must have been a familiar gesture to the Green Scarves as several moved to her side. Moghavi sniffed at the air, looked left over at a garbage lot and pointed at a heap of rusting metal. The Green Scarves rushed over, throwing aside junk until they found two men hiding underneath. Kasey was amazed. *Moghavi can smell the presence of men?* The men's cries and pleas were sheer agony to hear. Kasey had to turn away as Green Scarves finished them off with knives and machetes.

Moghavi put her attention back on Kasey and Nasir, "You two are the reason we here."

Kasey wished Moghavi hadn't told her. Since she did, it begged the question, "Why?"

"Saddam asked us to."

"Why would you risk it?

"It was a *request* from a *friend.*"

Leave it to Kasey, no matter the circumstances, always looking for information. It was suspected Moghavi had more than tacit approval from Saddam to operate from the Iraq desert near the Iran border. Now she knew there was more to their relationship.

"In this part of the world," Moghavi shrugged, "you take friends wherever you can find them." It wasn't a defense, or explanation. She recited it as a simple statistic. "He gives us land, some weapons too, but we do acquire most on our own. We please him by taking on his enemy."

Moghavi tossed off specifics nobody had been able to gather. Kasey's instinct said to find more, "Some think you provide more than that."

218

Kasey didn't intend it to come out that way. She learned Moghavi's demeanor could change in a blink.

"What do you mean?" Moghavi barked without waiting for an answer. "We are celibate. All energy goes into achieving our objectives."

That explained their rapacious intensity. Kasey wanted to clarify, "I meant to say some think you help keep him in power."

"If he goes, what happens to us? We were watching when they took you during the coup. We saved Saddam's ass once again when the CIA tried to take him out."

The words brought shuddering appall to Kasey. Moghavi was lying, or mistaken. She wanted to know which it was, "How can you say for sure it was the CIA that tried to take out Saddam?"

Moghavi was at first surprised at the doubt she perceived in Kasey's tone. Especially after what she had been through. Moghavi drilled her gaze into Kasey, an attempt to visually dissect her psyche, "Hard to believe? That's nothing. I could tell you stories."

Kasey connected all Moghavi told her, "Everybody knows where we are? How can you say that?"

Moghavi grasped what Kasey was getting at, "Does America know you're here?" She realized Kasey wouldn't believe the truth, "You'll find out for yourself."

A small commotion nearby broke Kasey's train of thought. The lanky woman was crawling under splintered plywood. She discovered hollow earth. The woman with childlike eyes shouted to all around.

Moghavi called out, "Find something, Sweet?" She turned to Kasey and Nasir, "We call her Sweet because of her lovely smile. Isn't she adorable?"

"Yes, charming," Nasir felt it best to concur.

Moghavi marched over, directing Kasey and Nasir to follow as the lanky one dug out the hole and the other threw off boards. It was an ammunition bunker.

"What have you got, Low?" There was great affection in the way Moghavi talked about her fellow warriors, "We call her Low because she likes to move close to the ground."

Sweet and Low? How strange could it get? Kasey knew Moghavi was serious. There was nothing droll about the woman.

Green Scarves flocked over and helped excavate until the profiles of Raza and Abbas emerged. They were clutching each other.

When Kasey saw them, her anger ignited. All their gleeful torture, the pain, the plans for death that just ended but already seemed ages ago, came back to her, "Those bastards kidnapped us!"

"I know," Moghavi understood Kasey's pain. "Show your face, thugs!"

Raza was pulled out by his collar and then Green Scarves prodded Abbas into the open with their rifle butts. They cringed on the ground, restrained by a tight circle of women.

"Please hear me," Raza tried to talk his way out of a terrifying fate, "the two, they killed my brother-"

Abbas interrupted, "It's all their fault!"

Moghavi nodded toward the intact gallows built for the execution of Kasey and Nasir. Green Scarves lifted up Abbas and shoved him down the road. He went shrieking and sobbing.

They were unable to bully Raza to his feet, so Moghavi sat on his back and drew her sword as Raza kept up his furious plea, "You see, we only wanted ransom-"

Moghavi set the knife under his neck, "You carry on like this and think yourself a man?"

She whacked his rear end, "Stop whining."

She pushed the knife hard against his throat and smacked his rear until Raza crawled on all fours toward the gallows with Moghavi riding him like a horse. Whenever he paused, or tried to speak, Moghavi would press on the sharp edge of the blade. Green Scarves strolled the route beside them as ahead Abbas was marched up the gallows platform, his wretched screeching perforating the hushed valley.

As Moghavi rode Raza down the road, women peeked around the destruction and watched, attempting to hold back children, some so bold they broke away and observed the progression close up, eventually joining the parade.

Kasey and Nasir kept a distance away as the noose was fixed around Abbas' neck. When Raza reached the platform stairs, it took a gun at his head to get him upright enough to be carried up.

The agonizing cries of the two became indistinguishable. Raza kept scheming, even as the noose tightened and tears ran down his face, "We can still ransom them together and all be rich-"

Abbas joined in the last desperate effort, "Think what it will buy your army ... " stopping cold when he saw Fajid's corpse, eyes open, staring up at him from the ground.

Moghavi took a seat on the platform stairs and rolled her eyes when Raza and Abbas continued pleading.

She circled a hand above her head.

Kasey and Nasir looked away.

A woman pulled the lever.

It took a long time for Kasey and Nasir to peek at the hanging corpses. By then, Moghavi was on the platform and Green Scarves grouped below in front of her. Kasey was curious. It seemed to be some kind of ceremony. She walked down the road, now inured to the carnage she passed. Nasir followed.

They beheld a woman handing Moghavi two black roses. Kasey watched the women congregate as if for a ritual. Moghavi held them up, "Reflect on this symbol of mourning for our sisters inside Iran." After a solemn pause, she pinned one to Raza's shirt, steadied Abbas' dangling body, and stuck the other inside his noose. "Men of Iran beware," she continued with pep talk enthusiasm, "we will hunt you until our veins are dry of blood."

The Green Scarves shouted approval. Some village women roamed closer and witnessed Moghavi shaking a fist, "We will contest them, now and forever!" Cheers and hand-clapping surged through the valley as soldiers holding the high and distant ground joined in.

Moghavi left the platform and approached the local women who shed their veils during the attack. They seemed relieved, like they were breathing outside air for the first time. Moghavi understood the look in their eyes, knew what was on their mind, "We are the National Revolutionary Army of Iran - Iranian citizens only."

It pained Moghavi to see their disappointment. She snapped her fingers and Green Scarves dashed over, offering their guns. The women were startled by the gesture. One hesitated, then grabbed a rifle. The rest took her cue, looking over the weapons with a sense of empowerment making them giddy.

"You can bury these men, but more will return," Moghavi told them. "You must make the valley yours while you have the chance. Take their arms, now. We'll show you how to use the big guns."

Kasey watched the village women break into smiles. Green Scarves lead them to the artillery in the hills, picking rifles and AK-47's from the corpses and handing them to women joining the march. Kasey knew she was bystander to something bursting out on a grand scale. The birth of a bold, muscular force to be reckoned with on the Mideast stage was exploding onto the radar screen. Moghavi was tapping into the deep subjugation of half the population, spreading discontent far past border skirmishes in the lonely desert. One day, somebody would have to significantly engage them. She pitied whoever had to. These women were much more savage, brave and irrational than any Mideast army of men she heard of. Maybe that was key to their success. How else could an army of women marauder across frontiers in a violent, unstable area of the world unless they were more ferocious than the men?

A girl stopped Moghavi and whispered in her ear. Moghavi patted her on the head and smiled, then hiked toward a kindling chest obstructed by a smoldering truck. Several Green Scarves followed. Moghavi waved off the oil fumes and opened the cover. She knew by the whimpering there was a man inside.

The women pulled him out. Kasey and Nasir watched, ready to turn away when it got ugly. Yet for now they couldn't help themselves. There was something so perversely compelling about the Green Scarves that was fascinating, even exhilarating in a morbid way that insisted attention.

They threw the man on the ground. Moghavi held her sword to the man's neck. She could smell fear on his breath, "Give me the right answer and you will live."

His eyes bulged, dreading the proposition.

Moghavi dropped her voice to a near whisper, "Can you *clean*?"

The man didn't say a word.

"I asked, can you *cl-ean*? Scrub and wash to perfection?"

"Yes ... yes," he hoped was the correct answer.

It was. Moghavi released the bewildered man and walked toward an outside latrine. Two Green Scarves towed him by his clothes along the ground behind Moghavi. Other women foraged through the wreckage of homes until they came up with a pail and scrub brush.

They filled the pail with well water, then thrust it and the brush into the man's hands in front of the outhouse.

"Go on," Moghavi spread her arms.

The man looked puzzled.

Moghavi grabbed him by the hair while two soldiers opened the door. Moghavi pushed him inside, on his knees and propelled his head into the filthy toilet.

"I want to see this place cleaned like it's never been cleaned before," Moghavi instructed, raising and plunging his head. "I want it cleaner than new!"

Waste matter and dirty water dripped from his face, "Yes, yes," he gagged.

Moghavi let him go. Green Scarves formed a circle, smirking while Moghavi reviewed his effort, "That doesn't look clean to me, better scrub harder."

Kasey and Nasir didn't need to speak about the grotesque events they were spectators to, only when their eyes met did they feel jolted from this surreal looking-glass world, rooted back to their reality by similar expressions communicating all a facial cast possibly could about these startling people.

Kasey noticed the village women's rapt attention on Moghavi grow bolder as they gradually joined the band of Green Scarves listening to Moghavi continuing to debase the man.

No matter what the future brought to Yanta, Kasey knew this visit by Moghavi would live on. The local women would either use it for inspiration to dominate the valley, bolstering their will with tales about the day the Green Scarves invaded. If the women instead were manipulated into subjugation by returning men, Moghavi's visit would always be remembered and displayed through some pattern of passive insubordination. In private moments, the Green Scarves exploits would be told to daughters, planting seeds for a more daring insurrection from a new generation. Regardless how the ramifications unfolded, the Bekka would never be the same.

No doubt, it was the birth of a legend. Human myth-making Kasey was certain Moghavi wouldn't care about if she had any sense of it underway. Of course, no myth is schemed. A legend is a material distillate wringing out a simple truth of existence, siphoning its energy so it forever spirals past the universally comprehended portentous time, place and circumstance of origin. What Kasey was witnessing this moment, as Moghavi again dunked and lifted the man's head at the toilet, was the truth about this legend in the making - she was a lunatic. The ritual at the latrine did more than hint at underlying psychological defect, it advertised it.

Kasey turned away and looked beyond the town to the airstrip where the seared skeleton of the plane sat. She put her head down and wiped away tears for the men who came for them, wondering how long they suffered and what, if anything, their families would learn about their heroism unless she returned to tell them.

Nasir placed a consoling arm around her. When Kasey looked up, Moghavi was punting the man onto his back and drawing her sword. Green Scarves pinned him down and held his mouth open. One grabbed his tongue and held it visible. Moghavi leaned over and before Kasey and Nasir could shield their eyes, she sliced it off.

It was so jarring and unbelievable a sight they refused to look toward the man contorting in agony. But they did hear Moghavi growl over his moans, "You go, go and tell-" Moghavi stopped, realizing the man wasn't going to be *telling* anybody anything, "you let the mullahs know we say they are cowards and we stand ready to have at them!"

With that, the Green Scarves backed away. The man got up holding his mouth and staggered off, in horrible pain yet emotionally elated to remain alive.

The Green Scarves loaded up. Moghavi headed to her tank, assigning another woman to drive and then calling to Kasey and Nasir. The Green Scarves amassed on foot and in vehicles near Moghavi, as her driver disappeared into the tank and revved its engine. Moghavi climbed on and took position peering out of the hatch. "Get on board, it's time to go home," she told Kasey and Nasir. They scrambled onto the tank and took positions on opposite sides of the cannon turret.

They left Yanta the way they came, on the north road. Moghavi's tank was in the middle of the convoy, nestling Kasey and Nasir in the bosom of one force no Mideast army of men wanted to encounter. Moving off, Kasey took a deep breath and savored the breeze on her face. For the first time since being kidnapped she felt protected.

Someone tuned a shortwave radio to an American golden oldies station and Kasey and Nasir watched foot soldiers do cartwheels and hand stands alongside them. Others sang along, mouthing words of songs in a language they didn't understand. Songs about young love, romantic envy and devotion between men and women. They would shimmy while hanging off transports and dance on the back of jeeps, gestures Kasey reasoned to be more a reaction to the joy of an emancipated life away from their fate inside Iran. She could grasp, even respect, why they were so ebullient. Anything was better than the destiny they left behind. They made a choice to live free and ready to die rather than to live long and enslaved.

The column slowed passing by the plane wreckage. Kasey stared, looking for a sign someone was miraculously alive. Moghavi absorbed the scene from her perch, "What went on here?"

"They came to rescue us," Kasey paused, choking up at the sight of human remains in the exposed interior.

"It was a set up," Nasir informed Moghavi.

"Stop!" Kasey yelled, jumping off the tank and running toward the plane. Moghavi ordered the convoy to halt.

Kasey leaned over the charred corpse of Bowers on the ground under the door of the plane. Nasir followed and stood over her, looking up at the bodies inside.

Moghavi approached trailed by foot soldiers.

"I want to bury them," Kasey said.

Moghavi paused, there was no sentimentality in her, but she was a soldier and held their valor and sacrifice in some regard.

Kasey insisted, "We have to do this."

"Without delay," Moghavi said, motioning for more soldiers.

They used a carrier with an attached trowel to start a hole on top of the nearest hill. A transport pulled up next to Kasey. She got on top of it and went into the

HONOR BOUND

plane, inching along intact sections of the frame. Nasir edged along behind her, wincing at what he saw. Green Scarves made shrouds out of tent awning and wrapped the corpses passed down a line of women.

On the airstrip, Kasey said a prayer over each soldier.

Moghavi joined Kasey, Nasir and others carrying the remains up the hill. Kasey went into the hole and arranged the soldiers next to each other. Extended hands pulled her out. She looked down at them, "Bowers, you were a better man than I ever thought. Moore, Harper ... all of you ... I will never forget what you did." Kasey had a blurry sense she was rambling. Inconsolable emotions made it a struggle to be coherent, "You were the best anyone could ever serve with," was all she could say to finish.

Moghavi snapped to attention and saluted. The Green Scarves followed her lead. Kasey and Nasir did the same. In that moment of stillness, Kasey couldn't help analyzing Moghavi's spontaneous gesture. She wondered, glancing indirectly at her, if those were tears in her eyes. Kasey faced her needing to know.

They were.

For a moment Kasey realized what this army saw in their unofficial leader, this anti-commander. Moghavi was pure out of control emotion, berserk over centuries of repression, serving as a lightning rod for the fury provoked by injustice, even if part of what was driving her came from some poisoned inner place. Kasey felt that under different circumstances she might have been one of them.

The carrier began filling the hole and the Green Scarves prepared to move out. Moghavi was gazing ahead on the road north, "I don't like this. These men were set up? We have a long trip ahead. I don't know what is out there waiting for us. We need to go through Syria. They already know we are here."

Kasey attentively listened to Moghavi's scheming. Her assessments had to be dazzling, if rate of success was any indication.

"We are too large to be contested by other than Syrian Berets. They won't risk losing any more to us. They need those divisions to protect the bosses," Moghavi surmised.

"Any more?" Kasey never heard of them battling with the Syrians.

226

"We took out a few Berets on the way here. Didn't plan to, but we had to," Moghavi paced. "Syria might be irritated about that, even though they know we're not out to have a war with them. My guess is logic will win out over anger. They'll keep Berets at home and if they come after us they'll only use grunts. It's only my guess."

Nasir knew it was a good one. No leader in the Mideast would forfeit a smidgen of protection for a bit of revenge.

"The wild card is how valuable the two of you are to them. Why did they have you brought to Lebanon? I don't think they would have been happy if you were executed. If we hadn't done in that bunch, Syria would have," Moghavi stopped and pondered. "I have a plan to guarantee safe passage."

Kasey watched a mad hell dance in Moghavi's eyes. She knew it was harbinger of havoc.

"Sweet, Low, over here," Moghavi shouted. Low lurched over and Sweet seemed to appear out of nowhere, spreading her deep smile to those around her.

"Take a hundred with you to Damascus. Bring dynamite and a change of clothes to blend in. Make some noise there. Do something to scare them so they'll keep security tight."

Interesting, Kasey thought. Moghavi left the plans vague enough for the women to be creative. It was confidence they would act in sum even when apart.

Nasir watched Sweet and Low get ready. He thought the plan could be bad news. Who knows what this pack might instigate? He had to address Moghavi, "Are you sure you want to do that?"

Moghavi got in his face, "I warned you, don't question me."

Nasir backed off.

Moghavi didn't, "Damascus is going to get a dose of Sweet and Low." She turned to the troops, "We're out of here!"

Sweet and Low rushed away ahead of them. Kasey and Nasir trailed Moghavi back to her tank and took their directed places flanking her.

Something made Kasey look behind when they left the Bekka for good. She had a fleeting view of the plane wreckage. When she lifted her eyes toward the burial site, a rolling wind kicked up and blew Bowers' hat over the mass grave.

She wished she could chase it down and bring it back to his family. But it drifted away.

Kasey stared at the horizon and shuddered at what could be ahead.

9

Rick briefly returned to the motel after trailing the trucks back to the laundry.
He took a shower, shaved and put on fresh jeans with a casual shirt. It was a calculated appearance to help him land a job at the laundry. He assumed they were seeking employees for the plant, not the office, so he wanted an appropriate look in place with applying for a job that likely paid little.

He went back to the laundry and parked in the rear by the loading dock. The three trucks that returned with barrels from the landfill remained in a corner of the lot. Rick walked in the front door to the reception desk, asked for an employment application and sat down to fill it out.

When he handed it back, the receptionist immediately led him into an office where he waited alone. Perfect, Rick thought, an instant interview. They probably needed help right away. Maybe he could start soon. He was ready with a fictional biography that had all the answers, right down to why he didn't have his Social Security card available (his wife just threw him out and a restraining order kept him away from the house where most of his things were).

Rick at once noticed the pictures mounted on the office wall. Most were framed photographs of an apparent career military man at different periods in his career.

He stood to inspect the more recent images. The military man resembled the person Rick witnessed overseeing activity at the dump around the laundry trucks.

"Hello, I'm Henry Coleman," a voice behind Rick said.

Rick spun around at who joined him in the office, the man in the photographs on the wall.

229

Suspicion confirmed - it was the white haired man he saw at the dump.

Rick extended his hand, "I'm Steve Andrews, glad to meet you."

Coleman went to his desk and Rick took the chair across from him. Coleman was reading the employment application, "I noticed you looking at the pictures. Were you in the service?"

"No." Rick gave an honest opinion, "It looks like you had quite a career."

"Retired a major. Ended my career here in my hometown at Fort Sellers," Coleman disclosed, looking over Rick's application. "I'd still be there if I wasn't forced out when the base changed over to a training ground. I came back to the family business and ended up taking it over when my brother retired. What's amusing about it all is that Fort Sellers then contracted out services and I ended up the laundry deal."

Rick couldn't have been happier. Coleman had no idea he was so divulging. "Well, it seems you've found a way to stay connected," Rick didn't know if he was trying too hard to be agreeable. Then again, it would it be unusual for a job applicant to act that way?

Coleman stood and looked over the photos. It seemed he did it often, judging how much sentiment he seemed to find in them, "Now I wash the uniforms of soldiers I once commanded," he said wistfully. He turned to Rick, "I'm willing to hire you. I can only pay minimum wage."

"I can't say I'll make a career out of it, but I need work right now. I'll start anytime."

"Is tomorrow good?"

"Hell, yes. Since my wife threw me out I've been looking for a job. I've been living out of my car. I need a job so I can get a place to live. I'd start right now if you wanted me to."

Coleman shrugged, "Might as well. We'll do your paperwork at the end of the day. Come on, I'll get someone to show you around."

Rick followed Coleman into the back where industrial sized washers and dryers hummed in aisles jammed with handcarts and wheeled racks. The place smelled like linen and soap powder. The employees at work seemed to be mostly recent immigrants. Except for the truck drivers who pulled in and out of the loading dock. They had the same cocked posture and swagger as Henry Coleman and were about his age. Maybe they were former military personnel? Coleman introduced the plant foreman. A man named Juan, probably from some Caribbean country, considering his accent. Juan explained the division of labor. Incoming is unloaded, invoiced and taken to the washers. Once done, they go to the dryers, then are either pressed, folded or racked and set aside in a corner by delivery route assignment.

Rick spent the rest of the morning unloading and washing the incoming. Through the receiving doors he was able to keep an eye on the three trucks with the barrels inside still parked where they were left in the early morning. Rick noticed the clean linens and clothes in the corner waiting to be trucked away. He saw racks of Army uniforms. Behind the rows of fatigues and formal dress, he caught sight of white lab coats and protective gear. He could see names of personnel tailored on them.

Late morning, an incoming truck brought a new load of wash from Fort Sellers. More uniforms. On separate racks, more protective clothing. Rick unloaded the truck, trying to remember the names he saw on the clothes as he pushed the laundry carts to the line waiting for free washers.

At noon, Juan explained that morning was all incoming from route drivers and afternoon work was loading the outgoing clean laundry. Drivers would be backing up trucks, the three trucks parked outside Juan pointed to, and the laundry loaded. For now, Juan said, it was time for a half-hour lunch break.

Rick watched the plant workers pile into vans outside and drive away. He lingered in a chair by the lockers in the rest room. All the machinery was turned off, so he listened. No footsteps, no voices, anywhere in the plant.

He quietly walked through the plant, looking to see anyone around. He strolled to the items heading out that afternoon, concluding the parked trucks would be loaded with the clothes, which would be delivered to Fort Sellers, where the barrels would be unloaded. He ran all the connecting events through his head. The barrels were from a textile plant, heading to a military base, a facility no longer involved in materials research and production. Then why was that section of the base active in the late hours of the night if Rick was told that part of the fort was inactive? There had to be cellulose acetate in those barrels.

What else could it be? Rick was so close ... but close to what? He fingered the uniforms and protective gear. This was evidence, he knew, scanning the names on the clothes ... Harris ... West ... O'Brien ... same names on the uniforms and gear, proving those wearing the lab clothes were soldiers. He looked over at the dirty wash from Fort Sellers. This could end up even better evidence. The clothes might have residue from whatever was happening in those late hours at the fort. If it had to do with plastic explosives, there might be indelible remains, those one of a kind markers Rick learned were as unique as DNA and even more telling because it could be date revealed by rate of decomposition. All he would ever need to know and to prove what was going on at Fort Sellers was here right now.

Rick looked over to the loading dock. The parking lot outside was quiet. He could see his car. He knew everybody would be returning soon.

This was his chance. He quickly wheeled the clean clothes onto the dock, then jogged back inside and brought out the soiled wash. He jumped off the platform and ran to his car, backing it up to the dock and leaving the engine idling. He popped the trunk and exited, climbing back onto the dock and tossing the clothes into the trunk. Then he leaped off, closed the trunk and drove off.

On the way out, he passed by those returning from lunch. Juan was driving a van. He locked eyes with Rick and laughed, probably guessing here was another guy who quickly decided the job wasn't for him. Rick turned onto the boulevard, dodging traffic without moving too fast. He kept checking behind him to see if anyone was on his tail as he thought out his plan. He was going to hurry back to the motel and check out. Then return his rented car in case someone quickly realized the theft and managed to remember his plate number while he was parked at work. He wasn't going to take a plane home. Someone might decide to stake out the airport. Unlikely, he knew, but that wasn't the only reason he decided to rent another car and drive all the way back. He didn't want to take the risk of shipping the clothes and having them lost or disappear mysteriously. He didn't want the items out of his possession, even it meant taking a pinch for stealing them. It was worth the risk for a story this big.

He was elated all his work was so close to a big payoff, smiling at how easy it was when the evidence was in front of him. Wasn't it just like the government?

Secrets being undone by bureaucratic compliance to contract out laundry services. Military secrets unattended inside a wash plant. Rick had a vision of Henry Coleman and his brigade of drivers fanning out in pursuit of him. Coleman would be livid because he'd probably be on the hook. Whatever mysterious relationship he had with covert activity going on at Sellers, he was into it up to his neck and no doubt would serve as fall guy. Whoever was ultimately behind it all would have to answer to another up the chain, and so on until they all piled on Coleman. Then again, the one Coleman was in league with was probably an Army cohort, someone who served with him before he was mustered out. They might scheme to cover up the theft and say nothing. In either case, the conspirators involved in illegal activity at Fort Sellers would know that someday, somehow, another shoe was going to drop regarding the matter.

***

After moving north out of Yanta, the Green Scarves slashed east through the Syrian desert, shunning the scene of the Beret massacre. They kept far north of Damascus, but did for a time commandeer the one thoroughfare leading there until they could pass laterally across. The occasional roadway traffic screeched to a halt well before the informal barriers once drivers detected scarves on the soldiers holding the ground. Cars, trucks, even a police wagon coming to investigate the situation all turned around and raced away.

The Green Scarves moved on through the night. Kasey and Nasir got into the back of a transport and tried to sleep among the women who took shifts as drivers and lookouts. They fought off exhaustion until late, apprehensive of dozing if an encounter with the Syrians broke out. It would have been a shorter route back to Iraq through Jordan, but Moghavi was wary. To her, Jordan was a "mushy" country, emasculated by outside influences. Everybody in the Mideast controlled some party lurking there, possibly ready to instigate destabilizing turmoil with a suicide attack aimed at them. Besides, Jordan was too near Israel and Moghavi had no desire to provoke their mettle.

233

Kasey and Nasir opened their eyes when the sun popped up in front of them on the horizon. Still no opposition from Syria. So far, Moghavi's judgment was sound.

The soldier's ritual was to have a morning break. They dug pits for their waste and handed around water jugs and sacks of fruit and nuts. Kasey nudged Nasir and pointed up at the vultures that seemed to follow the Green Scarves, as if aware that tagging along would eventually lead to a meal.

They pushed along under the scorching sun for hours without encountering a soul. In the early afternoon they paused at a small oasis to bathe, leaving it withered by the time they finished.

As the sun was setting, the Green Scarves approached the village of Al-Qarat, the only community in this wasteland, able to sustain a population only due to an ancient aqueduct channel built when the area was on a trade route. By the time they appeared on the desert horizon, their arrival had been announced by the scores of buzzards that already flew into in the village. They circled above, nestled in trees and perched on tops of buildings. They had come to know the Green Scarves very well. Precede them into the nearest population center and wait for the eventual feast. Once they appeared, the few cars and trucks in the village hurried in the opposite direction and a stream of men on foot fled in every direction but the one the vultures came from.

Rolling into Al-Qarat, girls and women lined the road gaping at Moghavi who stood up in her tank and declared, "Islam does not ask women to be men's servants! They do not own you! They lie about Islam, twisting it to make you believe what they demand!"

The females clustered around Moghavi's tank. Kasey sensed recognition in their eyes, confirmed when one woman pulled from under her robe a black rose, made from paper with a coat hanger stem. She handed it to Moghavi. The women following along who removed their veils were presented with guns by approving Green Scarves, who gave instant lessons on use, pointing out mechanics and firing bullets into the air.

Moghavi decided to camp for the night. Green Scarves set up guard posts on the perimeter and lit a bonfire in town after sunset. Kasey had an idea where they must be, determining that before another day went by they would be in

Iraq's Badiyat Ash-Sham section, the desert extension of the Saudi Arabia's Empty Quarter, only a figurative stone's throw from American forces on the Saudi side of the border. Kasey and Nasir sat with Moghavi by the fire under the cool, clear sky. Village women boiled kettles of rice and Green Scarves roasted chickens and vegetables over the flames. Moghavi tuned a radio to the BBC broadcast from Cypress, a good source of Mideast news. Kasey spent the time gawking at the Green Scarves' hardware. It was an astonishing piecemeal mishmash. Jerry-rigged artillery launchers patchworked from American, Soviet and French scraps. Tanks and transports assembled from different era bits of chassis and armor from British, Chinese, Italian, Cuban, American and Soviet, always American and Soviet pieces more than anything else, the two countries being the largest arms suppliers in the world. Nasir scanned the landscape of women stretching as far as he could see. "So huge," he said under his breath, almost to vent his amazement.

Moghavi heard him, "It didn't happen overnight," she informed him in a tone of portent.

"Remember ibn Saud, *what goes around, comes around.*"

He understood.

"You can't continue to be ignored for much longer," Kasey knew worse people than Moghavi had obtained political legitimacy in the world. "You need diplomacy to bring your cause to the international stage."

"We tried that," Moghavi shrugged, "the UN says we have no political base and others say we are too unstable." She stood up and spread her arms toward the Green Scarves, "Too unstable? Can you believe it!"

No following in world body politic meant any supporters of *significance.* Who would possibly champion their way of doing things? So, instead of being worked into the international system, they were becoming greater outlaws, which would, no doubt, stimulate more extreme methods for achieving goals or simply surviving. A never-ending circle, and another reason for them to get cozy with Saddam. Both understood the pariah psychology.

Moghavi sat down again, "If America recognized us, others would follow."
She let out a sour chuckle, "We all know America isn't Iran's enemy. They talk
as if they are while they act like chums."

Kasey felt Moghavi was way off base, "Not true. If you really knew America-"
Moghavi interrupted, "I *know* America quite well ... I am an American citizen."

It was traumatic, dismaying, baffling and so ... Mideast. Kasey stuttered,
"You're an American citizen?"

"Yes, but I prefer to be known as founder of the National Liberation Army of
Iran."

Kasey wondered if the US government knew Moghavi was a citizen. If they
did, they certainly weren't publicizing it.

Moghavi tossed a cup of cold coffee on the ground and seemed pensive, "I was
born in Tehran. When I was five, the Ayatollah came to power. My parents
were college teachers. My father ... "

The words gripped the air for a long time. Kasey swore she sensed burden in
Moghavi's pause.

" ... My father supported the revolution. My mother, like other women, was
thrown out of her job. Women in Iran aren't allowed to be productive outside
the home. Educating girls isn't a priority. They remain trapped in the chador,
forbidden to look a man in the eyes. The progress of women has been reversed."

The women nearby leaned closer to Moghavi, as if her story was the archetype
for all their lives.

"My mother refused to accept the new rules. She spoke out against the regime.
My father divorced her, cast us both from our home saying I was poisoned as
well. The rest of our family turned their backs on us. We lived as beggars. My
mother wouldn't be silenced, speaking out on the streets of Tehran. The
religious police warned her once. When she didn't stop they hauled her into an
alley and cut her tongue out," Moghavi stopped. Kasey thought she was looking
older as she took a subdued breath, "I was made to watch as a warning."

Nasir gazed at the Green Scarves and more than anything saw the glee of rage
in their eyes. He turned away to resist a creeping empathy, or fear.

"At the hospital, they treated a man with a sprained ankle before my mother.
After that, she decided to leave Iran. She did it for me. Borders were sealed, so

we went south and walked through the desert into Iraq. The Kurds let women coming over the border stay with them. A group of us walked to Baghdad. It took almost a month. Saddam let humanitarian organizations resettle us. We went to Turkey. It wasn't a friendly place. Then to Greece and finally America. A Christian church in Iowa gave us a place to live. My mother, with four college degrees, needed to work. She got a job cleaning septic tanks. She knew she could do better eventually, but a mute alien in a strange place with a child had to take whatever came along. Her first day on the job, she breathed too much methane, got dizzy and fell into a tank. People were nearby, but she couldn't scream. Before long, she was dead."

Moghavi pulled her head away from the light cast by the fire and disappeared into the privacy of darkness. Nobody was going to witness tears and nobody struggled to have a look at the disembodied voice, "I was adopted. They were good people. Made me a citizen. To assimilate, as it's called. Didn't work. I was out of control."

Her face darted into view, "When I was eighteen, I left America with money I saved from working a summer job. Flew to Athens and made my way to Iraq." Moghavi's timbre fluttered, "I wanted the mullahs to pay for what they did!" Passionate energy drove her to pace, which quieted her tone, "Saddam was at war with Iran. I volunteered to help. For a year, I went in and out of Iran as a spy and brought back information about their troop placements."

Moghavi picked at a piece of chicken, "I roughed it alone in the salt desert between Iraq and Iran. After every battle between them, I gathered up what was left behind, even if it was busted. I was the first person fleeing Iranian women met on the other side of the border. I knew their feelings. Many decided to stay with me. We learned how to repair things and fend for ourselves. Then that war ended. But things in Iran didn't change, so the women kept coming. We kept growing under Saddam's nose when he was preoccupied by his war with America. Women started leaving Iran because they heard about us. We learned together how to use guns, tanks and artillery and we trained hard."

It was getting cold. Moghavi again sat be by the fire. She looked weary to Kasey. There was no grandeur in her inflection, only toil and toll.

237

"We started making forays into Iran. We'd cross the border and hit a village. Take weapons, food, whatever we had to have. More women would join us. Eventually the men sent a division after us. We wiped them out. Even then, they had no idea of our size. Now we are over 25,000 strong. Some remain at our base camp in the desert. When we get back, there will be more waiting to join us. Saddam is happy we're there. We're his buffer."

Moghavi stared at Kasey and Nasir, "He asked us to find you. He knew he'd be blamed for anything that happened to you. He offered us things we need if we succeed. So we took up the offer. It was time to find out how good an army we are." Moghavi was silent. She slowly peered at the Green Scarves, "Not bad, I have found. Not bad at all."

During Moghavi's satisfied pause Nasir almost sympathized with this vagabond army. Moghavi had such a trenchant analysis of things, she had to know she was doomed. Changes were underway inside Iran. Moderates were gaining power and the country relaxing its strict Muslim fundamentalism. And did she think Saddam was really a friend? For now he may seem to be, but there were a million what ifs to that and someday one of those what ifs would test their relationship. Even if it didn't, a time would come when Saddam was no longer around. What would that mean for the Green Scarves? With no war to fight with Iran and no harbor inside Iraq, what would they do? Nasir saw no way they could disarm, go back home and lead normal, quiet lives. Iran would ever have them. No, Moghavi was in denial some place inside. Nasir shivered envisioning a massive suicide mission sending the Green Scarves and many others down in flames. There was no attitude but sorrow in his voice when he said, "Be careful, you are making new enemies."

"I weighed the factors," it was the first time Moghavi didn't address Nasir in a short-tempered way. "What we stand to gain outweighs the disadvantages."

"It was a big risk," Kasey meant it in gratitude. "You could have suffered losses."

"Saddam pledged future supplies of oil," Moghavi said with a trace of delight. "That got our attention."

It only took that to entice them? Nasir shrugged, "You say it as if he offered gold."

"It's worth more than that now."

It made no sense to Nasir, "In this part of the world? You know there's plenty." Moghavi felt he was being deceitful. She was annoyed, "Who are you kidding, ibn Saud? We both know it is *all but gone.*"

Kasey and Nàsir heard her, but refused to let the words sink in. To consider it, never mind believe it, would upset the paradigm of their reality. There was a slack-jawed void, a gawking non-acceptance outwardly directed at Moghavi, but in truth aimed at their defenses. A lag in reaction to brace the psyche for news that could change life in an instant.

Outrage finally exploded past Nasir's inner bulwark, "If it was true, I would know it!"

Moghavi didn't know what was behind his artifice. She did know no man raises his voice to her. She stood up and approached Nasir, "Then you have been fed lies. All that's left in Saudi Arabia is a trickle. Saddam's southern fields are dry. They feed from the same source. All he has left is in the north."

Nasir leaped to his feet, "It is you who have been fed lies!"

While he expressed insult, Kasey examined Moghavi's somber claim. "Wait a minute," she reasoned out, "when we met Saddam, it was at an abandoned refinery in the south." Her mind was racing to a conclusion, "He mentioned the other matter facing Iraq and Saudi Arabia. We wondered what it was. The meeting place, his words, were sending a message." Then another revelation, "Why, I remember the kidnappers having problems finding fuel."

Nasir was nauseous as his body hopelessly tried to fend off all he was hearing. The ground whirled and he almost lost balance when he put his hands over his ears and stumbled away. He was only a few feet from Kasey and Moghavi but in a hellish, isolating confrontation with himself. When he faced them, there was devastation carved into his face. "I saw my brother kill a man for only talking about the oil being gone," he whispered.

"That man knew something you don't seem to," Moghavi said it in pity. "When Saddam's fields went dry he discovered the plastic explosives passing through Iraq. He knew it was some kind of set up. He was trying to let you know he was on to it."

Kasey couldn't see any reason for Moghavi to lie. The logic was falling into place. "Please, let's not stop for the night," she urgently begged. "We need to get back. The United States needs to know this!"

Moghavi chuckled and shook her head, "You still don't get it. America is behind it all. They're helping the Saud's abdicate."

It was a vile accusation to Nasir, "You accuse my family of deserting the nation they created! Never!"

Kasey was furious, all but turning in circles, "Oil all gone? Why would America be hiding it? My country wouldn't do that!"

What a blinded pair, Moghavi thought, "America wants favor with Islamic fundamentalists. They believe it's the future of the region. A Saudi revolution has been planned inside Iran. It's going down while the Mecca pilgrims are there. America is the accommodating intermediary, even moving arms to the insurgents. Doing it through Iraq lets them blame Saddam if it's discovered. America told the royal family a revolt couldn't be put down. In exchange for negotiating the royals peacefully leaving, the Sauds will take the blame for hiding the facts about the oil being gone. America will get credit with the new regime in Arabia for avoiding bloodshed and effecting a smooth transition. And the US will say they knew nothing about the oil being gone. For fundamentalists, the symbol of a religious state in the homeland of Islam is all they care about. They believe it will incite more revolution."

Kasey screamed, as if it could block out what was striking her ears, "America would be ordering its people out! They would be warning the public at home to prepare for a fuel crisis!"

Nasir joined the howling, "Your lies are outrageous!" He shook a finger in Moghavi's face, "You slander my family!"

That's when the Green Scarves went for their guns. One flung herself at Nasir and knocked him on his back. Kasey and Nasir were surrounded, guns trained on them, bewildered, alarmed, denying, delirious and pulsating with countless other emotions leaving them red faced and cross-eyed.

Moghavi was calm. She motioned the soldiers to ease off.

"Believe whatever you wish," she told them both. "You'll see."

Nasir shouted, "Why should I believe you?" How do you know all this?"

I know what I need to know to survive," Moghavi explained, walking away. "We break camp at morning light."

Nasir's growing sympathy for the Green Scarves vanished. If Moghavi was right, it was not she who was doomed, it was he. He picked himself off the ground and watched her stroll away. If what Moghavi said was fact, then not only was there a place for the Green Scarves in the Mideast's future, they were the future. A boutique army held together by a uniting factor that was immutable - gender. While the rest of the Mideast would become impoverished due to loss of resources, the Green Scarves would endure. As the social fabric of fossil fuel nations broke down, the Green Scarves would endure. As anarchy took hold in countries unable to afford sustaining order, the Green Scarves would thrive. They could set terms, aligning with whatever party would do the most for them. They could even go it alone, likely able to grab land and call themselves a nation. No, Moghavi wasn't doomed, it was everybody else.

Kasey and Nasir were looking for warm place to talk things over when a BBC radio announcer started reporting the news of the day: "In Damascus, a bomb blast killed nine cabinet ministers today. Sixty others are reported dead. Syria vows retaliation against Israel, calling it new Zionist aggression ... "

The murmur among Green Scarves who understood English drowned out the rest of the words. The women translated for others. Kasey and Nasir watched collective smiles become giggles. Word quickly passed through the village and the murmur grew into laughter. Green Scarves tumbled, flipped and danced in ecstasy as the noise became a booming shriek of jubilation. Kasey and Nasir knew why. What happened in Damascus was, no doubt, the work of Sweet and Low.

Kasey gazed in frozen in amazement at the reaction. Nasir could only plant his head in hands. Each knew what a strange world the Mideast could be, but neither believed it would ever be an incomprehensible one.

***

Clayton Amfrick went directly to the American Embassy when he arrived in Saudi Arabia. He had Secretary of State Drake postpone her daily briefing with

General Zalman. Instead, Drake asked that a courier drop off the latest military intelligence. Personnel wise, it was getting even thinner at the embassy compound. All who remained were either soldiers staffing the perimeter gates, or Walker's people, "diplomatic security," who now performed the ordinary tasks, like meeting Amfrick and his escorts at the door.

Drake, Walker and Howe were looking over the intelligence when Amfrick entered the ambassador's office. There were spare greetings. His presence only amplified the unspoken tension they were feeling over what Zalman sent over.

Amfrick noticed the strained faces. He joined the three of them standing over the spread of aerial reconnaissance photos accompanied by Zalman's notes.

Howe was jittery. In equal parts due to Amfrick's company and the circumstances unfolding around him. He was the only one to try small talk, "How's the campaign going?"

"Very well," Amfrick was absorbed in analysis of the data.

"And the energy situation?"

Amfrick looked up at him, "Not a problem."

"Nobody's suspicious?"

Howe evidently wasn't going to be quiet without some calming words. Not good news to Amfrick. If the ambassador was already this uneasy, how would he hold up when a revolution broke out all around him? Amfrick had a seat and gestured for Howe to do the same. "Right now, the public is only experiencing price increases. The president has attributed it to OPEC, saying it is a temporary decrease in production to get a greater price for crude. It's happened before. No one is alarmed."

Drake watched Amfrick spin away. Things are getting bad when an administration has to spin its own, she thought. She disliked Amfrick, this party planner now orchestrating events on the world stage. Drake snickered inside at Amfrick's vanity. He was so intent on exhibiting his individuality that he had no idea his red, white and blue dotted bow tie made him look like a bad caricature of Uncle Sam. More like a cartoon character produced in a country with an exaggerated, off the mark idea of America. His eyeglass frames were so excessive his eyes looked like grain pellets. Drake looked over at Walker. He was staring at Amfrick from the moment he entered the room. Who could ever tell what Walker was thinking? She knew he was their man in Saudi Arabia, but was there any way he for him to welcome Amfrick's camaraderie?

Amfrick lingered over the intelligence, coming to see what was unsettling the others. He was having a hard time concentrating because Howe was tapping his fingers on the table. More annoying, there was no rhythm to it. Amfrick knew Howe was way out of his league dealing with what was happening in Saudi Arabia. He didn't know it was this bad, the man was all loose ends way too soon. When the president pushed Howe for the Saudi post, it was a manageably stable place, as far as America knew. When the truth was discovered, it became important not to make an ambassadorial change. It would attract attention, maybe not at the time, but later, when plausible deniability had to survive deconstruction. "Rest assured ambassador," Amfrick softly said, "it will be a while before any questions are asked. For some time, other oil producing countries will provide enough once Saudi Arabia is drip dry."

Maybe it was true. It could be a lie. Either way, it didn't matter. Howe wasn't curious or concerned about what was going on at home, he was terrified about his safety once things got dicey and he knew that day of reckoning was near. It was something he didn't have the courage to reveal, so he disclosed it by variant apprehension.

Amfrick had been keeping sharp eye on Saudi Arabia for months. Since Drake arrived, she had been faxing Zalman's intelligence to the White House, so Amfrick was quite up to speed. He knew how to interpret what he was in front of him and didn't like what he was seeing. "The army of women rocked in Lebanon," he grimaced. "What were they doing there? Isn't there war with Iraq?"

"Maybe they wanted at Hezbollah," Drake guessed.

"It's where our soldiers were lost. Is it a coincidence they would then show up there?" Amfrick got up and walked to a window. "We know they are tight with Saddam. Could he have sent them after Captain Lawrence?"

"All our people there are dead," Walked coldly said. To intimate otherwise was a threat to him and the agency. It insinuated they were passing along incorrect information.

Amfrick surprised them all with the alarm in his voice, "All we have is pictures. It's really not much proof."

"Are you afraid they'll drop Captain Lawrence on our doorstep?" Drake liked seeing Amfrick squirm.

"It would be ... *unanticipated*."

Amfrick went on, "The women are heading back into Iraq-"

Drake interrupted, "Wouldn't the return of any missing soldier be a great day for America?"

Walker knew Drake was goading Amfrick. He wouldn't let her idea be considered, "It's not going to happen."

"You say it like you don't want it to happen," Drake was now needling them both.

Amfrick knew exactly what was going on, "You're both right," he smiled. "Madam Secretary, it would be a great day if one of our presumed lost made it back. And our station chief is sadly correct, it's not going to happen."

Amfrick gazed out the window at the compound. The embassy grounds were quiet, the parking lot empty and the rest of the building silent. It was what he expected as indication things were progressing nicely. "I'm afraid if that army moves into the southern Iraq no-fly zone they could be a threat to our troops in Saudi Arabia," Amfrick faced the three. "Who know what they could be up to? The president will need to take action if that happens."

Drake knew what he was really saying. He would take no chance seeing Captain Lawrence return alive.

Walker also knew what Amfrick meant. That CIA analysis couldn't be trusted. There was no way Amfrick would be proved right. The agency wasn't going to have egg on their face over this one. He wouldn't permit the resurrection of his career being derailed.

***

Outside the palatial estate of King Khaled, a Guard division filled a moving van with the king's property. Prince Rakan directed the crew, made up of younger Guard members, while armed protectors shut off the surrounding area. Rakan ursurped curiosity by explaining the move as necessary for palace renovations. As one packed truck was ready to pull away, the driver leaned out the window and handed Rakan a thermos filled with coffee, "You've been here all day. You need this to keep going," he said before driving off.

Rakan put the thermos aside to direct another rig through the palace gates. He kept close watch on the men carting the valuables from the palace, lending a hand with those struggling to get the frame of a Louis XVI canopy bed up the truck ramp. Once it was inside, he invited them to take a break. One noticed the container and thought it was for them. He picked up the thermos, unscrewed the lid and poured coffee into the plastic cup. Steam rose as he moved it to his lips. Before he swallowed, there was an explosion. It detonated with such force it propelled the man through the granite palace wall and left him, or what was left of him, inside on the marble floor. Outside, men were strewn all over ground, either unconscious or contorting in agony.

Rakan was inside the palace when the bomb detonated. His ears were ringing as he ran to the entrance and saw the dead body. He stepped around it and found chaos outside.

Uninjured Guard members kneeled, tending the casualties. At least two more were dead.

He grabbed his pistol and shouted, "What happened!"

A wounded man looked up as blood trickled down his head, "Something blew up."

Rakan stared at the hole in granite. The Guard waited for his orders. He took too long.

An uninjured man took charge, "Get an ambulance!" Somebody was about to call for one when Rakan grabbed him, "No! We'll get the doctors to come here."

Rakan feared word of an attack at the royal palace would get out. It would lead to questions. People would whisper. The king was moving his property? A bomb at the palace? Combined with other recent events, who knows what would happen next? That's what was on Rakan's mind. The howls of the wounded men never struck his ears.

The Guard took initiative to disobey. They picked up the injured and started placing them in the truck.

"Don't do that," Rakan demanded.

They ignored him, pushing by and helping the less injured to their feet. The Guard hurled the king's belongings out of the truck. Rakan tried to stop the destruction of property. He darted about, pushing the items aside and ordering some to remain behind and continue the moving job.

A man pointed his rifle at Rakan and told him to shut up. He kept aim until all the injured were loaded. Then he jumped into the back and the truck drove away. Rakan was alone. He carefully wiped splattered flesh from the king's jewel studded armoire.

***

Moghavi watched a compass until certain the Green Scarves crossed over into Iraq. Back on friendly ground, she called the procession to a stop. Kasey and Nasir took water with the soldiers. It was only late morning, yet it felt as if the sun had evaporated every aqueous trace inside their bodies. Moghavi stood off alone, close enough to her base up north to establish radio contact with Green Scarves holding down the sanctuary. She held a receiver to her ear, learning Sweet and Low returned to the home redoubt. Peering at the southern skyline, she made a decision to send most of the women back to camp, telling them there was no need to move the whole army through the burning desert when they were so near the Saudi border. She kept a division of three hundred with her and the rest moved on. Moghavi watched them head north. Was something making her restive? Kasey wondered, sitting on the edge of Moghavi's tank and watching her roost on the hatch cover. Was there a vague dread in the air the way Moghavi kept looking over her shoulder at most of the disappearing army? Maybe it made her feel exposed, that's why she vigilantly squinted at the southern sky.

The unit forged southeast through the sand toward Saudi Arabia. Halfway through the afternoon, sonic booms thundered ahead in the shriveled expanse like distant fireworks. Moghavi called for a jeep to ride beside them. The noise roared again, this time closer and so loud Kasey and Nasir covered their ears and felt the earth tremble. Kasey tried to read Moghavi's countenance.

Was she contemplating? "Probably reconnaissance," Kasey clued her. "We must be near the no-fly."

"We've passed the 36th parallel," Moghavi already knew. "Less than two hundred kilometers to go."

A shrieking clatter sent all eyes upward. A squadron of military jets plunged from above and flew by them. Moghavi looked closely through binoculars. When she pulled them away, there was new unease etched in her visage.

Kasey heard them returning. She motioned for the binoculars and caught a quick glimpse, "US Air Force," her heart swelled with anticipation. "They know we're here!"

The planes vanished on the southern horizon. The Green Scarves moved forward. Again, jets descended, this time gliding lower and slower. Kasey stood on top of the tank and furiously waved as they went by.

Moghavi slowed the convoy's pace, warily observing the sky, "I sent the soldiers home so everybody could see we're not trying to be threatening," Moghavi spelled out gaps in her strategy. "They must know that."

Kasey sensed doubt in Moghavi's words. Then the desert semblance churned so violently it emptied the quivering ether from the vista as a different formation of jets dipped from the sky.

Kasey knew what they were, "Oh my god," she turned to Moghavi and shouted, "bombers!"

Moghavi screamed, "Everybody on the ground!"

Within seconds, they were hit with a sizzling barrage. One bomb scored a direct hit on a troop carrier, torching those inside.

The aircraft departed, but Moghavi ordered the Green Scarves to stay prone. Soon enough, the formation returned for another sortie and blistered them again. Moghavi jumped onto her tank in rage, shaking her fist above and howling, "One plane! All my tanks for one plane! Oh, what I could do!"

Kasey and Nasir were in front of her, crouched under the tank's chassis. They gaped at each other while listening to Moghavi's reckless wrath.

The planes answered her statement with an encore. Moghavi raged on, holding hands on hips and mocking them.

In a bizarre way, Nasir was comforted by Moghavi's actions as he tried to detect the direction of another nearing roar. Somehow, he knew the bombs would never hit Moghavi, that no aftermath would touch her. It never happens to those who challenge mayhem. Those who are taken out are the ones who righteously fear their predicament and run for shelter or try to flee the bedlam.

An explosion near the artillery regiment detonated ammunition, spraying it in random directions and crippling several women.

That was all Moghavi was going to take. She jumped from her tank and went to the jeep beside it, "This is as far I am going," she told Kasey and Nasir, gesturing to nearby soldiers for containers of gasoline and water. The women tied them in the back as the sky grumbled anew. "Take it and go," Moghavi demanded.

Nasir looked up and hesitated. Moghavi grabbed her gun, "Go now, I say! Go!"

Kasey and Nasir scrambled to the jeep and sped off as the aircraft bashed the Green Scarves again.

The jets roared away on the south horizon. Moghavi turned the division around and moved north. She avoided looking at the dead by turning at the fleeing Kasey and Nasir, "Two of a kind, they are. Thrown together to die together," she muttered to no one. Then she turned away and shrugged, "Good luck."

Nasir drove while Kasey caught a final glimpse at the Green Scarves disappearing on the northern horizon, "Command must have gotten nervous seeing Moghavi heading their way," Kasey decided. Then she produced the bullet Saddam gave them and handed it to Nasir, "You take this, you'll be in a better position to find out who made the marks on it." Kasey stared ahead, knowing the Saudi border wasn't far, "Just think Nasir, you will soon see your son."

Kasey paused when she noticed the anguish on his face. "I am taking him from that institution," he said with certainty.

"He's in an institution?" Kasey was stunned. "Why?"

"His legs," Nasir's voice cracked, "He'll never walk right."

"You sent him away because of that?" Kasey frowned in disbelief, "How come?"

"So his life would be easier."

"I was born with no opening between my nose and throat. No doctor gave my family hope I would overcome it. My father never set any limits on my life. She championed his son, "Do not lower expectations for him. Raise them!"

Nobody ever demanded such a thing from of Nasir, "You overcame problems like that?"

"Not problems, challenges. Accept no limits, Nasir. *No limits!*"

Nasir was silent. When he was about to say something when a sickeningly familiar sonic boom pulsated ahead of them. Then the planes emerged, developing like a ghostly vision. This time they flew so low Kasey and Nasir could make out the United States Air Force symbol on their tails.

Kasey knew the crew had a way to identify them. She leaped from the jeep and stood under the formation, waving and pointing at her uniform. The jets dropped a line of bombs. One exploded yards away from the jeep, propelling it off the ground and sending Kasey and Nasir into the air.

When Kasey came to, the last thing she remembered was crashing into the ground. She had no idea how long she was unconscious. Her head was pounding and her skin hurt from a deep burn caused by lying in scalding sand under a roasting sun. She sat up, unable to swallow due to dehydration. Before searching for water, she looked for Nasir. He was motionless on his back some distance away. Kasey stumbled over and found him breathing, but she couldn't rouse him. She had a look at the burned out jeep and saw a water jug siting next to it, tipped over and dribbling away a vital resource. She lurched over and wet her lips with a finger. When she picked up the container, she knew they were in trouble. It was near empty. She carried it to Nasir and sprinkled water over his face, checking his body for obvious injury. She alternated between sipping water and pouring some down Nasir's throat, calling his name and tapping his face. He didn't stir, except to briefly twitch, a good sign of no spinal damage. Kasey knew they had to be moving on. The border was somewhere ahead. They had to get there. They needed water, Nasir needed medical attention and neither would survive the elements for long.

HONOR BOUND

She prowled around the jeep wreckage and found some charred rope. She brought it over to where Nasir was and again unsuccessfully tried to awaken him. She pulled him up and tied his hands together in front of him. She finished off the remaining water by drinking some and splashing the rest on Nasir's face.

Kasey took a deep breath and stared south. Then she leaned down and draped Nasir over her back with his tied hands around her neck, a drill she knew from training as the way to transport casualties. She stood up. Nasir's feet scraped the ground as she walked. It wasn't his weight on her back that troubled her, it was the terrible quiet. She needed sound to engage her senses, impressions to stay alert. So she spoke out loud to sustain her consciousness, "We got into this together, we'll get out of it together, Nasir," she said, carrying on an imaginary conversation.

She took moderate, uniform strides under the wilting sunshine. Talking soon used up too much energy, so she focused on the sound of Nasir's dragging feet and kept her eyes peeled on the horizon.

Kasey began counting time. Seconds, minutes, hours. The sun was level on the western skyline. Dusk would soon come and that wasn't good news. Too easy to lose direction and even a slight veering would mean dire consequences.

Nasir's mass started to cause her knees to buckle. Pauses for breath became more frequent, eventually becoming panting for air as she relentlessly advanced. The first time she felt her eye lids shut sent her into another round of nervous verbalization meant to stimulate her wits. She broke into a chant female recruits would shout out during a long boot camp hike:

Used to wear a mini skirt
One ... Two ... Three ... Four
Now I'm rolling in the dirt
Two ... Three ... Four
Used to paint my pretty nails
Three ... Four
Now I'm crawling like a snail

She recited the rhyme until her mouth was dried out and her lips became parched and cracked. Every pause brought panic. Breathing became an unimaginable struggle. She was aware her eyes retracted for a moment. She wanted to shout, but could only whisper, "No ... never," and push ahead. After a few more steps, she fell to her knees and dropped face first into the sand with Nasir on her back.

Less than five miles away across the Saudi border, a US Army sergeant and corporal were positioned at the isolated outpost on the road to Badanah. They were the same two sentries that observed Kasey and Nasir go by on the way to meeting with Saddam. The corporal, surveying the Iraq frontier through binoculars, spotted vultures circling aloft in the distance, "Something is out there."

The sergeant took a look, "The Air Force was pounding earlier. Might be casualties."

Both stared, observing the vultures' orbit slightly descend. Neither liked the idea of someone hurt but alive so close to them. Each knew it was on the other's mind. "You know the orders," the sergeant reminded, "never cross the border."

"Yeah," the corporal knew what he had to do. "I'm calling Command." He tried to raise General Zalman in Badanah, but there was only static, "The bombers must have brought the skip in."

"Skip" is when transmissions through the atmosphere become erratically conveyed or interrupted. It could be due to storms, prevailing winds, the aurora borealis, sunspots, or what man sends into the sky. The sergeant kept an eye on the vultures while the corporal tried Command again. No luck. The corporal was troubled. He didn't want to stand by and allow someone to die, not even an Iraqi conscript. "I want to have a look," he said after thinking it over.

It was also eating away at the sergeant, "You'll need to say I was in the crapper when you left."

The corporal took his gun and radio to a Humvee, "I'll be quick."

It wasn't until he closed in under the vulture's orbit that he detected a speck in the sand. He accelerated once he saw it was a human. No, he saw two when he hit the brakes.. Rushing over, he saw they were wearing uniforms. He kneeled and saw Nasir's face. It seemed familiar. He recognized the Saudi insignia as he separated Nasir's hands from around the neck of the other body and examined the torso, "My god, it's Captain Lawrence!" He checked their vital signs. Both were alive, but with barely a pulse. He picked teeming scorpions from their exposed flesh, the insects raising their tails in strike mode as he pushed them away. The he quickly found a cloth to wipe off the vulture droppings covering them. He got on the radio, "Sergeant, do you hear me?" No reply.

"Sergeant ... Sergeant!"

Through the crackling interference he faintly heard, "Go on."

"It's Captain Lawrence and the Saudi. They're unconscious, but alive."

US military personnel tuned to the same frequency from the border to Badanah stopped all activity and listened. Did he say Captain Lawrence? One who heard the corporal loud and clear was the communications specialist on duty with the remaining members of Kasey's unit, who were still probing the silica between Badanah and the Empty Quarter. They heard nothing official about Captain Lawrence being missing, but there were rumors, and as far as they knew, Moore, Harper, Bowers and their buddies were still in Bahrain. The specialist shouted and the squad clustered around the radio. The gossip must have contained some truth. The captain seemed to be in trouble. They tried calling both the sergeant and corporal, but neither responded.

The corporal gave up trying to contact the sergeant. "I'm bringing them back," he declared on the off chance he could be heard. He lifted Kasey and carried her to the Humvee, upset with himself for not bringing water. He gently set her in the vehicle and ran to Nasir. Leaning over him, he felt airborn sand. His words must have gotten through. Help was coming. He motioned so the approaching speck could see him. Counting four of them, he noticed they weren't familiar vehicles, but some kind of civilian all terrain transportation.

The vehucles stopped and several men dashed out. The corporal had no idea who they were. Alexander Walker looked concerned marching over with his "diplomatic security" colleagues.

"Great job, corporal. We'll take over here," Walker said, directing his associates to get Kasey and Nasir.

The corporal didn't like the vibe, "Who are you?"

"CIA," Walker waved embassy identification. "Captain Lawrence is on assignment for us."

The corporal was leery. "You did a good job locating them," Walker complimented him as two of his men took Kasey from the Humvee. "But you'll get in trouble for being out here. We can get them help faster."

The corporal tried his radio again, "Sergeant, I have CIA here. They want to take them. Do you read?"

Nothing but white noise.

Kasey's unit didn't like what they heard in the corporal's tone. Again, they attempted to radio him and got no response. They made a collective decision to head over the border.

The corporal watched Kasey and Nasir being placed in Walker's vehicles. He went with his instinct and reached into the Humvee for his gun. Before he grabbed it, Walker shouted, "Don't do it!"

The corporal turned and found all the men aiming pistols at him. One walked to the Humvee and took the corporal's gun and radio. Another shot out the Humvee's tires. Walker tossed him a canteen of water, "You'll get back all right."

Walker's bunch sped off with Kasey and Nasir. The corporal watched them move southeast, a direction away from any road or guard post. Something told him it was the last time anyone would see Kasey and Nasir alive. He shivered as he stared.

Then he heard a mechanical roar far enough behind Walker's convoy he had to turn his head to see where it was coming from. Two Strikers raced behind four jeeps. The corporal watched Walker's crew take evasive action, but the mutts kept ramming away until disabling their prey.

Walker exited, furious and confrontational, even as the carriers caught up and soldiers streamed out. "You are interfering with a US government operation," he screamed. "The captain was working for us."

"You're not going anywhere," the lieutenant in charge told him.

One of Walker's men pulled a gun. Before he could point it, a soldier fired a rifle bullet an inch above the man's head.

The man let his pistol fall into the sand and put his hands up.

The troops secured Kasey and Nasir and on a stretcher and took off for the border. Nearing the guard station on the Saudi side, the communications specialist managed to get hold of Command in Badanah, "We have Captain Lawrence and the Saudi," he informed General Zalman's aide. "They need help. Notify the infirmary."

On the Saudi side of the border, personnel listening to the drama unfold dashed to the roadside and watched the convoy pass. A soldier leaned out of a jeep yelling, "She's alive! ... She's alive!" They were greeted with thumbs up, cheering and raised fists.

Walker kicked in frustration at one of his useless vehicles and led the others on foot back over the border.

The corporal had a longer walk, but an easier one. He had all the water.

10

A day later, Kasey opened her eyes. The first thing they focused on was a doctor standing over her. He smiled. Kasey looked around and found herself the only patient in the tent. She saw General Zalman over in a corner. Trying to sit up, she felt an IV needle in her arm. Her eyes followed the line up to the pouch filled with a hydrating solution. When she motioned Zalman over, she sensed gauze dressing covering several body parts.

The doctor urged her to remain still, but Kasey elevated herself to a sitting position as the general stood by.

"I need to talk to you," she told him.

The doctor gave them privacy.

"Where is Captain Saud?"

"He was moved to another hospital at his family's request."

"I have important information," Kasey's voice managed hardly a whisper.

Zalman didn't want to hear more, "I cannot engage in any debriefing until the embassy is notified."

"Then notify them."

"Let's wait until you're a bit better.

"This can't wait."

"Maybe one more day," Zalman suggested.

"No sir, now," Kasey insisted.

Zalman nodded and left.

Hours later in Riyadh, Nasir woke up in a private hospital suite. A team of doctors tentatively converged around him. Bandages covered his head down to

255

just above his eyes. A fractured skull had left him with brain swelling that led to a coma. His relatively quick return to consciousness was an excellent indication of recovery.

Abdul and Salih sat bedside and offered limp smiles when Nasir came to, their hearts torn by mixed feelings. Nasir was aware. He wanted to speak, needing to tell them everything, but his brain wouldn't execute the command. He stared blankly when one doctor asked, "Prince Nasir, can you hear me?"

The doctors patiently waited. "If you hear us, can you nod?"

He did. The doctors looked relieved.

Comprehension was intact, another favorable sign of recovery. The doctors left to give Nasir's family private time with him.

Abdul slumped in his chair, recalling moments of his son's life and the pride he felt when Nasir became the only royal in the armed services. Salih gazed with a furrowed brow at his brother, an expression scalded with pain. He knew their different paths now diverged so far they were lost to each other forever.

Nasir began to stir. First moving his arms and legs, then his head. He wasn't sure he could form words, but did know he could raise his body. He did it on first try. Salih motioned for him lie back. He refused and slowly asked, "Where is Captain Lawrence?"

"At a US Army infirmary," Salih said.

Nasir felt ease with the answer. He looked at his father. Abdul seemed forlorn. Only now did Nasir grasp he had been that way for a long time. Nasir watched Salih and beamed inside at his familiar glaring continence. Nothing appeared to please Salih. Even when they were children, he was never satisfied. Nasir smiled at him for a moment. Salih tilted his head and grimaced.

"I have vital things to tell you," Nasir forced the words out.

It tormented Abdul and Salih to hear it. It meant he knew what the two of them hoped he never would. "Not now, Nasir," Abdul said, resting a hand on his son's arm. "Regain your strength."

"There is little time," Nasir labored to say.

He was right, Salih thought, deciding it was time to tell the truth. Abdul knew that look of candor on Salih's face. "Wait," Abdul said to both of them. Then he stood and glared at Salih, "We will notify the king."

Salih stayed quiet and Nasir rested his head on a pillow. Abdul and Salih left him alone, knowing a time they dreaded was at hand.

Kasey started relating her story to Secretary Drake while sitting on the edge of the hospital bed. By the time she finished, Kasey and Drake were seated in chairs across from each other, both leaning forward alone in the tent.

The secretary reached for Kasey's hand, "I apologize for the attack by our Air Force. They were ordered to repel Moghavi's bunch. They were getting too close." Drake paused. She despised what she had to say, but cloaked it with a sincere mien, "The men who died in Lebanon were a rescue team we sent to get you. We were operating with information Mossad gave us."

"I am going to see to it to see their families know the heroes they are," Kasey looked at the floor, barely able to rub her face with her hands and wipe the away tears of anguish at witnessing their deaths.

Drake, still not sure of everything Kasey might know, made up her answers as she went along, "We needed to stay quiet until the matter with you was settled."

The secretary's lie about Mossad's role had the effect of confirming a truth for Kasey, "If Mossad gave you the information, then it was to set us up."

Drake hoped to get out of this meeting without saying much. She didn't know what might end up in conflict with what Kasey knew, "I don't know what happened. We'll take it up with Israel." Drake paced the tent, "As for some of the others things you were told," she drew a breath and hoped it would fly, "you know disinformation is a refined art in the Mideast." The secretary moved closer to Kasey for emphasis, "To say the oil is gone ... we would know about it. A revolution is Saudi Arabia? Our intelligence says nothing of the sort is going on." Drake was concerned for Kasey. How was everybody going to react when she told them what the captain knew?

Kasey pounded on the chair, "A revolt *is* about to happen!"

Drake raised her voice, "We would never leave Americans at risk!" She wasn't so much angry with Kasey as incensed at the person she had to be now.

"It's bigger than you can imagine," Kasey briskly spoke. "Saddam knows he's being set up for blame. Iran is behind it, with help. I don't know from where. There's evidence. Captain Saud has it-"

Drake had to curb what she couldn't stand to hear, "Saddam is a world class liar!" She could tell from Kasey's face that her tone went too far. Drake had to get out of there. "Captain Lawrence, I will pass all the information along," Drake moved to exit. "I hope you'll back on duty soon."

The secretary left. Kasey was at first bewildered, then worried over how the encounter unfolded.

Drake was escorted to the perimeter of the compound where her diplomatic security escort waited. She got into the car where Clayton Amfrick was waiting. Drake said nothing for a long time after they drove off, finally sighing, "She knows everything."

Amfrick was prepared, "We'll have a meeting as soon as we get back to the embassy."

"No, wait until morning," Drake said. "I have something to do when we get back."

Amfrick knew what.

King Khaled stayed away from the window in Nasir's suite, lingering not far from the door. Though the Saudi Guard enveloped the outside perimeter of the hospital and security was tight inside on every floor, the king had the instincts of a monarch in trouble. More than any other royal, he was at greatest risk right now. Taking out the king would be a symbol, possibly prematurely spurring the mob of Mecca pilgrims now swarming over just about every Saudi population center. Salih had no apprehension about standing by the window. That's where he placed himself the moment the king entered, as if to accuse Khaled of being cowardly. Abdul was next to Nasir's bed, subdued and occasionally propping the cushions Nasir leaned up on as he gave account of his ordeal.

The king wanted to be out of there, but it took Nasir a long time to tell everything. As far as Khaled was concerned, dealing with Nasir was a situation for Abdul's side of the family.

"It's nonsense," Khaled reassuringly said when Nasir finished. "Saddam never misses a chance to stir things."

His response was a shock to Nasir, "What proof do we have he is lying?" Talking took so much energy that Nasir had to pause. "We know plastic explosives did move through Iraq. I have new evidence, the bullet he gave me, in my pocket."

Khaled walked slightly closer to Nasir, "They checked your uniform at the hospital. Your pockets were empty."

The king fired a glance at Salih, who turned and looked out the window, "The Americans could have taken it ... or maybe it was lost," Salih tossed off over his shoulder.

"We are about to host one million pilgrims," Khaled was doing a good job at appearing tranquil, "do you think an uprising could stay secret?"

Nasir raised his voice as much as he could, "You know better-"

Khaled didn't permit him to go on, "Enough, Nasir" he firmly said. "Do you think I would let our family be targeted? Unrest is always the work of a few. No oil? Think who told you. Crazy Moghavi!"

Nasir was so shaken he struggled to get out of bed. Abdul held him back. "We'll talk more when you feel better," the king ended the meeting and left the suite. Male nurses entered as Abdul followed Khaled into the corridor. The nearby Guard backed away, giving them room to talk.

"I promised you I would not tell him the truth," the king was as sad a monarch preoccupied with abdication could be. "He will soon know, Abdul."

"You see how he is," Abdul was suffering. He knew how it would now end. "He loves his country too much. I want him to never know the shame. Let him die for honor rather than live a ruined man."

"Then so be it," the king sealed the judgment and walked away.

***

Immediately after returning to Riyadh, Secretary Drake flew to Bahrain on a private jet accompanied by a modest diplomatic security entourage. From there, a US Navy destroyer ferried them to Suniyafan Island, the eastern most deep water port accessible to the US in the Persian Gulf. A sterile, uninhabited place leased by the American military for maneuvers. The destroyer made its way to a spot outside the harbor while Drake waited with her protection in a vacant Navy office building near the pier. Long after dark, a commercial freighter sailed into port.

It docked at the illuminated wharf and Drake watched the crew take down one flag of registry and hoist a red, white and green flag, the colors of Iran.

Hashemi Rajavi exited the ship, attended by a retinue. They tramped down the plywood ramp and into the building where Drake was. Rajavi and Drake withdrew alone into a room. Rajavi took out and envelope and set a series of photographs on a table. Drake gathered them one by one, having a penetrating look at each.

"I thought these might be of interest to you," Rajavi believed Drake was smiling at the pictures of the forced sexu al encounter between Kasey and Nasir.

Drake was sneering, her hope the photos would be blurred or absent telling features now down the drain. She felt corrupted and soiled, "Yes, Mr. Rajavi, they do interest me," she told him, taking custody of the pictures. "But I wish I could tell you they didn't."

***

"Then I threw it all into the trunk and took off," Rick informed Denise while he gingerly placed each item of clothing into a separate garment tote and zipped it shut. "After that, I switched to a different rental car and drove home."

Denise didn't move from the kitchen table as she listened to Rick's account of what happened in North Carolina. He started narrating details hours ago, in the early evening when he returned home. He called before arriving, after she got in from work, and asked her to go and buy a few dozen garment bags right away. Soon after she returned, he walked into the house with arms full of clothing. He gave her a bracing kiss and smiled before heading back out to the car to get what remained in the trunk. After he put the last of the clothes on the table, he gave her a bracing kiss and said he missed her. For an instant, she believed the bounce in his step was a tingle he got from seeing her. She was unable to fool herself for long. When Rick began recounting his adventure, she knew what was inspiring his zeal. She found it a bit unsettling to learn he stole the clothing. Perhaps it was justified if the story turned out to be everything Rick thought it might be. Nonetheless, the idea of it made her tense. She never saw him take something that didn't belong to him and it was a bad time to learn new things about her husband that gave pause. She made a private decision not to touch the pilfered items, instead only watching Rick pack them away.

Still, she was thrilled he was home. Although she was incapable of sharing in his excitement and remained stumped by particulars real or imagined about their relationship, it was good to have him back. Whatever was going on in their marriage would be resolved when one of them (she preferred it be him) became determined to get some answers. She was ashamed for wondering if any love could be enduring. Her concern about their marriage had to be confirmation it was. He was gone only days, yet it felt like ages. Would she feel this way if she didn't love him? Would it hurt so deeply to feel as though they were becoming strangers? Or to ask if maybe they were always strangers? Would it be so agonizing if her emotions weren't so incisive?

"I'm going to have a chemical analysis done on the soiled clothes," Rick divulged his plan. "Denise, if it contains cellulose acetate residue, I'm going to have a huge story! Everybody will be talking about it."

He sure would, she thought. A notion it could be huge for their relationship crossed her mind. It was maddening not to know why.

"I'll have proof of the US Army manufacturing plastic explosives in violation of federal law. I'll have uniforms and protective clothing with the residue originating from a base supposed to be an infantry training facility. I have the names of the personnel and a trail of photographic evidence," Rick said in an ecstatic tone.

"Have you told your editor?"

"I want to wait until I know the truth. I know someone from a drug testing story I did way back who owns an independent chemical analysis business. I'm taking it to him."

Denise almost asked why he didn't want to inform the Examiner, but she held back. Maybe she didn't want the answer, but what reason could there be for that? Could be she simply wanted distance from the story. It probably was only unfounded fear, she decided as Rick took the garment bags upstairs into their bedroom saying, "I don't want these out of my sight."

She never heard him come downstairs. Denise was running her fingers through her hair, lost in reflection, when he leaned over her back, put a hand on her chin, tilted her head and slid his tongue into her mouth.

It was warm and dreamy, the way she felt fantasizing him elsewhere inside her. At the same time, it was stinging and tormenting. Does he have any sense of something going on with us? She couldn't help asking herself. Rick pulled away and delicately rubbed her shoulders.

Neither said a word as he massaged for a while.

He finally asked, "How are you Denise?"

She almost told him, but stayed quiet.

He leaned over and kissed her again. Then whispered, "I love you."

She stood up, faced him and reached for his hands. She slid them around her shoulders, "I missed you Rick."

They went upstairs and made love.

Both were awake long after they finished.

Rick turned to her, "Have you seen Gary?"

"I saw him yesterday morning for a minute at the coffee shop," Denise knew that wasn't what he wanted to know. "He still hasn't heard from Kasey since Ted died."

Rick didn't say anything. Once he fell asleep, Denise went into the bathroom and cried.

***

Drake returned to Riyadh in the middle of the night. Walker and Amfrick were waiting for her with Ambassador Howe. Walking into the conference room, the secretary sensed a tension so thick a machete couldn't hack through it. Walker's demeanor, as usual, was inscrutable. Amfrick looked irritated and Howe's face was red. Drake suspected some heated discussion was the cause. She guessed Howe was cracking under stress and Amfrick probably went off on him. If that was the case, Amfrick could only blame himself. He was the one who created the loop that gave each only limited access to information. It was time to come clean. The secretary knew Amfrick never would. So, she was going to do it.

"If we're not all straight with each other right now," she scanned the room, looking each in the eye, "then everything is going to fall apart."

Amfrick searched for a way to stop Drake, but she cut to the quick before he could open his mouth.

"It was my idea to send Captain Lawrence to meet with Saddam. I believed a woman on such a mission in the Mideast would be treated as a joke, or even better, an insult. The Saudi treated her that way, but Saddam didn't."

She stared at Amfrick. He wasn't happy. Walker, even though Amfrick's choice for the job in Riyadh, picked up the ball for reasons of agency preservation, "We knew she was there during the coup. It was planned before I got here and evidently before the captain was scheduled to meet Saddam. Nobody said a word about calling it off."

Howe was relieved to be learning the facts, "Nobody told me anything."

There was too much momentum now for Amfrick to shut anybody up. Drake went on, "Iran said they needed plastic explosives to facilitate a revolution as quickly and painlessly as possible. A few incidents of terror with plastic explosives could collapse resistance without battles in the street that would leave many more casualties."

Howe at last had enough information for insight, "So, we gave explosives to Iran so they could get them to Saudi Arabia in a way that would never implicate the United States."

Amfrick hated what was happening. His chest heaved from repressed hostility while istening to Howe continue, "Iraq was the perfect transportation route. If things were traced, the road would end at Saddam." It answered quite a bit, but Howe's case of nerves remained, "How much more time are we going to sit on pins and needles waiting for the royals to leave?"

Drake felt the same frustration, "They're still moving their wealth." The royals' determination to squeeze every riyal they could from the country was causing troubling delays. "But there was an incident at the palace. They may decide it's time," Drake hoped.

Amfrick finally boiled over. He raised a finger at them all, "None of you have mentioned the president. My concern and your concern is to protect him. You are to see to it that nobody knows the oil is gone until the royals have left the country. If word gets out beforehand, it will prove he knew all along the wells were dry. It will destroy his political future."

Drake knew Amfrick was leading up about what to do about the Lawrence matter, "All the president has to do is order Captain Lawrence to remain silent, if that's what is worrying you."

"She knows the stakes," Walker pointed out, doubting the secretary's solution. "She might risk disobeying an order if she believes Americans here are at risk."

"It's too late for any other strategy," Howe shrugged.

Drake pulled out the envelope with the photographs.

Amfrick yelled, "Don't!" He wanted it to be only between the two of them.

The secretary ignored his order and tossed the pictures across the table at Walker and Howe.

Amfrick squirmed as Walker smiled and Howe gaped in awe. Walker let out a laugh, "This is fabulous!"

Drake turned away from all of them. She was sick to her stomach.

"I know you feel it's too bad it has come to this, Madam Secretary," Amfrick saw her frowning profile. "It is sad, I admit. But we all know in politics there's always a victim."

***

Shortly after dawn, mosques around Saudi Arabia were packed. Worshippers listened to preaching mullahs brazenly criticize the monarchy, boldly challenging its right to exist in an Islamic society. There were murmurs among the gatherings at hearing words seldompublicly uttered. Outside, the air was filled with a knowing buzz that something was goingon. Something big.

Nasir felt stronger after another night's rest. Early in the morning, his wife Waddhi came for her first visit. When the two were alone in the room, she removed her veil and sat on the edge of his bed, hugging him. Nasir mentioned nothing about his time away. Mostly, he wanted to know about Ibrahim. He could see the sadness in Waddhi's eyes when she told him she didn't know how their son was adjusting to life in his new environment. Nasir's soul plunged into a fit of pain when he learned the institution preferred Ibrahim have no visitors until completely adapting to his new surroundings.

Waddhi washed Nasir's feet and hands, then set rugs on the floor so they could pray together. As they kneeled side by side and gave offering to Allah, Nasir was fighting off tears. By the time they finished praying, Waddhi was crying. Nasir went to the closet and found fresh linen robes waiting. He took the clothes and looked at Waddhi. She gently turned away, knowing his mind. Small gestures from a Saudi wife say all. Nasir went into the bathroom and dressed.

When he came out, Waddhi had covered her face, a signal she was ready to go with him. Nasir asked her Guard escort waiting outside the room to take her home. Waddhi linked eyes with Nasir for a long time before she slightly dipped her head and left.

The guards in the hallway were surprised to see Nasir leave his room. They said nothing, it not being their place to dissuade a royal from doing anything. They only followed him out of the hospital. Outside, a full Guard platoon controlled access in and out of the building. Nasir entered a car and told the driver where he wanted to go. A motorcade followed.

Before long, Nasir was marching into the facility where Ibrahim now lived. He went into the administration building, Guard members trailing along. Nasir was immediately taken to Ibrahim's dormitory. The boy had just finished praying in the mosque and was having breakfast in the cafeteria.

Ibrahim glowed when he saw his father. Nasir hugged him and took him into his arms.

"I love you, son," Nasir squeezed him. "I love you. You are coming home."

Ibrahim was elated. Nasir put the boy down and the two of them walked out hand in hand.

As they approached the waiting motorcade, several vehicles drove up. Prince Rakan got out along with armed members of the Guard. Nasir told Ibrahim to get into the car waiting for him.

Rakan refused to look his cousin in the eye, "Nasir, you are under arrest." Rakan could only guess Nasir's expression. "The charge is adultery. You will be tried forthwith."

HONOR BOUND

Nasir stiffened, immediately aghast, "Adultery! What obscenity is this!"

Rakan produced a set of handcuffs while the Guard went for their guns. Rakan waved off a show of force, "Not in front of the boy." He took Nasir's arm and led them a few feet away to talk privately, "There is evidence of the American woman and you."

"Pictures? They are not what they seem!"

"You said nothing about it," Rakan said, as if to bolster the accusation. Of course Nasir hadn't told the family. Yet. No matter the circumstances, such talk violates Saudi social propriety.

The earth under Nasir reeled, "Who gave you the pictures?"

"Save your questions for the trial," Rakan looked at the handcuffs he was holding.

Nasir got the message, "Wait one minute." He went over to Ibrahim and leaned inside the car, "Son, remember I love you."

Ibrahim smiled and flung open his arms. Nasir held him one more time, then closed the door.

Nasir watched the car disappear from sight. Then he walked to Rakan and held out his wrists. Rakan chose to look only at Nasir's hands. He handcuffed Nasir and helped him inside the vehicle. Rakan planned to ride with Nasir, but couldn't. He went to another car and led the convoy away.

***

In the morning, Kasey requested an immediate discharge from the infirmary. She was determined to resume duty so she could assert the gravity of the situation to Army superiors. Surely, they would embrace the veracity of an intelligence officer more than a civilian diplomat like Drake did. Even though she barely slept the night, she told the doctors she was feeling much better. They wanted to review the results of a few more tests before making a decision on her release. Kasey wandered back and forth from her bed to the sick bay entrance, staring outside at soldiers going about business. Those that got a look at her grinned, shouted encouragement or saluted. She offered back a tight smile or slight wave. There was a divide between their heartening gestures and

266

what she was feeling inside. Watching them was a tormenting reminder of Americans, civilian and military, inside Saudi Arabia and the danger facing them. Lives were in peril and someone had to believe her before it was too late. She sat in a chair next to her bed and prayed for Nasir's recovery. She was optimistic he was going to be all right and once he informed his family what was happening in the country they still might have time to put a stop to it. No doubt, the royals would demand greater attention on the matter from the US government.

A private brought Kasey a new uniform, a good sign of impending discharge. She began dressing and asked for a sewing kit. The private brought one from his own gear. Kasey began stitching letters with thread on the inside of her new coat. She finished - America, One Nation, One Destiny, and looked up to see General Zalman. He approached with another general and a junior officer.

Kasey put on the coat and jumped to attention, a display of alertness and resiliency she hoped they would notice.

"At ease, captain," Zalman said.

His face was filled with profound emotion as he gazed at her. He was probably gratified to see her so quickly on the mend, she thought. Maybe he would advocate for her discharge. Then she could tell him everything she knew. They served here together for months. It would be like unburdening to a family member. He'd know what to do with the information.

"Captain Lawrence, with your return my Army career has come to a end," Zalman said with a lump in his throat. "Retirement takes effect immediately. General Collins is your new commander."

Kasey pushed away the grinding in the pit of her stomach to again place herself at attention and salute the new man in charge.

General Collins returned her salute, "Remain at ease, captain."

Kasey had a long look at Zalman. She was already missing him. He turned away after a few seconds. At first, it puzzled Kasey. Then she guessed maybe his last moments as commander were filled with emotions he struggled not to show.

But Kasey expected no less a hearing from General Collins. She wasted no time in pressing her case, "Thank you for coming to see me, sir. I'm sure you know my account of events. I beg you to advise the diplomats on the urgency of the situation," the words rushed out of Kasey, but something was peculiar. Was it their expressions? Odd energy was flowing in a way she couldn't put a finger on as she continued, "It's imperative they recognize what is going on and order an immediate evacuation-"

General Collins interrupted her using a rehearsed declaration, "Captain Lawrence, as of this moment you are removed from duty pending investigation or arraignment."

Kasey frowned. *Am I hearing right?*

"You are charged with disobeying orders ... "

How can this be? She shook her head hard, side to side, an attempt to extricate herself from an auditory hallucination.

" ... dereliction of duty ... "

Her mouth fell open. *Why is this man slandering me?*

" ... and desertion."

Kasey couldn't catch her breath. How did this ghastly mistake come about? She stared at Zalman. She swore he was delicately nodding opposition to the accusations. Why was he staying silent? *Straighten this out, general.* You know it's not true. She felt more alone by the second, desperate for familiar cohorts ... Moore... Harper ... even Bowers.

Kasey fell into the chair by her bed. She was nauseous, her body responding to this threatening development while her mind stretched for the logic behind this startling blunder by the Army.

"Captain, it is alleged that you abandoned duty to disappear and engage in a sexual escapade with Captain Saud," Collins detailed. "There is photographic evidence-"

"Sir, I told the secretary all about it! The pictures, all of it. She knows!"

General Collins wanted her silence, "I urge you not to comment."

Did this general she never met believe it was all true? Kasey had no idea the bureaucratic trajectory of this misunderstanding. At this moment, she couldn't focus on anything.

"Right now, Lieutenant Moulton will serve as your counsel," Collins was finished. He pivoted and led the others away. The lieutenant stayed behind.

Kasey watched them go, mostly keeping her eyes on Zalman. He never looked back, but she knew he had to feel her gaze on him. She needed him to turn around. She didn't know after that what she expected of him, but Zalman represented her last grip on what was steadfast around her and she had to have someone who knew the truth there with her right now. When Zalman departed, Kasey's world suddenly became a precarious and isolating place. Maybe Zalman did defend her when he heard about the charges and it was too painful for him to face her without an explanation. Maybe the whole thing was sprung without his imput. He could have needed to simply walk away from it all so he could have a sane retirement. Whatever his reasons, Kasey felt she deserved more. It may have violated protocol, having an aside in front of the new commander, but what did Zalman care? He was all but out the door. What could they do to him?

Kasey felt in the company of strangers. She had no bonds with anyone around her. How could General Collins fashion these charges in so little time, especially since she hadn't given the Army a report yet? It must be Drake with the wrong idea about what happened. Kasey probed their meeting, searching for why the secretary made an astonishing miscalculation about the events. Was that why she sloughed off what Kasey told her? Drake must have seen Kasey's entire story as a concoction to disguise an affair. Did they really have the photos? Kasey couldn't see how they would have gotten them.

Lieutenant Moulton sat next to Kasey as she ran it all through her head. Eventually, she glanced at him. A pup of an officer, she thought. Probably right out of law school.

The lieutenant said nothing for some time after Kasey turned away. He understood well enough to remain quiet until she wasn't so overwhelmed.

An uncomfortable amount of time passed. Moulton had no idea if the allegations were true, but was sure about something she'd be relieved to hear, "At least you got the bad news first."

Kasey snapped at him, "Why, is there some *good* news?"

"Yes," the lieutenant gently smiled, "since the alleged affair took place outside the country, Saudi Arabia has agreed not to prosecute you under their laws for

269

fornicating with a married man. Technically they could, but I got them to agree not to."

"*Oh, my god, Nasir,*" Kasey shrieked to herself in realization. If this was what she was facing, then what about him?

"It could have been a death sentence for you," Moulton had a notion it might be on her mind. "Same as the adultery charge Captain Saud is facing. I feel for him. His trial going on right now at the Council of Ministers."

Kasey's feet moved quicker than her mind. An adrenaline rush propelled her from the chair and out of the infirmary.

The lieutenant could only gawk while she disappeared from his sight in a flash. By the time he got to his feet and chased after her, Kasey had ordered a soldier out of the first jeep she saw, jumped behind the wheel and drove toward the post perimeter.

The guards grinned when they saw her pull up behind an exiting truck. Egress was temporarily unobstructed as the sentries walked over to Kasey. Before they got close, Kasey hammered the acceleration and zoomed away. The shocked guards hurdled out of her path and stared at the jeep's dust.

One of the guards shook his head, "Where does she think she's going?"

"The Saudi Guard will stop her if we can't," the other said, radioing the base.

General Collins declined to send a team after her, citing safety concerns. In a quick meeting with the outpost security officer, Collins elaborated that since Captain Lawrence was removed from duty, there was technically no infraction in her leaving the base and the military wasn't responsible for her well being. He also pointed out all matters regarding foreigners away from their restricted communities were strictly Saudi concerns. Collins was confident some Saudi law enforcement agency, either local police, the Guard, or a patrol of moral wardens would soon apprehend her.

If that's what the general truly believed, he couldn't have been more wrong. Kasey roared through the desert, cutting south and bursting onto the highway that emptied into Riyadh. She dodged in and out of traffic past gawking motorists and buses crammed with Mecca pilgrims. There was no mistaking the obvious sight of a female American solider in a military vehicle to any authorities spotting her, but during the three hours it took Kasey to reach the outskirts of Riyadh, she encountered no police of any sort. It was not a source of relief to her, but worry. Saudi Arabia was always well watched over by layers of enforcement authorities. Their absence was indication something was amiss. The door was wide open for whatever chaos was ready to erupt. It was additional confirmation of the truth Kasey was finding nobody wanted to hear.

Kasey was even more rattled to find no police on the streets of Riyadh. The sidewalks were packed with pilgrims glaring in disbelieving anger at Kasey while she ignored traffic signals, as much out fear of encountering a mob as urgency to find Nasir. She didn't know exactly how, but she was determined to have her say before something disgraceful happened to Nasir. Inside the Council of Ministers, ten royal family members, assigned by age, comprised the jury hearing the case against Nasir. Prince Rakan, as leader of the Guard, functioned as prosecutor. Only the most loyal Guard members were brought in to form a block long protective loop around the Council of Ministers. There was debate among the royals whether they should submit to the constitutional provision the trial be held there. Abdul insisted on it, citing the promise made that his son never learn the truth. Holding the trial anyplace else would clue Nasir that things weren't right. The family agreed, although all knew the reason was to appease Abdul's sense of denial. They also granted Abdul's request that Nasir only be tried for adultery. Charges of desertion and dereliction of duty unacceptably impinged on Nasir's patriotism. No royal dared object to that appeal.

Rakan spent most of the day presenting the case while the jury quietly listened. He set out the circumstances and submitted facts about Nasir's assignment with the American woman. Rakan outlined their first joint mission and succeeding extended time in each other's company to underscore the opportunity for a sexual liaison.

Nasir tuned out Rakan and stared into the faces around him. People he knew his entire life, his blood, now seemed strangers. He needed to find out why all this was happening.

He stalked eyes too timid to meet his for an answer. Could this trial be at the king's urging? Khaled, the adept monarch, sat immobile, as if portraying a role on stage. He always was a forthright man and Nasir knew him as one to be up front with any accusation. He couldn't believe his uncle the king would bring such charges. Nasir's heart wrenched when he gazed at his father. Abdul seemed bent and knotted in contorted agony. It had to be as much a mystery to Abdul who was behind the allegations. Nasir thought a lot about Salih, who was sitting next to Abdul. Yes, much divided Nasir and Salih, but brotherly love always transcended their worldly disagreements. Salih was the most blunt person Nasir ever met. It was impossible that he would be driving these proceedings. Might Rakan be behind it? A laughable idea. Rakan, the most Westernized in the family? No way it could be him. Especially since rumors of his escapades often followed him back from out of country. Gossip about his affairs was never pursued. Why would he insist on an investigation of such complaints against Nasir?

It was an exasperating exercise for Nasir as he then considered every present cousin and uncle as the source of the charges. He couldn't envision it coming from any of them. Nasir figured if he could pin down who was behind the trial, the why would follow. How many times had those in attendance called him a source of pride for all of them? Was it an expression of hidden jealousy on someone's part? A resentment of Nasir by another royal who never served in the military? That included everybody there. And what about the photographs? Once the family saw them, there was no choice but to invoke the law. Who provided them? It was infuriating for Nasir to know the answer had to be in front of him.

Rakan finished the process of establishing the opportunity for an adulterous affair. By statute, all he needed to do now was furnish the physical evidence.

He passed the photos to the jury. Nasir watched each member closely, dissecting any indication of what they might be thinking.

It was in these moments something began to churn in Nasir's marrow. The way the jury looked at the pictures and then gazed at Abdul unbuckled the tracks of Nasir's straight ahead reasoning. The jury's looks seemed to be asking his father ... *Are you sure?* A distressing perception was simmering, still pushed from consciousness, that this was not a sincere trial. For the first time, Nasir's focus wasn't on the gathering. He slipped into a void where a dire struggle was beginning.

"The photos are proof of the affair," Rakan said after the jury examined the evidence. "I rest my case."

Rakan's words brought Nasir back to the here and now. Why did the jury give more attention to Abdul than the photos? Nasir hunted for an answer different from the one curdling in his gut. The pictures were certainly too immodest for any Saudi. Maybe far too mortifying for a royal when it involved one of the family. Perhaps the jury's concentration shifted to Abdul as a way to avoid lingering on the visually jarring images in front of them.

"Nasir ibn Saud," Rakan announced, "your defense."

Nasir hesitated, or possibly stuttered. It was time to refute the indictment, but for the first time a part of him wasn't sure he could. The photos were irrefutable, but he always thought the particular circumstances obliged exoneration. Until now. He stood before the jury, queasy over a dawning awareness the trial was a show, the judgment decided, and he was going to *die*.

"We were forced at gun point into the encounter," Nasir's subdued voice quivered through empty nooks of the Council chamber. He couldn't concentrate on what he was saying. If this was merely a stage spectacle, then all he learned while away about the oil being gone and the family ready to abdicate rule, was true. "It was a blackmail plot by kidnappers," Nasir stopped to combat his inner turmoil. He stared at the jury, then the king, then Salih and Abdul. Could it be no one of them behind it, but all of them?

"We had vital evidence Saddam gave us. I had to do all I could to stay alive and bring it back," Nasir continued, speaking with a tone that made most turn away. When heads rotated back, Nasir saw only distant expressions. It was a collective tune out, an emotional severing from what sounded too close to begging.

Nasir responded to their perceived indifference by placing more urgency in his assertions, "Saddam gave us a bullet with teeth marks on it. He said it belonged to the contact in Jordan who was receiving the explosives. Saddam thought we had a chance to find out the identity of the Saudi the smugglers were on the way to meet if we could find out whose bite matched the notches on the bullet. It would tell us who was planning the revolt."

Rakan interrupted Nasir's increasingly manic fight for life with a question, "This bullet ... where is it?"

"I cannot locate it," Nasir spoke in a vulnerable tone. "I had it in my uniform. When I came to in the hospital, it was gone."

There were raised eyebrows and indignant scowls from the jury. The silent gestures inspired the ultimate insight for Nasir. He saw unmistakable affectation in their manner, as if it was some kind of peculiar, rehearsed drill. Nasir watched his father tremble and Salih grab his hand to calm him. Suddenly, Nasir's emotions were liberated from the unfolding scene. All anxiety emptied from his visage. He felt composed and at ease. He knew what he was going to do. For a moment, his essence floated above the surroundings, giving him a feeling that all this was happening to somebody else.

Then gunshots rang out. They seemed to come from outside the Council alcazar. Nasir heard shouts from the Guard as fidgety royals ran for cover. Only Salih remained where he was. It was a telling retreat to Nasir, affirming his decision to end this sham. The moment was the chance for Nasir to verify one final thing. He wanted to see if a mob was storming the chambers. Curiosity propelled him toward the exit until the Guard blocked his way.

More rapid fire pumped up the tension. Even the Guard ducked, leaving the way clear for Nasir to walk away until the Guard regrouped and gave chase.

Nasir began running when he heard a familiar voice. Between the pilasters in front of the building he saw Kasey wrestling with the Guard. She was furiously demanding entrance into Council chambers. She was so inflamed it took an entire squad to subdue her. A soldier fired another volley into the air to dissuade her from struggling.

"Back off her," Nasir raged before being tackled by the pursuing Guard.

Kasey and Nasir bore a gaze into each other that persisted even as the Guard overpowered them.

"Let me go," Kasey ordered. "I want to testify."

She was being dragged away when Rakan appeared behind Nasir. There was no way this American woman was going to be allowed inside the Council. That's what Rakan decided.

The racket drew a lingering crowd on the other side of the barricades. It was distant enough so they remain in the dark about the source of the commotion, but Rakan was worried. The Guard was outnumbered. He ordered Kasey away as Salih emerged, raised his arms and bellowed, "No, let her in!"

Everybody froze. Rakan was stunned. Salih, *of all people,* calling for this foreigner, this woman, to be brought into Council chambers? This was no time for him to persist as the relentless contrarian.

Salih, of such strident emotion and frowning candor, needed to defend his role in what was to befall his brother. He wanted ease from the spasms of remorse and sorrow he unpleasantly discovered festering in his core as the trial went on. He knew what it would take to end it, "Let us hear her!"

There was indecision among the Guard as they waited for Rakan's cue. Kasey and Nasir traveled a million miles away during the delay. Seeing each other again brought back the entire ordeal. They thought about what they went through together. Only now, feelings for each other surged to the fore. Nasir didn't want her there. He couldn't stand her seeing what became of the House of Saud. It wasn't what the two of them risked their lives for. Nor did he want her to know what he intended to do about it. Kasey still held the notion what they were going through was an aberration that would inevitably be rectified. It was humiliating, what her country's officials concluded happened. She wasn't sure she could look at Nasir, knowing what so many thought about them. It turned out they couldn't stop looking at each other. Nasir needed her help now. If she could convince them with her testimony, or somehow stall things long enough, the truth would finally win out. Nasir was experiencing an affection he just now comprehended or admitted he had for Kasey. That's why he finally, slowly, nodded at her, signaling opposition to her presence. He didn't want her to see what he was going to do. He knew Kasey was there out of the same tenderness for him that he felt for her. He also knew neither would ever have the chance to express it.

Rakan still wanted Kasey hauled off, but Salih was staring him down and the crowd was making him nervous. The Guard was anxious for a decision. Rakan motioned the Guard to bring her inside and led the way to Council chambers. The Guard, out of deference to Nasir's status as a royal, removed their hands from him and allowed him to walk in on his own. Kasey was ushered in, closely flanked by soldiers. Salih entered last.

Kasey spent no time focusing on the resplendent corridors and sculpted marble halls inside the Council. Even the king's gold throne made no impression. She was there for one purpose, to save Nasir's life.

Kasey knew her presence would not be tolerated for long. She had to make the most of it. She ran all she wanted to say through her head while the king took his place and the jury was seated. Salih's eyes darted about as he comforted Abdul. None were on to the fact he was the one seeking solace.

Everyone was on edge in different ways by Kasey's attendance. She stood in a corner, surrounded by soldiers. Nasir took his place in the midst of it all. Rakan took over, "As magistrate of this tribunal, I sanction a witness for the defense."

Kasey didn't know what she was expected to do. She longed to speak with Nasir. She would have to do it with words in open court. Wary attention was all over her. Nasir wanted her to have her say and go. Her presence was a wrenching interruption. It would have no effect on the proceedings. Kasey cautiously stepped to the center of the chamber, not knowing how long she paused before beginning, "Captain Saud is not an adulterer. We were blackmailed and threatened with death. There was no corrupt intent. He did it for love of country." She felt an oozing hostility from the jury and could only hope it wouldn't cloud their search for justice. She went on, her voice cracking, "*I* convinced him to do it. His choice was death. Captain Saud is a noble man and a proud citizen of his country. Acquit him of the shame I brought to him and all of you."

Salih agreed with everything Kasey said. If an amiable man, he would have felt sorry for her. She would never understand what she said in his defense was why he must be convicted. Kasey's testimony appeased his fleeting distress, but in a way he did not expect.

Nasir prayed for Kasey to quickly finish. He needed her out of there so he could finish family business. He wanted it over with before hated truth consumed him. It wasn't a revolution that was imminent, it was an abdication. All he believed to be a lie was the truth. That's why he was on trial. They didn't want him to know it. They were a disgrace to the blood of Ibn Saud and were nothing but depraved, greedy, conniving villains with a plan to do him in before escaping. They wanted his life, not to save him shame, but because to ever look at him again would be reminder of their dishonor.

Kasey tried to say more, but Nasir couldn't stand to see her pleading with scoundrels. He marched in front of her, "Kasey, no."

Someone gasped at his unceremonious address. It wasn't a sincere reaction. Nasir snickered, it was time to end this bogus trial,

"Captain Lawrence, do not glory these fools with your appeal."

Her heart sank trying to avoid hearing what he really was saying.

Why was he talking this way? He needed them to see the facts. Insulting them would be no help. Kasey wanted to band with Nasir for another struggle, but he was going a different way, a way she didn't comprehend.

It was his wisdom about Kasey's strength that ultimately made him close in on the jury, "Give me your verdict. I will embrace death before living with your humiliation."

His decree shocked Kasey. Nasir stood with his back to her while she tried to understand. What humiliation? Was he saying he believed this trial was a fraud? Was he affirming all they learned on their mission was the truth? Maybe Nasir was certain what he submitted in defense before she arrived was enough for acquittal? She stared at Nasir's back, needing to see his face.

Nasir wouldn't turn around. They made their choices in life and he made his.

Rakan called out, "Verdict!"

The first juror mumbled, "Guilty," and looked away from Nasir. The next kept his eyes on Rakan, "Guilty." The following juror glared at Nasir and barked, "Guilty!" Tears gushed from Abdul long before the other seven agreed. The entire reason for the trial was to keep Nasir from knowing the truth. There was no doubt it had failed. Abdul buried his head in Salih's torso. For a moment, Salih lost his scowl, his demeanor fusing into something murkier.

Kasey was appalled. Her world was upside down and out of control. American and Saudi officials were seized by some astonishing misimpression and if it didn't stop a lot more people than the two of them were to suffer. Nasir still wouldn't look at Kasey. He remained fixed on the jury.

Rakan then asked, "Penalty?"

This time, there was no drawn out tally. All together, the jury said, "Death." A hush draped over the chamber. Kasey was writhing inside, silently screaming in utter agony. Why was Nasir silent? She couldn't stand the quiet. She started to say something, but Nasir severed her words, "So be it," he growled. "I accept the sentence. Carry it out now. I cannot bear another moment knowing your disgrace."

His words stole Kasey's breath. She was awed by his courage and overwhelmed by its consequences.

The Guard converged on Nasir. Kasey couldn't stand it. She made a run at him, shouting his name, but was quickly held back.

Before the Guard took Nasir, he wheeled around, looked into Kasey's eyes and saluted. He lingered, firm and erect until the Guard snatched his arms.

Kasey didn't know what to make of what she saw in his eyes. They were absent of sentiment or message. Nasir was on his way to another world and his gesture completed his business on this earth. No human could reach him now, Kasey realized. He belonged to the Absolute. His salute, a one soldier to another homage. She felt strangled, like a noose tightening around her neck, as another intimate part of her universe set to disappear.

The Guard led Nasir toward the plaza outside the Council. Abdul never looked at his son as he passed. Salih did. He coupled his gaze with Nasir's, and in the instant decided his brother was due the whole truth. Salih exhibited the bullet from Saddam, holding it up for Nasir to see. Then he placed it in his mouth, spreading his lips to show the marks on it perfectly fit his bite. There was no surprise from Nasir, only a gentle nod. He understood. The waning moments of his life were gifted with undiluted awareness. No rancor, no resentment, stained him. The nation belonged to those who saw as Salih did. Nasir wished Allah's blessings on them.

As he disappeared, Kasey's emotions detonated with a howling protest. Rakan ordered her ejected and the Guard hauled her from chambers and out into the plaza. She witnessed a small circle of soldiers forming around Nasir. One held a pair of handcuffs. Nasir shook him off, kneeled on the ground and willfully placed his hands behind his back, no restraints necessary. The executioner stood in front of him with a long, arched sword. Kasey screamed at sight of it while the Guard pulled her away in another direction. Nasir never moved. Kasey witnessed the sword rising high into the air. She bit her tongue and closed her eyes as it plunged.

Kasey couldn't believe Nasir was dead within the mere seconds it took the Guard to push her into the custody of US diplomatic security agents waiting in a rear byway near a car sent by the embassy. Somebody must have notified them she was there, or else they figured it out for themselves. They directed Kasey into the vehicle and took a back route out to avoid the Mecca pilgrims all over the main streets. Shattered, Kasey shut out the world the only way left for her, by dropping her head between her knees.

11

Rick took the most visibly stained lab coat from North Carolina for analysis. It had a dark powdery streak along the elbow sleeve as well as a round splotch of something above a pocket. Tom was Rick's acquaintance who operated a substance analysis facility on the second floor of a strip mall above an auto parts store. Tom worked primarily examining evidence in legal proceedings, usually for defense purposes. There was nothing outside to indicate what went on upstairs and for the most part Tom worked alone. That was perfect for Rick, who only gave out details relevant to what he needed to know. Tom asked no prying questions when Rick said he needed b establish the presence of combustible substances on the clothing.

"That's easy," Tom smiled, "I can find that out pretty quick."

And he did. Less than one hour later, they had a positive result. Rick shouted, "Yes!"

Now Tom performed a component analysis to reveal what the incendiary elements were. This breakdown took longer. A few hours later the summary came up on the computer screen. To Rick, they were only confusing symbols. He was in a hurry to know, "What do we have?"

"Lots on inert filler ... not surprising," Tom scrolled down the screen, "and synthetic polymers ... Wow! ... it's cellulose acetate."

Rick near danced around the room. No doubt, this was a life changing moment. Not only for him, but for many people who didn't know it yet.

Tom knew more than Rick thought, "This is vicious stuff. Used by people up to no good. What else do you want to know?"

"The dynamic ratio."

This impressed Tom. Rick knew what he wanted and how to ask for it. This test took even longer, as the component elements needed to undergo primary separation.

Late in the afternoon, Tom's eyes widened the moment he got the results, "It's thirty percent cellulose acetate."

"Can you believe it?" Rick whistled, "C-30."

"Somebody's been cooking up something heinous," Tom raised a brow. "Let's find out when they were doing it."

Tom rubbed his hands together and started the diffusion study. This surveyed the rate of atomic depletion from the time the elements were compounded. Tom put on his glasses and used a pencil and paper to calculate the raw data streaming from the printer.

He occasionally looked up to see Rick pacing so excitedly the walls barely contained him. Evidently, this was quite important.

"Rick, this stuff was put together two or three weeks ago."

"That's all I need to know," he told Tom as he snatched up the clothing. "For now."

"Guess I don't have to ask if you found out what you wanted to know."

"No you don't," Rick beamed on the way out, "I'll be back with more tomorrow."

Denise didn't need to ask what happened at the lab. Rick's expression told her. However, she quietly listened to his account of the day.

Listened, yes, but without always hearing. Too many other things were on her mind, mostly relating to their shaky relationship. At least it was to her. Rick acted as if he had no idea, which is why she decided it was time to start pressing issues, if she could only find a way. She wanted his whole attention tonight, and waited out the minutiae of his narration. Maybe getting out of the house would help, "Why don't we go out for dinner?" she asked when Rick finished.

"Not tonight," he instantly shot back.

He probably wanted to tell his editor the news. Maybe after that she'd have his focus, "Then I'll go out and pick something up for us."

281

When Denise returned, Rick was in his upstairs office adding the test results to his expanding folders of research notes, interviews, photographs and swatches of clothing snipped from the coat he took to the lab.

Rick came down to the kitchen. For a while, both ate in preoccupied silence.

"What did Carl have to say?"

"I want to wait ... a little longer before I tell him."

"I thought that's why you wanted to stay home," Denise was rattled, feeling as though she knew her husband less by the minute, "so you could talk with him."

Rick said nothing. Denise obsessed over the pause halfway between his last words. That's how bad this was getting.

"It's such a big story and I know you're excited about it," Denise said to preface her inquiry. "Why wait to tell your editor?"

"To get more test results ... and round out the story."

A logical answer. Yet, there was another one of those lags.

Wait ... a little longer ... round out the story?

Denise sensed a subtext in the words. Was he hoping to talk to Kasey? This had to be outright paranoia, Denise thought, fed up with herself. Kasey was nowhere around. Even her brother had no idea where she was. Still, Denise couldn't let go of suspicion. Did he want to talk with Kasey to expand the story? It already seemed huge enough to make the career of any reporter. Then again, Kasey put him onto it and might have something important to add. But Rick's dilated phrasing hinted maybe it wasn't the information Kasey might have that held him back. Could it be he wanted Kasey to be the first to know what he learned ... so he could ... see her face? Now why did Denise think that? Did Rick have a score to settle with Kasey over ancient differences in how they saw the world? It was a weird idea to consider for many reasons. If it were true, why would Kasey put him on to the story in the first place? Denise veered to the looming issue in their marriage. Why did that introspection so often come up in a bizarre tandem with musing about Kasey? She blamed herself for anxiety eating away at her. If only Rick would see a doctor and get the answer the two of them needed. To bring the subject up again right now ... he'd only put her off, saying it was a bad time. At least he recently looked over specialists in the phone book. Perhaps all he needs is a little more time.

Awake in bed that night while Rick worked down the hall in his office, Denise felt haunted by unease. So, she made a decision.

The next day Rick took two more pieces of clothing for analysis. Each test confirmed the results of the day before. It was becoming an embarrassment of riches, evidence wise, and so much more remained. He left the lab late in the afternoon, fatigued, yet continuing to pump adrenaline.

Denise took the day off work. She searched medical information sites on her computer, gathering data and submitting questions. Later, she made phone calls to doctors, making an appointment for Rick with one she knew he'd be comfortable with.

She made dinner and again listened to him detail the day, this time absorbing much more of the account. Rick hadn't eaten since last night. He stuffed himself between words. After doing the dishes, he plopped down on the couch next to Denise.

She draped her arms around his neck. He grabbed her tight. They spent a long time kissing. Denise ended up on Rick's lap. She felt so good, she began vacillating about bringing up the subject.

Then all the ugly strangeness crept back into her head. She pulled her mouth away from Rick's lips. He gave her a deep look.

"What are you thinking about?"

That was her cue, "Getting an answer."

This is my husband, Denise thought, *I should be able to bring this up with him.*

Wide emotions swirled in the silent air until Denise bridged her reply, "I made an appointment with a doctor."

It stunned Rick. Denise knew it, "I knew you were looking for a doctor. I figured you were too busy right now to keep at it, so I stayed home from work today and did some research. I found a specialist who-"

He staved off hearing more, trying hard to disguise anger, "It isn't a good time for me to go right now."

Denise got up, "When will it ever be, Rick?"

"I need all my time for this story-"

"You always have an excuse."

"Denise, I told you, this story is going to be huge. I need to-"

"We need to know. I've been patient. It's time." Denise left the room.

He called out, "It's *my* situation, who are *you* to make the appointment?"

The defensive reared its head, not a good sign for either of them. There was real trouble in their relationship and big story or not, they had to confront it. And dealing with it started with candor. Denise decided none of this was going to eat away at her any longer. Even if it meant seeming suspicious or doubting, she wasn't going to let them drift apart by doing nothing.

She walked back into the room, determined to let it all out, "Tell me, who knows you had a vasectomy?"

Denise had no conscious idea why everything festering inside manifested with this question. A sour cast subverted Rick's demeanor, offering a silent opinion it was a bizarre thing for her to ask. He scratched his head, "My ex-wife knows."

"Goes without saying, I'd imagine," Denise was more aggressive than Rick had ever seen her. "Anybody else?"

"Well, I was young when I had it. It wasn't something you discussed with college pals."

She was startled. *How young was he when he had it done?*

"How old were you?"

The urgency of her grilling upset Rick. He remained composed, judging it was the best way to navigate this intense subject, "I was eighteen."

A pervading fog of mystery set to lift for Denise. All she needed was answer to one question, "Does Kasey know?"

Rick winced and looked away. The thought of lying made his lip quiver. He whispered, "Yes."

Denise placed a hand over her mouth and froze. Everything fell into place in her mind and Rick knew it. Both were near tears. She dropped her hand, "You had a vasectomy ... while you ... were still a teenager?"

Rick had nothing to say. Denise wasn't angry, hurt or disappointed. She could see agony in his soul.

"You had a vasectomy because Kasey didn't go away to college with you," Denise said gently. "You did it because she went to West Point instead. You were furious ... felt the country, the establishment, took her away from you," the

284

JOHN RATTI

words came out synchronal to her insight. "It was your payback to the world ... an act negating hope in the future."

My god, could somebody actually do that? Have a vasectomy for an ideological reason because they were mad at the country over a relationship? Evidently, at least one person could. Rick must have told Kasey not long after the procedure to prove a point about the country's future. He was still at it with this story, acting out something going on between him and Kasey forever. His entire career as a journalist was spent challenging the establishment, how much due to natural disposition as to show Kasey his view of the world was the correct, and hers was wrong?

"You know Rick," Denise's voice filled with compassion, "even if you both went to the same college, the relationship probably wouldn't have worked out. You both are just too different."

Rick knew it. He always did. That's what made the effect of his long ago decision so painful. Denise had it right.

"Did your first wife figure this out?"

The way he looked at her said it all.

"That's why your marriage broke up," Denise concluded.

It's what Rick was terrified of having happen again.

"Well, it won't break up this marriage," Denise resolutely asserted, "*if you don't want it to.*"

Denise went up to the bedroom. There was too much contorted energy in the air for them to share proximity right now. Rick wished the truth brought relief instead of burden. *Why do I keep putting off finding out if it can be reversed?* If it can't, at least we'd know. The maybe we could adopt, or else live as two, or Denise could make another choice ... one being divorce. He cringed at the thought. But what if the answer was yes, it could be reversed? Something about that notion made him recoil even more. Could Rick permit himself to be a father? He wasn't sure. The way he saw the world hadn't changed. It came from his essence. Nobody can change that about themselves. Yet, a part of him behaved otherwise when he promised Denise an answer about reversing the procedure.

285

Rick was scared. Denise left the door open in the relationship. It remained up to him. He had to hazard lurking demons. He didn't know if he could.

Rick grabbed a quilt from the closet and spread out on the couch for the night. He turned off the lights and tried to sleep.

The phone rang a little later. Nobody picked it up. Gary's message echoed through the quiet house loud enough for both Rick and Denise to hear, "Hi, calling to tell you I just heard from Kasey. She'll be home tomorrow. Talk to you soon."

Neither one of them said anything, nor slept a wink after.

***

The next afternoon, Gary went to pick up Kasey at the airport. When he spotted her in the terminal, he did a double take. *Is that Kasey?* He masked surprise at her haggard bearing. She looked evaporated and hollow. A jarring sight for Gary, Kasey was always invulnerable. He almost asked if she had been ill, imagining some exotic affliction picked up abroad. Could be that's why she came home. He decided to wait for what she had to say.

Kasey was a jumble of nerves inside. It was getting late for Americans in Saudi Arabia and the situation facing them. This cloud of doom permeated all her impressions. It seemed to be getting late for everything - making relationships right, pursuing dreams, even for being alive.

Gary met her with a wide smile and deep squeeze. They locked their free hands as they walked to the car. "I didn't expect you to be on leave so soon," Gary said when they hit the highway.

"It's a little different kind of time off," Kasey tried hard to sound poised. "I've been temporarily relieved of duty."

"Are you ill?"

She noted the concern in Gary's voice, "I'm fine."

There was a hint of something he didn't like in her tone, "Then what happened?"

"I can't talk about it right now."

Gary was accustomed to her silence about military matters.

Kasey wanted to change the subject, "You look great."

"The business is back on track," he finally informed her. "Doing better than it has for years. Even with energy costs driving up the price of everything."

The news walloped Kasey in the gut. More confirmation of the truth by its effect already on things at home. Gary wondered about her troubled stare. He hoped some more positive news might help her disposition, "Wait until you see the store. I put a new coat of paint on the place." She didn't seem to be listening. Maybe hearing from an old friend would bring a grin, "I left a message with Rick saying you were coming home. He caught up to me at work this morning. He wants to see you."

It was Kasey's first time back since her father died. The house felt empty even before she walked in. She went to her room while Gary made something for them to eat.

Kasey fell onto her bed. It took better part of a day in the air to get home. The grim knowledge she held with no outlet for and desperate career situation left her numb. A few minutes to unwind and she'd be able to conceal the basket case she was. She fell asleep and awoke upright in a cold sweat. She gazed at her journals piled around the room, then went downstairs.

Kasey grew more at ease sitting in the kitchen with Gary. The door to the yard was open and spring air drifted in with a gentle evening breeze. Still, Gary saw Kasey trying to hide puzzling turmoil. He didn't press the subject, long accustomed to her silence about military matters.

They eventually went into the living room. Kasey sprawled out on the couch. Gary never saw her do that before. Usually she was a bundle of energy when home. She crunched up, knees folded toward her chest and head on a pillow. Gary sat in the recliner and turned on the TV. The news, with an image of an oil refinery on the screen and a reporter standing close by, *"The White House says this long price spike in crude should soon subside, but the damage is already done. Inflation for the year is at seventeen percent and unemployment has soared past eight. Today, both NASDAQ and the Dow fell to lowest level in five years. It will be a long time before the American economy again becomes bullish, even if oil prices drop tomorrow. Not a good sign for an incumbent president down in the polls and fighting for reelection."*

It was too much to hear. Kasey closed her eyes knowing today's news is nothing compared to what was ahead. Everything here connected to what happened to her there, yet she had no way to describe the complete picture. Anyway, she couldn't say a word about it. She was under orders not to. It was an unimaginable aloneness, knowing the peril for Americans in Saudi Arabia and no place to go with it.

The news anchor droned on without her paying attention, *"Leading international news tonight is a story from the Mideast. It centers on a startling disclosure from the US Army about an affair between an American female Army captain and a married Saudi Arabian Air Force officer who was a prince. The incident has led to the Saudi's beheading after a conviction for adultery. Will it now also mean the end on the Army captain's career?"*

A still photograph of Kasey flashed on the screen.

Kasey bolted up, eyes wide. She looked over at Gary and watched his jaw drop. Neither said a word as the reporter's voice kicked in, *"This is US Army Captain Kasey Lawrence, an intelligence officer attached to a chemical and biological detection unit inside Saudi Arabia near the Iraq border. Today, the Army publicly revealed charges she vacated duty while on an undisclosed mission to engage in a sexual relationship with married Saudi Air Force Captain Prince Nasir ibn Saud ... "*

Kasey jumped in front of the set. Incoherent noise burst from her fissured spirit before she shut off the TV. "It's all a big misunderstanding," she spit out.

Gary swallowed the lump in his throat, "I know it must be."

Stress pulled Kasey so tight she was ready to snap and bounce off the walls. A growl erupted from the entrails of her being, "What is happening?" She threw her arms over her face, finally realizing she stood in the midst of something way out of her control.

Gary grabbed her by the arms, "What happened, Kasey? Tell me what happened!"

She wanted to unburden. She tried to speak, but only gibberish came out. Gary sat her down, got her a glass of water and wiped her brow with a towel.

288

His sister was having a breakdown. He felt a pernicious atmosphere engulfing them. He held Kasey tight, not quite believing his sister needed him to be strong.

"We were on a mission," Kasey panted, " ... kidnapped inside Iraq ... taken to Iran ... and other places ... we escaped once ... "

Gary softly swayed in embrace with Kasey. She felt hot.

" ... in Lebanon, we were put on trial...then, only minutes from execution ... " Kasey gulped air and gagged on her words.

"You don't have to tell me," Gary whispered. "Not now."

Kasey gave in to her seizure, flinging her head back on the couch and letting out a moan that vibrated the ceiling. Then tears flowed down her cheeks like a monsoon's deluge down a mountain. Gary gripped her wrists until the flood ended a long time later.

Then Kasey slumped into a fetal position. Gary caressed her cheek and pushed hair out of her eyes. She stared at him, but he wasn't sure what she saw. What he was sure of was that his sister would come out of this. This was Kasey, the strongest person in the world.

Late in the night, Gary shut the kitchen door to keep out the cold deep night air. When he came back, Kasey was sitting up.

"Are you all right?"

"Yes."

Said like the old Kasey. He smiled and sat beside her.

"Gary, it's a misunderstanding on the Army's part. It's all going to straighten itself out in time."

He nodded, although he had doubts.

"For now, I'll give you a hand with the business."

"I don't want you to do that. I can-"

"I should. I want to. Dad would want me to."

No, he wouldn't, Gary thought. *He would want you fighting for your Army career.*

They talked a while longer. Gary delicately questioned why the Army went public, but Kasey stubbornly maintained it was only a mistake. Gary gave in to her. She could help him with the business. It would keep her busy.

After midnight, Kasey decided, "I'm going for a walk."

"I'll go with you."

"Let me have some alone time. I want to clear my head."

Gary knew where she needed to go.

"I'm staying awake until you come back."

"Don't worry about me," Kasey got up, kissed Gary on the forehead and left the house.

She drew a deep breath in the crisp outside air. She looked up at the gleaming sky and thought about the times over the years she stood under this unchanging firmament. She needed reminders of the enduring. She closed the gate to the yard, grinned at its familiar creaking noise and strolled onto the bridge. Her throbbing pulse mellowed soon as she began treading the planks to her favorite spot halfway over the river. She leaned over the rail and watched the flowing tide slap against the pilings. In a trance of memories, she glanced at the house and up to window where she saw her father alive for the last time. She shivered and turned away.

Footsteps headed her way. Kasey never looked. She knew the stride. It was Rick. Kasey gave a furtive peek as he stepped from a mist. The moon illuminated the empathy in his eyes. It meant he knew. She gazed ahead over the water. Rick stopped a few feet away. Kasey preferred not to face him. It would expose her to the effortless insight they had into each other. Even as both stared ahead, a current stronger than the tide below arched the space between them. There was never a vacuum when they were together.

Yes, Rick knew. He had so much to say before finding out, but now he struggled for words.

"I thought you could use a friend right now."

She had no idea what she needed anymore. Maybe nothing more than to let the wandering surf lull her into a stupor.

"I take it you saw the news tonight," she finally said.

"I know it has to be a lie," Rick at once shot back.

"Not a lie, a *misunderstanding*," Kasey quickly fired back, already tired of correcting mistaken notions.

As usual, it didn't take long for their immutable differences to arise. Kasey dropped her head and glared into the dark water. For a moment, she wished it a churning abyss she could throw herself into.

Rick abhorred this wretched beast keeping endless vigil on the borderline separating them, "I'm worried about you. Talk to me."

"What can I say? The truth will come out."

He wanted to connect with her and offer support, but Kasey never had the needs he wanted her to have. In all the years they knew each other, barely did a day pass without them aware of the agony of knowing each other. Rick knew she would never open up.

"The information you told me to check out has led to a story," he watched her become still. "It's a big one."

Kasey didn't admit to herself she wanted to know more. She kept quiet, probing mirages in the cloaking fog.

Rick was certain she wanted him to go on, "I have proof the Army is manufacturing plastic explosives. I possess the material evidence. Irrefutable as a stain on a dress. I'm writing the story now."

The disclosure fueled Kasey's inner storm. *Could Army manufactured plastic explosives be used against American citizens in the Mideast?* She flinched and pushed away the thought, the logic simply too revolting to be fact. "Good luck with it." Then she quickly changed the subject, "how's Denise?"

"I see ... small talk."

"I want to know."

Rick kicked the railing and raised his voice, "Wake up, will you! Somebody's out to ruin your life. Better protect yourself."

Kasey turned her back to him and battled an urge to scream back.

"I know something important is behind all this," Rick evened his tone, "I think what you're going through now is part of it."

She bit her tongue, stifling the instinct to protect her denial with an accusation of paranoia. She worried what might come out of her mouth.

"Tell me, Kasey," Rick pleaded, for her good rather than his ambition. "Tell me."

Kasey faced him and waved her hands, "There's nothing to tell."

They locked eyes. Kasey couldn't lie, Rick would see through it. She went with a minor truth, if only to keep him from haunting her, "We had reports of unusually potent plastic explosives turning up in the hands of terrorists."

She should have known. Rick instantly became the journalist, "You suspect they came from America?"

Kasey shrugged, "One intercepted shipment weighed exactly 45.35 kilograms."

"Meaning?"

"Well, by weight standards used here that comes out to precisely one hundred pounds ... "

Kasey stopped. Why did she reveal so much?

Too late. Rick rubbed his chin, "That's the reason you think it came from America?"

"At the time I did. Later I realized it may have come from a place using that measurement standard to hide its source," Kasey backtracked. It was no lie. She had no proof where the stuff came from. "After all, if you were trying to hide plastic explosives coming from America, wouldn't it be stupid to use the weight standard used almost exclusively here?" She hoped to confuse Rick by muddling his thinking with hazy data.

It didn't work, "Stupid? I wasn't long ago NASA lost the Mars Climate Orbiter because someone forgot to transfer navigational measurements to metric. Three hundred million dollars down the drain. Another government agency could make a similar mistake."

He hit the nerve Kasey didn't want touched. Every unfailing explanation had a repudiation.

"I know there's more you can tell me, Kasey."

"There's nothing to say," she gave a let's-end-it-gesture.

"If I only had the slightest residual trace of the explosives, I could tell if they matched what I have. I could even find out when they were made."

Kasey didn't respond. He didn't expect her to. He was simply sketching out a defense for things he had no firm knowledge about. She knew it and the cost - the whole story.

Rick took a step back, "I'll leave you with your thoughts."

Neither one of them moved. Kasey looked away for a moment. Turning back, Rick was gone. She peered into the mist and bent her head until detecting parting footsteps. She lingered until it was quiet.

She heard the television in Gary's room tuned to the news when she walked into the house. Heading up the stairs, she heard him mute the sound.

Kasey switched the light on in her bedroom. She sat on the edge of her bed and stared at the pile of journals winding along the wall. She reached over and picked up the unfinished one, flipping to the page where she taped the bit of uniform sleeve wrapped in plastic. The part she wiped after handling the cellulose acetate Saddam gave them. She fingered the cloth through its casing. Her frowning eyes stared.

I have to destroy this ... it violates the edict against appropriating data from an intelligence mission. She closed the diary. Why did I keep it in the first place? She shook *her* head. *I'm going to destroy this right now.*

She didn't. Instead, she slid into the chair at her desk and began the account of everything that happened since she was last home. Kasey filled the journal, then another, and most of one more before dawn peeked through the window behind her. She leaned back in the chair and rubbed her aching wrist. Existing in a revitalized zone beyond fatigue, she eased downstairs and let the screen door fall against her back to hush its sound while she walked outside.

Songbirds warbled around Kasey in the emerging daylight as she strolled up to the hill to the cemetery, stopping at the aisle at the top row. She saluted each headstone memorializing ancestors who served in the military. Nearing her father's grave, her hand fell from her brow. His plot was at the end of the row, spaced a distance away from the rest. Baffled emotion launched Kasey to the still unmarked site. She understood it took some time to set the headstone, but why was he buried away from the others? He should be next to his father,

Casey IV, who died in Korea. She stood over the freshly heaped earth until the knawing pain receded. She couldn't stop thinking about how close he was to her right now, but all she could do connect with him was reach down and touch the dirt. She crouched, gripping a handful in a tight fist and realizing this was as close as she would ever again get to her father. She stood up and looked down over the river, only now hearing the ocean she could see in the distance. Fishing boats in the cove by her house were leaving their moorings and neighbors living along the water were leaving for work in their cars. The new day had seized her solitary time. She let the soil slide from her hand and walked home.

Gary was drinking coffee in the kitchen when Kasey came in. "Why is dad buried at the end of the row?" she asked right away.

"It's what he wanted." Gary watched her trying to figure why. "I didn't know it until we took him to the plot," he shrugged.

It would have been different if I was there, Kasey at first thought. Pouring some coffee, she realized it was best she wasn't there. Who was she to impose her will over her father's?

Kasey sat across from Gary, aware he had more facts about the charges against her than he did last night. Gary looked away, "Dad felt the military family should be buried in a continuous line."

She knew what he meant. One vacant plot remained to complete the unbroken sequence. For her. Colliding emotions made her eyes soggy. Gary got up and hugged her from behind. "I know, Kasey," he whispered, resting his head on her back and keeping it there until her heart relaxed.

"Are you going to be all right?"

Kasey cleared her throat, "We'll get through the day."

"You're not coming to work with me."

"I told you, I'm going to-"

"Not today you won't."

"Yes, I want-"

"You look really tired. You must have been up all night."

"I'm fine."

"Stop arguing with me," Gary smiled. "Not today. You only got back yesterday."

Kasey again tried to speak, but Gary gently lunged and put a finger on her lip, "Get some sleep."

She gave up. Gary kissed her and left. Kasey made her way upstairs with heavy feet. Fatigue caught up with her. She cursed Gary. It was only because he reminded her of it. She collapsed on her bed without taking off any clothes.

Kasey woke up all spun around on the bed. The afternoon sun on her face interrupted a dream she couldn't remember. Something about a plane crashing on top of a crowd of people? Her mouth was dry and her bones cracked when she lifted herself off the bed and to her desk. She started writing again. Only without mindfulness could Kasey tell her story. Maybe to relieve the pressure of what never went away - it was a very late hour for Americans in Saudi Arabia and she didn't know what to do. She stopped after cramming another diary. She needed to get out of the house. After a shower, she drove off to see Gary in her father's car. Before pulling out of the driveway, Jack the mailman walked into the yard on his rounds. He didn't seem to notice her. Kasey kept quiet, for the first time wondering what acquaintances might have heard.

She passed by *Uncle Moe's* before heading up the hill to the store. Uncle Moe stood outside talking to somebody. She beeped the horn when he spotted her. He never smiled. Or waved. He squinted, maybe unable to tell who it was.

Kasey got out of the car and looked over the grounds. The store sparkled, clean and kept. Did Gary even paint the fence, or was it new? He said business was good, but there was no one parked in the lot. Could be due to near closing time?

Approaching the entrance, Kasey saw Gary inside sitting on a stool wearing a blank expression. A puzzling image. When Kasey walked in, he livened up. Still, there was an odd vibe.

Kasey tried to avoid it and make nice, "You did a great job," she said, strolling the tidy aisles.

"Thanks," he replied in a curious monotone.

"Not busy today?"

"No."

She went behind the counter and faced him, "What's eating you?"

A customer walked in. Donna, a friend of Kasey's for over twenty years.

"Hi," Kasey smiled and approached her, never noticing the sudden unease in the air. Kasey cut short the limp embrace she received. Now she knew something was wrong.

Kasey asked, "How's your family?" and wondered what it was

"We're all doing well," Donna looked at the floor.

Kasey wanted to shout - *It's me, remember? We went through twelve years of school together. I was at your wedding. My father baked brownies for us during sleepovers at my house.*

Gary broke the excruciating pause, "Did you want the loam today?"

Donna was relieved, "Could you bring it?"

"I planned to after I close. It's already in the truck."

Donna quickly scribbled a check. She wanted out of there, but did pause by the door, "I hope it all works out for you, Kasey." She didn't wait for a response. The sound of bell tacked to the door was her goodbye.

Through the window, Kasey watched Donna drive away. *She treated me like I have an infectious disease.* She glanced at Gary. He looked away. Kasey marched outside, slamming the door behind her. She headed down the long driveway to *Uncle Moe's.*

Everybody inside iced up in when they saw her coming. Kasey entered with a tense smirk and probing eyes. She nodded at the faces and walked up to Uncle Moe behind the grill, "Uncle Moe, I missed you." She plunged into one of the bear hugs he was famous for dishing out. It was a corrosive gesture, not one of sweeping emotion. A test of an inconceivable assumption - that people she knew an entire lifetime were now strangers.

Uncle Moe's arms never left his side during her embrace. Kasey pulled back and looked around. Everybody stared back as if she stepped into the place from another planet.

Kasey slowly moved backwards, nodding and mumbling, " ... OK ... OK ... fine ... " before bumping into the door. She left without closing it, jogged up to the car and peeled away.

JOHN RATTI

Passing *Uncle Moe's,* everybody inside watched as she sped by.
Kasey careened into the yard back home, furiously seeking refuge in the last familiar place in her world. She sat inside the car, unable to gain control of mind or body. It took several deep breaths before she could slide out. Kasey picked up the newspaper on the doorstep and saw a word on the front page that made her cringe. She ripped away the band and opened the paper.

LOCAL WOMAN SNARED IN ARMY SEX SCANDAL

An inferno erupted in her viscera, a retching hatred of everything. Birds, sun, flowers, sea, everything she could glimpse and one thing she couldn't - herself. She opened the screen door. A book fell at her feet, *The United Nations Standards of International Military Code.* No doubt put there by Rick.
Inside, she flung the newspaper against a wall and pitched the book on the couch. Then Kasey stood fixed in the middle of the living room until her knees buckled or earth gyrated. She couldn't tell which. The universe was now so bizarre it could have been both. At the same time, she felt stretched like rubber in opposite directions, on one hand consciously insisting everything would work out while an alternative she couldn't consider urgently bid to be heard.
Kasey stumbled onto the couch and stared at the book. Was Rick trying to provoke her anger by rubbing salt into their wounding differences with preposterous insinuations? Or did he truly believe she needed to consider its content?
She thumbed through the pages stating ratified precepts of acceptable military conduct. Most of it chartered during the trials of German Nazis in Nuremberg after World War Two. Something caught her eye, motivating her to mark a page and read more thoroughly. An hour into it, the phone rang. Kasey hesitated, then picked it up, "Hello."
"Hi."
Could it be it person Kasey thought it was during the ensuing silence?
"Thank you for not hanging up," the hesitant voice said.
Yes, it was her mother.

"I just want to tell you I know the charges cannot be true. No child of Ted would ever disgrace the uniform."

Kasey wanted to say something sarcastic, but held back.

"I have never been more proud to say my daughter is a Lawrence. All the way!"

Kasey never recalled having a tender emotion for her mother. She wasn't going to allow
one now, "It's ... nice to hear."

"Kasey, I'm praying for you."

" ... Thank you ... "

A pause made each realize it best to end the conversation here.

"Goodbye, *mother.*"

Cutty hadn't heard the word for a long time. She knew her daughter well enough to leave it at that. "Goodbye," Cutty replied, hanging on the line for a few seconds before hanging up.

Kasey stared at the phone. The call unsettled her, further proof of how peculiar her world had become.

She went back to reading the manual, engrossed enough to forget the crisis around her as she pondered sections she outlined. She put the book down after glancing at the clock, wanting to make dinner before Gary got home. She foraged around the kitchen and found pasta to boil. She wasn't the cook Gary was, but he never complained.

Gary walked in. Kasey peeked out from the kitchen, "Hi, I'm making dinner for us."

He gave her a thin smile. She noticed a misery in his eyes she didn't know how to access. He went to his room and closed the door.

Kasey gave him some time, then yelled up, "Come and get it!" She sat at the table and waited, finally shouting, "Gary!"

No response. A horrible image flashed in her mind that suddenly propelled Kasey from the table and up the stairs. Her heart beat wildly with thoughts about what happened to her father. She pushed open the bedroom door and saw Gary face down on his bed. She stopped over him and screamed, "Gary!"

He immediately stirred, but it gave her no relief. She rolled him over and Gary covered his eyes.

Kasey tugged at his hands, "What's wrong?"

He dropped his arms. His face looked raw and he let out a wail, "I can't believe what they're saying about you!"

Gary started weeping, needing to release the strain over things they weren't communicating about. Kasey blamed herself, wishing she could tell him everything. Her lawyer told her to keep quiet right now, but the truth was Kasey had no idea how to discuss allegations of sexual misconduct. Especially with her brother. She could only hold him until he let it all out.

In time, Gary composed himself and got up. Kasey searched for words to ease what he was going through. She failed. "Come on, dinner's getting cold," was all she said.

Kasey went downstairs. Gary soon followed.

The emotional upheaval over, they went back to not communicating.

Gary sullenly picked at his food.

Kasey smiled, "Is it that bad?"

He briefly grinned, "No ... actually, it tastes very good."

Kasey gave him a yeah-sure look.

"I'm just not hungry," Gary explained.

He nibbled a bit more, lingering over the plate until Kasey finished her meal. Once she did, Gary went into the living room and picked up the newspaper sitting on the floor. He sat on the couch, glancing at the headline. A second later he tossed it aside. He wasn't going to turn on the news either. He folded his arms while Kasey did the dishes. He was in that position when Kasey came into the room and sat in the recliner.

The house was quiet. There was too much going on for the silence to be comfortable. Kasey reflected on life for Gary, living here alone with memories of the father he took care of without getting much credit for while his ever absent sister was adored. She gazed at him. He wasn't looking her way.

"I love you."

Gary snapped out of his daze, aiming a wide smile at her, "I love you, too."

The room felt better. It was getting dark. Kasey switched on a light. Gary stood up, "I'm going out for a while."

Kasey nodded. Let him get air. He went to the bathroom, then left. Kasey stayed in the chair, continuing to read the manual. Eventually she took it to her room and sat at her desk, pouring over the marked segments, mouthing words until committing them to memory.

Gary went to a bar downtown. An old haunt he kept away from since his father died. When he walked in, the bartender switched the TV from the news to something else. Gary sat on a stool by the door, ordered a shot of whiskey and stared at the glass for a long time. People began to notice him. Gary nodded at the faces turning his way. None were friends, but the several he knew were usually happy to shoot the breeze over a drink. This time, they all stayed aloof, looking away or at the TV when his eyes met theirs. Gary noticed those clustered in booths nudging each other and muttering. He grabbed the shot glass in a fist and downed it in one gulp. Then he asked for another round. Gary knocked back three shots in ten minutes, growing angrier at the sneaky looks he sensed. Then he ordered a beer, sighing at the warm comfort the liquor brought in his stomach. He picked up pieces of conversations around him. Words no doubt about Kasey. A man he knew since high school sat at the opposite end of the bar. When Gary ordered a second beer, the man staggered his way.

"Sorry to hear about your sister."

"Thanks," somebody finally acknowledged him, "I am too." Gary sipped his drink, "The truth will eventually come out."

"Yeah," the man said, "then the whore will get what she deserves for disgracing the uniform."

Gary briefly turned, then plunged at him, knuckling away. Both rolled onto the floor. The bartender hurled over the counter and tried to break them up. Gary flailed at the man, even while in a headlock. Someone sitting at the bar flung himself on Gary and pulled his hair. A woman ran over and hit Gary in the face with a bottle. The bartender called the police as Gary took on all comers, ducking flying furniture and bursting bottles. Anyone sympathetic to Gary stood by and watched or ran into the street. Gary was pinned on the floor when the police came. After statements from the bartender and patrons naming him as instigator, they hauled Gary away.

Kasey was alone on the bridge when she heard a vehicle turn onto the street along the quiet cove. She watched from darkness as a car stopped in front of her house. The lights on inside cast enough glow for her to see the government license plates. Two men wearing Army uniforms got out and walked into the yard. She labored for a better look. *A general? A general and a major? A late night visit?* She didn't like sensations the image roused and decided to stay put while they knocked on the door. Then rang the bell. And knocked again. And rang the bell again. The major peeked through a window. *If they try the door, they could walk in.* The chill up her spine was abrupt conscious awareness at the significance of what she left alone inside. After a long pause on the stoop, they went back to the car. She was only yards away. If they took a good look around they might even see her. They slowly drove away.

When the sound of the car's engine faded, Kasey started walking home, picking up the pace once she stepped off the bridge.

Inside the house, she locked the door behind her and scrambled around the kitchen until she found some airtight plastic freezer bags. Then she hurried to her room, sealed her journals inside, cleaned out her duffel bag and packed the diaries.

She peeked out the front door before hauling the bag onto the bridge. Halfway across she kneeled over the side and sheltered the bag in a nook formed by pilings. The tide was rising and she wasn't sure where the water level would top off, but she needed these things out of the house right away. Self-preservation finally won out over denial. Kasey secured the bag as best she could, then ran back toward the house.

In the yard, she lowered the American flag from the pole, turned it upside down, and raised it high. A reversed American flag – the symbol of distress. Kasey dashed into the house and for the phone.

Rick was working late in his home office, the story almost done. He spent most of the day *Examiner* going over a draft. Rick's account electrified Carl. The paper planned to serialize the story in three parts soon as they had a look at the evidence. They were due to see it in the morning. Denise's ultimatum remained on hold. She waited, but wouldn't forever, as their non-communication constantly reminded him. He was working full speed and still sleeping on the couch. Denise had taken to not coming home from work until late to minimize their time together. It was not a pleasant atmosphere. Especially since Rick quietly left the house last night to visit Kasey on the bridge. He hoped Denise was asleep when he slithered away. She wasn't.

Rick rushed to grab the phone on the second ring. Immediately sensing who it was, he didn't want Denise to hear.

"Hello," he near whispered.

"Rick, *remember our letters.*"

"Huh? Kasey, what do you mean? Is everything all right?"

Kasey was so paranoid she thought it possible her line was tapped, "Rick, *remember our love letters.*" She wouldn't be any more specific.

"Tell me what you mean. Spell it out. What's-"

The dial tone stopped him. She didn't sound right. *Something is going on over there and* it's *not good.* Rick glanced toward the bedroom down the hall.

Kasey went upstairs, stripped and put on her uniform. Then she sat in the living room, watching the door. She knew they would be back. It sounded as if they were coming now.

Rick grabbed his head wracking his brain. *What was she telling me? Why didn't she say more? Letters ... the letters we used to leave under the bridge?* ...

He had to find out what was going on. He left his room and sneaked down the hall. The bedroom door flew open.

Denise glared, "That was Kasey, wasn't it?"

He said nothing. He didn't have to.

Denise pointed a finger at him, "You go," then she aimed a thumb at her chest, "and I'm gone."

Rick tried to explain, but Denise was emphatic, "You go ... I'm gone. Understand?"

She closed the bedroom door. Rick stared at it. Something was wrong in his house, something was wrong down the street ... something was wrong ... *what should I do?*

Kasey opened the door when she heard the footsteps in the yard. The general and major shook their heads at the upside down flag as her silhouette emerged in the doorway. Kasey stepped out and saluted.

"Captain Lawrence," the general snapped, "I remind you even presently adjourned of duty you continue under Army jurisdiction."

Kasey continued at attention, "Yes, sir."

"Your orders are to accompany us."

"Yes, sir. I am ready, sir."

She marched between them. Another major waited behind the wheel of the car. Kasey remembered what counsel said, that the Army might try to gain incriminating evidence by asking for a further mission debriefing. She figured that's what they were up to, intimidating her by calling in the middle of the night. Her Army attorney in Saudi Arabia said another lawyer would contact her back home, but it hadn't happened yet. He also urged her to engage civilian counsel, but she hadn't done that, only being home for two days. She got into the car and braced herself for an eventual masked interrogation.

Rick ferociously paced in his living room. If he left the house, Denise would be gone when he returned. But something was desperately wrong over at Kasey's. He was in a vise, squeezed harder by the second. He thought about running upstairs and again trying to explain. He decided he never could. That was the problem. He never could explain his relationship with Kasey to his first wife, or Denise, or even himself. He had to accept that maybe he never would, just as he had to accept Kasey may be in danger and he was the one she reached out to. If he did nothing, what would happen to her? *I gotta go.* He scampered out the door and broke into a sweat before jogging by the old lamp posts and arched sidewalks leading to the cove.

He veered onto Kasey's street as the car hit the intersection. Rick looked as it briefly slowed down. Too dark to see inside, but he saw the government plates. *She's in that car.*

The lights were on in Kasey's house. He didn't notice the flag until running into the yard. The sight erased any doubt. *There's trouble.* He raced to the door and knocked, "Kasey! Are you there! Gary! Kasey!"

Rick didn't intend to wait. He walked in, checked around, then hurdled up the stairs. He looked in Kasey's room. Her civilian clothes were on the floor. She'd never leave them like that. It was time to head for the bridge.

He hustled outside, squinting around into the dark until his feet hit the wood planks. He twisted his head every which way. *I don't see anything.* He slid face down and started looking underneath at the posts. Rising water drizzled on his face. He crawled along, bending his head and feeling around.

Rick felt something. A strap. Pulling on it, more weight. Looking hard, he saw the duffel bag on a ledge, but the tide was too high to haul it away without a soaking. Rick jumped into the neck high river and allowed the current to draw him under the bridge. He clutched the bag with both hands, held it over his head, and struggled toward shore. He tossed the bag on land, climbed a granite bank, grabbed it and rushed home.

During the ride, nobody explained anything to Kasey and she didn't ask. They moved west on the highway for over an hour. She knew the only Army base for hundreds of miles was north. Determined not to let what they do throw her off guard, she stayed calm, watched and waited. They exited the main road into deep rural night until faint lights emerged ahead. *Why, this is Fort Davis.* An Army base decommissioned long ago. Last she heard, it was occasionally used for National Guard housing.

Tonight the place resembled its past days. Brightly illuminated grounds and a guarded perimeter. Waved through the access, the car stopped at the administrative complex. The general escorted Kasey inside former headquarters to a long room near what must have once been the Commander's suite. He told Kasey to sit and wait, then left her alone. Kasey absorbed every detail of the space. The peeling paint, cobwebs, musty odor and antiquated furniture. Time slowly passed. She felt composed, eager to get on with whatever they wanted. Confinement with only thoughts made her reflect on Nasir, Bowers, Harper, Moore and all the others who gave their lives to save her. She thought about where she found herself now. And about what must be going on in Saudi Arabia. More time went by. She thought about her father, the mission inside Iraq and everything happening now. She thought about Americans in Saudi Arabia. More time passed. Hours. *Are they trying to rattle me?* She wondered if Rick understood her message. If he did, then right now he'd know more then she ever believed she could tell him, or tell anybody. And he would tell the world. The idea shook her up. But it was too late now and she couldn't let anything make her uneasy. She thought about Americans in Saudi Arabia. The lights outside dimmed. *More mind games?* Kasey was angry. She thought about Americans in Saudi Arabia. Emotion beyond anger. Saudi Arabia. Americans at risk. Nobody is doing a thing about it.

Secretary of State Drake tilted away from Amfrick and Cunningham. The three were in a limousine, near the rear of a motorcade heading toward Fort Davis. The men hadn't stopped firing declarations at her since she entered the car. Drake tuned them out miles back, allowing her mind to fall into a void to distance her hostility.

"Make sure she really understands the consequences," Amfrick said, as if instructing a subordinate. "Make her know how hot it'll get for her."

Drake refused to look at him, "You've said that six times."

"Be firm," Cunningham dictated, "not diplomatic."

"Excuse me," the secretary's blood rushed into her cheeks as she turned Cunningham's way, "was that an insult?"

He glared back.

"Get this straight," Drake abandoned her polished civility, "I don't like either of you. I've served administrations for twenty years and watched spin idiots like you two come and go. The career personnel are the ones holding everything together. I cannot tell you how many times I've been asked to carry out orders in the enlightened self-interest of some cretin. Usually at the country's expense.

HONOR BOUND

I suffer them because between all the crap I do what I can to see the country stays on course."

Amfrick blossomed in corrosive atmospheres. He readied to rip into Drake, but Cunningham motioned him quiet. Drake finally said what both knew she always thought. Drake wasn't done and Cunningham wanted her to get it out of her system - now.

"When I'm told to destroy someone, I deaden myself and do it," Drake was almost musing. "It's the only way to survive politics. And every time I bring the bad news, another bit of me dies. Public service in the interests of a great nation and a better world - the government hasn't been about that for a long time. You can't even form bonds with colleagues. One day you may need to destroy them. Or them you. It's getting worse all the time, even in the Foreign Service. Now ambassadors are appointed due to the dollars they raise a party or president. They have no experience in the countries they serve in. We clean up the mess they make." Drake's lip curled with malice, "Or people like you make."

Amfrick heard enough, "You talk like that when we're doing you a favor? You wanted a chance to help her. We're giving it to you."

Cunningham didn't want to see his associate raising his voice. He smiled and smoothed the tension with his low baritone, "Judith, you do your job well. So do we. When push comes to shove, we all know it's not you the president will listen to. We're the ones who get him elected. That's just how it is. There are parts of all our jobs none of us like. For you, it's cleaning up the mess. Maybe you can come away feeling good about something. You need that right now. Take your shot with her before we have to."

That's what scared Drake. An election was coming up with the president in desperate straits, according to polls. These two would go any length to win another term.

The motorcade entered Fort Davis and stopped in front of the administration complex. Cunningham held the door open for Drake. The procession of black cars idled in a semi -circle after severe looking civilians excited and swarmed around the buildings. The general met Drake at the entrance and led her inside. The secretary set foot alone into the conference room. Kasey remembered the surprise she experienced first time she walked into a meeting and came across Drake. It seemed a lifetime ago. Kasey's reaction this time proved it was. Last time she was impressed. This time she was offended. The secretary knew the truth. She had to. Her presence now represented something menacing. Drake even looked different. All the trappings of her position melted away. Drake seemed smaller and older.

Kasey stood up and shook Drake's hand, "Good evening, or should I say *good morning,* Madam Secretary."

Drake got the sarcasm, "I'm sorry, Captain Lawrence. I came a long way." Drake slid a chair across the floor close to Kasey and had a seat after Kasey did.

"Captain, I asked for this meeting with you," Drake sounded like a doctor ready to deliver a somber prognosis. "I'm not out to question you about your mission. This is no attempt to trick evidence out of you. You don't take orders from me."

The secretary folded her hands on the table, "I am bringing you a proposal. One the Army will sign off on. I hope you will agree to it. Here is the deal: Never say a word about the mission, about anything that went on before, during and after it. Do that and all charges against you will be dropped. The Army *will* say it was a mistake. In return, we need your silence."

Kasey no longer trusted Drake, or the Army. The threat of revealing everything at court martial was her only retort against the Army's miscalculation. Somewhere down the line, conceding it would come back to haunt her. Apart from that, the secretary's offer failed to address the most important thing, "I want you to tell me why the president will not order evacuation of Americans in Saudi Arabia?"

This was not what Drake wanted to hear. She sighed, "As I've told you before, our information indicates there is no reason for concern," she had to look away from Kasey. "You have been misled by those you met."

"Stop lying," Kasey went on the offensive. "If I didn't know the truth, this meeting would not be happening."

Kasey couldn't see this was for her benefit and the alternative something much worse. The secretary was determined to make Kasey take the deal, even if it took more lies, "The Army believes, mistakenly or not, you deserted to have an affair. The Army doesn't need or want the issues this kind of trial would raise. They're not the only ones that feel that way. After all, there's an election soon-"

In an instant, the big picture emerged. Kasey wanted to slap a palm against her forehead for not figuring it out much earlier, "If the president orders an evacuation before the Saudis abdicate, then he'll be forced to admit the oil is gone." Kasey jumped from the pivoted around and jumped from her chair, "I don't care about the election. Thousands of Americans are in danger right now! They need to know what's about to happen." Kasey leaned over the table, "If they're not warned, and something happens, I'll see it comes out at my trial. There is no deal!"

Drake's strategy backfired. The attempt to get Kasey to reach a settlement only exposed the sickening reality she didn't know. The secretary's instinct was to persist, but the look on Kasey's face left her lost for words. A distressing silence passed between them.

The door to the room slowly opened. Kasey glanced over and saw shadows, strange faces and bustling activity. The president emerged from this cyclone of energy and walked alone into the room. Kasey leaped to her feet, poised at attention. Drake stood, hiding the clenched fist liberating bristling anger at the realization a listening device must be in the room.

Drake nodded at the president and exited. Kasey kept unblinking eyes on him. Her mind focused to an occasional fantasy of meeting the president at a ceremony promoting her to general.

"At ease, Captain Lawrence."

Kasey barely moved, unable to halt racing images. Pictures from television, newspapers and history books. Memories of important events and moments somber to exhilarating. Inescapably evoked by proximity to one holding the office.

The president took a seat and gestured for Kasey to do the same. *He looks different in person.* The president glanced as if sensing her impression. *He must know people often think that.* What struck Kasey even more was how he moved. Affected ... forced ... unreal. As if physically pulled and prodded for a lifetime by endless manipulators until his pelvic center got all quivery and wobbled up, down and sideways. Kasey felt no weight to his stare. He didn't seem to absorb anything. The room felt hollow with him in it.

"The secretary made you aware of the Army's offer?"

"She did, sir."

Even one on one, the president spoke from a dais. He reminded Kasey of the performer from another era who went town to town forever reprising the same role. A role that brought droves to see the celebrity, even after he became a rote caricature. Curiously, the observation spurred Kasey to reflect on her journals. Why would she hide them and call Rick if she believed this was only a masked interrogation? Instead, her behavior resulted from her world being turned upside down too many times and fears it would happen again. A horror of a worst that was yet to come, that once they came back for her, she would disappear forever. What for so long she needed to believe a misunderstanding on the Army's part was much more sinister, and her heart gasped at the reality.

"Captain Lawrence," the president lowered his voice, "take the Army's offer."

"I can't, sir."

"You are facing twenty years in prison. I'm asking you to reconsider." He phrased it as a personal plea, but it felt like an order.

Kasey briefly paused, "I just did, sir. I decline."

The president saw her quick response as insolence, "Then this is how we'll do it - I hereby order your silence about all events that occurred in service before, during and after the charges against you."

She saw his determination to box her into a corner and force her to accept the deal. Somebody expertly prepared him how to react to all her objections. *Well, we'll see about that.*

"It'll have to come out in order for me to defend myself, sir."

"Military trials are not public proceedings. The order I'm giving you is not to discuss what went on before, during, or after your mission while in active service."

The media. *That's what he is afraid of.* Twisting her arm with threats cloaked in facts about closed tribunals and decades in prison, locked away in silence.

The president stood up, "If do not accept my order, I will immediately have you held until trial as a matter of national security. Do you understand, captain?"

"Yes, sir."

"I'm *ordering* your silence."

"I hear you, sir."

"You hear me? Tell me you will comply."

"I can't, sir."

"You intend to disobey my order."

"I'm saying I can't obey it, sir."

One word worried the president, "*Can't*?"

"Sir, the United States is signatory to international military law that compels a soldier to disobey an order in association with acts codified as immoral."

The president dropped his jaw, stupefied, his foaming rage the first genuine sentiment Kasey witnessed, "How dare you!" The president stammered, thrown off script until discovering a retort in his ire, "You challenge my order by invoking a law used to prosecute Nazis after World War Two?" He shook his head, "It won't work."

He got in her face. She could smell his breath, his body. He's only a man. Her soul grimaced. *A delusive one.* She looked at the floor. *My Commander-in-Chief.*

"Captain, I forgive your obstinance," the president calmed and employed a new strategy. "It's likely you were brainwashed by your captors. Maybe you need to be committed for a time instead of put on trial."

Another threat. Kasey didn't care anymore.

"Again, I am ordering your silence."

"Yes, I hear you, sir."

"I'll have you taken away right now."

This was going nowhere. She sensed the president wouldn't let this continue much longer. Kasey decided it was time to lead this dance, "You can't keep the facts from being revealed, sir."

"You're threatening to disobey my order by going to the media? I won't-"

310

"A reporter already knows, sir. He found out our military is manufacturing plastic explosives and has evidence from an Army base in North Carolina. He also knows everything that happened to me, sir."

Behind the livid scowl, Kasey saw the dread in his eyes. The panic at losing another term because everything didn't go as planned. In the moment, everything became clear to Kasey. The country she served, loved and invested her life in is hostage to individuals who believe their personal gain is in the country's best interests. Then *give him a way to get what he wants, but force him to do the right thing.*

The president strained to mimic authority, but his tone betrayed the effort, "How can you do that?"

"Sir, if you give an order to evacuate all Americans inside Saudi Arabia within twenty-four hours, I can see to it the story never reaches the public. If you wait any longer, it'll be too late for me to stop it."

Surprisingly, the president seemed to grasp what she was up to, probably seeing it as familiar back room hardball. His pretense faded, his body almost relaxed. They were now conniving peers, "Never comes to light? How do I know you can guarantee that?"

"I am honor bound by my word, sir," Kasey followed his eyes when she said it. "Court martial or not."

The president walked a circle around her, hands behind his back, "You spoke to a reporter? Before your case is adjudicated? The Army could sanction you for that alone."

"I never spoke about it, sir. The reporter found my diaries."

The president smirked. A technicality. Clever. "How do I know any of this is true, that there's any story at all?"

"I am an honest soldier. You know that, sir. If you doubt me, then wait and see."

He scrutinized her without scorn or anger. When he paraded into the room, it was a take the deal or be hauled away in confined silence proposition. But now? She was home only two days. It didn't seem likely what she said about a reporter, a coincidentally relevant story, and discovered diaries could be true.

Could he risk it wasn't? The president tapped a finger on his chin, "That will be all, Captain Lawrence. *For now.*"

Kasey saluted, "Yes, sir."

In a blink, the president disappeared from the room.

Rick raced toward home with the bag, desperately hoping Denise would still be there. He was away only minutes. Would she leave so quickly? Maybe she decided not to go at all. *I can talk her out of it. I'll get the test, tomorrow, if possible.* No matter what else must be put off. Coiled within every thought about his marriage were questions; Where is Kasey? Why is the flag in her yard upside down? What's in the bag? Why didn't she simply hand over its contents if she wanted him to have what's inside? Something serious was underway and instinct said it somehow linked to his story.

He caught a glimpse of the driveway. Denise's car was gone. Rick bolted through the door and shouted, "Denise!" as if conjuring her by name would cause denial to magically prevail over fact.

Rick dropped the bag in the living room, heart in mouth and feet spinning around. Maybe she went for a drive and would return. *She's throwing a scare into me, showing she means business this time.* He dashed up into the bedroom. His eyes went to the open closet. Half empty. *Oh, god ... she's gone. She really left.*

He walked downstairs and slumped onto the couch. He tilted his head and stared at the ceiling for a long time. Then he looked at the bag, grabbed it and set it on his lap. He paused, foolishly wondering if he never peeked inside and put it back under the bridge Denise might reappear with his undoing the act. He shook his head. It wasn't going to happen. He slid the zipper open and saw diaries wrapped in plastic. He knew Kasey kept records of everything. He inspected the top journal as he carefully removed its casing. Then Rick opened it to the first page:

Three days ago, I met Saddam Hussein.

Rick's eyes shot wide open.

312

It turned out a curious duty General Zalman assigned. A mission into Iraq with Saudi Air Force Captain Prince Nasir ibn Saud.

A mission inside Iraq? Meeting Saddam Hussein with the late Saudi officer? The words exploded in Rick's psyche.

Saddam had a disturbing present for us. One hundred pounds of cellulose acetate. In thirty percent concentration, turns out. C-30, a density likely only possible to manufacture in America.

C-30. Made in America. Ending up in Iraq. The diary revealed a story far greater than the one Rick had. Menacing facts, dangerous to know. Feeling exposed, his eyes darted around the room.

Saddam said they caught smugglers taking it to Jordan. One of them gave testimony before me it was heading for Saudi Arabia.

Rick labored to understand the significance.

Saddam kept repeating the batch weighed 45.35 kilograms. I got his point. The mass was one hundred pounds in units of US measure.

The information stirred paranoia. Rick suddenly grew aware of every sound. A page later he discovered the portion of Kasey's sleeve taped inside the diary. He gazed at it, astounded. *If this evidence connects to mine, it will be the biggest story since Watergate!* Rick jumped up, locked all the doors and shut off every light but the table lamp he sat near. Then he immersed himself in Kasey's ensuing words.

Gary slumped on a bench, alone in the holding cell at the police station. His alternating sobs and curses were familiar drunken prattle to the overnight desk sergeant. Another officer lingered, checking on Gary and trying to soothe him until he passed out. Drunks hauled in late at night need close attention. It doesn't take much for someone intoxicated and in jail to do something impulsive. The officer reassured Gary he'd be transported to court first thing in the morning and probably be released on personal recognizance. He would be home before the morning ended. Gary tossed insults at the officer and slapped at the wall whenever he appeared.

The sergeant took two aspirins and leaned back in his chair. The other officer rolled his eyes, "Will he ever tire himself out?"

"He's been dealing with a lot," the sergeant shrugged. "His father died not too long ago and now his sister has blown her Army career by running off to get poked by a towel head."

Immediately after the president departed, the general entered and ordered Kasey to wait. The room grew smaller with her increasing anxiety about getting home. That is, if they allowed her to go. There was no longer certainty to any moment in Kasey's life. She had to get home and find out if Rick retrieved her diaries. Kasey prayed he hadn't, that she could hide them elsewhere for a day until seeing what the president would do. If he didn't order Americans out of Saudi Arabia, then she would hand deliver them to Rick and hope it wasn't too late for him to get the story out and avert a tragedy for America. The number of Mecca pilgrims in Saudi Arabia was peaking. Zero hour for an uprising. Word of Saud family abdication the sign it was too late for foreigners to escape.

If Rick found the journals, things became complicated. She'd have to get him to sit on it, maybe ultimately even kill the story. Not only what he gleamed from her account, but his entire story about Army production of plastic explosives. She flinched, thinking about what it might mean to his career. He'd have to be persuaded to give up the chance to do what he lusted to do for years, destroy the biggest public figure imaginable.

The general finally returned and told Kasey to follow him. Outside, lights were dim and the administration complex quiet. All imprint of eventfulness gone. One car waited. The general dismissed Kasey.

She got into the car as saw only the driver, a lieutenant. He drove out through the now unguarded gate. He knew something significant went on involving Kasey and obliquely made an effort to learn more.

JOHN RATTI

Kasey told him nothing. Her palms started to sweat. *Why doesn't he drive faster?* She tapped her feet. *I could jog home quicker.* Kasey tipped her head, rubbed her eyes and sighed. Home for two days and it felt like two years.

Kasey got out in front of her house. Gary's truck wasn't there. She carefully looked inside every room of the house. It seemed just as when she left. She turned out all the lights and peeked out a window. All quiet. Kasey stepped out the front door and stood for a long time. It was an hour before dawn. Kasey strolled toward the bridge, listening and watching.

She put light feet on the planks. Halfway across she slithered onto her knees and gazed under the bridge.
Rick has it.

Kasey stood up and paused. She leaned on the rail and considered the brightening horizon. The last time she witnessed this time of day on the bridge was the morning after her senior prom. With Rick. She told him she was going to attend West Point.

Almost twenty years later, she had to again tell him something he would to find hard to hear and she had to do it now.

Kasey walked off the bridge. She wouldn't chance the direct route to Rick's. She went home. Then out the back door. She hopped the fence into a neighbor's yard and ran through a field at the end of their property. Then she dashed through a grove into another yard, climbed a fence and emerged near Rick's. His house was dark. She knew he had to be awake. Kasey circled around and saw drawn shades. She tapped on a living room window.

Rick froze in place on the couch, his ears focused on the sound. Tentatively, he got up and crept over to the window, sitting on the floor next to it with his back against the wall. He heard another knock on the glass, then a whisper.

"Rick?"

Kasey watched the front door slowly open. Looking around, she ran inside the house and Rick locked the door behind her.

They stood facing each other in silence. Kasey could tell Rick knew everything by the storm in his eyes. Rick thought Kasey seemed frazzled, almost terrified.

315

"Rick, I just met with the president."

Her announcement didn't stun him. *That's what happened with her? Then it's more I can use for the story.*

Kasey planted weight on her feet, took a deep breath and looked him in the eye, "You need to kill your story for now. Maybe forever."

"*What?*"

Rick walked a circle numb with confusion, "Americans are in danger. The government knows it and is doing nothing. You hid your diaries so I would find out, and now you're saying I need to stop the story?" He stopped in front of her, "What happened to you is incredible. This story is huge! And I may be able to prove it all with the evidence you gave me."

Kasey struggled to keep composed. Somewhere inside she sensed that for Rick it was about more than this story. She grabbed his hand and they both sat on the couch, "I was taken to meet the president. He ordered me to keep quiet about the mission. I had to tell him it was too late. I said a reporter had a separate story about the Army manufacturing plastic explosives, that he found my diaries and had physical evidence about all of it."

Rick's broke into a panicked expression similar to Kasey's, "They know I have the story?"

"They don't know who has it."

Rick jumped up, "They'll figure it out. Why did you tell him?"

"They were ready to take me away. To a hospital or to solitary as a security threat I told the president that if he ordered evacuation of all Americans in Saudi Arabia within a day, I could stop the story."

"The president agreed?"

"He didn't say anything. Then I was escorted home."

"You made a promise you can't keep."

Kasey knew this was coming. She battled to keep from erupting and sending the encounter to a place she didn't want to go.

Rick filled her pause, "The country needs to know what's been going on."

"Is it more important than having citizens return in body bags, if at all?"

"So he evacuates everybody, I could still go ahead with the story."

"It would create big problems. For me - possibly you, too."

"The public has a right to-"
She curbed his rejoinder, "What's more important, *your* story or *their* safety?"
Rick stopped, but Kasey could read his face like a map. She knew he intended to rattle off every compelling reason for publishing the story, all the justifications a reporter knew by heart. She dodged the harangue, "Does the newspaper know what you have?"
"They know about the Army manufacturing plastic explosives in North Carolina." Rick hesitated, then decided to divulge the whole picture, "They haven't seen my evidence yet. I'm bringing to them today."
Kasey felt his tone change and understood what it meant. Backing off this story, his first at a newspaper with national standing, would cost his job and forever ruin his reputation. Doubtful any explanation he gave would make him seem anything but a liar. Still, he hadn't yet said outright he wouldn't halt the story. Kasey needed to appeal to his integrity. "Rick, you must agree. Thousands of Americans are in harm's way," Kasey heard her fissure. She reeled away, then came back at him, "Is reporting this story more important than their lives?"
"If I hold the story, and the president orders everyone home, I'm finished at the *Examiner*. And nobody will ever know the truth."
Kasey held back tears, "What do you want me to say, Rick? What do you want me to say? Lives are at stake! In the instant, Kasey recognized it wasn't about everybody knowing the truth, it was about *her* knowing the truth. Rick's *truth*. "Rick, do you want to hear me say you are right and I am wrong? That everything I believed, no, was sure of about our country, is a lie?"
Rick couldn't stand to hear it, "Kasey, we don't go there with each other."
"We don't? Every second we're together, that's where we are."
"Maybe for you-"
"Be real, Rick," Kasey shouted, stopped and looked around.
"I'm sorry. I don't want to wake up Denise."
"She's not here."
Kasey hesitated, wondering why. Rick turned away. Ache filled the space and a new dynamic formed. "Rick, I invested my life in things I'm learning may be more fiction than fact," Kasey said in sorrow. "I was always afraid of hearing

what you thought about the world. You're too smart to fool. I couldn't stand to know. I should have listened. Things wouldn't be so hard to take now."

She sounded as if she believed it. Rick continued looking away. "Please, hold the story," Kasey voiced like a prayer. "Agree to kill it if you have to."

Rick snapped back, scowling, "I will agree to nothing."

His bitter tone stunned Kasey.

"You made your choice years ago, Kasey. And now I get to make mine."

It blew Kasey away. *Would Rick hazard lives for emotional retribution?* A twisted idea. *That's not him.* He didn't say he wouldn't kill the story. And where is Denise? Kasey had an uneasy sense of trouble between them. She remembered something Rick said not long ago, "Rick, it's not about a free press, or about ripping apart elected officials. It's not about you and me. It's all about *your* demons." Kasey felt dire sadness, "Go ahead, write the story. Take someone down, win an award. Just don't think, even for a second, it's about anything but what you can't face about yourself."

They stared at each other. Then Kasey walked out of the house. Outside, parents escorted children to the school bus and streets were alive with the new day. Disparaging eyes surveyed Kasey when she was unaware, all without a clue about the remarkable drama going on in the quiet cove.

***

In Saudi Arabia, it was back to business as usual for American employees at refineries and ports. Corporations called meetings at work sites and reiterated what all Americans learn before accepting a Mideast assignment - sporadic incidents happen. The eruptions of days ago faded into memory as transports gradually renewed accustomed routes to and from the virtual cities. Nobody said anything as the number of Guard escorts decreased and took on a different look. The regiments became composed of either younger or older soldiers. A few times, none showed up at all. Americans quickly seek complacency and fell back into relaxed ways, seeing less security as sign things were under control. All was again calm, and for Americans there was no such thing as too quiet. Living cloistered as they did, the Americans had no idea of the crisis underway as Saudi Arabia teemed with Mecca pilgrims and the big plan neared furious explosion. In the rugged places, all government control was now absent. The clerics immediately filled the void, no longer only challenging the monarchy, but setting up provisional rule and establishing their own moral police to keep order using weapons taken from royal loyalists wise enough to flee. Those employed in supporting the monarchy for generations heard nothing from the royals, but many sensed impending upheaval. They either took to the highway, jamming roads looking for a safe haven forever out of grasp, or hunkering down with their kind in suburban enclaves, barricading neighborhoods and even arming women and children.

Riyadh was detonation point for the looming conflagration. Once open strife engulfed Saudi Arabia's largest city and cultural hub, all would see the end was near. That's why Rakan, still acting as head of the Guard, raced around directing squads of boys and elderly men who dispersed crowds, put out fires, and tried to nip plundering in the bud. Rakan knew time was running out and prayed for word from Khaled that it was time to leave. Rakan had a plane and pilot waiting to take him to Switzerland. He kept no longer than a few minutes dash away. The abdication should have already happened, but a problem with transfer of funds out of country held up their departure. Even though the royals moved out tens of billions the past weeks, most were hungry for more. The National Reserve froze all new international appropriations, at first nervously defying the royals, then outright denying transfers after meeting only verbal opposition. His family's intransigence disturbed Rakan. They were consulting lawyers, accountants and computer experts trying to circumvent the Reserve. Rakan wanted it to be over, the amounts haggled over represented but a trifling of their fortune. He was the only royal who knew what was happening on the streets, but nobody would listen. So Rakan decided, as the siren of his motorcade prodded aside the swarm on Riyadh's jammed boulevards, to leave tomorrow, no matter what. They were on the way to quell a new disturbance, word that a gathering was defacing the memorial to Ibn Saud in the government plaza. To allow such disrespect could be the straw that breaks the camel's back. It all could come undone that fast.

Rakan raced from his car as the Guard jostled aside the crowd, who pushed back. The soldiers barely created space for Rakan to reach the plaza. He found a row of mullahs kneeling around the memorial, a symbol of expunging the past, as hundreds of men bowed in prayer.

Rakan stood in front of the mullahs and ordered them to leave or face arrest, shouting they were disobeying martial law edict. They ignored him. Frustrated, Rakan directed the Guard to arrest the clerics. The troops hesitated.

Rakan reached down and seized a mullah by the arm. The crowd closed in on him, and his squad melted away. He fired a pistol into the air, bringing everyone to a standstill. The bullet ricocheted off a building and struck a man. Dozens scrambled to his aid while the rest shouted at Rakan. He spun around in a cold sweat with fidgety eyes as the mob circled.

Then Salih appeared. Rakan drew a breath of relief. The horde paused when he walked up to Rakan. He expected Salih to get him out of this. No doubt he was as baffled as Rakan, albeit for different reasons, over the royal's dawdling. Still, Salih had an agreement with the family and Rakan expected him to keep his end of it.

Salih threw his hands up and cried out, "Our time is *now!*"

The crowd roared. Rakan looked around and saw his squad standing by the clerics in a defensive posture. The energy unleashed by their act shook the ground. Rakan knew this was Salih's show, a coming out, so to speak, and he wanted theatrics. After some spectacle, Salih would squire him away to safety. Rakan then intended to get directly on the plane. Things were beyond nasty, they were rapidly moving toward lethal.

Rakan didn't understand the depth of Salih's ire at the family. After bleeding the country's riches, they were picking at its bones. Salih intended to put an end to it by sending them a message. And Rakan would deliver it. Salih howled, "We are ready to end the reign of those with contempt for Islam!"

The drove hemmed in Rakan. He soothed his racing heart by smirking inside and admiring how Salih could play the crowd.

Salih grabbed Rakan in a tight squeeze and whispered in his ear, "May Allah forgive you."

Then he pushed Rakan into the mob and lifted his voice, "Let the new era begin!"

The gathering stampeded Rakan. Salih watched his face plead until he disappeared, punched and kicked to the ground. Salih stared ahead, refusing to blink as Rakan was bludgeoned by sticks, rods and clubs rhythmically rising in the air. Salih wet his lips while Rakan shrieked and begged. When his cries ended, all grew silent. A path cleared as Salih marched over, looked down and kneeled by his cousin. Rakan lay curled up, his flesh red moist, clothes soaked and eyes frozen open. Salih watched until convinced Rakan's spirit was gone. Then he closed his cousin's eyes, "Drop him in front of the palace."

They tossed Rakan's corpse into the back of a Guard truck. His former underlings took him away with some of the crowd hanging off the convoy.

Salih seized the plaza stage, hurling his arms at the crowd and initiating the chant, "The end of infidels! ... end of infidels!" Soon, nearly all imitated Salih's gestures and words. Others hurried away to spread news about the events in Riyadh and the rest began tearing apart all traces of royal rule.

On the boulevard, a train of vehicles emerged on the outskirts of the city and converged with the swarm on the plaza. Salih pointed and broke into a wide smile, convinced their timing was an omen of great things to come. White robed men carrying automatic weapons streamed out of trucks and personnel carriers. The Army of Allah's Arabia, existing in small cells until now, disclosed itself to the public by falling into attention behind Salih. The crowd murmured with giddy excitement until Salih addressed them, "This land is Allah's! This new nation, his dominion! Make it truth, my brothers!"

The mob thundered in approval. Salih led the soldiers to the caravan and took his place in the front. The mob watched the Army of Allah's Arabia drive away until they vanished on the horizon. Then the gathering scattered, reeling with vigor and set to embark on chaos in the name of a devoted cause.

Allah's Army geared up for the five hundred mile destiny crusade to Mecca. First, they stopped at Salih's residence. Thousands more troops waited inside his compound in a newly deserted suburb where royals used to live. Salih arrived to delirious cheers and led an elitesquad into his courtyard where a hooded pallet sat surrounded by guards.

Salih pulled off the cover, exposing stacked rows of wafer thin plastic the size of dinner plates. Salih picked up one and summoned the unit closer. He looked each one in the eye, "Is everybody prepared to execute their assignment?"

The question met with nods and whispered assent. They were unlike the other soldiers, a cadre Salih chose and trained for this mission. An unruffled bunch aware this was somber business.

"The roads into Mecca ... the airports ... the palace of the king and the borders around all the American cities," the locations rolled from Salih's tongue while the soldiers set the explosives into metal bins. "Once we arrive in Mecca and seal it off, the king will know he must go. And after some Americans die, the rest will beg to leave. See to it they stay confined within their areas until I give word their country promises no intervention."

Salih watched the pile disappear. *But for the greed of the family, it would have never come to this.* He threw open his prayer rug and stooped on his knees, prompting the squad to a final liturgy together before starting the war.

***

Returning from Rick's, Kasey stopped in front of the flag hanging upside down on the pole. She left it that way, went inside and turned on the television. Kasey paced while switching between morning news shows. Lots of chitchat and segments merely filling time. A slow news day, so far. She finally realized Gary hadn't been home all night. She sat down to brace her anxiety. *He's been doing so well, please let this be only a fleeting return to old ways.* Kasey stared at the phone. Should I call and see if he made it to work? She decided no. If he wasn't there, it would only add to her raging torment.

Kasey roamed the channels, settling on an all news station as the morning wore on. *What is Rick doing? Is he at the keyboard, delighted and inspired?* Maybe he's having the evidence I gave him analyzed. Instead of appealing to his conscience, she could have simply demanded back her diaries. But groveling for their return would give him too much sway. She wouldn't cower before him. No way. He'd have given them back if he planned to kill the story.

Kasey's mouth became so dry she filled a pitcher of water and drank it dry standing in the kitchen. Then she made toast to settle her stomach, but the few bites she took made her queasy.

Late in the morning, Kasey was staring and cringing at mail that came from the police department, a notice that she could come and pick up the gun her father used to kill himself. She stuffed the letter into a kitchen drawer when she heard Gary's truck pull into the driveway. The moment he stumbled in Kasey knew he couldn't have made it to work. His face was bruised and an eye swollen shut. She raced for some ice.

"What happened to you?"

Gary pressed the wrap against his face, "I don't want to talk about it."

"Fall off the wagon?"

"You don't look so good yourself."

He frowned and went upstairs. Kasey regretted her words. This wasn't the time for a confrontation. Screwing up one time after pulling himself together didn't deserve a harangue.

She heard him taking a shower. Probably best he wasn't there when they came for her in the night. Who knows what he might have done? At the right time she would tell him everything.

Kasey listened to Gary go into his bedroom and close the door. She knew his routine. Time to sleep off the carousing.

Minutes before noon, a commercial was interrupted for a quick return to the woman at the anchor desk:

"We have just received word the president will be making an important announcement from the Oval Office."

Kasey leaned forward, her nervous system tense and acidy.

"The White House has given no information about the subject of the address, only that the president has something urgent to tell the American public. This notification came to us ... I'm sorry, it's time to switch to the Oval Office and the president."

Kasey held her breath as the president appeared displaying an emphatically somber cast.

HONOR BOUND

"As I speak, the process of evacuating all American civilian and military personnel from Saudi Arabia is underway. Over the past few days, we received alarming intelligence reports about circumstances inside the country that has necessitated this act. We have also shared this information with nations having substantial populations inside Saudi Arabia. They are also evacuating their citizens. A rebellion against the Saudi monarchy is at hand and the royal family at this moment is in the process of abdicating the country."

The president paused and the camera closed in on his face. Kasey clenched a hand, appalled at the manipulation. For her, there was no relief until knowing all Americans made it out safely.

"There is another thing the American people need to know. When the Saudi royal family admitted to us their intent to abdicate, they also disclosed that nearly all their nation's petroleum reserve is depleted, a fact kept even from Saudi citizens. It had been estimated Saudi Arabia held up to one quarter of the world's oil supply, a figure provided to the world by the Saudi government. I don't want Americans alarmed. Even with world oil consumption of seven hundred million barrels per day, we expect little effect on the American consumer. There are still stable sources for world crude. If I need to order tapping the National Petroleum Reserve and dropping restrictions on domestic exploration, I will. America shall endure this situation and continue to prosper. This is all I can say at the moment. I will have more to tell you later. God bless America."

The screen cut back to the anchor desk with chaos underway in the background. In a few monumental minutes, the world had changed forever.

Kasey leaned back on the couch, angrier than ever. Even forced to order the evacuation, the president managed to put exactly the spin he wanted on the situation.

At last, someone on television shook off bewilderment; *"You have just heard a startling announcement from the president ... "*

324

Kasey's fury blocked out the talking head. The president's people were relentless. Utterly precise in scheming every crisis to the president's benefit. It sickened her. *He could have done it all sooner. If so much as a single American is lost or harmed ...*
She refused to finish the thought, only going so far as admitting that Rick writing the story could be a moral thing to do. After all, she did make a promise she couldn't keep. She swerved from that view once her hostility subsided. The president did what she needed him to do and her word had to count for something if she was to salvage her military career. No matter how furious it made her to realize they would find a way to somehow make the president appear a hero in all this. Probably portraying him as the one who decisively led when Americans were at risk and took us through an energy crisis sprung on him without notice.
Kasey kicked the footstool by the sofa as media gasbags referred to as experts explained what was underway. None had any clue. She turned off the television. A few minutes later she passed out.

* * *

Salih's intended mayhem never got underway. Yet by the time the president made his announcement, chaos ruled in Saudi Arabia. Marines stationed on aircraft carriers in the Gulf flew into the virtual cities in helicopters to assist Army and Air Force personnel already there. They escorted civilians to transport planes arriving at three airports. The Marines maintained secure perimeters, wrangling with other evacuating foreign nationals as the Army escorted buses and the Air Force ferried Americans away from the tops of apartment buildings in virtual cities. By midnight, the cities were empty and airports jammed. On tarmacs, planes packed with Americans vied for takeoff side by side with jets hauling away royals pursued by furious citizens. Pilots argued with other pilots over who would leave first, even racing ahead of each other in desperate games of chicken. Americans working in the port cities when the president gave the evacuation order sat tight until Navy SEALS scurried in and emptied everybody out, taking them onto destroyers just offshore. By dawn, all Americans were gone from Saudi Arabia without a single casualty. Cunningham and Amfrick gloated when they received word. It wasn't going to take much on their part to make the president seem a great leader.

***

Kasey woke up and found Gary sitting across the room staring at the television screen. Her bleary eyes focused on faces racing their mouths on split screens from distant places around the globe.

Germany - "The State Department has just said the evacuation is complete ... "

Washington - "We are still waiting to hear again from the president ..."

London - "The world spot market for crude just went through the roof ... "

New York - "Wall Street analysts expect gasoline to retail at over five dollars per gallon within sixty days ... "

Kasey looked around. *How long was I asleep?* It felt dark outside. How long *has Gary been watching all this?* One glance and his inquiring expression said it was time.
    She told him the entire story.

***

After Kasey left, Rick reached Tom as he walked into his office. Holding Kasey's evidence, Rick asked to have some immediate work done in the lab. Then he called a friend of Denise's and asked if his wife was there. She said no. Rick grimaced. The tone in her voice gave him inkling many would soon suspect trouble in their marriage.

Rick dashed to the lab. Explaining nothing, he asked Tom for an incendiary residue analysis of the uniform sleeve. Once Tom got to work, Rick went into another room and shut the door.

He called Denise at work. No answer on her line. He called someone else there and found out Denise was taking the day off. Then Rick reached Carl at the *Examiner* and notified him he had to have more time before they could see the story and evidence.

Carl was beyond disappointed. With a hint of suspicion, he questioned Rick's explanation that this was on the verge of being a story "bigger than you can believe" but the paper had to wait just a little longer to see everything. Tension rose during their exchange until it sounded as if both were ready to blow-up. Then Carl backed off, citing frustration over waiting with such high hopes.

Rick let out a deep breath, then joined Tom in the lab. Unable to be still while waiting for the results, Rick paced, nervously looking out a window at the parking lot, tapping his hands on tables and desks, and even doing push-ups against a wall. Tom remained oblivious to the mannerisms, focusing on the task at hand.

Again, Rick stepped into the office, this time searching his phone book and calling another friend of Denise's. What the hell, he thought, all her friends probably know by now. Nobody answered. Rick left a message asking Denise to get in touch if she turned up there. He left the office.

Tom swiveled around in his chair, "I have positive cellulose acetate residue on this material."

Rick's nervous system fired up, "I need to know how it compares with what you previously analyzed."

Tom motioned him over while the printer pushed out symbols, numbers and graphs, "I figured that was next."

He grabbed the data, went to a file cabinet and pulled out test results of the previous evidence. Tom spread everything on a table, moving his head back and forth and making notations in pencil along paper margins. Rick watched, longing for the ability to decipher the information himself. He looked at the wall clock. Almost noon. Time was running out for the president.

Tom turned to Rick, "The sample you gave me comes from the same source as the previous evidence."

"No mistake about it?"

"It's far more than ninety-nine percent certain," Tom pointed at a series of number sequences. "They coincide in ratio of C-30 along with six inert filler compositions by more than nine decimal points. Isotope degeneration indicates this new sample was manufactured earlier, but no doubt at the same place."

"Absolutely no doubt?"

"Criminal evidence and paternity tests are accepted by courts on far less percentage of certainty."

The confirmation gave Rick a story sure to make him a journalistic legend. He had everything necessary to cause enough heat to ruin an administration. And he intended to do just that, no matter the president's decision about Americans in Saudi Arabia. He felt utterly disquieted by the power he had right now.

Tom smiled at him, "Are you satisfied?"

Rick seemed temporarily absent, "Of course ... sure."

Tom made duplicates of the results for Rick, then put the originals back into folders.

"Give me everything, Tom."

"I should hold on to-."

"Believe me, you don't want to have them in your possession."

Tom was puzzled, "Shouldn't the originals be in another location in case something happens?"

"The newspaper will be sending everything to a different lab to verify your results."

"Still, shouldn't-"

"Trust me, you don't want to keep them."

Tom shrugged and handed over all the files.

Rick put them under his arm, "I'm ready to pay you."

"I'll send you the bill."

"Don't. Call me with the figure and I'll pay cash." Rick noted vague alarm when the words hit Tom's ears, "In time, you'll know why."

Tom watched Rick take everything and leave. Wondering what he got himself into, he watched from a window as Rick got into his car and drove away.

Rick immediately turned on the radio. The airwaves were filled with talk about the president's announcement. *So, he's pulling them out.* In a way that's even better. There will be less they can deny.

Rick went right to work when he got home. He kept a television on to keep informed and sat at the computer screen and listening to a frenzied press conference going on at the White House. *They're already spinning, making the president into a hero.*

Rick grinned. *Well, there's a whole different side to what they're putting out, and everyone's going to hear about it from me.*

For a time, Rick stared at his fingers on the keyboard. He had a new lead to write but the words wouldn't come. Probably due to excitement. He watched television, then tried again, opening the document with his last version of the story on it. The words remained blocked. He couldn't even insert a new lead into what he already written. Scanning the evidence scattered around the room finally freed his psyche:

Today, the president of the United States ordered the evacuation of all American citizens from Saudi Arabia. In his address to the nation, the president referred to an impending revolt, the imminent abdication of the Saudi royal family and the stunning fact that Saudi oil reserves were all but depleted. The president announced he had just learned these facts.

It was a lie.

Rick stopped. Not by intent, but from inner coercion. It wasn't a loss for words, more like a lock on expressing them. Rick stood up. *It must be the other things on my mind.*

The phone rang. Hoping it was Denise, Rick raced to pick it up.

"Rick, we need what you have right away," Carl quickly said.

"You'll have it tomorrow."

"I don't want you holding onto it."

"Nothing's going to happen."

"Bring it to us."

"Carl, I'll finish the story today. As big as I've told you it is, it's bigger."

"As in relating to what's all over the news now?"

"You'll see."

"Just tell me - I'm getting very nervous."

"I have testimony and evidence the president is managing the events. Providing explosives for the revolt, knowing the oil is gone and orchestrating the abdication. All of it."

Carl stayed quiet for a long time, "You mean that? Testimony and *evidence?*"

"That's right."

"Incredible!"

"Wait until you see it."

"I want to. Now."

Rick didn't sense the pleading doubt in Carl's voice, "In the morning, Carl. First thing."

"First thing meaning what time?"

"By seven."

"We're going to have our analysis done on the evidence and fact checkers waiting."

"I'll see you then."

Rick hung up thinking Carl had asserted the *Examiner's* hunger to get the story out fast. He went back to work as images of the initial American evacuees arriving in Germany unfolded on the television screen.

Rick again froze at the keyboard. *Why is this happening to me?* It must be Denise. He went to the phone and called her line at work. *Maybe she decided to go in after all.* No answer. He called friends of hers again. None answered. This time, he left no messages.

Back to the computer. He still couldn't write. Rick got back on the phone and called more friends of Denise's. None answered. Again, he left no messages.

To the keyboard. His fingers nervously jiggled over the letters.

US Army Captain Kasey Lawrence ...

330

Already, he felt emptied. Rick marched to the bedroom, found Denise's phone book and made more calls looking for her, a futile search among old associates and faint acquaintances.

Over to the computer-

US Army Captain Kasey Lawrence, the woman accused of dereliction of duty and desertion days before the president's announcement, has come forward ...

Rick stopped. His fingers wouldn't move. "Arrgghh!" he shouted, gnashing his teeth in anguish and banging on the desk.

He switched from the open document to the Internet, seeking medical information about male fertility. He learned encouraging and discouraging facts about his situation, then found listings of nearby fertility specialists. He held the phone in his hand for a long time. Rick hadn't been to a doctor since his vasectomy. He groaned and made the call, getting an appointment for next week.

Now I can get back to work. He went to the keyboard as the television network released results of a poll determining public opinion of the president's leadership during the crisis. *Americans haven't even been completely evacuated yet!*

Rick bristled when preliminary conclusions showed the president's approval rating going through the roof.

He returned to the story. Resting fingers on the keys, he stared at what he wrote, unable to pull his eyes away from the words-

US Army Captain Kasey Lawrence...

Rick's essence was suddenly flooded by emotions surging from murky depths and seeping out of long cinched vaults. Inner apparitions seized his anima, dictating his introspection. For the first time, he sincerely considered what this story would do to Kasey. Was her promise of silence really an attempt to salvage her military career? *Do I really believe that?* What would happen if they mustered her out, or worse, put her on trial? Rick resisted the empathy.

Kasey might have to end up paying the price of her political naiveté. Nothing could save her career now. One day, she'd see his story as the payback they deserved.

Rick again tried to write. *US Army Captain Kasey Lawrence* stayed in his range of vision burned into his brain even as he looked away. Everything Kasey believed in and lived for had crashed down around her. The promise of silence, the promise she couldn't keep, was no effort to save her career. It was simply to save American lives. Rick knew it in his heart. *The media will swarm her like killer bees after the story is published.* Then the resisting Rick gained the upper hand. *She can handle it. She'll have to. It's only a matter of time before they seek her out over the sex scandal anyway.*

Rick tried to work. Words refused him. He jumped out of the chair and once more went to Denise's phone book. He couldn't find anyone to call. *Relax, sooner or later she'll get in touch. At least she must know I'm trying to find her.*

Back to the computer-

US Army Captain Kasey Lawrence...

Rick rapidly shook his head from side to side but nothing changed. *I have to write this story, there will never be another like it in my career.*

He turned away from the screen. *It'll mak* keyb *e things difficult for Kasey.* He faced the keyboard. *After what I told Carl, if I don't produce what I promised, I'm done* He looked up at the screen-

Kasey Lawrence...

He decided to scroll the page so he wouldn't see her name but his fingers stiffened. I can't do this to her. Then he settled it - *Hey, what has happened to Kasey isn't my fault. I have to write this story.*

Rick tried to find the words-

Am I really going to do this to her?

I must.

I can't.

What happened to her isn't my fault.

What happens to her next might be.

If I don't tell the story, Denise will never understand.

Can I take from Kasey the last thing she has left, her word?

Why not? Look what she took from me.

Rick's world suddenly came to a halt. The story, his marriage, the president, the evacuation, even sense of time melted away so he could at last hear the quiet voice he never listened to.

She took nothing from me. I took it from myself.

A stream of tears fell down his cheeks and stained his shirt.

I did it to myself.

The act hardened youthful non-conformist, anti-establishment sentiment into something permanent, forging unrelenting bitterness toward institutions important to Kasey. God, country, military tradition, elected leaders. *I hate them all because of what I did to myself.* And now he had the power to make Kasey hate herself by showing her word meant nothing. He had a chance to emotionally impale Kasey and force upon her the humiliation he long ago forced on himself. Self-loathing rage, disgust, disappointment, sorrow, he could bring all of it on Kasey now.

He buried his head on the desk, weeping while the feelings he denied for years were laid bare.

***

Salih's plan for isolating resistance to gain a political upper hand ended up thwarted by the president's evacuation order. Ultimately, it didn't matter to Salih. The president's order had the same result. The royal family and Westerners were officially gone and American military presence vanished. Rakan, assumed next in line to the Saudi throne, no longer existed as a possible threat in exile. On the road to Mecca, Allah's Army swelled to a procession covering miles. By the time they neared the city, over one million packed the highway awaiting their arrival. All semblance of previous Saudi authority either disappeared or shed Guard uniforms and donned the white linen of Allah's Army.

Mecca now belongs to Allah, Salih thought with a luminous grin. The caravan inched toward the Grand Mosque, the roaring ecstasy of the masses thundering so loud he couldn't hear what was going on inside his head.

Outside the mosque, people cleared a path for Salih leading to a line of senior mullahs. Salih bowed to the clerics who precisely set the groundwork according to plan, gradually promoting resistance to the royal family. Images of Salih flexing before them were graphed long before the strategy of open revolt. With as many foreign pilgrims as Saudi citizens jamming Mecca, the picture inspired rabid dreams of similar miracles happening elsewhere. Salih gave no speech and the mullahs said no words. This was time for symbol and spectacle. Salih followed the clerics into the mosque, crowded by trailing worshippers until the mosque seemed to expand. As everyone inside kneeled to pray, those outside also went prone like rows of toppling dominoes. The Grand Mosque, the burning air, sweltering sun, the steaming pavement and the empty sky all seemed to quiver under the ground rattling vibration of the chants with a seismic jolt felt across the world.

America next heard from their president in the middle of the night, his face on the television screen dotted with whisker shadow and slightly tousled hair in an attempt to show preoccupation with the crisis. Truth was, his handlers woke him and a make-up expert went to work fashioning his look, down to the dark circles under his eyes. Amfrick and Cunningham timed his appearance for a when most Americans had finally collapsed in front of their set or went to sleep.

Today, under my command, our military completed a perilous mission with a rapidity and precision that should make every American proud. The evacuation of all our citizens from Saudi Arabia is now complete. At great risk, every branch of our armed forces participated in the evacuation without a single casualty. Americans with loved ones in Saudi Arabia can now be assured of their safety. In the next days, they will be returning home from locations in Turkey, Germany and England.

There is something else I need to tell the American public. To avoid further instability in the Mideast, the Swiss government has agreed to accept the abdicating Saudi royal family under the condition they agree to give up all claim of rule in the nation they left behind in the Arabian Peninsula. They have agreed and are now in Switzerland. Although the Saudi royal family precipitated this crisis by failing to reveal depleted oil reserves and covering up impending revolt, America played a role in finding them a safe haven. It is the right thing to do. This is a dangerous period in an important part of the world and America must do all it can to bring stability to the region. To balance this, I will agree to recognize the new state in the Arabian peninsula, so long as they agree to public elections and abide by the will of the electorate. We hope this can be an opportunity for a new democracy in the Mideast.

It's also important that Americans do not to panic about reports citing immediately rising oil costs and declining availability. As I told you, I am determined to see there will be no energy shortages. While I spent today directing safe evacuation of Americans in Saudi Arabia, I also ordered immediate development of a detailed policy to address our new energy situation. Let me tell you once more: if necessary, I will order use of our national petroleum reserves and I am asking Congress to lift bans on exploratory oil drilling in environmentally sensitive areas. We are also undertaking something long overdue, a comprehensive policy outlining potential new energy sources.

In a few hours, I will be at Andrews Air Force base to meet with the first homecoming Americans. Over the next days, you'll be hearing more from my administration about the continuing events. Until then, goodnight, and God bless America.

Then he fired off a reassuring smile. Kasey, one of those awake and watching, felt her gut churn at his gesture. *Our leader, taking control during a dangerous time brought upon by a deceptive monarchy. Hard at work saving Americans and our nation's future by creating a new energy policy.* Yet still finding time to stand on the tarmac and meet returning Americans. There was something awesomely sinister and frightening about the orchestration of his public image. Choosing the wee hours to divulge a deal sending the Saudi royal family to a neutral country and already offering recognition to the new regime in the place he now referred to as the Arabian Peninsula. Deals made long ago covered up, a mere sidebar to the pictures of him the world will see tomorrow hugging returning Americans. The result of it all diverting attention from everything negative his administration had represented. Inflation. Unemployment. Incompetent appointees and mismanagement of the Federal Reserve, to name only what Kasey often heard. Never mind leaving Americans at risk to hide the truth about exhausted oil wells in Saudi Arabia. OPEC never cut production to increase price as the president always maintained. Kasey knew he would at sometime claim the Saudi royal family spent years lying to America. Frustration at his disappointing administration was about to disappear, washed away in patriotic images and calls to rally around a president dealing with a crisis.

Kasey turned off the television and sat in the dark.

***

As foreign nationals and the royal family deserted Saudi Arabia, Salih brought the world media to Mecca. Allah's Army seized control of planes at the airport near Mecca used for chartering pilgrims and waiting pilots set out for Germany, France and England to bring in film crews. In some places, aircraft taking off with Westerners heading for Saudi Arabia vied for air space with jets in exodus. In Mecca, representatives of television networks were put up in a hotel previously used to house notable visitors. A haven from the tumult on the streets, invited correspondents enjoyed lavish meals and a full bar while waiting to meet emissaries of the new state called Allah's Arabia.

Hours after the president spoke to the American public in the deep night, Salih, calling himself a delegate for an interim ruling committee, escorted reporters to a staging area close by the Grand Mosque. There, film crews recorded a panel of mullahs surrounded by a teeming multitude. Back in the hotel, Salih sat down individually with selected correspondents and introduced the world to the new nation.

Salih looked grief ridden when discussing the royal family's refusal to heed warnings about citizen discontent over lack of influence in government affairs. He sighed as he mentioned public anger over the royal's foibles, shedding a tear while he talked about his brother Nasir, put to death because of an adulterous affair. "That's when people had enough," Salih told a reporter, who consoled him with a touch of a hand. Then he grimaced when he spoke of disappointment at learning only days ago about the nation's depleted oil reserves. He covered his face and broke down as he revealed how he tried to stop a mob from beating his cousin to death.

It was a media perfect story. A former Saudi royal defying family ties and casting his lot with a revolution by a fed up populace. A media superstar was born overnight as Salih related his account over and again in Arabic as well as English, Spanish, French and German, languages he spent recent weeks learning. He ended each interview by expressing regret over America's reaction to the events, claiming nobody was at risk and Allah's Arabia wanted peace with the world, even pleading for immediate US aid now that the country had little oil and rapidly declining natural gas reserves.

Salih took the media for a ride they were all too willing to go on. Nobody questioned the astonishing timing of the president's late night speech recognizing the new government only hours before its proclamation to the world in a consummately staged pageant.

***

Kasey refused to read a newspaper, listen to the radio or turn on the television all day. She admitted her disgust but denied the fear that lurked from witnessing the menacing deceit played out by old and new powers-that-be. She accompanied Gary to a meeting with an attorney hired to handle the assault charges against him. After, Gary went to open the store and Kasey consulted with another lawyer, one she hired to work in tandem with her military counsel on her court martial. She still hadn't told her attorneys the entire truth. She considered doing it now and getting over the waiting-for-the-other-shoe-to-drop feeling she had anticipating Rick's story. She held back. *They'll be learning about it soon enough. Then what happens?* The lawyers certainly would use that in her defense. What personal destruction do those threatened by the truth have schemed up as come back? It was sinking in - her military career was finished. She had no control over any of it now. Americans were safe and the truth was in other hands. She did what she had to do. Everything now was aftermath.

Kasey made dinner that night, but Gary never came home after work. He was likely sitting on a stool in another haunt drowning frustrations the only way he knew how. Kasey stewed about it, blaming herself. He was doing so well until I came back. The perception compelled Kasey confront the unthinkable: this place was no longer her home. Once her case closed, she'd have to find another place to live. Besides Gary's problems, there was the peculiar way people these days reacted to her. Her presence in town affected the family business, and that was Gary's livelihood.

Kasey walked onto the bridge in the deep night. She took a deep breath. Only surrounded by the inanimate elements of sky and water did she feel at ease. The tide was a low-drainer, the table so scant she saw the river's bottom. She didn't need to look up to know it was a full moon. Kasey sighed, longing for the sound of waves stroking the pilings.

From a corner of her eye she saw movement and quickly glanced over. Rick stood leaning on the rail looking over the water. Kasey turned away.

"I've been so preoccupied lately that I've neglected spring cleaning," Rick said softly after a long time passed.

Kasey wouldn't face him. He came here to tell me this?

"I need to rake the yard and get rid of the leaves ... do some burning. If your around in the morning, I could use help."

Help him tend his yard? Kasey almost laughed. *Is he crazy? Awkward small talk? That's not him. A muddled peace offering?* Something had to be up. Denise is the one who takes care of the landscaping.

"Why don't you just say what's on your mind?"

No reply. She eventually looked in his direction.

Rick wasn't there.

Unable to sleep, Kasey sprawled on her back in bed and stared at the ceiling. Hearing Gary come in brought some comfort. At least he didn't end up in jail again. She yawned and turned over, hoping to finally get some rest. If she dozed, it was briefly. Rick's appearance on the bridge ruffled any tranquillity. *What was he really talking about? He must be done with the story. You'd think he'd be celebrating over what was happening.* The president's actions only bolstered the evidence. He should be ecstatic. Why did he sound so subdued?

Kasey was at the kitchen table when Gary walked in to grab a cup of coffee before work. She inspected his demeanor. He looked better than she felt. He gave her a quick grin.

She smiled back, "Can I help you at the store today?"

"I'll be fine."

That was all they said. Each coveted a read of the other, but neither tended to reveal much. It was simply a way they were the same, regardless of any inner turmoil.

Gary left. Kasey couldn't get Rick out of her mind. She stood gazing out the screen door, noting two robins skipping around collecting twigs. They flew back and forth to an eave on the house where they were building a nest. *I guess there's only one way to know.*

Kasey shut the door behind her and marched down the street. A usually chatty neighbor heading her way turned around. Kasey smirked. *Even during a national crisis, they don't forget.* Nearing the corner, a car backed out of a driveway. The driver, living there since the day Kasey was born, kept his head facing away as she walked behind him. She swore eyes were upon her. She faced ahead, choosing to believe it was paranoia, but couldn't help a fast glance toward a window she passed. The curtains swayed as if somebody moved away.

Approaching Rick's, she noticed Denise's car wasn't there. Her motorcycle sat by the garage, still too early for riding season. She must have gone to work. Kasey spurned her intuition, an apprehension that told her of trouble in Rick's marriage. She ignored it to keep from facing the absolute insight they had into each other's lives. Time, space, words - nothing destroyed their pure cognition. A lusciously tart, hulking dilemma that precipitated distance mostly, but today brought her here. Her core knew why Rick wanted her there.

She walked toward his front door and curved around the side of the house when she heard scraping noise in the back yard. Kasey saw neat piles of foliage around a metal barrel. Rick threw aside his rake and reached for a shovel sitting on the ground.

Kasey stood behind him holding it.

Rick faced her, "Hello."

"Seems everything got done without my help."

Rick headed inside, "Not quite."

He held up a finger and disappeared into the house. Kasey began shoveling leaves into the barrel. Before she knew it, Rick was next to her, holding a box with her diaries.

Rick dropped them into the barrel.

Countless emotions unraveled in silence as they stared at each other. Rick fired up some kindling and lingered over the barrel. Kasey wasn't sure what she wanted him to do. She closed her eyes. When she opened them, the inside of the barrel was on fire.

Rick walked away. Kasey stoked the blaze. Rick came back, arms full of clothing he pilfered in North Carolina. One by one, he tossed each piece into the fire while Kasey scooped up leaves. It took Rick three trips to bring everything outside and over an hour until everything became sooty shreds and cinder. Then Rick dumped the folder with all the lab results into the barrel. They watched until the fire put itself out.

"Never felt so good," Rick smiled at Kasey, "doing yard work."

Kasey couldn't believe it. *He seems ... liberated.*

Rick sauntered away, "I'll get us a drink."

Kasey merely gazed at him in astonishment. She settled down on the porch stoop.

Soon Rick came out twisting open a bottle of beer, "It's the only thing in my refrigerator." He had a seat next to Kasey, took a drink and handed her the bottle.

Kasey held it and they both observed the smoldering fire. She had a sip of beer and handed the bottle back to Rick.

"What did you tell the paper?"

"That I had good reasons to back off the story and not make the evidence available."

"How'd they respond?"

"They wanted to know the reasons."

"You told them?"

"No."

Kasey cringed.

Rick was serene, "They think I'm a phony ... that I never had a story to begin with."

"You could have convinced them Americans were at risk if you went ahead."

"I could have," Rick looked at Kasey, "but it was about more than that."

"More?"

Both of them stared ahead with shoulders touching. "Better to protect one person in this world whose word means something rather than destroy someone nobody has any faith in anyway," Rick said with a curling, feathery resonance.

341

What had made him so emotionally surprising? Kasey tried to hide her utter astonishment with a somber tone, "But you're ruined."

"That makes two of us," Rick delicately grinned.

Everything coming out of his mouth sounded surreal, making it hard to believe this was Rick. She turned and gazed into his eyes, "Tell me what I don't know."

"There's nothing you don't know."

Kasey looked away. There wasn't a thing they didn't know about each other. A long time went by so each could confront that pain.

"I'm worried about you," Rick briefly touched her knee. "Forcing the president to do the right thing ... the price they'll make you pay for that scares me."

"Maybe they'll let go of it," Kasey shrugged. "Things seem to have worked out well for him."

Rick shook his head, "They won't forget. When you're at the top of the political food chain, everything's a meal."

His words brought Nasir to mind and what happened to him. Then Bowers, Harper, Moore and the others buried in Lebanon grabbed her thoughts. Then there were Gary's problems, and Rick's, and hers.

"I never saw it as taking on the president," Kasey had to explain, if only to herself. "It was about saving Americans. Watching Captain Saud go to his death, I was overwhelmed by his courage. He wouldn't yield to those without integrity. He seemed so at ease about it ..." Kasey didn't know how to finish.

"Are you at ease about what you did?"

"Completely," she said almost a minute later.

"So am I." Rick eventually let out a soft sigh, "What now?"

"We'll see what my lawyers can do."

Rick raised his eyebrows, "You still have hopes for life in the Army?"

"It's hard to picture my life without it," Kasey wistfully ached. "The Army has always been a completing thing in my family. Being a good soldier is all I ever wanted. It's the foundation of the Lawrence's ... it's us ... it's me."

"What happens when that is taken away? I can't bear to see you lost."

"I'm not lost," Kasey snapped.

"That's not what I should have said." Rick clarified, "Of course you're not lost. America is. I should have told you a long time ago I felt the country could handle a skeptic like me only because we had a patriot like you."

Maybe he never said it, but Kasey knew it, "I always felt so long as we had someone like you to keep everyone in line, I could afford to have faith and believe the best about our country."

They became quiet, aware it was a sign to part. Both were sad, even fretful, never sure what the dynamic would be at their next encounter.

"Kasey, I can't figure it out ... why would our government provide plastic explosives to harm Americans? The abdication was already a done deal."

"To guarantee the royal family would abide by the agreement. If they didn't, it would destroy the scenario for claiming the president didn't know the oil was gone."

For a moment, it brought back Rick's hardened loathing, "And kill his chances at another term."

Not much for either to say after that insight.

"I need to go," Kasey stood up. "I'm waiting to hear from my lawyer."

Rick looked up at her.

Kasey wanted, no needed, to ask him about Denise, but Rick got to his feet and moved to the door.

Kasey slowly walked away. She turned around. Rick was watching.

He saluted her, "You're a good soldier, Captain Lawrence."

Rick went inside, not waiting for a reaction. Kasey paused until the door shut, then she went home.

***

Kasey waited another day before hearing from Army counsel. Lieutenant William Baker called from Washington and apologized for news that the Army offered a five-year prison sentence as plea bargain to avoid a trial. The stern proffer incensed Kasey. No way would she agree to doing time. She swallowed hard before refusing the terms, realizing with the evidence now gone she was twisting in the wind. She guessed the Army carried on unaware of the entire truth and was simply proposing what they thought fair under the circumstances. Like civilian courts, once someone ends up in the military justice system, it rarely just lets go. The Army had to be merely processing data coming their way from civilian sources. Things were working out for the president better than any of his people could have imagined. Would they continue vindictiveness through a trial? Lieutenant Baker informed her of the court martial start date and asked what she wanted to do.

"We'll take it to trial," Kasey said in a flinty tone.

"What's your defense?"

"I was blackmailed."

"The evidence?"

She paused, eventually stammering, "The truth will come out."

Baker reiterated, "The *evidence*?"

"I'll come up with some." Kasey desperately hunted for any trace of documentation she could use in defense.

"Can you, really?" the lieutenant sounded exasperated. "I've asked you to tell me what happened ...They have the pictures ... You were found in the desert with Captain Saud not far from where you disappeared. Are you keeping me in the dark about something? If you won't help me, I can't help you. Losing at trial could mean twenty years in jail."

Kasey wavered before replying, loathing the idea of throwing in the towel. "The offer ... that's open to negotiation ... right?"

"What will you accept?"

"An honorable discharge."

"I'm sorry to tell you that will never happen."

"I won't accept a dishonorable one. I'll go to trial first."

"Even a general discharge is probably more than we can get."

Kasey clamped her jaw.

Baker pleaded, "What do you want me to put on the table?"

Kasey let out air and groaned, "Take it to them. A general discharge."

Kasey's civilian attorney, Rich Lowen, was more upbeat about her situation. She felt encouraged and relieved after meetings in his office. Being apart from

Army culture, he had no need to tread lightly to protect a budding career or fell to unconsciously deferring to copious stripes. He seemed to grasp the reasons behind Kasey's reluctance to be forthcoming with details. He was even ready to take it all the way to trial.

"Can you tell me how they got the photographs?"

"I'm not sure," Kasey truthfully told him.

"Without disclosing what you don't want me to know, could they have been in the hands of civilian sources? Maybe inside the government?"

"Possibly."

"Maybe high profile civilian leaders?"

"They may have come down that road."

Lowen rubbed his hands, "We'll call them staged photos and force prosecution to establish full chain of custody. Let's see who had hands on them. Maybe they don't want that known."

Kasey gave him a fleeting smile. She needed someone to play hardball. "All I want back is my good name."

"You won't serve a day, I can promise you that."

"I did tell Army counsel I'd accept a general discharge."

"Let's see if we can do better."

Kasey spent most of the next several weeks in meetings with Baker and Lowen. The two lawyers met a few times with Army prosecutors, getting them to budge their offer down to a three-year sentence. Lieutenant Baker asked Kasey to consider it, telling her the Army called it a final offer. Attorney Lowen still believed they could do better. Kasey insisted she wouldn't serve time. Her lawyers tried a good cop-bad cop routine in negotiations. Baker claimed he was doing all he could to get Captain Lawrence to settle but Lowen wanted a trial. The lieutenant privately told the Army's lead prosecutor that civilian counsel intended to aggressively pursue acquittal, challenging the photographic evidence by shedding light on chain of custody and calling as witnesses everybody who knew anything about Captain Lawrence's mission and its purpose. They were flying blind with the strategy since neither lawyer was privy to the facts Kasey kept to herself. Lowen's instinct told him there was something there the Army, or someone else, didn't want revealed. He was certain they would never take it to trial.

After two months, the court martial date loomed. Kasey's legal bills were piling up with still no resolution to her case. America was changing, and not for the better. The country struggled to provide an uninterrupted energy supply. Even in places without shortages, panic caused lines at gas pumps, bringing incidents of price gouging and violence. Though it was summer, home heating oil reserves dried up in stampedes of frightened buying. Prospects for the winter looked bleak. Those switching to natural gas found backlogs of up to a year. Extended gas pipelines broke down, sending prices spiraling up comparable to the costs of oil. Electrical power plants, using oil and gas for generators, had to charge three times the price to consumers from only months before. Inflation pushed up over fifteen percent. Stock market quivered through three "energy corrections" as unstrung investors cut losses and capital for new businesses dried up as fast as mutual funds went defunct. Unemployment flew beyond nine percent on the same day the president's popularity ratings went through the roof, reaching heights usually seen only during wartime.

Kasey occasionally helped Gary at the store, mainly tending the register when he needed to make deliveries. Business wasn't good, hard to tell if it had to do with a poor economy or Kasey's notoriety. Gary braved the circumstances, never uttering a discouraging word, but Kasey could see no peace or haven for either of them anymore in the place always called home. Gary must have drawn the same conclusion in a tacit way. He stayed away from the bars, hitting the liquor store after work and sitting alone in the yard, drinking. When the weather was bad, he'd get into his truck parked in the driveway and stare ahead, gulping beer.

Kasey grew weary of being shunned. She took to doing errands after nightfall whenever possible, eyes peeled straight ahead, a cipher oblivious to all around her. Her only serenity came when she was on the bridge in the dark. Kasey would gaze at the sky and river, sometimes glancing at homes lining the embankment or at the tower of city hall downtown. It was time to keenly absorb everything, the way a person takes in final impressions when a time of life nears an end. Days here now were numbered by the duration it took resolve her case. Then she would be leaving. *Could Gary feel the same way? I hope he'll sell the business and get out.* She wondered how things were working out for Rick. Since destroying the evidence, they seldom spoke. One night a while back Kasey walked by and spotted him leaving his house. She stopped to talk. Rick mentioned all the employment opportunities coming his way. Maybe he would be staying put. Kasey hadn't seen Denise around for ages and the yard appeared unkempt. She didn't broach the subject then. Sometime later Kasey noticed Denise's motorcycle wasn't around. She called Rick, hoping he'd open up about what was happening. He made sure the dialogue didn't go there. She knew what he was doing and backed off. Rick guided the exchange toward Kasey's court martial. She told him they were ready for a trial. He wished her luck.

Once the Saudi royal family abdicated and revealed the depletion of the country's oil reserves, allegations of Kasey's affair slipped from the headlines. The media later picked up on it in drips and drabs. A regional weekly newspaper, two national television magazine shows and a scandal sheet sniffed around, approaching neighbors and others in town. Their presence certainly didn't ease Kasey's estrangement from the community. One network news program showed up with trucks, cameras, producers and reporters. En masse they canvassed nearly the entire town, even knocking on the door while Kasey was home and walking into the store with Gary there. They asked probing questions, attempting to connect the "Captain Lawrence affair" with the Saudi abdication. Then they trekked down to Washington pursuing Army officials and badgering them with inquiries about the "curious timing" between Kasey's mission, the charges against her, and the events that so soon after took place in Saudi Arabia. The Army learned the account, slated for broadcast as the court martial took place, might include interviews with Saudi royalty in exile.

Attorney Lowen was the off-record source behind it all. He correctly assumed many details Kasey wouldn't divulge and wet the network's appetite for controversy in an attempt to scare the Army away from going ahead with a trial. It worked. The protracted negotiations ended a day before the trial with an "absolutely final offer" of general discharge. Kasey's lawyers urged her to accept it.

She did.

The purging release Kasey witnessed in Rick when they burned the evidence ebbed over time into disappointment and sorrow. He spent the next days unsuccessfully trying to track down Denise. Either friends had closed ranks around her, or she went someplace he couldn't guess. She finally called Rick a day before his appointment with the fertility specialist. Denise wanted a divorce. Rick refused to hear the conviction in her voice. With slobbering optimism, he enthusiastically apologized and promised things would change in their relationship. Denise didn't waver. Rick was sure she would. He pleaded for a meeting. They had things to discuss, so she agreed. She made him wait a week for it to happen.

She met him in a diner by the highway. Denise politely inquired when the Examiner intended to publish his story. Rick said he abandoned it.

"Why?" a shocked Denise asked.

"To put a lot of things to rest."

"Did the paper go along?"

"No."

Rick hoped Denise would see it as an ending to whatever she perceived going on between Kasey and him. "I lost my job," he tightened his focus on her, "but I have faith it'll save us."

Denise shook her head and avoided his gaze, "It's over, Rick."

Both were quiet. She didn't know when it would sink in for him.

Neither did he.

"I want to set up a time to come over and get my belongings," Denise found it harder to say then she thought. "Probably better if it's a time when you're not home."

"Denise, I-"

"Please ... Rick, I want it to be easy for you ... for both of us. No communal property settlement, you owned the house way before you married me. Just let me get my things ... so we can disentangle our lives."

Disentangle our lives? Her words swallowed up Rick, awakening him from denial and forcing him to consider life without Denise, even if what came out of his mouth indicated otherwise, "I love you. We can get past this."

Denise extended her hand across the table and gently placed it on his arm, "Rick ... it's over. It really is. You may not see it now, but it's better for both of us."

Her melancholy tone pierced his heart. It was no less agonizing to Denise. She had believed Rick was emotionally hers. When she discovered he wasn't, she could never trust it would be different. Not out of deception on his part, but from her fear there had to be other hidden nooks in his psyche. She would never be able to go through life speculating about them.

The part of Rick still hoping to get Denise back pushed an envelope across the counter in front of her, "I saw a doctor ... had some tests ... got some answers."

Denise looked at the envelope and paused. She was curious, but opening it would only encourage Rick and somewhere inside she was scared it would make her rethink her decision.

"Go ahead," Rick gestured, "have a look."

With tears in her eyes Denise pushed the envelope back at him, "Rick, it's something about your life that's personal. It's for another woman's eyes at some future time."

Rick watched her get up. She only offered a sad smile, "Let's end this respecting each other."

Then Denise walked out of the diner.

Pumping adrenaline left Rick's mouth dry. His anatomy throbbed as his spirit became vulnerable over the permanent growing distance he couldn't avoid experiencing with his wife. Sometime later Rick stopped by for a visit at the *Tribune*, the newspaper he quit to go to work at the *Examiner*. Ostensibly, he dropped in for a social call with former colleagues, but with an agenda to explore the possibility of rejoining the staff. Sitting in the editor's office, Rick explained the culture at a major metropolitan daily wasn't for him, regardless of its reputation. He had an idea the *Tribune* would welcome him back. After all, his work brought them prestige they had never known. No job offer came his way. He walked out speculating word about his brief stint at the *Examiner* had filtered through journalistic circles. He winced, thinking that the ones slapping his back minutes ago might now be bad mouthing him.

He hunkered down at home for a while, leaving only the day Denise came over in a truck to remove her belongings. He cried when he first saw the emptied house. Eventually he went on with his life, taking a series of temporary jobs while searching for something permanent. He wrote copy for software manuals, proofread classifieds for a buying and selling guide and researched statistics for an insurance company.

None of his networking with publishing contacts and resumes sent to editors harvested a single interview. A reporter with his award and experience should easily find work. Something no doubt had happened to his reputation. Rick extended his job hunt to include out of state magazines and newspapers as well as Internet news services. He omitted his brief term at the *Examiner* when he listed past employment, but came to presume what happened there would haunt him for a long time. He considered writing a book about the relationship between the media and public officials. It would have to be another time. He needed steady work - now.

Rick finally received an offer to edit the *Outlet Consumer.* As the only full time employee, he did layout (mainly ads) of the free weekly and contributed brief paragraphs of shopping tips. It paid far less than he was used to, but it would do for a while.

Personal and professional matters consumed Rick. In his head, he kept planning to talk with Kasey. But his heart avoided the encounter. This dichotomy forged into a subconscious awareness their relationship required distance as a matter of emotional survival.

Kasey didn't seem to feel the same. Maybe it was her curiosity about Rick's marriage that made her walk by his house the night he stepped out for a late appointment with his divorce lawyer. Rick writhed at the sight of her appearing so sunken and hollow. He watched her eyes probing him and the surroundings while talking about her lawyers continuing to be optimistic about settling the case. Rick didn't remember what he said to her, only her clipped smile. Weeks after, she gave him a call, curious about what he was up to. Rick said he was still sorting through his options. He asked Kasey about the progress of her case.

No news. When Rick got off the phone he stared at it for a long time. It was the day after Denise took her motorcycle away. *Who is Kasey trying to kid? She's pumping me for information about my marriage.*

Rick grinned. *The two of us ... forever destined to know each other better than we should.*

On the 4th of July, Rick spent the morning sitting on his front porch watching the neighborhood being decorated for the afternoon parade. American flags dangled from utility poles and street vendors vied with spectators for prime space along the route. Cookout aromas filled the air well before guests arrived at family picnics along the block. Rick couldn't stop thinking of Kasey. *I really should go and see her today.*

He wrestled with the idea until red, white and blue saturated the town. Not only on flags, but balloons, pennants, clothes, even the stilts a man dressed as Uncle Sam walked on. Band members heading for the start of the parade course passed by him. Then a group of military veterans. He studied their VFW caps.

It was time for a stroll.

Gary smiled for the first time in ages as he dodged the crowd on Main Street. Yesterday, the assault charges against him were continued without a finding, and Kasey had reached a settlement in her case. No trial and a general discharge, it could have ended a lot worse. After the final administrative hearing in a few days, it would all be official. Now the decks were clear for them to go on with their lives.

Gary picked up some groceries at the supermarket. He knew Kasey would stay away from the parade. She stayed out of sight in her room all morning. Certainly a rough day for her from the start. He was content to barbecue for just the two of them.

Kasey was standing in front of a mirror in her room when she heard Gary leave the house. She was in Army uniform for the last time but for the upcoming final hearing. Staring at her form, she noticed a slack button on the jacket. She got a sewing kit and stitched it tight while sitting on the edge of her bed. Then she walked out of the house.

Kasey hiked up the hill toward the cemetery, the summer heat forming beads of sweat around her hairline. She made her way to "relative's row" as she always thought of it. She turned and took a long look at the distant ocean, the river below and the people swarming and darting around town. She listened to the remote voices and musicians getting ready for the parade. Kasey unbuttoned her coat and gazed at the lining.

America, One Nation, One Destiny

Then she pivoted toward the headstones, holding a salute for each ancestor before slowly moving on to the next memorial.

Rick ambled into Kasey's yard and saw the front door half open. He gave a quick knock and waited. He called out for Kasey, then Gary, even though his truck wasn't in the yard. No answer. Rick went inside and called their names again. Only a brief gust of wind punctuated the silence. He didn't like the feeling coming over him, though he didn't know why.

Gary pulled into the driveway. Rick stepped outside, slightly relieved. He helped Gary with the bags, "Where's Kasey?"

"She's been in her room all day," Gary shrugged.

"The door was open when I got here."

Rick followed Gary into the kitchen. Once everything was in the refrigerator, Gary went upstairs. Rick didn't like the look on Gary's face when he came down.

"She's not up there."

Both of them felt troubled in a way they couldn't express. Rick stepped outside. Something compelled his eyes up the hill. Ready to look away, he saw a figure in the cemetery, only the movement revealing a presence on the manicured grounds. He knew it was Kasey. Rick turned around. Gary stood behind him gazing at the same sight.

Without a word, they headed her way as the parade began. Music, firecrackers and floating helium balloons suddenly filled the air as Rick and Gary paced, jogged and finally raced up the hill.

Kasey reached the end of relative's row after striding past the empty space next to her father's grave. She crouched in front of his memorial, kissed a finger and touched the stone with it. She stood up and saluted him. Then Kasey slid a hand into her coat pocket and took out her old .22. She sat down on the ground next to her father's tomb and pushed the gun deep into her mouth.

She didn't acknowledge the approaching shouts. Rick and Gary were near enough to have a good look. They charged at her, scrambling up burial rows and lurching between headstones.

They stopped a few feet in front of her.

Tears raced down Gary's face, "Kasey, don't do it! I need you, sister ... you're all I have."

Rick clasped his hands in supplication, "Have hope, Kasey. Things will get better. Put the gun down."

Kasey stared at them, her finger resting on the trigger. Rick and Gary stared back, unsure of what they saw in her eyes ...

THE END

Printed in the United States
2026

9 781931 391351